John Habberton

Little Guzzy and Other Stories

John Habberton

Little Guzzy and Other Stories

ISBN/EAN: 9783744750486

Printed in Europe, USA, Canada, Australia, Japan

Cover: Foto ©Andreas Hilbeck / pixelio.de

More available books at **www.hansebooks.com**

AND OTHER STORIES.

BY

THE AUTHOR OF

"HELEN'S BABIES."

WITH ILLUSTRATIONS.

NEW YORK:

Copyright, 1878, by

G. W. Carleton & Co., Publishers.

LONDON: S. LOW, SON & CO.

MDCCCLXXVIII.

To FRANK LESLIE,

Who, while other publishers were advising the writer
of these sketches to write, supplied the author with
encouragement in the shape of a publishing medium
and the lucre which all literary men despise but long
for, this volume is respectfully dedicated by

THE AUTHOR.

THE SCHOOLTEACHER AT BOTTLE FLAT.

IT certainly *was* hard. What was the freedom of a country in which the voice of the original founders was spent in vain? Had not they, the "Forty" miners of Bottle Flat, really started the place? Hadn't they located claims there? Hadn't they contributed three ounces each, ostensibly to set up in business a brother miner who unfortunately lost an arm, but really that a saloon might be opened, and the genuineness and stability of the camp be assured? Hadn't they promptly killed or scared away every Chinaman who had ever trailed his celestial pig-tail into the Flat? Hadn't they cut and beaten a trail to Placerville, so that miners could take a run to that city when the Flat became too quiet? Hadn't they framed the squarest betting code in the whole diggings? And when a 'Frisco man basely attempted to break up the camp by starting a gorgeous saloon a few miles up the creek, hadn't they gone up in a body and cleared him out, giving him only ten minutes in which to leave the creek for ever? All this they had done, actuated only by a stern sense of duty, and in the patient anticipation of the reward which traditionally crowns virtuous action. But now—oh, ingratitude of republics!—a schoolteacher was to be forced upon Bottle Flat in spite of all the protest which they, the oldest inhabitants, had made!

Such had been their plaint for days, but the sad excitement had not been productive of any fights, for the few married men in the camp prudently absented themselves at night from "The Nugget" saloon, where the matter was fiercely discussed every evening. There was, therefore, such an utter absence of diversity of opinion, that the most quarrelsome searched in vain for provocation.

On the afternoon of the day on which the opening events of this story occurred, the boys, by agreement, stopped work two hours earlier than usual, for the stage usually reached Bottle Flat about two hours before sundown, and the one of that day was to bring the hated teacher. The boys had wellnigh given up the idea of further resistance, yet curiosity has a small place even in manly bosoms, and they could at least *look* hatred at the detested pedagogue. So about four o'clock they gathered at The Nugget so suddenly, that several fathers, who were calmly drinking inside, had barely time to escape through the back windows.

The boys drank several times before composing themselves into their accustomed seats and leaning-places; but it was afterward asserted, and Southpaw—the one-armed bar-keeper—cited as evidence, that none of them took sugar in their liquor. They subjected their sorrow to homeopathic treatment by drinking only the most raw and rasping fluids that the bar afforded.

The preliminary drinking over, they moodily whittled, chewed, and expectorated; a stranger would have imagined them a batch of miserable criminals awaiting transportation.

The silence was finally broken by a decided-looking red-haired man, who had been neatly beveling the door-post with his knife, and who spoke as if his words only by great difficulty escaped being bitten in two.

"We ken burn down the schoolhouse right before his face and eyes, and then mebbe the State Board 'll git our idees about eddycation."

"Twon't be no use, Mose," said Judge Barber, whose legal title was honorary, and conferred because he had spent some time in a penitentiary in the East. "Them State Board fellers is wrong, but they've got grit, ur they'd never hev got the schoolhouse done after we rode the contractor out uv the Flat on one of his own boards. Besides, some uv 'em might think we wuz rubbin' uv it in, an' next thing you know'd they'd be buildin' us a jail."

"Can't we buy off these young uns' folks?" queried an angular fellow from Southern Illinois. "They're a mizzable pack of shotes, an' I b'leeve they'd all leave the camp fur a few ounces."

"Ye—es," drawled the judge, dubiously; "but thar's the Widder Ginneys—*she'd* pan out a pretty good school-room-full with her eight young uns, an' there ain't ounces enough in the diggin's to make *her* leave while Tom Ginneys's coffin's roostin' under the rocks."

"Then," said Mose, the first speaker, his words escaping with even more difficulty than before, "throw around keards to see who's to marry the widder, an' boss her young uns. The feller that gits the fust Jack's to do the job."

"Meanin' no insult to this highly respectable crowd," said the judge, in a very bland tone, and inviting it to walk up to the bar and specify its consolation, "I don't b'leeve there's one uv yer the widder'd hev." The judge's eye glanced along the line at the bar, and he continued softly, but in decided accents—"Not a cussed one. But," added the judge, passing his pouch to the barkeeper, "if anything's to be done, it must be done lively, fur the stage is pretty nigh here. Tell ye what's ez good ez ennything. We'll crowd around the stage, fust throwin' keards for who's to put out his hoof to be accidently trod onto by the infernal teacher ez he gits out. Then satisfaction must be took out uv the teacher. It'll be a mean job, fur these teachers hevn't the spunk of a coyote, an' ten to one he won't hev no shootin' irons, so the job 'll hev to be done with fists."

"Good!" said Mose. "The crowd drinks with me to a square job, and no backin'. Chuck the pasteboards, jedge —— The—dickens!" For Mose had got first Jack.

"Square job, and no backin'," said the judge, with a grin. There's the stage now—hurry up, fellers!"

The stage drew up with a crash in front of The Nugget, and the passengers, outside and in, but none looking teacherish, hurried into the saloon. The boys scarcely knew whether to swear from disappointment or gratification, when a start from Mose drew their attention again to the stage. On the top step appeared a small shoe, above which was visible a small section of stocking far whiter and smaller than is usual in the mines. In an instant a similar shoe appeared on the lower step, and the boys saw, successively, the edge of a dress, a waterproof cloak, a couple of small gloved hands, a bright muffler, and a pleasant face covered with brown hair, and a bonnet. Then they heard a cheerful voice say:

"I'm the teacher, gentlemen—can any one show me the schoolhouse?"

The miserable Mose looked ghastly, and tottered. A suspicion of a wink graced the judge's eye, but he exclaimed in a stern, low tone: "Square job, an' no backin'," upon which Mose took to his heels and the Placerville trail.

The judge had been a married man, so he promptly answered:

"I'll take yer thar, mum, ez soon ez I git yer baggage."

"Thank you," said the teacher; "that valise under the seat is all."

The judge extracted a small valise marked "Huldah Brown," offered his arm, and he and the teacher walked off before the astonished crowd as naturally as if the appearance of a modest-looking young lady was an ordinary occurrence at the Flat.

The stage refilled, and rattled away from the dumb and staring crowd, and the judge returned.

"Well, boys," said he, "yer got to marry *two* women, now, to stop that school, an' you'll find this un more particler than the widder. I just tell yer what it is about that school—it's agoin' to go on, spite uv any jackasses that wants it broke up; an' any gentleman that's insulted ken git satisfaction by——"

TOLEDO AND THE COMMITTEEMEN'S VISIT TO THE SCHOOLTEACHER.

"Who wants it broke up, you old fool?" demanded Toledo, a man who had been named after the city from which he had come, and who had been from the first one of the fiercest opponents of the school. "I move the appointment uv a committee of three to wait on the teacher, see if the school wants anything money can buy, take up subscriptions to git it, an' lay out any feller that don't come down with the dust when he's went fur."

"Hurray!" "Bully!" "Good!" "Sound!" "Them's the talk!" and other sympathetic expressions, were heard from the members of the late anti-school party.

The judge, who, by virtue of age, was the master of ceremonies and general moderator of the camp, very promptly appointed a committee, consisting of Toledo and two miners, whose attire appeared the most respectable in the place, and instructed them to wait on the schoolmarm, and tender her the cordial support of the miners.

Early the next morning the committee called at the schoolhouse, attached to which were two small rooms in which teachers were expected to keep house.

The committee found the teacher "putting to rights" the schoolroom. Her dress was tucked up, her sleeves rolled, her neck hidden by a bright handkerchief, and her hair "a-blowin' all to glory," as Toledo afterward expressed it. Between the exertion, the bracing air, and the excitement caused by the newness of everything, Miss Brown's pleasant face was almost handsome.

"Mornin', marm," said Toledo, raising a most shocking hat, while the remaining committee-men expeditiously ranged themselves behind him, so that the teacher might by no chance look into their eyes.

"Good-morning, gentlemen," said Miss Brown, with a cheerful smile; "please be seated. I suppose you wish to speak of your children?"

Toledo, who was a very young man, blushed, and the whole committee was as uneasy on its feet as if its boots had been soled with fly-blisters. Finally, Toledo answered:

"Not much, marm, seein' we ain't got none. Me an' these gentlemen's a committee from the boys."

"From the boys?" echoed Miss Brown. She had heard so many wonderful things about the Golden State, that now she soberly wondered whether bearded men called themselves boys, and went to school.

"From the miners, washin' along the crick, marm—they want to know what they ken do fur yer," continued Toledo.

"I am very grateful," said Miss Brown; "but I suppose the local school committee——"

"Don't count on them, marm," interrupted Toledo; "they're livin' five miles away, and they're only the preacher, an' doctor, an' a feller that's j'ined the church lately. None uv 'em but the doctor ever shows themselves at the saloon, an' *he* only comes when there's a diffikilty, an' he's called in to officiate. But the boys—the boys hez got the dust, marm, an' they've got the will. One uv us 'll be in often to see what can be done fur yer. Good-mornin', marm."

Toledo raised his hat again, the other committee-men bowed profoundly to all the windows and seats, and then the whole retired, leaving Miss Brown in the wondering possession of an entirely new experience.

"Well?" inquired the crowd, as the committee approached the creek.

"Well," replied Toledo, "she's just a hundred an' thirty pound nugget, an' no mistake—hey, fellers?"

"You bet," promptly responded the remainder of the committee.

"Good!" said the judge. "What does she want?"

Toledo's countenance fell.

"By thunder!" he replied, "we got out 'fore she had a chance to tell us!"

The judge stared sharply upon the young man, and hurriedly turned to hide a merry twitching of his lips.

That afternoon the boys were considerably astonished and scared at seeing the schoolmistress walking quickly

toward the creek. The chairman of the new committee was
fully equal to the occasion. Mounting a rock, he roared:
"You fellers without no sherts on, git. You with shoes
off, put 'em on. Take your pants out uv yer boots. Hats
off when the lady comes. Hurry up, now—no foolin'."

The shirtless ones took a lively double-quick toward
some friendly bushes, the boys rolled down their sleeves and
pantaloons, and one or two took the extra precaution to
wash the mud off their boots.

Meanwhile Miss Brown approached, and Toledo stepped
forward.

"Anything wrong up at the schoolhouse?" said he.

"Oh, no, replied Miss Brown, "but I have always had a
great curiosity to see how gold was obtained. It seems as
if it must be very easy to handle those little pans. Don't
you—don't you suppose some miner would lend me his pan
and let me try just *once*?"

"Certingly, marm; ev'ry galoot ov 'em would be glad of
the chance. Here, you fellers—who's got the cleanest pan?"

Half a dozen men washed out their pans, and hurried off
with them. Toledo selected one, put in dirt and water, and
handed it to Miss Brown.

"Thar you are, marm, but I'm afeared you'll wet your
dress."

"Oh, that won't harm," cried Miss Brown, with a laugh
which caused one enthusiastic miner to "cut the pigeon-
wing."

She got the miner's touch to a nicety, and in a moment
had a spray of dirty water flying from the edge of the pan,
while all the boys stood in a respectful semicircle, and
stared delightedly. The pan empty, Toledo refilled it
several times; and, finally, picking out some pebbles and
hard pieces of earth, pointed to the dirty, shiny deposit in
the bottom of the pan, and briefly remarked:

"Thar 'tis, marm."

"Oh!" screamed Miss Brown, with delight; "is that
really gold-dust?"

"That's it," said Toledo. "I'll jest put it up fur yer, so yer ken kerry it."

"Oh, no," said Miss Brown, "I couldn't think of it—it isn't mine."

"You washed it out, marm, an' that makes a full title in these parts."

All of the traditional honesty of New England came into Miss Brown's face in an instant; and, although she, Yankee-like, estimated the value of the dust, and sighingly thought how much easier it was to win gold in that way than by forcing ideas into stupid little heads, she firmly declined the gold, and bade the crowd a smiling good-day.

"Did yer see them little fingers uv hern a-holdin' out that pan?—did yer see her, fellers?" inquired an excited miner.

"Yes, an' the way she made that dirt git, ez though she was useder to washin' than wallopin'," said another.

"Wallopin'!" echoed a staid miner. "I'd gie my claim, an' throw in my pile to boot, to be a young 'un an' git walloped by them playthings of han's."

"Jest see how she throwed dirt an' water on them boots," said another, extending an enormous ugly boot. "Them boots ain't fur sale now—them ain't."

"Them be durned!" contemptuously exclaimed another. "She tramped right on my toes as she backed out uv the crowd."

Every one looked jealously at the last speaker, and a grim old fellow suggested that the aforesaid individual had obtained a trampled foot by fraud, and that each man in camp had, consequently, a right to demand satisfaction of him.

But the judge decided that he of the trampled foot was right, and that any miner who wouldn't take such a chance, whether fraudulently or otherwise, hadn't the spirit of a man in him.

Yankee Sam, the shortest man in camp, withdrew from the crowd, and paced the banks of the creek, lost in thought.

Within half an hour Sam was owner of the only store in the place, had doubled the prices of all articles of clothing contained therein, and increased at least six-fold the price of all the white shirts.

Next day the sun rose on Bottle Flat in his usual conservative and impassive manner. Had he respected the dramatic proprieties, he would have appeared with aston-ished face and uplifted hands, for seldom had a whole community changed so completely in a single night.

Uncle Hans, the only German in the camp, had spent the preceding afternoon in that patient investigation for which the Teutonic mind is so justly noted. The morning sun saw over Hans's door a sign, in charcoal, which read, "SHAVIN' DUN HIER"; and few men went to the creek that morning without submitting themselves to Hans's hands.

Then several men who had been absent from the saloon the night before straggled into camp, with jaded mules and new attire. Carondelet Joe came in, clad in a pair of pants, on which slender saffron-hued serpents ascended graceful gray Corinthian columns, while from under the collar of a new white shirt appeared a cravat, displaying most of the lines of the solar spectrum.

Flush, the Flat champion at poker, came in late in the afternoon, with a huge watch-chain, and an overpowering bosom-pin, and his horrid fingers sported at least one seal-ring each.

Several stove-pipe hats were visible in camp, and even a pair of gloves were reported in the pocket of a miner.

Yankee Sam had sold out his entire stock, and prevented bloodshed over his only bottle of hair-oil by putting it up at a raffle, in forty chances, at an ounce a chance. His stock of white shirts, seven in number, were visible on manly forms; his pocket combs and glasses were all gone; and there had been a steady run on needles and thread. Most of the miners were smoking new white clay pipes, while a few thoughtful ones, hoping for a repetition of the events of the previous day, had scoured their pans to a dazzling brightness.

As for the innocent cause of all this commotion, she was fully as excited as the miners themselves. She had never been outside of Middle Bethany, until she started for California. Everything on the trip had been strange, and her stopping-place and its people were stranger than all. The male population of Middle Bethany, as is usual with small New England villages, consisted almost entirely of very young boys and very old men. But here at Bottle Flat were hosts of middle-aged men, and such funny ones! She was wild to see more of them, and hear them talk; yet, her wildness was no match for her prudence. She sighed to think how slightly Toledo had spoken of the minister on the local committee, and she piously admitted to herself that Toledo and his friends were undoubtedly on the brink of the bottomless pit, and yet—they certainly were very kind. If she could only exert a good influence upon these men—but how?

Suddenly she bethought herself of the grand social centre of Middle Bethany—the singing-school. Of course, she couldn't start a singing-school at Bottle Flat, but if she were to say the children needed to be led in singing, would it be very hypocritical? She might invite such of the miners as were musically inclined to lead the school in singing in the morning, and thus she might, perhaps, remove some of the prejudice which, she had been informed, existed against the school.

She broached the subject to Toledo, and that faithful official had nearly every miner in camp at the schoolhouse that same evening. The judge brought a fiddle, Uncle Hans came with a cornet, and Yellow Pete came grinning in with his darling banjo.

There was a little disappointment all around when the boys declared their ignorance of "Greenville" and "Bonny Doon," which airs Miss Brown decided were most easy for the children to begin with; but when it was ascertained that the former was the air to "Saw My Leg Off," and the latter was identical with the "Three Black Crows," all friction was removed, and the melodious howling attracted the few remaining boys at the saloon, and brought them up in a body, led by the barkeeper himself.

The exact connection between melody and adoration is yet an unsolved religio-psychological problem. But we all know that everywhere in the habitable globe the two intermingle, and stimulate each other, whether the adoration be offered to heavenly or earthly objects. And so it came to pass that, at the Bottle Flat singing-school, the boys looked straight at the teacher while they raised their tuneful voices; that they came ridiculously early, so as to get front seats; and that they purposely sung out of tune, once in a while, so as to be personally addressed by the teacher.

And she—pure, modest, prudent, and refined—saw it all, and enjoyed it intensely. Of course, it could never go any further, for though there was in Middle Bethany no moneyed aristocracy, the best families scorned alliances with any who were undegenerate, and would not be unequally yoked with those who drank, swore, and gambled—let alone the fearful suspicion of murder, which Miss Brown's imagination affixed to every man at the Flat.

But the boys themselves—considering the unspeakable contempt which had been manifested in the camp for the profession of teaching, and for all who practiced it—the boys exhibited a condescension truly Christian. They vied with each other in manifesting it, and though the means were not always the most appropriate, the honesty of the sentiment could not be doubted.

One by one the greater part of the boys, after adoring and hoping, saw for themselves that Miss Brown could never be expected to change her name at their solicitation. Sadder but better men, they retired from the contest, and solaced themselves by betting on the chances of those still "on the track," as an ex-jockey tersely expressed the situation.

There was no talk of "false hearted" or "fair temptress," such as men often hear in society; for not only had all the tenderness emanated from manly breasts alone, but it had never taken form of words.

Soon the hopeful ones were reduced to half a dozen of these. Yankee Sam was the favorite among the betting men, for Sam, knowing the habits of New England damsels, went to Placerville one Friday, and returned next day with a horse and buggy. On Sunday he triumphantly drove Miss Brown to the nearest church. Ten to one was offered on Sam that Sunday afternoon, as the boys saw the demure and contented look on Miss Brown's face as she returned from church. But Samuel followed in the sad footsteps of many another great man, for so industriously did he drink to his own success that he speedily developed into a bad case of *delirium tremens*.

Then Carondelet Joe, calmly confident in the influence of his wonderful pants, led all odds in betting. But one evening, when Joe had managed to get himself in the front row and directly before the little teacher, that lady turned her head several times and showed signs of discomfort. When it finally struck the latter that the human breath might, perhaps, waft toward a lady perfumes more agreeable than those of mixed drinks, he abruptly quitted the school and the camp.

Flush, the poker champion, carried with him to the singing-school that astounding impudence which had long been the terror and admiration of the camp. But a quality which had always seemed exactly the thing when applied to poker seemed to the boys barely endurable when displayed toward Miss Brown.

One afternoon, Flush indiscreetly indulged in some triumphant and rather slighting remarks about the little teacher. Within fifteen minutes, Flush's final earthly home had been excavated, and an amateur undertaker was making his coffin.

An untimely proposal by a good-looking young Mexican, and his prompt rejection, left the race between Toledo and a Frenchman named Lecomte. It also left Miss Brown considerably frightened, for until now she had imagined nothing more serious than the rude admiration which had so delighted her at first.

But now, who knew but some one else would be ridiculous? Poor little Miss Brown suffered acutely at the thought of giving pain, and determined to be more demure than ever.

But alas! even her agitation seemed to make her more charming to her two remaining lovers.

Had the boys at the saloon comprehended in the least the cause of Miss Brown's uneasiness, they would have promptly put both Lecomte and Toledo out of the camp, or out of the world. But to their good-natured, conceited minds it meant only that she was confused, and unable to decide, and unlimited betting was done, to be settled upon the retirement of either of the contestants.

And while patriotic feeling influenced the odds rather in Toledo's favor, it was fairly admitted that the Frenchman was a formidable rival.

To all the grace of manner, and the knowledge of women that seems to run in Gallic blood, he was a man of tolerable education and excellent taste. Besides, Miss Brown was so totally different from French women, that every development of her character afforded him an entirely new sensation, and doubled his devotion.

Toledo stood his ground manfully, though the boys considered it a very bad sign when he stopped drinking, and spent hours in pacing the ground in front of his hut, with his hands behind him, and his eyes fixed on the ground.

Finally, when he was seen one day to throw away his faithful old pipe, heavy betters hastened to "hedge" as well as they might.

Besides, as one of the boys truthfully observed, "He couldn't begin to wag a jaw along with that Frenchman."

But, like many other young men, he could talk quite eloquently with his eyes, and as the language of the eyes is

always direct, and purely grammatical, Miss Brown understood everything they said, and, to her great horror, once or
twice barely escaped talking back.

The poor little teacher was about to make the whole
matter a subject of special prayer, when a knock at the
door startled her.

She answered it, and beheld the homely features of the
judge.

"I just come in to talk a little matter that's been
botherin' me some time. Ye'll pardon me ef I talk a little
plain?" said he.

"Certainly," replied the teacher, wondering if he, too,
had joined her persecutors.

"Thank ye," said the judge, looking relieved. "It's all
right. I've got darters to hum ez big ez you be, an' I want
to talk to yer ez ef yer was one uv 'em."

The judge looked uncertain for a moment, and then
proceeded :

"That feller Toledo's dead in love with yer—uv course
you know it, though 'tain't likely he's told yer. All I want
to say 'bout him is, drop him kindly. He's been took so
bad sence you come, that he's stopped drinkin' an' chewin'
an' smokin' an' cussin', an' he hasn't played a game at The
Nugget sence the first singin'-school night. Mebbe this all
ain't much to you, but you've read 'bout that woman that
was spoke well uv fur doin' what she could. He's the fust
feller I've ever seen in the diggin's that went back on all
the comforts uv life, an'—an' I've been a young man myself,
an' know how big a claim it's been fur him to work. I ain't
got the heart to see him spiled now; but he *will* be ef, when
yer hev to drop him, yer don't do it kindly. An'—just one
thing more—the quicker he's out of his misery the better."

The old jail-bird screwed a tear out of his eye with a
dirty knuckle, and departed abruptly, leaving the little
teacher just about ready to cry herself.

But before she was quite ready, another knock startled
her.

She opened the door, and let in Toledo himself.

"Good-evin', marm," said he, gravely. "I just come in to make my last 'fficial call, seein' I'm goin' away to-morrer. Ez there anything the schoolhouse wants I ken git an' send from 'Frisco?"

"Going away!" ejaculated the teacher, heedless of the remainder of Toledo's sentence.

"Yes, marm; goin' away fur good. Fact is, I've been tryin' to behave myself lately, an' I find I need more company at it than I git about the diggin's. I'm goin' some place whar I ken learn to be the gentleman I feel like bein'—to be decent an' honest, an' useful, an' there ain't anybody here that keers to help a feller that way—nobody."

The ancestor of the Browns of Middle Bethany was at Lexington on that memorable morning in '75, and all of his promptness and his courage, ten times multiplied, swelled the heart of his trembling little descendant, as she faltered out:

"There's one."

"Who?" asked Toledo, before he could raise his eyes.

But though Miss Brown answered not a word, he did not repeat his question, for such a rare crimson came into the little teacher's face, that he hid it away in his breast, and acted as if he would never let it out again.

Another knock at the door.

Toledo dropped into a chair, and Miss Brown, hastily smoothing back her hair, opened the door, and again saw the judge.

"I jest dropped back to say——" commenced the judge, when his eye fell upon Toledo.

He darted a quick glance at the teacher, comprehended the situation at once, and with a loud shout of "Out of his misery, by thunder!" started on a run to carry the news to the saloon.

*   *   *   *   *   *   *

Miss Brown completed her term, and then the minister,

who was on the local Board, was called in to formally make
her tutor for life to a larger pupil. Lecomte, with true
French gallantry, insisted on being groomsman, and the
judge gave away the bride. The groom, who gave a name
very different from any ever heard at the Flat, placed on his
bride's finger a ring, inscribed within, "Made from gold
washed by Huldah Brown." The little teacher has
increased the number of her pupils by several, and her
latest one calls her grandma.

I.

"YE don't say?"

"I do though."

"Wa'al, I never."

"Nuther did I—adzackly."

"Don't be provokin', Ephr'm—what makes you talk in that dou'fle way?"

"Wa'al, ma, the world hain't all squeezed into this yere little town of Crankett. I've been elsewheres, some, an' I've seed some funny things, and likewise some that wuzn't so funny ez they might be."

"P'r'aps ye hev, but ye needn't allus be a-settin' other folks down. Mebbe Crankett ain't the whole world, but it's seed that awful case of Molly Capins, and the shipwreck of thirty-four, when the awful nor'easter wuz, an'——"

"Wa'al, wa'al, ma—don't let's fight 'bout it," said Ephr'm, with a sigh, as he tenderly scraped down a new ax-helve with a piece of glass, while his wife made the churn-dasher hurry up and down as if the innocent cream was Ephr'm's back, and she was avenging thereon Ephr'm's insults to Crankett and its people.

Deacon Ephraim Crankett was a descendant of the founder of the village, and although now a sixty-year old farmer, he had in his lifetime seen considerable of the world. He had been to the fishing-banks a dozen times, been whaling twice, had carried a cargo of wheat up the Mediterranean, and had been second officer of a ship which

had picked up a miscellaneous cargo in the heathen ports
of Eastern Asia.

He had picked up a great many ideas, too, wherever he

JIM HOCKSON'S REVENGE. —"HE HELD IT UNDER THE LIGHT, AND
EXAMINED IT CLOSELY."

had been, and his wife was immensely proud of him and
them, whenever she could compare them with the men and
ideas which existed at Crankett; but when Ephr'm displayed

his memories and knowledge to her alone—oh, that was a
very different thing.

"Anyhow," resumed Mrs. Crankett, raising the lid of the
churn to see if there were any signs of butter, "it's an everlastin' shame. Jim Hockson's a young feller in good
standin' in the Church, an' Millie Botayne's an unbeliever—
they say her father's a reg'lar infidel."

"Easy, ma, easy," gently remonstrated Ephr'm. " When
he seed you lookin' at his pet rose-bush on yer way to
church las' Sunday, didn't he hurry an' pull two or three an'
han' 'em to ye?"

"Yes, an' what did he hev' in t'other han'?—a Boasting
paper, an' not a Sunday one, nuther! Millicent ain't a
Christian name, nohow ye can fix it—it amounts to jest
'bout's much ez she does, an' that's nothing. She's got a
soft face, an' purty hair—ef it's all her own, which I powerfully doubt—an' after that ther's nothin' to her. She's never
been to sewin' meetin', an' she's off a boatin' with that New
York chap every Saturday afternoon, instead of goin' to the
young people's prayer-meetin's."

"She's most supported Sam Ransom's wife an' young
uns since Sam's smack was lost," suggested Ephr'm.

" That's you, Deac'n Crankett," replied his wife, "always
stick up for sinners. P'r'aps you'd make better use of your
time ef you'd examine yer own evidences."

" Wa'al, wife," said the deacon, "she's engaged to that
New York feller, ez you call Mr. Brown, so there's no danger of Jim bein' onequally yoked with an onbeliever. An' I
wish her well, from the bottom of my heart."

" I don't," cried Mrs. Crankett, giving the dasher a
vicious push, which sent the cream flying frantically up to
the top of the churn; "I hope he'll turn out bad, an' her
pride 'll be tuk down ez——"

The deacon had been long enough at sea to know the
signs of a long storm, and to know that prudence suggested
a prompt sailing out of the course of such a storm, when
possible; so he started for the door, carrying the glass and

ax-helve with him. Suddenly the door opened, and a female
figure ran so violently against the ax-helve, that the said
figure was instantly tumbled to the floor, and seemed an
irregular mass of faded pink calico, and subdued plaid
shawl.

"Miss Peekin!" exclaimed Mrs. Crankett, dropping the
churn-dasher and opening her eyes.

"Like to ha' not been," whined the figure, slowly arising
and giving the offending ax-helve 'a glance which would have
set it on fire had it not been of green hickory; "but—*hev* you
heerd?"

"What?" asked Mrs. Crankett, hastily setting a chair for
the newcomer, while Ephr'm, deacon and sixty though he
was, paused in his almost completed exit.

"*He's* gone!" exclaimed Miss Peekin.

"Oh, I heerd Jim hed gone to Califor——"

"Pshaw!" said Miss Peekin, contemptuously; " that was
days ago! I mean Brown—the New York chap—Millie
Botayne's lover!"

"Ye don't?"

"But I do; an' what's more, he *had* to. Ther wuz men
come after him in the nighttime, but he must hev heard
'em, fur they didn't find him in his room, an' this mornin'
they found that his sailboat was gone, too. An' what's
more, ther's a printed notice up about him, an' he's a
defaulter, and there's five thousand dollars for whoever
catches him, an' he's stole *twenty-five*, an' he's all described
in the notice, as p'ticular as if he was a full-blood Alderney
cow."

"Poor fellow," sighed the deacon, for which interruption
he received a withering glance from Miss Peekin.

"They say Millie's a goin' on awful, and that she sez
she'll marry him now if he'll come back. But it ain't likely
he'll be such a fool; now he's got so much money, he don't
need hern. Reckon her an' her father won't be so high an'
mighty an' stuck up now. It's powerful discouragin' to the
righteous to see the ungodly flourishin' so, an' a-rollin' in

ther wealth, when ther betters has to be on needles all year
fur fear the next mack'ril catch won't 'mount to much. The
idee of her bein' willin' to marry a defaulter! I can't
understand it."

"Poor girl!" sighed Mrs. Crankett, wiping one eye with
the corner of her apron. "I'd do it myself, ef I was her?"

The deacon dropped the ax-helve, and gave his wife a
tender kiss on each eye.

II.

PERHAPS Mr. Darwin can tell inquirers why, out of very
common origin, there occasionally spring beings who are
very decided improvements on their progenitors; but we
are only able to state that Jim Hockson was one of these
superior beings, and was himself fully aware of the fact. Not
that he was conceited at all, for he was not, but he could
not help seeing what every one else saw and acknowledged.

Every one liked him, for he was always kind in word and
action, and every one was glad to be Jim Hockson's friend;
but somehow Jim seemed to consider himself his best
company.

His mackerel lines were worked as briskly as any others
when the fish were biting; but when the fish were gone, he
would lean idly on the rail, and stare at the waves and clouds;
he could work a cranberry-bog so beautifully that the
people for miles around came to look on and take lessons;
yet, when the sun tried to hide in the evening behind a
ragged row of trees on a ridge beyond Jim's cranberry-
patch, he would lean on his spade, and gaze until everything
about him seemed yellow.

He read the Bible incessantly, yet offended alike the
pious saints and critical sinners by never preaching or
exhorting. And out of everything Jim Hockson seemed to
extract what it contained of the ideal and the beautiful; and
when he saw Millicent Botayne, he straightway adored the
first woman he had met who was alike beautiful, intelligent
and refined. Miss Millie, being human, was pleased by the

admiration of the handsome, manly fellow who seemed so far
the superior of the men of his class; but when, in his
honest simplicity, he told her that he loved her, she declined
his further attentions in a manner which, though very delicate and kind, opened Jim's blue eyes to some sad things he
had never seen before.

He neither got drunk, nor threatened to kill himself, nor
married the first silly girl he met; but he sensibly left the
place where he had suffered so greatly, and, in a sort of sad
daze, he hurried off to hide himself in the newly discovered
gold-fields of California. Perhaps he had suddenly learned
certain properties of gold which were heretofore unknown
to him; at any rate, it was soon understood at Spanish
Stake, where he had located himself, that Jim Hockson got
out more gold per week than any man in camp, and that it
all went to San Francisco.

"Kind of a mean cuss, I reckon," remarked a newcomer,
one day at the saloon, when Jim alone, of the crowd present,
declined to drink with him.

"Not any!" replied Colonel Two, so called because he
had two eyes, while another colonel in the camp had but
one. "An' it's good for *you*, stranger," continued the
colonel, "that you ain't been long in camp, else some of the
boys 'ud put a hole through you for sayin' anything 'gainst
Jim; for we all swear by him, *we* do. He don't carry
shootin'-irons, but no feller in camp dares to tackle him; he
don't cuss nobody, but ev'rybody does just as he asks 'em to.
As to drinkin', why, I'd swear off myself, ef 'twud make me
hold a candle to him. Went to old Bermuda t'other day,
when he was ravin' tight and layin' for Butcher Pete with a
shootin'-iron, an' he actilly talked Bermuda into soakin' his
head an' turnin' in—ev'rybody else was afeared to go nigh
old Bermuda that day."

The newcomer seemed gratified to learn that Jim was so
peaceable a man—that was the natural supposition, at least
—for he forthwith cultivated Jim with considerable assiduity,
and being, it was evident, a man of considerable taste and

experience, Jim soon found his companionship very agreeable, and he lavished upon his new acquaintance, who had been nicknamed Tarpaulin, the many kind and thoughtful attentions which had endeared Jim to the other miners.

The two men lived in the same hut, staked claims adjoining each other, and Tarpaulin, who had been thin and nervous-looking when he first came to camp, began to grow peaceable and plump under Jim's influence.

One night, as Jim and Tarpaulin lay chatting before a fire in their hut, they heard a thin, wiry voice in the next hut inquiring:

"Anybody in this camp look like this?"

Tarpaulin started.

"That's a funny question," said he; "let's see who and what the fellow is."

And then Tarpaulin started for the next hut. Jim waited some time, and hearing low voices in earnest conversation, went next door himself.

Tarpaulin was not there, but two small, thin, sharp-eyed men were there, displaying an old-fashioned daguerreotype of a handsome-looking young man, dressed in the latest New York style; and more than this Jim did not notice.

"Don't know him, mister," said Colonel Two, who happened to be the owner of the hut. "Besides ef, as is most likely, he's growed long hair an' a beard since he left the States, his own mother wouldn't know him from George Washington. Brother o' yourn?"

"No," said one of the thin men; "he's—well, the fact is, we'll give a thousand dollars to any one who'll find him for us in twenty-four hours."

"Deppity sheriffs?" asked the colonel, retiring somewhat hastily under his blankets.

"About the same thing," said one of the thin men, with a sickly smile.

"Git!" roared the colonel, suddenly springing from his bed, and cocking his revolver. "I b'lieve in the Golden Rule, *I* do!"

The detectives, with the fine instinct peculiar to their profession, rightly construed the colonel's action as a hint, and withdrew, and Jim retired to his own hut, and fell asleep while waiting for his partner.

Morning came, but no Tarpaulin; dinner-time arrived, but Jim ate alone, and was rather blue. He loved a sociable chat, and of late Tarpaulin had been almost his sole companion.

Evening came, but Tarpaulin came not.

Jim couldn't abide the saloon for a whole evening, so he lit a candle in his own hut, and attempted to read.

Tarpaulin was a lover of newspapers—it seemed to Jim he received more papers than all the remaining miners put together.

Jim thought he would read some of these same papers, and unrolled Tarpaulin's blankets to find them, when out fell a picture-case, opening as it fell. Jim was about to close it again, when he suddenly started, and exclaimed :

"Millicent Botayne ! "

He held it under the light, and examined it closely.

There could be no doubt as to identity—there were the same exquisite features which, a few months before, had opened to Jim Hockson a new world of beauty, and had then, with a sweet yet sad smile, knocked down all his fair castles, and destroyed all his exquisite pictures.

Strange that it should appear to him now, and so unexpectedly, but stranger did it seem to Jim that on the opposite side of the case should be a portrait which was a duplicate of the one shown by the detectives !

"That rascal Brown ! " exclaimed Jim. "So he succeeded in getting her, did he ? But I shouldn't call him names ; he had as much right to make love to her as I. God grant he may make her happy ! And he is probably a very fine fellow—*must* be, by his looks."

Suddenly Jim started, as if shocked by an electric battery. Hiding all the hair and beard of the portrait, he stared at it a moment, and exclaimed :

"*Tarpaulin !* "

III.

"Both gone!" exclaimed Colonel Two, hurrying into the saloon, at noon.

"*Both* gone?" echoed two or three men.

"Yes," said the colonel; "and the queerest thing is, they left ev'rything behind—every darned thing! I never *did* see such a stampede afore—*I* didn't! Nobody's got any idee of whar they be, nor what it's 'bout neither."

"Don't be *too* sartain, colonel!" piped Weasel, a self-contained mite of a fellow, who was still at work upon his glass, filled at the last general treat, although every one else had finished so long ago that they were growing thirsty again—"don't be *too* sartain. Them detectives bunked at my shanty last night."

"The deuce they did!" cried the colonel. "Good the rest of us didn't know it."

"Well," said Weasel, moving his glass in graceful circles, to be sure that all the sugar dissolved, "I dunno. It's a respectable business, an' I wanted to have a good look at 'em."

"What's that got to do with Jim and Tarpaulin?" look at demanded the colonel, fiercely.

"Wait, and I'll tell you," replied Weasel, provokingly, taking a leisurely sip at his glass. "Jim come down to see 'em——"

"What?" cried the colonel.

"An' told 'em he knew their man, an' would help find him," continued Weasel. "They offered him the thousand dollars——"

"Oh, Lord! oh, Lord!" groaned the colonel; "who's a feller to trust in this world! The idee of Jim goin' back on a pardner fur a thousand! I wouldn't hev b'lieved he'd a-done it fur a million!"

"An' he told 'em he'd cram it down their throats if they mentioned it again."

"Bully! Hooray fur Jim!" shouted the colonel.

"What'll yer take, fellers? Fill high! Here's to Jim! the feller that b'lieves his friend's innercent!"

The colonel looked thoughtfully into his glass, and remarked, as if to his own reflection therein, "Ain't many such men here nur nowhars else!" after which he drank the toast himself.

"But that don't explain what Tarpaulin went fur," said the colonel, suddenly.

"Yes, it does," said the exasperating Weasel, shutting his thin lips so tightly that it was hard to see where his mouth was,

"What?" cried the colonel. "'Twould take a four-horse corkscrew to get anything out o' you, you dried-up little scoundrel!"

"Why!" replied Weasel, greatly pleased by the colonel's compliment, "after what you said about hair and beard hidin' a man, one of them fellers cut a card an' held it over the picture, so as to hide hair an' chin. The forehead an' face an' nose an' ears wuz Tarpaulin's, an' nobody else's."

"Lightning's blazes!" roared the colonel. "Ha, ha, ha! why, Tarpaulin hisself came into my shanty, an' looked at the pictur', an' talked to them 'bout it! Trot out yer glassware, barkeeper—*got* to drink to a feller that's ez cool ez all that!"

The boys drank with the colonel, but they were too severely astonished to enjoy the liquor particularly. In fact, old Bermuda, who had never taken anything but plain rye, drank three fingers of claret that day, and did not know of it until told.

The colonel's mind was unusually excited. It seemed to him there were a number of probabilities upon which to hang bets. He walked outside, that his meditation might be undisturbed, but in an instant he was back, crying:

"Lady comin'!"

Shirt-sleeves and trowsers-legs were hurriedly rolled down, shirt-collars were buttoned, hats were dusted, and then each man went leisurely out, with the air of having merely happened to leave the saloon—an air which imposed upon no disinterested observer.

Coming up the trail beside the creek were a middle-aged gentleman and a young lady, both on horseback.

The gentleman's dress and general style plainly indicated that he was not a miner, nor a storekeeper, nor a barkeeper; while it was equally evident that the lady was neither a washerwoman, a cook, nor a member of either of the very few professions which were open to ladies on the Pacific Coast in those days.

This much every miner quickly decided for himself; but after so deciding, each miner reached the uttermost extremity of his wits, and devoted himself to staring.

The couple reined up before the saloon, and the gentleman drew something small and black and square from his pocket.

"Gentlemen," said he, "we are looking for an old friend of ours, and have traced him to this camp. We scarcely know whether it would be any use to give his name, but here is his picture. Can any one remember having seen the person here?"

Every one looked toward Colonel Two, he being the man with the most practical tongue in camp.

The colonel took the picture, and Weasel slipped up behind him and looked over his shoulder. The colonel looked at the picture, abruptly handed it back, looked at the young lady, and then gazed vacantly into space, and seemed very uncomfortable.

"Been here, but gone," said the colonel, at length.

"Where did he go, do you know?" asked the gentleman, while the lady's eyes dropped wearily.

"Nobody knows—only been gone a day or two," replied the colonel.

The colonel had a well-developed heart, and, relying on what he considered the correct idea of Jim Hockson's mission, ventured to say:

".He'll be back in a day or two—left all his things."

Suddenly Weasel raised his diminutive voice, and said:
" The detec—— "

The determined grip of the colonel's hand interrupted the
communication which Weasel attempted to make, and the
colonel hastily remarked :

" Ther's a feller gone for him that's sure to fetch him
back."

" Who—who is it?" asked the young lady, hesitatingly.

" Well, ma'am," said the colonel, " as yer father—I s'pose,
leastways—said, 'tain't much use to give names in this part
of the world, but the name he's goin' by is Jim Hockson."

The young lady screamed and fell.

IV.

" WHETHER to do it or not, is what bothers me," soliloquized Mr. Weasel, pacing meditatively in front of the
saloon. " The old man offers me two thousand to get
Tarpaulin away from them fellers, and let him know where
to meet him an' his daughter. Two thousand's a pretty
penny, an' the bein' picked out by so smart a lookin' man is
an honor big enough to set off agin' a few hundred dollars
more. But, on t'other hand, if they catch him, they'll come
back here, an' who knows but what they'll want the old
man an' girl as bad as they wanted Tarpaulin? A bird in
the hand's worth two in the bush—better keep near the
ones I got, I reckon. Here they come now!"

As Mr. Weasel concluded his dialogue with himself, Mr.
Botayne and Millicent approached, in company with the
colonel.

The colonel stopped just beyond the saloon, and said :

"Now, here's your best p'int—you can see the hill-trail
fur better'n five miles, an' the crick fur a mile an' a half.
I'll jest hev a shed knocked together to keep the lady from
the sun. An' keep a stiff upper lip, both of yer—trust Jim
Hockson; nobody in the mines ever knowed him to fail."

Millicent shivered at the mention of Jim's name, and the

colonel, unhappily ignorant of the cause of her agitation, tried to divert her mind from the chances of harm to Tarpaulin by growing eloquent in praise of Jim Hockson.

Suddenly the colonel himself started and grew pale. He quickly recovered himself, however, and, with the delicacy of a gentleman, walked rapidly away, as Millicent and her father looked in the direction from which the colonel's surprise came.

There, handcuffed, with beard and hair singed close, clothes torn and face bleeding, walked Ethelbert Brown between the two detectives, while Jim Hockson, with head bowed and hands behind his back, followed a few yards behind.

Some one gave the word at the saloon, and the boys hurried out, but the colonel pointed significantly toward the sorrowful couple, while with the other hand he pointed an ugly pistol, cocked, toward the saloon.

Millicent hurried from her father's side, and flung her arms about the sorry figure of her lover; and Jim Hockson, finding his pathway impeded, raised his eyes, and then blushed violently.

"Sorry for you, sir," said one of the detectives, touching his hat to Mr. Botayne, "but can't help being glad we got a day ahead of you."

"What amount of money will buy your prisoner?" demanded the unhappy father.

"Beg pardon, sir—very sorry, but—we'd be compounding felony in that case, you know," replied one of the officers, gazing with genuine pity on the weeping girl.

"Don't worry," whispered the colonel in Mr. Botayne's ear; "we'll clean out them two fellers, and let Tarpaulin loose again. Ev'ry feller come here for somethin', darn it!" with which sympathizing expression the colonel again retired.

"I'll give you as much as the bank offers," said Mr. Botayne.

"Very sorry, sir; but can't," replied the detective. "We'd be just as bad then in the eyes of the law as before.

Reward, five thousand, bank lose twenty-five thousand — thirty thousand, in odd figures, is least we could take. Even *that* wouldn't be reg'lar; but it would be a safe risk, seeing all the bank cares for's to get its money back."

Mr. Botayne groaned.

"We'll make it as pleasant as we can for you, sir," continued the detective, "if you and the lady'll go back on the ship with us. We'll give him the liberty of the ship as soon as we're well away from land. We'd consider it our duty to watch him, of course; but we'd try to do it so's not to give offense—we've *got* hearts, though we *are* in this business. Hope you can buy him clear when you get home, sir?"

"I've sacrificed everything to get here—I can never clear him," sighed Mr Botayne.

"*I* can!" exclaimed a clear, manly voice.

Millicent raised her eyes, and for the first time saw Jim Hockson.

She gave him a look in which astonishment, gratitude and fear strove for the mastery, and he gave her a straightforward, honest, respectful look in return.

The two detectives dropped their lower jaws alarmingly, and raised their eyebrows to their hat-rims.

"The bank at San Francisco has an agent here," said Jim. "Colonel, won't you fetch him?"

The colonel took a lively double-quick, and soon returned with a business-looking man.

"Mr. Green," said Jim, "please tell me how much I have in your bank?"

The clerk looked over a small book he extracted from his pocket, and replied, briefly :

"Over two thousand ounces."

"Please give these gentlemen a check, made whatever way they like it, for the equivalent of thirty thousand dollars. I'll sign it," said Jim.

The clerk and one of the detectives retired to an adjacent hut, and soon called Jim. Jim joined them, and immediately he and the officer returned to the prisoner.

"It's all right, Maxley," said the officer ; "let him go."
The officer removed the handcuffs, and Ethelbert Brown
was free. His first motion was to seize Jim's hand.

"Hockson, tell me why you helped those detectives,"
said he.

"Revenge !" replied Jim.

"For what?" cried Brown, changing color.

"Gaining Millie Botayne's love," replied Jim.

Brown looked at Millicent, and read the story from her
face.

He turned toward Jim a wondering look, and asked,
slowly:

"Then, why did you free me ?"

"Because she loved you," said Jim, and then he walked
quietly away.

V.

"WHY, Miss Peekin !"

"It's a fact : Eben Javash, that went out better'n a year
ago, hez got back, and he wuz at the next diggins an' heerd
all about it. 'T seems the officers ketched Brown, an' Jim
Hockson gave 'em thirty thousand dollars to pay them an'
the bank too, and then they let him go. Might's well ha
kept his money, though, seein' Brown washed overboard on
the way back.

"I ain't a bettin' man," said the deacon, "but I'd risk
our white-faced cow that them thirty thousand dollars
preached the greatest sermon ever heerd in Californy—ur in
Crankett either."

Miss Peekin threw a withering glance at the deacon; it
was good he was not on trial for heresy, with Miss Peekin
for judge and jury. She continued :

"Eben says there was a fellow named Weasel that hid
close by, an' heerd all 'twas said, and when he went to the
rum-shop an' told the miners, they hooray'd for Jim ez ef
they wuz mad. Just like them crazy fellers—they hain't no
idee when money's wasted."

"The Lord waste all the money in the world that way!" devoutly exclaimed the deacon.

"An' that feller Weasel," continued Miss Peekin, giving the deacon's pet cat a vicious kick, "though he'd always been economical, an' never set a bad example before by persuadin' folk to be intemprit, actilly drored a pistol, and fit with a feller they called Colonel Two—fit for the chance of askin' the crowd to drink to Jim Hockson, an' then went aroun' to all the diggins, tellin' about Jim, an' wastin' his money treatin' folks to drink good luck to Jim. Dis—graceful!"

"It's what *I'd* call a powerful conversion," remarked the deacon.

"But ther's more," said Miss Peekin, with a sigh, and yet with an air of importance befitting the bearer of wonderful tidings.

"What?" eagerly asked Mrs. Crankett.

"Jim's back," said Miss Peekin.

"Mercy on us!" cried Mrs. Crankett.

"The Lord bless and prosper him!" earnestly exclaimed the deacon.

"Well," said Miss Peekin, with a disgusted look, "I s'pose He will, from the looks o' things; fur Eben sez that when Weasel told the fellers how it all wuz, they went to work an' put gold dust in a box fur Jim till ther wus more than he giv fur Brown, an' fellers from all round's been sendin' him dust ever since. He's mighty sight the richest man anywhere near this town."

"Good—bless the Lord!" said the deacon, with delight.

"Ye hain't heerd all of it, though," continued Miss Peekin, with a funereal countenance. "They're going to be married."

"Sakes alive!" gasps Mrs. Crankett.

"It's so," said Miss Peekin; "an' they say she sent for him, by way of the Isthmus, an' he come back that way. Bad enough to marry him, when poor Brown hain't been dead six months, but to *send* for him——"

"Wuz a real noble, big-hearted, womanly thing to do," declared Mrs. Crankett, snatching off her spectacles; "an' I'd hev done it myself ef I'd been her."

The deacon gave his old wife an enthusiastic hug; upon seeing which Miss Peekin hastily departed, with a severely shocked expression of countenance and a nose aspiring heavenward.

BLACK HAT was, in 1851, about as peaceful and well-regulated a village as could be found in the United States.

It was not on the road to any place, so it grew but little; the dirt paid steadily and well, so but few of the original settlers went away.

The march of civilization, with its churches and circuses, had not yet reached Black Hat; marriages never convulsed the settlement with the pet excitement of villages generally, and the inhabitants were never arrayed at swords' point by either religion, politics or newspapers.

To be sure, the boys gambled every evening and all day Sunday; but a famous player, who once passed that way on a prospecting-trip, declared that even a preacher would get sick of such playing; for, as everybody knew everybody else's game, and as all men who played other than squarely had long since been required to leave, there was an utter absence of pistols at the tables.

Occasional disagreements took place, to be sure—they have been taking place, even among the best people, since the days of Cain and Abel; but all difficulties at Black Hat which did not succumb to force of jaw were quietly locked in the bosoms of the disputants until the first Sunday.

Sunday, at Black Hat, orthodoxically commenced at sunset on Saturday, and was piously extended through to working-time on Monday morning, and during this period of thirty-six hours there was submitted to arbitrament, by knife or pistol, all unfinished rows of the week.

On Sunday was also performed all of the hard drinking at Black Hat; but through the week the inhabitants worked as steadily and lived as peacefully as if surrounded by church-steeples, court-houses and jails.

Whether owing to the inevitable visitations of the great disturber of affairs in the Garden of Eden, or only in the due course of that developement which affects communities as well as species, we know not, but certain it is that suddenly the city fathers at Black Hat began to wear thoughtful faces and wrinkled brows, to indulge in unusual periods of silence, and to drink and smoke as if these consoling occupations were pursued more as matters of habit than of enjoyment.

The prime cause of the uneasiness of these good men was a red-faced, red-haired, red-whiskered fellow, who had been nicknamed " Captain," on account of the military cut of the whiskers mentioned above.

The captain was quite a good fellow; but he was suffering severely from "the last infirmity of noble minds"— ambition.

He had gone West to make a reputation, and so openly did he work for it that no one doubted his object; and so untiring and convincing was he, that, in two short weeks, he had persuaded the weaker of the brethren at Black Hat that things in general were considerably out of joint. And as a little leaven leaveneth the whole lump, every man at Black Hat was soon discussing the captain's criticisms, and was neglecting the more peaceable matters of cards and drink. which had previously occupied their leisure hours.

The captain was always fully charged with opinions on every subject, and his eloquent voice was heard at length on even the smallest matter that interested the camp. One day a disloyal miner remarked :

" Captain's jaw is a reg'lar air-trigger; reckon he'll run the camp when Whitey leaves."

Straightway a devout respecter of the "powers that be" carried the remark to Whitey, the chief of the camp.

Now, it happened that Whitey, an immense but very peaceable and sensible fellow, had just been discussing with some of his adherents the probable designs of the captain, and this new report seemed to arrive just in time, for Whitey instantly said:

"Thar he goes agin, d'ye see, pokin' his shovel in all aroun'. Now, ef the boys want me to leave, they kin say so, an' I'll go. 'Tain't the easiest claim in the world to work, runnin' this camp ain't, an' I'll never hanker to be chief nowhar else; but seein' I've stuck to the boys, an' seen 'em through from the fust, 'twouldn't be exactly gent'e-manly, 'pears to me."

And for a moment Whitey hid his emotions in a tin cup, from which escaped perfumes suggesting the rye-fields of Kentucky.

"Nobody wants you to go, Whitey," said Wolverine, one of the chief's most faithful supporters. "Didn't yer kick that New Hampshire feller out of camp when he kept a-sayin' the saloon wuz the gate o' hell?"

"Well," said the chief, with a flush of modest pride, " I don't deny it; but *I* won't remind the boys of it, ef they've forgot it."

"An' didn't yer go to work," said another, "when all the fellers was a-askin' what was to be done with them Chinesers—didn't yer just order the boys to clean 'em out to wunst?"

"That ain't the best thing yer dun, neither!" exclaimed a third. "I wonder does any of them galoots forgit how the saloon got a-fire when ev'rybody was asleep—how the chief turned out the camp, and after the barkeeper got out the door, how the chief rushed in an' rolled out all three of the barrels, and then went dead-bent fur the river with his clothes all a-blazin'? Whar'd we hev been for a couple of weeks ef it hadn't bin fur them bar'ls?"

The remembrance of this gallant act so affected Wolverine, that he exclaimed:

" Whitey, we'll stick to yer like tar-an'-feather, an' ef cap'n an' his friends git troublesome we'll jes' show 'em the trail, an' seggest they're big enough to git up a concern uv their own, instid of tryin' to steal somebody else's."

The chief felt that he was still dear to the hearts of his subjects, and so many took pains that day to renew their allegiance that he grew magnanimous—in fact, when the chief that evening invited the boys to drink, he pushed his own particular bottle to the captain—an attention as delicate as that displayed by a clergyman when he invites into his pulpit the minister of a different creed.

Still the captain labored. So often did the latter stand treat that the barkeeper suddenly ran short of liquor, and was compelled, for a week, to restrict general treats to three per diem until he could lay in a fresh stock.

The captain could hit corks and half-dollars in the air almost every time, but no opportunity occurred in which he could exercise his markmanship for the benefit of the camp.

He also told any number of good stories, at which the boys, Whitey included, laughed heartily ; he sang jolly songs, with a very fair tenor voice, and all the boys joined in the chorus ; and he played a banjo in style, which always set the boys to capering as gracefully as a crowd of bachelor bears.

But still Whitey remained in camp and in office, and the captain, who was as humane as he was ambitious, had no idea of attempting to remove the old chief by force.

On Monday night the whole camp retired early, and slept soundly. Monday had at all times a very short evening at Black Hat, for the boys were generally weary after the duties and excitements of Sunday ; but on this particular Monday a slide had threatened on the hillside, and the boys had been hard at work cutting and carrying huge logs to make a break or barricade.

So, soon after supper they took a drink or two, and sprinkled to their several huts, and Black Hat was at peace,

There were no dogs or cats to make night hideous—no uneasy roosters to be sounding alarm at unearthly hours—no horrible policemen thumping the sidewalks with clubs—no fashionable or dissipated people rattling about in car-

THEY FOUND HIM SENSELESS, AND CARRIED HIM TO THE SALOON, WHERE THE CANDLES WERE ALREADY LIGHTED. ONE OF THE MINERS, WHO HAD BEEN A DOCTOR, PROMPTLY EXAMINED HIS BRUISES.

riages. Excepting an occasional cough, or sneeze, or over-loud snore, the most perfect peace reigned at Black Hat.

Suddenly a low but heavy rumble, and a trembling of

the ground, roused every man in camp, and, rushing out of their huts, the miners saw a mass of stones and earth had been loosened far up the hillside, and were breaking over the barricade in one place, and coming down in a perfect torrent.

They were fortunately moving toward the river on a line obstructed by no houses, though the hut of old Miller, who was very sick, was close to the rocky torrent.

But while they stared, a young pine-tree, perhaps a foot thick, which had been torn loose by the rocks and brought down by them, suddenly tumbled, root first, over a steep rock, a few feet in front of old Miller's door. The leverage exerted by the lower portion of the stem threw the whole tree into a vertical position for an instant; then it caught the wind, tottered, and finally fell directly on the front of old Miller's hut, crushing in the gable and a portion of the front door, and threatening the hut and its unfortunate occupant with immediate destruction.

A deep groan and many terrible oaths burst from the boys, and then, with one impulse, they rushed to the tree and attempted to move it; but it lay at an angle of about forty-five degrees from the horizontal, its roots heavy with dirt, on the ground in front of the door, and its top high in the air.

The boys could only lift the lower portion; but should they do so, then the hut would be entirely crushed by the full weight of the tree.

There was no window through which they could get Miller out, and there was no knowing how long the frail hut could resist the weight of the tree.

Suddenly a well-known voice was heard shouting:

"Keep your head level, Miller, old chap—we'll hev you out of that in no time. Hurry up, somebody, and borrow the barkeeper's ropes. While I'm cuttin', throw a rope over the top, and when she commences to go, haul all together and suddenly, then 'twill clear the hut."

In an instant later the boys saw, by the bright moonlight, the captain, bareheaded, barefooted, with open shirt, standing on the tree directly over the crushed gable, and chopping with frantic rapidity.

" Hooray for cap'en!" shouted some one.

" Hooray!" replied the crowd, and a feeble "hooray" was heard from between the logs of old Miller's hut.

Two or three men came hurrying back with the ropes, and one of them was dexterously thrown across a branch of the tree. Then the boys distributed themselves along both ends of the rope.

" Easy!" screamed the captain. " Plenty of time. I'll give the word. When I say, 'Now,' pull quick and all together. I won't be long."

And big chips flew in undiminished quantity, while a commendatory murmur ran along both lines of men, and Whitey, the chief, knelt with his lips to one of the chinks of the hut, and assured old Miller that he was perfectly safe.

" Now!" shrieked the captain, suddenly.

In his excitement, he stepped toward the top instead of the root of the tree; in an instant the top of the tree was snatched from the hut, but it tossed the unfortunate captain into the air as easily as a sling tosses a stone.

Every one rushed to the spot where he had fallen. They found him senseless, and carried him to the saloon, where the candles were already lighted. One of the miners, who had been a doctor, promptly examined his bruises, and .exclaimed :

" He's two or three broken ribs, that's all. It's a wonder he didn't break every bone in his body. He'll be around all right inside of a month."

" Gentlemen," said Whitey, " I resign. All in favor of the cap'en will please say 'I.' "

" I," replied every one.

" I don't put the noes," continued Whitey, "because I'm a peaceable man, and don't want to hev to kick any man mean enough to vote no. Cap'en, you'r boss of this camp, and I'm yourn obediently."

The captain opened his eyes slowly, and replied :

"I'm much obliged, boys, but I won't give Whitey the trouble. Doctor's mistaken—there's someting broken inside, and I haven't got many minutes more to live."

" Do yer best, cap'en," said the barkeeper, encouragingly. "Promise me you'll stay alive, and I'll go straight down to 'Frisco, and get you all the champagne you can drink."

" You're very kind," replied the captain, faintly ; " but I'm sent for, and I've got to go. I've left the East to make my mark, but I didn't expect to make it in real estate. Whitey, I was a fool for wanting to be chief of Black Hat, and you've forgiven me like a gentleman and a Christian. It's getting dark—I'm thirsty—I'm going—gone ! "

The doctor felt the captain's wrist, and said :

" Fact, gentlemen, he's panned his last dirt."

" Do the honors, boys," said the barkeeper, placing glasses along the bar.

Each man filled his glass, and all looked at Whitey.

" Boys," said Whitey, solemnly, " ef the cap'en hed struck a nugget, good luck might hev spiled him ; ef he'd been chief of Black Hat, or any other place, he might hev got shot. But he's made his mark, so nobody begrudges him, an' nobody can rub it out. So here's to 'the cap'en's mark, a dead sure thing.' Bottoms up."

The glasses were emptied in silence, and turned bottoms uppermost on the bar.

The boys were slowly dispersing, when one, who was strongly suspected of having been a Church member, remarked :

" He was took of a sudden, so he shouldn't be stuck up."

Whitey turned to him, and replied, with some asperity :

" Young man, you'll be lucky ef *you're* ever stuck up as high as the captain."

And all the boys understood what Whitey meant.

TWO o'clock A. M. is supposed to be a popular sleeping hour the world over, and as Flatfoot Bar was a portion of the terrestrial sphere, it was but natural to expect its denizens to be in bed at that hour.

Yet, on a certain morning twenty years ago, when there was neither sickness nor a fashionable entertainment to excuse irregular hours in camp, a bright light streamed from the only window of Chagres Charley's residence at Flatfoot Bar, and inside of the walls of Chagres Charley's domicile were half a dozen miners engaged in earnest conversation.

Flatfoot Bar had never formally elected a town committee, for the half-dozen men aforesaid had long ago modestly assumed the duties and responsibilities of city fathers, and so judicious had been their conduct, that no one had ever expressed a desire for a change in the government.

The six men, in half a dozen different positions, surrounded Chagres Charley's fire, and gazed into it as intently as if they were fire-worshipers awaiting the utterances of a salamanderish oracle.

But the doughty Puritans of Cromwell's time, while they trusted in God, carefully protected their powder from moisture, and the devout Mohammedan, to this day, ties up his camel at night before committing it to the keeping of the higher powers ; so it was but natural that the anxious ones at Flatfoot Bar vigorously ventilated their own ideas while they longed for light and knowledge.

"They ain't ornaments to camp, no way you can fix it.

them Greasers ain't," said a tall miner, bestowing an effective kick upon a stick of firewood, which had departed a short distance from his neighbors.

"Mississp's right, fellers," said the host. "They ain't got the slightest idee of the duties of citizens. They show themselves down to the saloon, to be sure, an' I never seed one of 'em a-waterin' his liquor; but when you've sed that, you've sed ev'rythin'."

"Our distinguished friend speaks truthfully," remarked Nappy Boney, the only Frenchman in camp, and possessing a nickname playfully contracted from the name of the first emperor. "*La gloire* is nothing to them. Comprehends any one that they know not even of France's most illustrious son, *le petit caporal?*"

"That's bad, to be sure," said Texas, cutting an enormous chew of tobacco, and passing both plug and knife; "but that might be overlooked; mebbe the schools down in Mexico ain't up with the times. What I'm down on is, they hain't got none of the eddication that comes nateral to a gentleman, even ef he never seed the outside of a schoolhouse. Who ever heerd of one of 'em hevin' a difficulty with any gentleman, at the saloon or on the crick? They drar a good deal of blood, but it's allers from some of their own kind, an' up there by 'emselves. Ef they hed a grain of public spirit, not to say liberality, they'd do some of their amusements before the rest of us, instead of gougin' the camp out of *its* constitutional amusements. Why, I've knowed the time when I've held in fur six hours on a stretch, till there could be fellers enough around to git a good deal of enjoyment out of it."

"They wash out a sight of dust!" growled Lynn Taps, from the Massachusetts shoe district; "but I never could git one of 'em to put up an ounce on a game—they jest play by 'emselves, an' keep all their washin's to home."

"Blarst 'em hall! let's give 'em tickets-o'-leave, an' show 'em the trail!" roared Bracelets, a stout Englishman, who had on each wrist a red scar, which had suggested his name and unpleasant situations. "I believe in fair play, but I darsn't keep my eyes hoff of 'em sleepy-lookin' tops, when their flippers is anywheres near their knives, you know."

"Well, what's to be done to 'em?" demanded Lynn Taps. "All this jawin's well enough, but jaw never cleared out anybody 'xcep' that time Samson tried, an' then it came from an individual that wasn't related to any of this crowd."

"Let 'em alone till next time they git into a muss, an' then clean 'em all out of camp," said Chagres Charley. "Let's hev it onderstood that while this camp cheerfully recognizes the right of a gentleman to shoot at sight an' lay out his man, that it considers stabbin' in the dark's the same thing as murder. Them's our principles, and folks might's well know 'em fust as last. Good Lord! what's that?"

All the men started to their feet at the sound of a long, loud yell.

"That's one of 'em now!" ejaculated Mississip, with a huge oath. "Nobody but a Greaser ken holler that way— sounds like the last despairin' cry of a dyin' mule. There's only eight or nine of 'em, an' each of us is good fur two Greasers apiece—let's make 'em git this minnit."

And Mississip dashed out of the door, followed by the other five, revolvers in hand.

The Mexicans lived together, in a hut made of raw hides, one of which constituted the door.

The devoted six reached the hut, Texas snatched aside the hide, and each man presented his pistol at full cock.

But no one fired: on the contrary, each man slowly dropped his pistol, and opened his eyes.

There was no newly made corpse visible, nor did any Greasers savagely wave a bloody stiletto.

But on the ground, insensible, lay a Mexican woman, and about her stood seven or eight Greasers, each looking even more dumb, incapable, and solemn than usual.

The city fathers felt themselves in an awkward position, and Mississip finally asked, in the meekest of tones:

"What's the matter?"

"She Codago s wife," softly replied a Mexican. "They fight in Chihuahua—he run away—she follow. She come here now—this minute—she fall on Codago—she say something, we know not—he scream an' run."

"He's a low-lived scoundrel!" said Chagres Charley, between his teeth. "Ef *my* wife thort enough of me to follow me to the diggin's, I wouldn't do much runnin' away. He's a reg'lar black-hearted, white-livered——"

"Sh—h—h!" whispered Nappy, the Frenchman. "The lady is recovering, and she may have a heart."

"*Maria, Madre purissima!*" low wailed the woman. "*Mi nino—mi nino perdido!*"

"What's she a-sayin'?" asked Lynn Taps, in a whisper.

"She talk about little boy lost," said the Mexican.

"An' her husband gone, too, poor woman!" said Chagres Charley, in the most sympathizing tones ever heard at Flatfoot Bar. But a doctor'd be more good to her jes' now than forty sich husbands as her'n. Where's the nearest doctor, fellers?" continued Chagres Charley.

"Up to Dutch Hill," said Texas; an' I'll see he's fetched inside of two hours."

Saying which, Texas dropped the raw-hide door, and hurried off.

The remaining five strolled slowly back to Chagres Charley's hut.

"Them Greasers hain't never got nothin'," said Mississip, suddenly; "an' that woman'll lay thar on the bare ground all night 'fore they think of makin' her comfortable. Who's got an extra blanket?"

"I!" said each of the four others; and Nappy Boney expressed the feeling of the whole party by exclaiming:

"The blue sky is enough good to cover man when woman needs blankets."

Hastily Mississip collected the four extra blankets and both of his own, and, as he sped toward the Mexican hut, he stopped several times by the way to dexterously snatch blankets from sleeping forms.

"Here you be," said he, suddenly entering the Mexican hut, and startling the inmates into crossing themselves violently. "Make the poor thing a decent bed, an' we'll hev a doctor here pretty soon."

SUDDENLY, BY THE GLARE OF A FRESH LIGHT, THE BOYS SAW THE FACE OF A RATHER DIRTY, LARGE-EYED, BROWN-SKINNED MEXICAN BABY.

Mississip had barely vanished, when a light scratching was heard on the door.

A Mexican opened it, and saw Nappy Boney, with extended hand and bottle.

"It is the *eau-de-vie* of *la belle France*," he whispered. "Tenderly I have cherished, but it is at the lady's service."

Chagres Charley, Lynn Taps and Bracelets were composing their nerves with pipes about the fire they had surrounded early in the morning. Lynn Taps had just declared his disbelief of a soul inside of the Mexican frame, when the door was thrown open and an excited Mexican appeared.

"Her tongue come back!" he cried. "She say she come over mountain—she bring little boy—she no eat, it was long time. Soon she must die, boy must die. What she do? She put round boy her cloak, an' leave him by rock, an' hurry to tell. Maybe coyote get him. What can do?"

"What can we do?" echoed Lynn Taps; "turn out every galoot in camp, and foller her tracks till we find it. Souls or no souls, don't make no diff'rence. I'll tramp my legs off, 'fore that child shall be left out in the snow in them mountains."

Within five minutes every man in camp had been aroused.

Each man swore frightfully at being prematurely turned out—each man hated the Greasers with all his heart and soul and strength; but each man, as he learned what was the matter, made all possible haste, and fluently cursed all who were slower than himself.

In fact, two or three irrepressible spirits, consuming with delay, started alone on independent lines of search.

Chagres Charley appeared promptly, and assumed command.

"Boys," said he, "we'll sprinkle out into a line a couple of miles long, and march up the mountain till we reach the snow. When I think it's time, I'll fire three times, an' then each feller'll face an' tramp to the right, keepin' a keerful lookout for a woman's tracks p'intin' t'ward camp. Ther can't be no mistakin' 'em, for them sennyritas hez the littlest kind o' feet. When any feller finds her tracks, he'll fire, an' then we'll rally on him. I wish them other fellers, instid of goin' off half-cocked, hed tracked Codago, the low-lived skunk. To think of him runnin' away from wife, an' young one, too! Forward, git!"

"They *hain't* got no souls—that's what made him do it, Charley," said Lynn Taps, as the men deployed.

Steadily the miners ascended the rugged slope; rocks, trees, fallen trunks and treacherous holes impeded their progress, but did not stop them.

A steady wind cut them to the bone, and grew more keen and fierce as they neared the snow.

Suddenly Chagres Charley fired, and the boys faced to the right—a moment later another shot rallied the party; those nearest it found Nappy Boucy in a high state of excitement, and leaning over a foot-print.

"*Mon Dieu!*" he cried; "they have not the *esprit*, those Mexicans; but her footprints might have been made by the adorable feet of one of my countrywomen, it is so small."

"Yes," said Mississip; "an' one of them fellers that started ahead hez found it fust, fur here's a man's track a-goin' up."

Rapidly the excited miners followed the tracks through the snow, and found them gradually leading to the regular trail across the mountain, which trail few men ventured upon at that season. Suddenly the men in advance stopped.

"Here 'tis, I reckon!" cried Mississip, springing across a small cleft in the rocks, and running toward a dark object lying on the sheltered side of a small cliff. "Good God!" he continued, as he stooped down; "it's Codago! An' he's froze stiff."

"Serve him right, cuss him," growled Lynn Taps. "I almost wish he *had* a soul, so he could catch it good an' hot, now he's gone!"

"He's got his pack with him," shouted Mississip, "and a huggin' it ez tight ez ef he could take it to—to wherever he's gone to."

"No man with a soul could hev ben cool enough to pack up his traps after seein' that poor woman's face," argued Lynn Taps.

Mississip tore off a piece of his trowsers, struck fire with flint and steel, poured on whisky, and blew it into a flame.

Rapidly the miners straggled up the trail, and halted opposite Mississip.

"Well, I'll be burned!" shouted the latter; "he ain't got no shirt on, an' there's an ugly cut in his arm. It beats anything I ever seed!"

One by one the miners leaped the cleft, and crowded about Mississip and stared.

It was certainly Codago, and there was certainly his pack, made up in his poncho, in the usual Greaser manner, and held tightly in his arms.

But while they stared, there was a sudden movement of the pack itself.

Lynn Taps gave a mighty tug at it, extricated it from the dead man's grasp, and rapidly undid it.

Suddenly, by the glare of a fresh light, the boys saw the face of a rather dirty, large-eyed, brown-skinned Mexican baby; and the baby, probably by way of recognition, raised high a voice such as the boys never heard before on that side of the Rocky Mountains.

"Here's what that cut in his arm means," shouted a miner who had struck a light on the trail; "there's a finger-mark, done in blood on the snow, by the side of the trail, an' a-pintin' right to that ledge; an' here's his shirt a-flappin' on a stick stuck in a snow-bank lookin' t'ward camp."

"There ain't no doubt 'bout what the woman said to him, or what made him yell an' git, boys," said Chagres Charley, solemnly, as he took a blanket from his shoulders and spread it on the ground.

Mississip took off his hat, and lifting the poor Mexican from the snow, laid him in the blanket. Lynn Taps hid the baby, rewrapped, under his own blanket, and hurried down the mountain, while four men picked up Codago and followed.

Lynn Taps scratched on the rawhide door; the doctor opened it.

Lynn Tapps unrolled the bundle, and its occupant again raised its voice.

The woman, who was lying motionless and with closed eyes, sprang to her feet in an instant, and as Lynn Taps laid his burden on the blankets, the woman, her every dull feature softened and lighted with motherly tenderness, threw her arms about the astonished Yankee, and then fell sobbing at his feet.

"You've brought her the only medicine that'll do her any good," said the doctor, giving the baby a gentle dig under the ribs as he picked up his saddle-bags.

Lynn Taps made a hasty escape, and reached the saloon, which had been hurriedly opened as the crowd was heard approaching.

The bearers of the body deposited it gently on the floor, and the crowd filed in quietly.

Lynn Taps walked up to the bar, and rapped upon it.

"Walk up, boys," said he; "fill high; hats off. Here's Codago. Maybe he *didn't* have a soul, but if he *didn't*, souls ain't needed in this world. Buttoms up, every man."

The toast was drunk quietly and reverently, and when it was suggested that the Greasers themselves should have participated, they were all summoned, and the same toast was drank again.

The next day, as the body of Codago was being carried to a newly dug grave, on the high ground overlooking the creek, and the Mexicans stood about, as if dumb staring and incessant smoking were the only proprieties to be observed on such occasions, Lynn Taps thoughtfully offered his arm to the weeping widow, and so sorrowful was she throughout the performance of the sad rites, that Lynn Taps was heard to remark that, however it might be with the men, there could be no doubt about Mexican women's possessing souls. As a few weeks later the widow became Mrs. Lynn Taps, there can be no doubt that her second husband's final convictions were genuine.

THE LAST PIKE AT JAGGER'S BEND.

WHERE they came from no one knew. Among the farmers near the Bend there was ample ability to conduct researches beset by far more difficulties than was that of the origin of the Pikes; but a charge of buckshot which a good-natured Yankee received one evening, soon after putting questions to a venerable Pike, exerted a depressing influence upon the spirit of investigation. They were not bloodthirsty, these Pikes, but they had good reason to suspect all inquirers of being at least deputy sheriffs, if not worse ; and a Pike's hatred of officers of the law is equaled in intensity only by his hatred for manual labor.

But while there was doubt as to the fatherland of the little colony of Pikes at Jagger's Bend, their every neighbor would willingly make affidavit as to the cause of their locating and remaining at the Bend. When humanitarians and optimists argued that it was because the water was good and convenient, that the Bend itself caught enough drift-wood for fuel, and that the dirt would yield a little gold when manipulated by placer and pan, all farmers and stockowners would freely admit the validity of these reasons ; but the admission was made with a countenance whose indignation and sorrow indicated that the greater causes were yet unnamed. With eyes speaking emotions which words could not express, they would point to sections of wheatfields minus the grain-bearing heads—to hides and hoofs of cattle unslaughtered by themselves—to mothers of promising

calves, whose tender bleatings answered not the maternal
call—to the places which had once known fine horses, but
had been untenanted since certain Pikes had gone across
the mountains for game. They would accuse no man
wrongfully, but in a country where all farmers had wheat
and cattle and horses, and where prowling Indians and Mexicans were not, how could these disappearances occur?

But to people owning no property in the neighborhood
—to tourists and artists—the Pike settlement at the Bend
was as interesting and ugly as a skye-terrier. The architecture of the village was of original style, and no duplicate
existed. Of the half-dozen residences, one was composed
exclusively of sod; another of bark; yet another of poles,
roofed with a wagon-cover, and plastered on the outside
with mud; the fourth was of slabs, nicely split from logs
which had drifted into the Bend; the fifth was of hide
stretched over a frame strictly gothic from foundation to
ridgepole; while the sixth, burrowed into the hillside, displayed only the barrel which formed its chimney.

A more aristocratic community did not exist on the Pacific Coast. Visit the Pikes when you would, you could
never see any one working. Of churches, school-houses,
stores and other plebeian institutions, there were none; and
no Pike demeaned himself by entering trade, or soiled his
hands by agriculture.

Yet unto this peaceful, contented neighborhood there
found his way a visitor who had been everywhere in the
world without once being made welcome. He came to the
house built of slabs, and threatened the wife of Sam Trotwine, owner of the house; and Sam, after sunning himself
uneasily for a day or two, mounted a pony, and rode off for
a doctor to drive the intruder away.

When he returned he found all the men in the camp
seated on a log in front of his own door, and then he knew
he must prepare for the worst—only one of the great influences of the world could force every Pike from his own
door at exactly the same time. There they sat, yellow-faced,

bearded, long-backed and bent, each looking like the other, and all like Sam ; and, as he dismounted, they all looked at him.

"How is she?" said Sam, tying his horse and the doctor's, while the latter went in.

"Well," said the oldest man, with deliberation, "the wimmin's all thar ef that's any sign."

Each man on the log inclined his head slightly but positively to the left, thus manifesting belief that Sam had been correctly and sufficiently answered. Sam himself seemed to regard his information in about the same manner.

Suddenly the raw hide which formed the door of Sam's house was pushed aside, and a woman came out and called Sam, and he disappeared from his log.

As he entered his hut, all the women lifted sorrowful faces and retired ; no one even lingered, for the Pike has not the common human interest in other people's business ; he lacks that, as well as certain similar virtues of civilization.

Sam dropped by the bedside, and was human ; his heart was in the right place ; and though heavily intrenched by years of laziness and whisky and tobacco, it *could* be brought to the front, and it came now.

The dying woman cast her eyes appealingly at the surgeon, and that worthy stepped outside the door. Then the yellow-faced woman said :

"Sam, doctor says I ain't got much time left.

"Mary," said Sam, "I wish ter God I could die fur yer. The children——"

"It's them I want to talk about, Sam," replied his wife. 'An' I wish they could die with me, rather'n hev 'em liv ez I've hed to. Not that you ain't been a kind husband to me, for you hev. Whenever I wanted meat yev got it, somehow ; an' when yev been ugly drunk, yev kep' away from the house. But I'm dyin', Sam, and it's cos you've killed me."

"Good God, Mary!" cried the astonished Sam, jumping up; "yure crazy—here, doctor!"

"Doctor can't do no good, Sam; keep still, and listen, ef yer love me like yer once said yer did; for I hevn't got much breath left," gasped the woman.

"Mary," said the aggrieved Sam, "I swow to God I dunno what yer drivin' at."

"It's jest this, Sam," replied the woman: "Yer tuk me, tellin' me ye'd love me an' honor me an' pertect me. You mean to say, now, yev done it? I'm a-dyin', Sam—I hain't got no favors to ask of nobody, an' I'm tellin' the truth, not knowin' what word'll be my last."

"Then tell a feller where the killin' came in, Mary, for heaven's sake," said the unhappy Sam.

"It's come in all along, Sam," said the woman; "there is women in the States, so I've heerd, that marries fur a home, an' bread an' butter, but you promised more'n that, Sam. An' I've waited. An' it ain't come. An' there's somethin' in me that's all starved and cut to pieces. An' it's your fault, Sam. I tuk yer fur better or fur wuss, an' I've never grumbled."

"I know yer hain't, Mary," whispered the conscience-stricken Pike. "An' I know what yer mean. Ef God'll only let yer be fur a few years, I'll see ef the thing can't be helped. Don't cuss me, Mary—I've never knowed how I've been a-goin'. I wish there was somethin' I could do 'fore you go, to pay yer all I owe yer. I'd go back on everything that makes life worth hevin'."

"Pay it to the children, Sam," said the sick woman, raising herself in her miserable bed. "I'll forgive yer everything if you'll do the right thing fur them. Do—do—everything!' said the woman, throwing up her arms and falling backward. Her husband's arm caught her; his lips brought to her wan face a smile, which the grim visitor, who an instant later stole her breath, pityingly left in full possession of the rightful inheritance from which it had been so long excluded.

Sam knelt for a moment with his face beside his wife—
what he said or did the Lord only knew, but the doctor, who
was of a speculative mind, afterward said that when Sam
appeared at the door he showed the first Pike face in which
he had ever seen any signs of a soul.

Sam went to the sod house, where lived the oldest woman
in the camp, and briefly announced the end of his wife.
Then, after some consultation with the old woman, Sam rode
to town on one of his horses, leading another. He came
back with but one horse and a large bundle ; and soon the
women were making for Mrs. Trotwine her last earthly robe,
and the first new one she had worn for years. The next day
a wagon brought a coffin and a minister, and the whole camp
silently and respectfully followed Mrs. Trotwine to a home
with which she could find no fault.

For three days all the male Pikes in the camp sat on the
log in front of Sam's door, and expressed their sympathy as
did the three friends of Job—that is, they held their peace.
But on the fourth their tongues were unloosed. As a con-
versationalist the Pike is not a success, but Sam's actions
were so unusual and utterly unheard of, that it seemed as if
even the stones must have wondered and communed among
themselves.

"I never heard of such a thing," said Brown Buck; "he's
gone an' bought new clothes for each of the four young
'uns."

"Yes," said the patriarch of the camp, "an' this mornin',
when I went down to the bank to soak my head, 'cos last
night's liquor didn't agree with it, I seed Sam with all his
young 'uns as they wuz a washin' their face an' hands with
soap. They'll ketch their death an' be on the hill with
their mother 'fore long, if he don't look out ; somebody ort
to reason with him."

" 'Twon't do no good," sighed Limping Jim. "He's lost
his head, an' reason just goes into one ear and out at t'other.
When he was scrapin' aroun' the front door t'other day, an'
I asked him what he wuz a-layin' the ground all bare an'

desolate for, he said he was done keepin' pig-pen. Now everybody but him knows he never had a pig. His head's gone, just mark my words."

On the morning of the fourth day Sam's friends had just secured a full attendance on the log, and were at work upon their first pipes, when they were startled by seeing Sam harness his horse in the wagon and put all his children into it.

"Whar yer bound fur, Sam?" asked the patriarch.

Sam blushed as near as a Pike could, but answered with only a little hesitation :

"Goin' to take 'em to school to Maxfield—goin' to do it ev'ry day."

The incumbent of the log were too nearly paralyzed to remonstrate, but after a few moments of silence the patriarch remarked, in tones of feeling, yet decision :

"He's hed a tough time of it, but he's no bizness to ruin the settlement. I'm an old man myself, an' I need peace of mind, so I'm goin' to pack up my traps and mosey. When the folks at Maxfield knows what he's doin', they'll make him a constable or a justice, an' I'm too much of a man to live nigh any sich."

And next day the patriarch wheeled his family and property to parts unknown.

A few days later Jim Merrick, a brisk farmer a few miles from the Bend, stood in front of his own house, and shaded his eyes in solemn wonder. It couldn't be—he'd never heard of such a thing before—yet it was—there was no doubt of it—there was a Pike riding right toward him, in open daylight. He could swear that Pike had often visited him —that is, his wheatfield and corral—after dark, but a daylight visit from a Pike was as unusual as a social call of a Samaritan upon a Jew. And when Sam—for it was he— approached Merrick and made his business known, the farmer was more astonished and confused than he had ever been in his life before. Sam wanted to know for how much money Merrick would plow and plant a hundred and sixty

acres of wheat for him, and whether he would take Sam's
horse—a fine animal,brought from the States, and for which
Sam could show a bill of sale—as security for the amount
until he could harvest and sell his crop. Merrick so well
understood the Pike nature, that he made a very liberal
offer, and afterward said he would have paid handsomely
for the chance.

A few days later, and the remaining Pikes at the Bend
experienced the greatest scare that had ever visited their
souls. A brisk man came into the Bend with a tripod on
his shoulder, and a wire chain, and some wire pins, and a
queer machine under his arm, and before dark the Pikes
understood that Sam had deliberately constituted himself a
renegade by entering a quarter section of land. Next morning two more residences were empty, and the remaining
fathers of the hamlet adorned not Sam's log, but wandered
about with faces vacant of all expression save the agony of
the patriot who sees his home invaded by corrupting influences too powerful for him to resist.

Then Merrick sent up a gang-plow and eight horses, and
the tender green of Sam's quarter section was rapidly
changed to a dull-brown color, which is odious unto the eye
of the Pike. Day by day the brown spot grew larger, and
one morning Sam arose to find all his neighbors departed,
having wreaked their vengeance upon him by taking away
his dogs. And in his delight at their disappearance, Sam
freely forgave them all.

Regularly the children were carried to and from school,
and even to Sunday-school—regularly every evening Sam
visited the grave on the hillside, and came back to lie by the
hour looking at the sleeping darlings—little by little farmers
began to realize that their property was undisturbed—little
by little Sam's wheat grew and waxed golden; and then
there came a day when a man from 'Frisco came and
changed it into a heavier gold—more gold than Sam had
ever seen before. And the farmers began to stop in to see
Sam, and their children came to see his, and kind women

were unusually kind to the orphans, and as day by day Sam took his solitary walk on the hillside, the load on his heart grew lighter, until he ceased to fear the day when he, too, should lie there.

HANNEY'S DIGGINGS certainly needed a missionary, if any place ever did; but, as one of the boys once remarked during a great lack of water, "It had to keep on a-needin'." Zealous men came up by steamer *via* the Isthmus, and seemed to consume with their fiery haste to get on board the vessel for China and Japan, and carry the glad tidings to the heathen. Self-sacrificing souls gave up home and friends, and hurried across, overland, to brave the Pacific and bury themselves among the Australasian savages. But, though they all passed in sight of Hanney's, none of them paused to give any attention to the souls who had flocked there. Men came out from 'Frisco and the East to labor with the Chinese miners, who were the only peaceable and well-behaved people in the mines; but the white-faced, good-natured, hard-swearing, generous, heavy-drinking, enthusiastic, murderous Anglo-Saxons they let severely alone. Perhaps they thought that hearts in which the good seed had once been sown, but failed to come up into fruit, were barren soil; perhaps they thought it preferable to be killed and eaten by cannibals than to be tumbled into a gulch by a revolver-shot, while the shootist strolled calmly off in company with his approving conscience, never thinking to ascertain whether his bullet had completed the business, or whether a wounded man might not have to fight death and coyotes together.

At any rate, the missionaries let Hanney's alone. If any one with an unquenchable desire to carry the Word where it is utterly unknown, a digestion without fear, and a full-proof article of common sense (these last two requisites are absolute), should be looking for an eligible location, Hanney's is just the place for him, and he need give himself no trouble for fear some one would step in before him. If he has several dozens of similarly constituted friends, they can all find similar locations by betaking themselves to any mining camp in the West.

As Hanney's had no preacher, it will be readily imagined it had no church. With the first crowd who located there came an insolvent rumseller from the East. He called himself Pentecost, which was as near his right name as is usual with miners, and the boys dubbed his shop "Pentecost Chapel" at once. The name, somehow, reached the East, for within a few months there reached the post-office at Hanney's a document addressed to "Preacher in charge of Pentecost Chapel." The postmaster went up and down the brook in high spirits, and told the boys; they instantly dropped shovel and pan, formed line, and escorted the postmaster and document to the chapel. Pentecost acknowledged the joke, and stood treat for the crowd, after which he solemnly tore the wrapper, and disclosed the report of a certain missionary society. Modestly expressing his gratification at the honor, and his unworthiness of it, he moved that old Thompson, who had the loudest voice in the crowd, should read the report aloud, he, Pentecost, volunteering to furnish Thompson all necessary spirituous aid during the continuance of his task. Thompson promptly signified his acquiescence, cleared his throat with a glass of amber-colored liquid, and commenced, the boys meanwhile listening attentively, and commenting critically.

"Too much cussed heavenly twang," observed one, disapprovingly, as one letter largely composed of Scriptural extracts was read.

"Why the deuce didn't he shoot?" indignantly demanded another, as a tale of escape from heathen pursuers was read.

"Shet up wimmen in a derned dark room! Well, *I'll* be durned!" soliloquized a yellow-haired Missourian, as Thompson read an account of a Zenana. "Reckon they'd set an infernal sight higher by wimmen if they wuz in the diggins' six months—hey, fellers?"

"You bet!" emphatically responded a majority of those present.

Before the boys became very restive, Thompson finished the pamphlet, including a few lines on the cover, which stated that the society was greatly in need of funds, and that contributions might be sent to the society's financial agent in Boston. Thompson gracefully concluded his service by passing the hat, with the following net result: Two revolvers, one double-barreled pistol, three knives, one watch, two rings (both home-made, valuable and fearfully ugly), a pocket-inkstand, a silver tobacco-box, and forty or fifty ounces of dust and nuggets. Boston Bill, who was notoriously absent-minded, dropped in a pocket-comb, but, on being sternly called to order by old Thompson, cursed himself most fluently, and redeemed his disgraceful contribution with a gold double-eagle. "The Webfoot," who was the most unlucky man in camp, had been so wrought upon by the tale of one missionary who had lost his all many times in succession, sympathetically contributed his only shovel, for which act he was enthusiastically cursed and liberally treated at the bar, while the shovel was promptly sold at auction to the highest bidder, who presented it, with a staggering slap between the shoulders, to its original owner. The remaining non-legal tenders were then converted into gold-dust, and the whole dispatched by express, with a grim note from Pentecost, to the society's treasurer at Boston. As the society was controlled by a denomination which does not understand how good can come out of evil, no detail of this contribution ever appeared in print. But a few months thereafter there *did* appear at Hanney's a thin-chested, large-headed youth, with a heavily loaded mule, who announced himself as duly accredited by the aforementioned society to

preach the Gospel among the miners. The boys received
him cordially, and Pentecost offered him the nightly hospitality of curling up to sleep in front of the bar-room fire-
place. His mule's load proved to consist largely of tracts,
which he vigorously distributed, and which the boys used to
wrap up dust in. He nearly starved while trying to learn to
cook his own food, so some of the boys took him in and fed
him. He tried to persuade the boys to stop drinking, and
they good-naturedly laughed ; but when he attempted to
break up the " little game " which was the only amusement
of the camp—the only *steady* amusement, for fights were
short and irregular—the camp rose in its wrath, and the
young man hastily rose and went for his mule.

But at the time of which this story treats a missionary
would have fared even worse, for the boys where wholly
absorbed by a very unrighteous, but still very darling,
pleasure. A pair of veteran knifeists, who had fought each
other at sight for almost ten years every time they met, had
again found themselves in the same settlement, and Hamney's
had the honor to be that particular settlement. "Judge "
Briggs, one of the heroes, had many years before discussed
with his neighbor, Billy Bent, the merits of two opposing
brands of mining shovels. In the course of the chat they
drank considerable villainous whisky, and naturally resorted
to knives as final arguments. The matter might have
ended here, had either gained a decided advantage over the
other ; but both were skillful—each inflicted and received so
near the same number of wounds, that the wisest men in
camp were unable to decide which whipped. Now, to
average Californians in the mines this is a most distressing
state of affairs ; the spectators and friends of the combatants waste a great deal of time, liquor, and blood on the
subject, while the combatants themselves feel unspeakably
uneasy on the neutral ground between victory and defeat.
At Sonora, where Billy and the Judge had their first encounter, there was no verdict, so the Judge indignantly
shook the dust from his feet and went elsewhere. Soon

"THOMPSON GRACEFULLY CONCLUDED HIS SERVICE BY PASSING THE HAT."

Billy happened in at the same place, and a set-to occurred at sight, in which the average was not disarranged. Both men went about, for a month or two, in a patched-up condition, and then Billy roamed off, to be soon met by the Judge with the usual result. Both men were known by reputation all through the gold regions, and the advent of either at any " gulch," or " washin'," was the best advertisement the saloon-keepers could desire. In the East, hundreds of men would have tried to reason the men out of this feud, and some few would have forcibly separated them while fighting; but in the diggings any interference in such matters is considered impertinent, and deserving of punishment.

Hanney's had been fairly excited for a week, for the Judge had arrived the week before, and his points had been carefully scrutinized and weighed, time and again, by every man in the camp. There seemed nothing unusual about him—he was of middle size, and long hair and beard, a not unpleasant expression, and very dirty clothes; he never jumped a claim, always took his whisky straight, played as fair a game of poker as the average of the boys, and never stole a mule from any one whiter than a Mexican. The boys had just about ascertained all this, and made their " blind " bets on the result of the next fight, when the whole camp was convulsed with the intelligence that Billy Bent had also arrived. Work immediately ceased, except in the immediate vicinity of the champions, and the boys stuck close to the chapel, that being the spot where the encounter should naturally take place. Miners thronged in from fifty miles around, and nothing but a special mule express saved the camp from the horror of Pentecost's bar being inadequate to the demand. Between " straight bets " and " hedging " most of the gold dust in camp had been " put up," for a bet is the only California backing of an opinion. As the men did not seem to seek each other, the boys had ample time to "grind things down to a pint," as the camp concisely expressed it, and the matter had given excuse for a dozen minor fights, when order was suddenly restored one after-

noon by the entrance of Billy and his neighbors, just as the
Judge and *his* neighbors were finishing a drink.

The boys immediately and silently formed a ring, on the
outer edge of which were massed all the men who had been
outside, and who came pouring in like flies before a shower.
No one squatted or hugged the wall, for it was understood
that these two men fought only with knives, so the spectators were in a state of abject safety.

The Judge, after settling for the drinks, turned, and saw
for the first time his enemy.

" Hello, Billy !" said he, pleasantly ; " let's take a drink
first."

· Billy, who was a red-haired man, with a snapping-turtle
mouth, but not a vicious-looking man for all that, briefly
replied, "All right," and these two determined enemies
clinked their glasses with the unconcern of mere social
drinkers.

But, after this, they proceeded promptly to business ;
the Judge, who was rather slow on his guard, was the owner
of a badly cut arm within three minutes by the bar-keeper's
watch, but not until he had given Billy, who was parrying a
thrust, an ugly gash in his left temple.

There was a busy hum during the adjustment of bets on
" first blood," and the combatants. very considerately refrained from doing serious injury during this temporary
distraction; but within five minutes more they had exchanged
chest wounds, but too slight to be dangerous.

Betting became furious—each man fought so splendidly,
that the boys were wild with delight and enthusiasm. Bets
were roared back and forth, and when Pentecost, by virtue
of his universally conceded authority, commanded silence,
there was a great deal of finger-telegraphy across the circle,
and head-shaking in return.

Such exquisite carving had never before been seen at
Hanney's—that was freely admitted by all. Men pitied
absent miners all over the State, and wondered why this
delightful lingering, long-drawn-out system of slaughter was

not more popular than the brief and commonplace method of the revolver. The Webfoot rapturously and softly quoted the good Doctor Watt's:

> "My willing soul would stay
> In such a place as this,
> And——"

when suddenly his cup of bliss was dashed to the ground, for Billy, stumbling, fell upon his own knife, and received a severe cut in the abdomen.

Wounds of this sort are generally fatal, and the boys had experience enough in such matters to know it. In an instant the men who had been calmly viewing a life-and-death conflict bestirred themselves to help the sufferer. Pentecost passed the bottle of brandy over the counter; half a dozen men ran to the spring for cold water; others hastily tore off coats, and even shirts, with which to soften a bench for the wounded man. No one went for the Doctor, for that worthy had been viewing the fight professionally from the first, and had knelt beside the wounded man at exactly the right moment. After a brief examination, he gave his opinion in the following professional style:

"No go, Billy; you're done for."

"Good God!" exclaimed the Judge, who had watched the Doctor with breathless interest; "ain't ther' no chance?"

"Nary," replied the Doctor, decidedly.

"I'm a ruined man—I'm a used-up cuss," said the Judge, with a look of bitter anguish. "I wish I'd gone under, too."

"Easy, old hoss," suggested one of the boys; "*you* didn't do him, yer know."

"That's what's the matter!" roared the Judge, savagely; "nobody'll ever know which of us whipped."

And the Judge sorrowfully took himself off, declining most resolutely to drink.

Many hearts were full of sympathy for the Judge; but the poor fellow on the bench seemed to need most just then.

He had asked for some one who could write, and was dictating, in whispers, a letter to some person. Then he drank some brandy, and then some water; then he freely acquitted the Judge of having ever fought any way but fairly. But still his mind seemed burdened. Finally, in a very thin, weak voice, he stammered out:

" I don't want—to make—to make it uncomfortable—for —for any of—you fellers, but—is ther' a—a preacher in the camp?"

The boys looked at each other inquiringly; men from every calling used to go to the mines, and no one would have been surprised if a backsliding priest, or even bishop, had stepped to the front. But none appeared, and the wounded man, after looking despairingly from one to another, gave a smothered cry.

" Oh, God, hez a miserable wretch got to cut hisself open, and then flicker out, without anybody to say a prayer for him?"

The boys looked sorrowful—if gold-dust could have bought prayers, Billy would have had a first-class assortment in an instant.

" There's Deacon Adams over to Pattin's," suggested a bystander; " an' they do say he's a reg'lar rip-roarer at prayin'! But 'twould take four hours to go and fetch him."

" Too long," said the Doctor.

" Down in Mexico, at the cathedral," said another, " they pray for a feller after he's dead, when yer pay 'em fur it, an' they say it's jist the thing—sure pop. I'll give yer my word, Billy, an' no go back, that I'll see the job done up in style fur yer, ef that's any comfort."

" I want to hear it myself," groaned the sufferer; " 1 don't feel right; can't nobody pray—nobody in the crowd?"

Again the boys looked inquiringly at each other, but this time it was a little shyly. If he had asked for some one to go out and steal a mule, or kill a bear, or gallop a buck-jumping mustang to 'Frisco, they would have fought for the chance; but praying—praying was entirely out of their line.

The silence became painful: soon slouched hats were hauled down over moist eyes, and shirt-sleeves and bare arms seemed to find something unusual to attend to in the boys' faces. Big Brooks commenced to blubber aloud, and was led out by old Thompson, who wanted a chance to get out of doors so he might break down in private. Finally matters were brought to a crisis by Mose—no one knew his other name. Mose uncovered a sandy head, face and beard, and remarked :

"I don't want to put on airs in this here crowd, but ef nobody else ken say a word to the Lord about Billy Bent, I'm a-goin' to do it myself. It's a bizness I've never bin in, but ther's nothin' like tryin'. This meetin' 'll cum to order to wunst."

"Hats off in church, gentlemen!" commanded Pentecost.

Off came every hat, and some of the boys knelt down, as Mose knelt beside the bench, and said :

"Oh, Lord, here's Billy Bent needs 'tendin' to ! He's panned out his last dust, an' he seems to hev a purty clear idee that this is his last chance. He wants you to give him a lift, Lord, an' it's the opinion of this house thet he needs it. 'Tain't none of our bizness what he's done, an' ef it wuz, you'd know more about it than we cud tell yer ; but it's mighty sartin that a cuss that's been in the diggins fur years needs a sight of mendin' up before he kicks the bucket."

"That's so," responded two or three, very emphatically.

" Billy's down, Lord, an' no decent man b'lieves that the Lord 'ud hit a man when he's down, so there's one or two things got to be done—either he's got to be let alone, or he's got to be helped. Lettin' him alone won't do him or any-body else enny good, so helpin's the holt, an' as enny one uv us tough fellers would help ef we knew how to, it's only fair to suppose thet the Lord 'll do it a mighty sight quicker. Now, what Billy needs is to see the thing in thet light, an' you ken make him do it a good deal better than we ken. It's mighty little fur the Lord to do, but it's meat an' drink an' clothes to Billy just now. When we wuz boys, sum uv us read some promises ef you'rn in thet Book thet wes writ a good spell ago by chaps in the Old Country, an' though Sunday-school teachers and preachers mixed the matter up in our minds, an' got us all tangle-footed, we know they're dar, an' you'll know what we mean. Now, Lord, Billy's jest the boy—he's a hard case, so you can't find no better stuff to work on—he's in a bad fix, thet we can't do nuthin' fur, so it's jest yer chance. He ain't exactly the chap to make an A Number One Angel ef, but he ain't the man to forget a friend, so he'll be a handy feller to hev aroun'."

"Feel any better, Billy?" said Mose, stopping the prayer for a moment.

"A little," said Billy, feebly; "but you want to tell the whole yarn. I'm sorry for all the wrong I've done."

"He's sorry for all his deviltry, Lord——"

"An' I ain't got nothin' agin the Judge," continued the sufferer.

"An' he don't bear no malice agin the Judge, which he shouldn't, seein' he generally gin as good as he took. An' the long an' short of it, Lord, is jest this—he's a dyin', an' he wants a chance to die with his mind easy, an' nobody else can make it so, so we leave the whole job in your hands, only puttin' in, fur Billy's comfort, thet we recollect hearing how yer forgiv' a dyin' thief, an' thet it ain't likely yer a-goin' to be harder on a chap thet's alwas paid fur what he got. Thet's the whole story. Amen."

Billy's hand, rapidly growing cold, reached for that of Mose, and he said, with considerable effort:

"Mose, yer came in ez handy as a nugget in a gone-up claim. God bless yer, Mose. I feel better inside. Ef I get through the clouds, an' hev a livin' chance to say a word to them as is the chiefs dar, thet word 'll be fur *you*, Mose. God bless yer, Mose, an' ef my blessin's no account, it can't cuss yer, ennyhow. This claim's washed out, fellers, an' here goes the last shovelful, to see ef ther's enny gold in it er not."

And Billy departed this life, and the boys drank to the repose of his soul.

THE NEW SHERIFF OF BUNKER COUNTY.

HE suited the natives exactly. What they would have done had he not been available, they shuddered to contemplate. The county was so new a one that but three men had occupied the sheriff's office before Charley Mansell was elected. Of the three, the first had not collected taxes with proper vigor; the second was so steadily drunk that aggrieved farmers had to take the law in their own hands regarding horse-thieves ; the third was, while a terrible man on the chase or in a fight, so good-natured and lazy at other times, that the county came to be overrun with rascals. But Charley Mansell fulfilled every duty of his office with promptness and thoroughness. He was not very well known, to be sure, but neither was any one else among the four or five thousand inhabitants of the new county. He had arrived about a year before election-day, and established himself as repairer of clocks and watches—an occupation which was so unprofitable at Bunkerville, the county town, that Charley had an immense amount of leisure time at his disposal. He never hung about the stores or liquor-shop after dark ; he never told doubtful stories, or displayed unusual ability with cards ; neither did he, on the other hand, identify himself with either of the Bunkerville churches, and yet every one liked him. Perhaps it was because, although short, he was straight and plump, whereas the other inhabitants were thin and bent from many discouraging tussles with ague ; perhaps it was because he was always the first to see the actual merits and demerits of any subject of con-

versation; perhaps it was because he was more eloquent in
defense of what he believed to be right than the village
pastors were in defense of the holy truths to which they
were committed; perhaps it was because he argued Squire
Backett out of foreclosing a mortgage on the Widow Worth
when every one else feared to approach the squire on the
subject; but, no matter what the reason was, Charley Mansell became every one's favorite, and gave no one an excuse
to call him enemy. He took no interest in politics, but one
day when a brutal ruffian, who had assaulted a lame native,
escaped because the easy-going sheriff was too slow in pursuing, Charley was heard to exclaim, "Oh, if I were
sheriff!" The man who heard him was both impression-
able and practical. He said that Charley's face, when he
made that remark, looked like Christ's might have looked
when he was angry, but the hearer also remembered that the
sheriff-incumbent's term of office had nearly expired, and he
quietly gathered a few leading spirits of each political party,
with the result that Charley was nominated and elected on
a "fusion" ticket. When elected, Charley properly declined,
on the ground that he could not file security bonds; but,
within half an hour of the time the county clerk received
the letter of declination, at least a dozen of the most solid
citizens of the county waited upon the sheriff-elect and
volunteered to go upon his bond, so Charley became sheriff
in spite of himself.

And he acquitted himself nobly. He arrested a murderer
the very day after his sureties were accepted, and although
Charley was by far the smaller and paler of the two, the
murderer submitted tamely, and dared not look into Charley's eye. Instead of scolding the delinquent tax-payers,
the new sheriff sympathized with them, and the county
treasury filled rapidly. The self-appointed "regulators"
caught a horse-thief a week or two after Charley's install-
ment into office, and were about to quietly hang him, after
the time-honored custom of Western regulators, when Charley dashed into the crowd, pointed his pistol at the head of

Deacon Bent, the leader of the enraged citizens, remarked that *all* sorts of murder were contrary to the law he had sworn to maintain, and then led the thief off to jail. The regulators were speechless with indignation for the space of five minutes—then they hurried to the jail; and when Charley Mansell, with pale face but set teeth, again presented his pistol, they astonished him with three roaring cheers, after which each man congratulated him on his courage.

In short, Bunkerville became a quiet place. The new sheriff even went so far as to arrest the disturbers of camp-meetings; yet the village boys indorsed him heartily, and would, at his command, go to jail in squads of half a dozen with no escort but the sheriff himself. Had it not been that Charley occasionally went to prayer-meetings and church, not a rowdy at Bunkerville could have found any fault with him.

But not even in an out-of-the-way, malarious Missouri village, could a model sheriff be for ever the topic of conversation. Civilization moved forward in that part of the world in very queer conveyances sometimes, and with considerable friction. Gamblers, murderers, horse-thieves, counterfeiters, and all sorts of swindlers, were numerous in lands so near the border, and Bunkerville was not neglected by them. Neither greenbacks nor national bank-notes were known at that time, and home productions, in the financial direction, being very unpopular, there was a decided preference exhibited for the notes of Eastern banks. And no sooner would the issues of any particular bank grow very popular in the neighborhood of Bunkerville than merchants began to carefully examine every note bearing the name of said bank, lest haply some counterfeiter had endeavored to assist in supplying the demand. At one particular time the suspicions had numerous and well-founded grounds; where they came from nobody knew, but the county was full of them, and full, too, of wretched people who held the doubtful notes. It was the usual habit of the Bunkerville merchants

to put the occasional counterfeits which they received into
the drawer with their good notes, and pass them when unconscious of the fact; but at the time referred to the bad
notes were all on the same bank, and it was not easy work
to persuade the natives to accept even the genuine issues.
The merchants sent for the sheriff, and the sheriff questioned
hostlers, liquor-sellers, ferry-owners, tollgate-keepers, and
other people in the habit of receiving money; but the questions were to no effect. These people had all suffered,
but at the hands of respectable citizens, and no worse by
one than by another.

Suddenly the sheriff seemed to get some trace of the
counterfeiters. An old negro, who saw money so seldom
that he accurately remembered the history of all the currency in his possession, had received a bad note from an
emigrant in payment for some hams. A fortnight later, he
sold some feathers to a different emigrant, and got a note
which neither the store-keeper or liquor-seller would accept;
the negro was sure the wagon and horses of the second emigrant were the same as those of the first. Then the sheriff
mounted his horse and gave chase. He needed only to ask the
natives along the road leading out of Bunkerville to show
him any money they had received of late, to learn what
route the wagon had taken on its second trip.

About this time the natives of Bunkerville began to
wonder whether the young sheriff was not more brave than
prudent. He had started without associates (for he had
never appointed a deputy); he might have a long chase,
and into counties where he was unknown, and might be
dangerously delayed. The final decision—or the only one
of any consequence—was made by four of the "regulators,"
who decided to mount and hurry after the sheriff and volunteer their aid. By taking turns in riding ahead of their own
party, these volunteers learned, at the end of the first day,
that Charley could not be more than ten miles in advance.
They determined, therefore, to push on during the night, so
long as they could be sure they were on the right track.

An hour more of riding brought them to a cabin where they received startling intelligence. An emigrant wagon, drawn by very good horses, had driven by at a trot which was a gait previously unheard of in the case of emigrant horses; then a young man on horseback had passed at a lively gallop; a few moments later a shot had been heard in the direction of the road the wagon had taken. Why hadn't the owner of the house hurried up the road to see what was the matter?—Because he minded his own business and staid in the house when he heard shooting, he said.

"Come on, boys!" shouted Bill Braymer, giving his panting horse a touch with his raw-hide whip; "perhaps the sheriff's needin' help this minute. An' there's generally rewards when counterfeiters are captured—mebbe sheriff 'll give us a share."

The whole quartet galloped rapidly off. It was growing dark, but there was no danger of losing a road which was the only one in that part of the country. As they approached a clearing a short distance in front of them, they saw a dark mass in the centre of the road, its outlines indicating an emigrant wagon of the usual type.

"There they are!" shouted Bill Braymer; "but where's sheriff? Good Lord! The shot must have hit *him!*"

"Reckon it did," said Pete Williamson, thrusting his head forward; "there's some kind of an animal hid behind that wagon, an' it don't enjoy bein' led along, for it's kickin' mighty ·lively—shouldn't wonder if 'twas Mansell's own pony."

"Hoss-thieves too, then?" inquired Braymer; "then mebbe there'll be *two* rewards!"

"Yes," said Williamson's younger brother, "an' mebbe we're leavin' poor Charley a-dyin' along behind us in the bushes somewhere. Who'll go back an' help hunt for him!"

The quartet unconsciously slackened speed, and the members thereof gazed rather sheepishly at each other through the gathering twilight. At length the younger

Williamson abruptly turned, dismounted, and walked slowly backward, peering in the bushes, and examining all indications in the road. The other three resumed their rapid gallop, Pete Williamson remarking:

"That boy alwus *was* the saint of the family—look out for long shot, boys!—and if there's any money in this job, he's to have a fair share of—that *is* sheriff's horse, sure as shootin'—he shall have half of what *I* make out of it. How'll we take 'em, boys?—Bill right, Sam left, and me the rear? If I should get plugged, an' there's any money for the crowd, I'll count on you two to see that brother Jim gets my share—he's got more the mother in him than all four of us other brothers, and—why don't they shoot,-do you s'pose?"

"P'r'aps ther ain't nobody but the driver, an' he's got his hands full, makin' them hosses travel along that lively," suggested Bill Braymer. "Or mebbe he h'ain't got time to load. Like enough he's captured the sheriff, an' is a-takin him off. We've got to be keerful how *we* shoot."

The men gained steadily on the wagon, and finally Bill Braymer felt sure enough to shout ·

"Halt, or we'll fire!"

The only response was a sudden flash at the rear of the wagon; at the same instant the challenger's horse fell dead.

"*Hang* keerfulness about firin'!" exclaimed Braymer. "*I'm* a-goin' to blaze away."

Another shot came from the wagon, and Williamson's horse uttered a genuine cry of anguish and stumbled. The indignant rider hastily dismounted, and exclaimed:

"It's mighty kind of 'em not to shoot *us*, but they know how to get away all the same."

"They know too much about shootin' for *me* to foller 'em any more," remarked the third man, running rapidly out of the road and in the shadow caused by a tree.

"They can't keep up that gait for ever," said Bill Braymer. "I'm goin' to foller 'em on foot, if it takes all night; I'll get even with em for that hoss they've done me out of."

"I'm with you, Bill," remarked Pete Williamson, "an' mebbe we can snatch *their* hosses, just to show 'em how it feels."

The third man lifted up his voice. "I 'llow I've had enough of this here kind of thing," said he, "an' I'll get back to the settlement while there's anything for me to get there on. I reckon you'll make a haul, but—I don't care— I'd rather be poor than spend a counterfeiter's money."

And off he rode, just as the younger Williamson, with refreshed horse, dashed up, exclaiming :

"No signs of him back yonder, but there's blood-tracks beginnin' in the middle of the road, an' leanin' along this way. Come on!"

And away he galloped, while his brother remarked to his companion :

"Ef *he* should have luck, an' get the reward, you be sure to tell him all the good things I've said about him, won't you?"

Jim Williamson rode rapidly in the direction of the wagon until, finding himself alone, and remembering what had befallen his companions, he dismounted, tied his horse to a tree, and pursued rapidly on foot. He soon saw the wagon looming up in front of him again, and was puzzled to know how to reach it and learn the truth, when the wagon turned abruptly off the road, and apparently into the forest.

Following as closely as he could under cover of the timber, he found that, after picking its way among the trees for a mile, it stopped before a small log cabin, of whose existence Jim had never known before.

There were some groans plainly audible as Jim saw one man get out of the wagon and half carry and half drag another man into the hut. A moment later, and a streak of light appeared under the door of the hut, and there seemed to be no windows in the structure ; if there were, they were covered.

Jim remained behind a sheltering tree for what seemed two hours, and then stealthily approached the wagon. No

one was in it. Then he removed his boots and stole on tip-
toe to the hut. At first he could find no chink or crevice
through which to look, but finally, on one side of the log
chimney, he spied a ray of light. Approaching the hole and
applying his eye to it, Jim beheld a picture that startled
him into utter dumbness.

On the floor of the hut, which was entirely bare, lay a
middle-aged man, with one arm bandaged and bleeding.
Seated on the floor, holding the head of the wounded man,
and raining kisses upon it, sat Bunker County's sheriff!

Then Jim heard some conversation which did not in the
least allay his astonishment.

"Don't cry, daughter," said the wounded man, faintly,
"I deserve to be shot by you—I haven't wronged any one
else half so much as I have you."

Again the wounded man received a shower of kisses, and
hot tears fell rapidly upon his face.

"Arrest me—take me back—send me to State's prison,"
continued the man ; "nobody has so good a right. Then I'll
feel as if your mother was honestly avenged. I'll feel better
if you'll promise to do it."

"Father, dear," said the sheriff, "I might have suspected
it was you—oh! if I *had* have done! But I thought—I
hoped I had got away from the reach of the cursed business
for ever. I've endured everything—I've nearly died of loneliness, to avoid it, and then to think that I should have hurt
my own father."

"You're your mother's own daughter, Nellie," said the
counterfeiter ; "it takes all the pain away to know that I
haven't ruined *you*—that *some* member of my wretched
family is honest. I'd be happy in a prisoner's box if I
could look at you and feel that you put me there."

"You sha'n't be made happy in that way," said the
sheriff. I've got you again, and I'm going to keep you to
myself. I'll nurse you here—you say that nobody ever
found this hut but—but the gang, and when you're better
the wagon shall take us both to some place where we can live

or starve together. The county can get another sheriff easy enough."

"And they'll suspect you of being in league with counterfeiters," said the father.

"They may suspect me of anything they like!" exclaimed the sheriff, "so you love me and be—be your own best self and my good father. But this bare hut—not a comfort that you need—no food—nothing—oh, if there was only some one who had a heart, and could help us!"

"*There is!*" whispered Jim Williamson, with all his might. Both occupants started, and the wounded man's eyes glared like a wolf's.

"Don't be frightened," whispered Jim; "I'm yours, body and soul—the devil himself would be, if he'd been standin' at this hole the last five minutes. I'm Jim Williamson. Let me help you miss—sheriff."

The sheriff blew out the light, opened the door, called softly to Jim, led him into the hut, closed the door, relighted the candle and—blushed.. Jim looked at the sheriff out of the top of his eyes, and then blushed himself—then he looked at the wounded man. There was for a moment an awkward silence, which Jim broke by clearing his throat violently, after which he said:

"Now, both of you make your minds easy. Nobody'll never find you here—I've hunted through all these woods, but never saw *this* cabin before. Arm broke?"

"No," said the counterfeiter, "but—but it runs in the family to shoot ugly."

Again the sheriff kissed the man repeatedly.

"Then you can move in two or three days, said Jim, "if you're taken care of rightly. Nobody'll suspect anything wrong about the sheriff, ef he don't turn up again right away. I'll go back to town, throw everybody off the track, and bring out a few things to make you comfortable."

Jim looked at the sheriff again, blushed again, and started for the door. The wounded man sprang to his feet, and hoarsely whispered:

"Swear—ask God to send you to hell if you play false— swear by everything you love and respect and hope for, that you won't let my daughter be disgraced because she happened to have a rascal for her father!"

Jim hesitated for a moment; then he seized the sheriff's hand.

"I ain't used to swearin' except on somethin' I can see," said he, "an' the bizness is only done in one way," with this he kissed the little hand in his own, and dashed out of the cabin with a very red face.

Within ten minutes Jim met his brother and Braymer.

"No use, boys," said he, "might as well go back, There ain't no fears but what the sheriff 'll be smart enough to do 'em yet, if he's alive, an' if he's dead we can't help *him* any."

"If he's dead," remarked Bill Braymer, "an' there's any pay due him, I hope part of it 'll come for these horses. Mine's dead, an' Pete's might as well be.

"Well," said Jim, "I'll go on to town. I want to be out early in the mornin' an' see ef I can't get a deer, an' it's time I was in bed." And Jim galloped off.

The horse and man which might have been seen threading the woods at early daybreak on the following morning, might have set for a picture of one of Sherman's bummers. For a month afterward Jim's mother bemoaned the unaccountable absence of a tin pail, a meal-bag, two or three blankets, her only pair of scissors, and sundry other useful articles, while her sorrow was increased by the fact that she had to replenish her household stores sooner than she had expected.

The sheriff examined so eagerly the articles which Jim deposited in rapid succession on the cabin-floor, that Jim had nothing to do but look at the sheriff, which he did industriously, though not exactly to his heart's content. At last the sheriff looked up, and Jim saw two eyes full of tears, and a pair of lips which parted and trembled in a manner very unbecoming in a sheriff.

"Don't, please," said Jim, appealingly. "I wish I could have done better for *you*, but somehow I couldn't think of nothin' in the house that was fit for a woman, except the scissors."

"Don't think about me at all," said the sheriff, quickly. "I care for nothing for myself. Forget that I'm alive."

"I—I can't," stammered Jim, looking as guilty as forty counterfeiters rolled into one. The sheriff turned away quickly, while the father called Jim to his side.

"Young man," said he, "you've been as good as an angel could have been, but if you suspect *her* a minute of being my accomplice, may heaven blast you! I taught her engraving, villain that I was, but when she found out what the work really was, I thought she'd have died. She begged and begged that I'd give the business up, and I promised and promised, but it isn't easy to get out of a crowd of your own kind, particularly when you're not so much of a man as you should be. At last she got sick of waiting, and ran away—then I grew desperate and worse than ever. I've been searching everywhere for her; you don't suppose a smart—smart counterfeiter has to get rid of his money in the way I've been doing, do you? I traced her to this part of the State, and I've been going over the roads again and again trying to find her; but I never saw her until she put this hole through my arm last night."

"I hadn't any idea who you were," interrupted the sheriff, with a face so full of mingled indignation, pain and tenderness, that Jim couldn't for the life of him take his eyes from it.

"Don't let any one suspect her, young man," continued the father. "I'll stay within reach—deliver me up, if it should be necessary to clear *her*."

"Trust to me," said Jim. "I know a man when I see him, even if he *is* a woman."

Two days later the sheriff rode into town, leading behind him the counterfeiter's horses, with the wagon and its contents, with thousands of dollars in counterfeit money. The counterfeiter had escaped, he said, and he had wounded him.

Bunkerville ran wild with enthusiasm, and when the sheriff insisted upon paying out of his own pocket the value of Braymer's and Williamson's horses, men of all parties agreed that Charley Mansell should be run for Congress on an independent ticket.

But the sheriff declined the honor, and, declaring that he had heard of the serious illness of his father, insisted upon resigning and leaving the country. Like an affectionate son, he purchased some dress-goods, which he said might please his mother, and then he departed, leaving the whole town in sorrow.

There was one man at Bunkerville who did not suffer so severely as he might have done by the sheriff's departure, had not his mind been full of strange thoughts. Pete Williamson began to regard his brother with suspicion, and there seemed some ground for his feeling. Jim was un-naturally quiet and abstracted; he had been a great deal with the sheriff before that official's departure, and yet did not seem to be on as free and pleasant terms with him as before. So Pete slowly gathered a conviction that the sheriff was on the track of a large reward from the bank injured by the counterfeiter; that Jim was to have a share for his services on the eventful night; that there was some disagreement between them on the subject, and that Jim was trying the unbrotherly trick of keeping his luck a secret from the brother who had resolved to fraternally share any-thing he might have obtained by the chase. Finally, when Pete charged his brother with the unkindness alluded to, and Jim looked dreadfully confused, Pete's suspicions were fully confirmed.

The next morning Jim and his horse were absent, ascer-taining which fact, the irate Peter started in pursuit. For several days he traced his brother, and finally learned that he was at a hotel on the Iowa border. The landlord said that he couldn't be seen; he, and a handsome young fellow,

with a big trunk, and a tall, thin man, and ex-Judge Bates,
were busy together, and had left word they weren't to be
disturbed for a couple of hours on any account. Could Pete
hang about the door of the room, so as to see him as soon
as possible ?—he was his brother. Well, yes ; the landlord
thought there wouldn't be any harm in that.

The unscrupulous Peter put his eye to the keyhole ; he
saw the sheriff daintily dressed, and as pretty a lady as ever
was, in spite of her short hair ; he heard the judge say :

" By virtue of the authority in me vested by the State of
Iowa, I pronounce you man and wife ;" and then, with vacant
countenance, he sneaked slowly away, murmuring :

" *That's* the sort of reward he got, is it ? And," continued Pete, after a moment, which was apparently one of
special inspiration, " I'll bet that's the kind of *deer* he said
he was goin' fur on the morning after the chase."

EAST PATTEN was one of the quietest places in the world. The indisposition of a family horse or cow was cause for animated general conversation, and the displaying of a new poster or prospectus on the post-office door was the signal for a spirited gathering of citizens.

Why, therefore, Major Martt had spent the whole of three successive leaves-of-absence at East Patten, where he hadn't a relative, and where no other soldier lived, no one could imagine. Even professional newsmakers never assigned any reason for it, for although their vigorous and experienced imaginations were fully capable of forming some plausible theory on the subject of the major's fondness for East Patten, they shrank from making public the results of any such labors.

It was perfectly safe to circulate some purely original story about any ordinary citizen, but there was no knowing how a military man might treat such a matter when it reached his ears, as it was morally sure to do.

Live military men had not been seen in East Patten since the Revolutionary War, three-quarters of a century before the villagers first saw Major Martt; and such soldiers as had been revealed to East Patten through the medium of print were as dangerously touchy as the hair-triggers of their favorite weapons.

So East Patten let the major's private affairs alone, and was really glad to see the major in person. There was a scarcity of men at East Patten—of interesting men, at least,

EAST PATTEN WAS ONE OF THE QUIETEST PLACES IN THE WORLD.

for the undoubted sanctity of the old men lent no special graces to their features or manners; while the young men were merely the residuum of an active emigration which had for some years been setting westward from East Patten.

When, therefore, the tall, straight broad-shouldered, clear-eyed, much-whiskered major appeared on the street, looking (as he always did) as if he had just been shaved, brushed and polished, the sight was an extremely pleasing one, except to certain young men who feared for the validity of their titles to their respective sweethearts should the major chance to be affectionate.

But the major gave no cause for complaint. When he first came to the village he bought Rose Cottage, opposite the splendid Wittleday property, and he spent most of his time (his leave-of-absence always occurring in the Summer season) in his garden, trimming his shrubs, nursing his flowering-plants, growing magnificent roses, and in all ways acting utterly unlike a man of blood. Occasionally he played a game of chess with Parson Fisher, the jolly ex-clergyman, or smoked a pipe with the sadler-postmaster; he attended all the East Patten tea-parties, too, but he made himself so uniformly agreeable to all the ladies that the mothers in Israel agreed with many sighs, that the major was not a marrying man.

It may easily be imagined, then, that when one Summer the major reappeared at East Patten with a brother officer who was young and reasonably good-looking, the major's popularity did not diminish.

The young man was introduced as Lieutenant Doyson, who had once saved the major's life by a lucky shot, as that chieftain, with empty pistols, was trying to escape from a well-mounted Indian; and all the young ladies in town declared they *knew* the lieutenant *must* have done something wonderful, he was *so* splendid.

But, with that fickleness which seems in some way communicable from wicked cities to virtuous villages, East Patten suddenly ceased to exhibit unusual interest in the

G

pair of warriors, for a new excitement had convulsed the village mind to its very centre.

It was whispered that Mrs. Wittleday, the sole and widowed owner of the great Wittleday property, had wearied of the mourning she wore for the husband she had buried two years previously, and that she would soon publicly announce the fact by laying aside her weeds and giving a great entertainment, to which every one was to be invited.

There was considerable high-toned deprecation of so early a cessation of Mrs. Wittleday's sorrowing, she being still young and handsome, and there was some fault found 'on the economic ground that the widow couldn't yet have half worn out her mourning-garments ; but as to the propriety of her giving an entertainment, the voices of East Patten were as one in the affirmative.

Such of the villagers as had chanced to sit at meat with the late Scott Wittleday, had reported that dishes with unremembered foreign names were as plenty as were the plainer viands on the tables of the old inhabitants; such East Pattenites as had not been entertained at the Wittleday board rejoiced in a prospect of believing by sight as well as by faith.

The report proved to have unusually good foundation. Within a fortnight each respectable householder received a note intimating that Mrs. Wittleday would be pleased to see self and family on the evening of the following Thursday.

The time was short, and the resources of the single store at East Patten were limited, but the natives did their best, and the eventful evening brought to Mrs. Wittleday's handsome parlors a few gentlemen and ladies, and a large number of good people, who, with all the heroism of a forlorn hope, were doing their best to appear at ease and happy.

The major and lieutenant were there, of course, and both in uniform, by special request of the hostess. The major. who had met Mrs. Wittleday in city society before her husband's death, and who had maintained a bowing-acquaintance with her during her widowhood, gravely presented the lieutenant to Mrs. Wittleday, made a gallant speech about the debt society owed to· her for again condescending to smile upon it, and then presented his respects to the nearest of the several groups of ladies who were gazing invitingly at him.

Then he summoned the lieutenant (whose reluctance to leave Mrs. Wittleday's side was rendered no less by a bright smile which that lady gave him as he departed), and made him acquainted with ladies of all ages, and of greatly varying personal appearance. The young warrior went through the ordeal with only tolerable composure, and improved his first opportunity to escape and regain the society of the hostess. Two or three moments later, just as Mrs. Wittleday turned aside to speak to stately old Judge Bray, the lieutenant found himself being led rapidly toward the veranda. The company had not yet found its way out of the parlors to any extent, so the major locked the lieutenant's arm in his own, commenced a gentle promenade, and remarked :

" Fred, my boy, you're making an ass of yourself."

" Oh, nonsense, major," answered the young man, with considerable impatience. "I don't want to know all these queer, old-fashioned people ; they're worse than a lot of plebes at West Point."

"I don't mean that, Fred, though, if you don't want to make talk, you must make yourself agreeable. But you're too attentive to Mrs. Wittleday."

" By George," responded the lieutenant, eagerly, "how can I help it? She's divine !"

"A great many others think so, too, Fred—I do myself —but they don't make it so plagued evident on short acquaintance. Behave yourself, now—your eyesight is good— sit down and play the agreeable to some old lady, and look at Mrs. Wittleday across the room, as often as you like."

The lieutenant was young ; his face was not under good

control, and he had no whiskers, and very little mustache to
hide it, so, although he obeyed the order of his superior, it
was with a visage so mournful that the major imagined,
when once or twice he caught Mrs. Wittleday's eye, that
that handsome lady was suffering from restrained laughter.

Humorous as the affair had seemed to the major before,
he could not endure to have his preserver's sorrow the cause
of merriment in any one else; so, deputing Parson Fisher to
make their excuse to the hostess when it became possible
to penetrate the crowd which had slowly surrounded her, the
major took his friend's arm and returned to the cottage.

" Major ! " exclaimed the subaltern, " I—I half wish I'd
let that Indian catch you; then you wouldn't have spoiled
the pleasantest evening I ever had—ever *began* to have, I
should say."

" You wouldn't have had an evening at East Patten then,
Fred," said the major, with a laugh, as he passed the cigars,
and lit one himself. " Seriously, my boy, you must be more
careful. You came here to spend a pleasant three months
with me, and the first time you're in society you act, to a
lady you never saw before, too, in such a way, that if it had
been any one but a lady of experience, she would have
imagined you in love with her."

" I *am* in love with her," declared the young man, with a
look which was intended to be defiant, but which was
noticeably shamedfaced. " I'm going to tell her so, too—
that is, I'm going to write her about it."

" Steady, Fred — steady !" urged the major, kindly.
" She'd be more provoked than pleased. Don't you suppose fifty men have worshiped her at first sight ? They
have, and she knows it, too—but it hasn't troubled her mind
at all : handsome women know they turn men's heads in
that way, and they generally respect the men who are sensible enough to hold their tongues about it, at least until
there's acquaintance enough between them to justify a little
confidence."

" Major," said poor Fred, very meekly, almost piteously,

" don't—don't you suppose I *could* make her care something
for me ? "

The major looked thoughtfully, and then tenderly, at the
cigar he held between his fingers. Finally he said, very
gently :

" My dear boy, perhaps you could. Would it be fair,
though? Love in earnest means marriage. Would you tor-
ment a poor woman, who's lost one husband, into wondering
three-quarters of the time whether the scalp of another isn't
in the hands of some villainous Apache ? "

The unhappy lieutenant hid his face in heavy clouds of
tobacco smoke.

" Well," said he, springing to his feet, and pacing the
floor like a caged animal, " I'll tell you what I'll do ; I'll
write her, and throw my heart at her feet. Of course she
won't care. It's just as you say. Why should she ? But
I'll do it, and then I'll go back to the regiment. I hate to
spoil *your* fun, major, if it's any fun to you to have such a
fool in your quarters ; but the fact is, the enemy's too much
for me. I wouldn't feel worse if I was facing a division. I'll
write her to-morrow. I'd rather be refused by her than
loved by any other woman."

" Put it off a fortnight, Fred," suggested the major ; " it's
the polite thing to call within a week after this party ; you'll
have a chance then to become better acquainted with her.
She's delightful company, I'm told. Perhaps you'll make up
your mind it's better to enjoy her society, during our leave,
than to throw away everything in a forlorn hope. Wait a
fortnight, that's a sensible youth."

" I can't, major ! " cried the excited boy. " Hang it !
you're an old soldier—don't you know how infernally uncomfortable it is to stand still and be shot at ? "

" I *do*, my boy," said the major, with considerable
emphasis, and a far-away look at nothing in particular.

" Well, that'll be my fix as long as I stay here and keep
quiet," replied the lieutenant.

" Wait a week, then," persisted the major. " You don't

want to be 'guilty of conduct unbecoming an officer and a gentleman,' eh? Don't spoil her first remembrances of the first freedom she's known for a couple of years."

"Well, call it a week, then," moodily replied the love-sick brave, lighting a candle, and moving toward his room. "I suppose it will take me a week, anyway, to make up a letter fit to send to such an angel."

The major sighed, put on an easy coat and slippers, and stepped into his garden.

"Poor Fred!" he muttered to himself, as he paced the walk in front of the piazza; "can't wait a fortnight, eh? Wonder what he would say if he knew I'd been waiting for seven or eight years—if he knew I fell in love with her as easily as he did, and that I've never recovered myself? Wonder what he'd do if some one were to marry her almost before his very eyes, as poor Wittleday did while I was longing for her acquaintance? Wonder what sort of fool he'd call me if he knew that I came to East Patten, time after time, just for a chance of looking at her—that I bought Rose Cottage merely to be near her—that I'd kept it all to myself, and for a couple of years had felt younger at the thought that I might, perchance, win her after all? Poor Fred! And yet, why shouldn't she marry him?—women have done stranger things; and he's a great deal' more attractive-looking than an old campaigner like myself. Well, God bless 'em both, and have mercy on an old coward!"

The major looked toward the Wittleday mansion. The door was open; the last guests were evidently departing, and their beautiful entertainer was standing in the doorway, a flood of light throwing into perfect relief her graceful and tastefully dressed figure. She said something laughingly to the departing guests; it seemed exquisite music to the major. Then the door closed, and the major, with a groan, retired within his own door, and sorrowfully consumed many cigars.

The week that followed was a very dismal one to the major. He petted his garden as usual, and whistled softly to himself, as was his constant habit, but he insanely pinched the buds off the flowering plants, and his whistling —sometimes plaintive, sometimes hopeless, sometimes wrathful, sometimes vindictive in expression—was restricted to the execution of dead-marches alone. He jeopardized his queen so often at chess that Parson Fisher deemed it only honorable to call the major's attention to his misplays, and to allow him to correct them.

The saddler post-master noticed that the major—usually a most accomplished smoker—now consumed a great many matches in relighting each pipe that he filled. Only once during the week did he chance to meet Mrs. Wittleday, and then the look which accompanied his bow and raised hat was so solemn, that his fair neighbor was unusually sober herself for a few moments; while she wondered whether she could in any way have given the major offense.

As for the lieutenant, he sat at the major's desk for many sorrowful hours each day, the general result being a large number of closely written and finely torn scraps in the waste-basket. Then coatless, collarless, with open vest and hair disarranged in the manner traditional among love-sick youths, he would pour mournful airs from a flute.

The major complained—rather frequently for a man who had spent years on the Plains—of drafts from the front windows, which windows he finally kept closed most of the time, thus saving Mrs. Wittleday the annoyance which would certainly have resulted from the noise made by the earnest but unskilled amateur.

For the major himself, however, neither windows nor doors could afford relief; and when, one day, the sergeant accidentally overturned a heavy table, which fell upon the flute and crushed it, the major enjoyed the only happy moments that were his during the week.

The week drew very near its close. The major had, with a heavy but desperate heart, told stories, sung songs, brought up tactical points for discussion—he even waxed enthusiastic in favor of a run through Europe, he, of course, to bear all the expenses; but the subaltern remained faithful and obdurate.

Finally, the morning of the last day arrived, and the lieutenant, to the major's surprise and delight, appeared at the table with a very resigned air.

"Major," said he, "I wouldn't mention it under any other circumstances, but—I saved your life once?"

"You did, my boy. God bless you!" responded the major, promptly.

"Well, now I want to ask a favor on the strength of that act. I'll never ask another. It's no use for me to try to write to her—the harder I try the more contemptible my words appear. Now, what I ask, is this: *you* write me a rough draft of what's fit to send to such an incomparable being, and I'll copy it and send it over. I don't expect any answer—all I want to do is to throw myself away on her, but I want to do it handsomely, and—hang it, I don't know how. Write just as if you were doing it for yourself. Will you do it?"

The major tried to wash his heart out of his throat with a sip of coffee, and succeeded but partially; yet the appealing look of his favorite, added to the unconscious pathos of his tone, restored to him his self-command, and he replied:

"I'll do it, Fred, right away."

"Don't spoil your breakfast for it; any time this morning will do," said the lieutenant, as the major arose from the table. But the veteran needed an excuse for leaving his breakfast untouched, and he rather abruptly stepped upon the piazza and indulged in a thoughtful promenade.

"Write just as if you were doing it for yourself."

The young man's words rang constantly in his ears, and before the major had thought many moments, he determined to do exactly what he was asked to do.

This silly performance of the lieutenant's would, of course, put an end to the acquaintanceship of the major and Mrs. Wittleday, unless that lady were most unusually gracious. Why should he not say to her, over the subaltern's name, all that he had for years been hoping for an opportunity to say? No matter that she would not imagine who was the real author of the letter—it would still be an unspeakable comfort to write the words and know that her eyes would read them—that her heart would perhaps—probably, in fact—pity the writer.

The major seated himself, wrote, erased, interlined, re-wrote, and finally handed to the lieutenant a sheet of letter-paper, of which nearly a page was covered with the major's very characteristic chirography.

"By gracious, major!" exclaimed the lieutenant, his face having lightened perceptibly during the perusal of the letter, "that's magnificent! I declare, it puts hope into me; and yet, confound it, it's plaguy like marching under some one else's colors."

"Never mind, my boy, copy it, sign it, and send it over, and don't hope too much."

The romantic young brave copied the letter carefully, line for line; he spoilt several envelopes in addressing one to suit him, and then dispatched the missive by the major's servant, laying the rough draft away for future (and probably sorrowful) perusal.

The morning hours lagged dreadfully. Both warriors smoked innumerable cigars, but only to find fault with the flavor thereof.

The lieutenant tried to keep his heart up by relating two or three stories, at the points of each of which the major forced a boisterous laugh, but the mirth upon both sides was visibly hollow. Dinner was set at noon, the usual military dinner-hour, but little was consumed, except a bottle of claret, which the major, who seldom drank, seemed to consider it advisable to produce.

The after-dinner cigar lasted only until one o'clock; newspapers by the noon-day mail occupied their time for but a scant hour more, and an attempted game of cribbage was speedily dropped by unspoken but mutual consent.

Suddenly the garden gate creaked. The lieutenant

sprang to his feet, looked out of the window, and exclaimed :

"It's her darkey—he's got an answer—oh, major!"

"Steady, boy, steady!" said the major, arising hastily and laying his hand on the young man's shoulder, as that excited person was hastening to the door. " 'Officer and gentleman,' you know. Let Sam open the door."

The bell rang, the door was opened, a word or two passed between the two servants, and Mrs. Wittleday's coachman appeared in the dining-room, holding the letter. The lieutenant eagerly reached for it, but the sable carrier grinned politely, said :

"It's for de major, sar—wuz told to give it right into his han's, and nobody else," fulfilled his instructions, and departed with many bows and smiles, while the two soldiers dropped into their respective chairs.

"Hurry up, major—do, please," whispered the lieutenant. But the veteran seemed an interminably long time in opening the dainty envelope in his hand. Official communications he opened with a dexterity suggesting sleight-of-hand, but now he took a penknife from his pocket, opened its smallest, brightest blade, and carefully cut Mrs. Wittleday's envelope. As he opened the letter his lower jaw fell, and his eyes opened wide. He read the letter through, and re-read it, his countenance indicating considerable satisfaction, which presently was lost in an expression of puzzled wonder.

"Fred," said he to the miserable lieutenant, who started to his feet as a prisoner expecting a severe sentence might do, "what in creation did you write Mrs. Wittleday?"

"Just what you gave me to write," replied the young man, evidently astonished.

"Let me see my draft of it," said the major.

The lieutenant opened a drawer in the major's desk, took out a sheet of paper, looked at it, and cried :

"I sent her your draft! *This* is my letter!"

"And she imagined *I* wrote it, and has accepted *me!*" gasped the major.

The wretched Frederick turned pale, and tottered toward a chair. The major went over to him and spoke to him sympathizingly, but despite his genial sorrow for the poor boy, the major's heart was so full that he did not dare to show his face for a moment; so he stood behind the lieutenant, and looked across his own shoulder out of the window.

"Oh, major," exclaimed Fred, "isn't it possible that you're mistaken ?"

" Here's her letter, my boy," said the major ; " judge for yourself."

The young man took the letter in a mechanical sort of way, and read as follows:

" *July* 23d, 185—.

" DEAR MAJOR—-I duly received your note of this morning, and you may thank womanly curiosity for my knowing from whom the missive (which you omitted to sign) came. I was accidentally looking out of my window, and recognized the messenger.

"I have made it an inflexible rule to laugh at declarations of 'love at first sight,' but when I remembered how long ago it was when first we met, the steadfastness of your regard, proved to me by a new fancy (which I pray you not to crush) that your astonishing fondness for East Patten was partly on my account, forbade my indulging in any lighter sentiment than that of honest gratitude.

"You may call this evening for your answer, which I suppose you, with the ready conceit of your sex and profession, will have already anticipated.

·" Yours, very truly,   HELEN WITTLEDAY."

The lieutenant groaned.

"It's all up, major ! you'll *have* to marry her. 'Twould be awfully ungentlemanly to let her know there was any mistake."

"Do you think so, Fred ?" asked the major, with a perceptible twitch at the corners of his mouth.

"Certainly, I do," replied the sorrowful lover; "and I'm sure you can learn to love her; she is simply an angel—a goddess. Confound it! you can't help loving her."

"You really believe so, do you, my boy?" asked the major, with fatherly gravity. "But how would *you* feel about it?"

"As if no one else on earth was good enough for her—as if she was the luckiest woman alive," quickly answered the young man, with a great deal of his natural spirit. "'Twould heal *my* wound entirely."

"Very well, my boy," said the major; "I'll put you out of your misery as soon as possible."

    *   *   *   *   *   *   *

Never had the major known an evening whose twilight was of such interminable duration. When, however, the darkness was sufficient to conceal his face, he walked quickly across the street, and to the door of the Wittleday mansion.

That his answer was what he supposed it would be is evinced by the fact that, a few months later, his resignation was accepted by the Department, and Mrs. Wittleday became Mrs. Martt.

In so strategic a manner that she never suspected the truth, the major told his *fiancee* the story of the lieutenant's unfortunate love, and so great was the fair widow's sympathy, that she set herself the task of seeing the young man happily engaged. This done, she offered him the position of engineer of some mining work on her husband's estate, and the major promised him Rose Cottage for a permanent residence as soon as he would find a mistress for it.

Naturally, the young man succombed to the influences exerted against him, and, after Mr. and Mrs. Doyson were fairly settled, the major told his own wife, to her intense amusement, the history of the letter which induced her to change her name.

HOW he came by his name, no one could tell. In the early days of the gold fever there came to California a great many men who did not volunteer their names, and as those about them had been equally reticent on their own advent, they asked few questions of newcomers.

The hotels of the mining regions never kept registers for the accommodation of guests—they were considered well-appointed hotels if they kept water-tight roofs and well-stocked bars.

Newcomers were usually designated at first by some peculiarity of physiognomy or dress, and were known by such names as "Broken Nose," "Pink Shirt," "Cross Bars," "Gone Ears," etc. ; if, afterward, any man developed some peculiarity of character, an observing and original miner would coin and apply a new name, which would afterward be accepted as irrevocably as a name conferred by the holy rite of baptism.

No one wondered that Buffle never divulged his real name, or talked of his past life ; for in the mines he had such an unhappy faculty of winning at cards, getting new horses without visible bills of sale, taking drinks beyond ordinary power of computation, stabbing and shooting, that it was only reasonable to suppose that he had acquired these abilities at the sacrifice of the peace of some other community.

He was not vicious—even a strict theologian could hardly have accused him of malice ; yet, wherever he went, he was promptly acknowledged chief of that peculiar class which renders law and sheriffs necessary evils.

He was not exactly a beauty—miners seldom were—yet a connoisseur in manliness could have justly wished there were a dash of the Buffle blood in the well-regulated veins of many irreproachable characters in quieter neighborhoods than Fat Pocket Gulch, where the scene of this story was located.

He was tall, active, prompt and generous, and only those who have these qualities superadded to their own virtues are worthy to throw stones at his memory.

He was brave, too. His bravery had been frequently recorded in lead in the mining regions, and such records were transmitted from place to place with an alacrity which put official zeal to the deepest blush.

At the fashionable hour of two o'clock at night, Mr. Buffle was entertaining some friends at his residence; or, to use the language of the mines, "there was a game up to Buffle's." In a shanty of the composite order of architecture—it having a foundation of stone, succeeded by logs, a gable of coffin misfits and cracker-boxes, and a roof of bark and canvas—Buffle and three other miners were playing "old sledge."

The table was an empty pork-barrel; the seats were respectively, a block of wood, a stone, and a raisin-box, with a well-stuffed knapsack for the tallest man.

On one side of the shanty was a low platform of hewn logs, which constituted the proprietor's couch when he slept; on another was the door, on the third were confusedly piled Buffle's culinary utensils, and on the fourth was a fire-place, whose defective draft had been the agent of the fine frescoing of soot perceptible on the ceiling. A single candle hung on a wire over the barrel, and afforded light auxiliary to that thrown out by the fireplace.

The game had been going largely in Buffle's favor, as was usually the case, when one of the opposition injudiciously played an ace which was clearly from another pack of cards,

"COME IN," ROARED BUFFLE'S PARTNER. "COME IN, HANG YER, IF YER LIFE'S
INSURED!" THE DOOR OPENED SLOWLY, AND A WOMAN ENTERED.

inasmuch as Buffle, who had dealt, had the rightful ace in his own hand. As it was the ace of trumps, Buffle's indignation arose, and so did his person and pistol.

"Hang yer," said he, savagely; "yer don't come that game on me. I've got that ace myself."

An ordinary man would have drawn pistol also, but Buffle's antagonist knew his only safety lay in keeping quiet, so he only stared vacantly at the muzzle of the revolver, that was so precisely aimed at his own head.

The two other players had risen to their feet, and were mentally composing epitaphs for the victim, when there was heard a decided knock on the door.

"Come in!" roared Buffle's partner, who was naturally the least excited of the four. "Come in, hang yer, if yer life's insured."

The door opened slowly, and a woman entered.

Now, while there were but few women in the camp, the sight of a single woman was not at all unusual. Yet, as she raised her vail, Buffle's revolver fell from his hands, and the other players laid down their cards; the partner of the guilty man being so overcome as to lay down his hand face upward.

Then they all stared, but not one of them spoke; they wanted to, but none knew how to do it. It was not usually difficult for any of them to address such specimens of the gentler sex as found their way to Fat Pocket Gulch, but they all understood at once that this was a different sort of woman. They looked reprovingly and beseechingly at each other, but the woman, at last, broke the silence by saying:

"I am sorry to disturb you, gentlemen, but I was told I could probably find Mr. Buffle here."

"Here he is, ma'am, and yours truly," said Buffle, removing his hat.

He could afford to. She was not beautiful, but she seemed to be in trouble, and a troubled woman can command, to the death, even worse men than free-and-easy miners. She had a refined, pure face, out of which two great brown eyes looked so tenderly and anxiously, that these men forgot themselves at once. She seemed young, not more than twenty-three or four; she was slightly built, and dressed in a suit of plain black.

"Mr. Buffle," said she, "I was going through by stage to San Francisco, when I overheard the driver say to a man seated by him that you knew more miners than any man in California—that you had been through the whole mining country."

"Well, mum," said Buffle, with a delighted but sheepish look, which would have become a missionary complimented on the number of converts he had made, "I *hev* been around a good deal, that's a fact. I reckon I've staked a claim purty much ev'rywhar in the diggins."

"So I inferred from what the driver said," she replied, " and I came down here to ask you a question."

Here she looked uneasily at the other players. The man who stole the ace translated it at once, and said:

"We'll git out ef yer say so, mum; but yer needn't be afraid to say ennything before us. We know a lady when we see her, an' mebbe some on us ken give yer a lift; if we can't, I've only got to say thet ef yer let out enny secrets, grizzlies couldn't tear 'em out uv enny man in this crowd. Hey, fellers?"

"You bet," was the firm response of the remaining two, and Buffle quickly passed a demijohn to the ace-thief, as a sign of forgiveness and approbation.

"Thank you, gentlemen—God bless you," said the woman, earnestly. "My story is soon told. I am looking for my husband, and I *must* find him. His name is Allan Berryn."

Buffle gazed thoughtfully in the fire, and remarked:

"Names ain't much good in this country, mum—no man kerries visitin'-cards, an' mighty few gits letters. Besides, lots comes here 'cos they're wanted elsewhere, an' they take names that ain't much like what their mothers giv 'em. Mebbe you could tell us somethin' else to put us on the trail of him?"

"Hez he got both of his eyes an' ears, mum?" inquired one of the men.

"Uv course he hez, you fool!" replied Buffle, savagely. "The lady's husband's a gentleman, an' 'tain't likely he's been chawed or gouged."

"I ax parding, mum," said the offender, in the most abject manner.

"He is of medium height, slightly built, has brown hair and eyes, and wears a plain gold ring on the third finger of his left hand," continued Mrs. Berryn.

"Got all his front teeth, mum?" asked the man Buffle had rebuked; then he turned quickly to Buffle, who was frowning suspiciously, and said, appeasingly, "Yer know, Buffle, that bein' a gentleman don't keep a feller from losin' his teeth in the nateral course of things."

"He had all his front teeth a few months ago," replied Mrs. Berryn. "I do not know how to describe him further —he had no scars, moles, or other peculiarities which might identify him, except," she continued, with a faint blush—a wife's blush, which strongly tempted Buffle to kneel and kiss the ground she stood on—"except a locket I once gave him, with my portrait, and which he always wore over his heart. I can't believe he would take it off," said she, with a sob that was followed by a flood of tears.

The men twisted on their seats, and showed every sign of uneasiness ; one stepped outside to cough, another suddenly attacked the fire and poked it savagely, Buffle impolitely turned his back to the company, while the fourth man lost himself in the contemplation of the king of spades, which card ever afterward showed in its centre a blotch which seemed the result of a drop of water. Finally Buffle broke the silence by saying :

"I'd give my last ounce, and my shootin'-iron besides, mum, ef I could put yer on his trail ; but I can't remember no such man ; ken you, fellers?"

Three melancholy nods replied in the negative.

"I am very much obliged to you, gentlemen," said Mrs.

Berryn. "I will go back to the crossing and take the next stage. Perhaps, Mr. Buffle, if I send you my address when I reach San Francisco, you will let me know if you ever find any traces of him?"

"Depend upon all of us for that, mum," replied Buffle.

"Thank you," said she, and departed as suddenly as she had entered, leaving the men staring stupidly at each other.

"Wonder how she got here from the crossin'?" finally remarked one.

"Ef she came alone, she's got a black ride back," said another. "It's nigh onto fourteen miles to that crossin'."

"An' she or ten't to be travelin' at all," said little Muggy, the smallest man of the party. "I'm a family man—or I wuz once—an' I tell yer she ort to be where she ken keep quiet, an' wait for what's comin' soon."

The men glanced at each other significantly, but without any of the levity which usually follows such an announcement in more cultured circles.

"This game's up, boys," said Buffle, rising suddenly. "The stage don't reach the crossin' till noon, an' she is goin' to hev this shanty to stay in till daylight, anyhow. You fellers had better git, right away."

Saying which, Buffle hurried out to look for Mrs. Berryn. He soon overtook her, and awkwardly said :

"Mum!"

She stopped.

"Yer don't need to start till after daylight to reach that stage, mum, an' you'd better come back and rest yerself in my shanty till mornin'."

"I am very much obliged, sir," she replied, "but——"

"Don't be afeard, mum," said Buffle, hastily. "We're rough, but a lady's as safe here as she'd be among her family. Ye'll have the cabin all to yerself, an' I'll leave a revolver with yer to make yer feel better."

"You are very kind, sir, but—it will take me some time to get back."

"Horse lame, p'r'aps?"

"No, sir; the truth is, I walked."

"Good God!" ejaculated Buffle; "I'll kill any scoundrel of a station-agent that'll let a woman take such a walk as this. I'll take you back on a good horse before noon to-morrow, and I'll put a hole through that rascal right before your eyes, mum."

Mrs. Berryn shuddered, at sight of which Buffle mentally consigned his eyes to a locality boasting a superheated atmosphere, for talking so roughly to a lady.

"Don't harm him, Mr. Buffle," said she. "He knew nothing about it. I asked him the road to Fat Pocket Gulch, and he pointed it out. He did not know but what I had a horse or a carriage. Unfortunately, the stage was robbed the day before yesterday, and all my money was taken, or I should not have walked here, I assure you. My passage is paid to San Francisco, and the driver told me that if I wished to come down here, the next stage would take me through to San Francisco. When I get there, I can soon obtain money from the East."

"Madame," said Buffle, unconsciously taking off his hat, "any lady that'll make that walk by dark is clear gold all the way down to bed-rock. Ef yer husband's in California, I'll find him fur yer, in spite of man or devil—*I* will, an' I'll be on the trail in half an hour. An' you'd better stay here till I come back, or send yer word. I don't want to brag, but thar ain't a man in the Gulch that'll dare molest anythin' aroun' *my* shanty, an' as thar's plenty of pervisions thar—plain, but good—yer can't suffer. The spring is close by, an' you'll allers find firewood by the door. An' ef yer want help about anythin', ask the fust man yer see, and say I told yer to."

Mrs. Berryn looked earnestly into his face for a moment, and then trusted him.

"Mr. Buffle," she said, "he is the best man that ever lived. But we were both proud, and we quarrelled, and he left me in anger. I accidentally heard he was in California, through an acquaintance who saw him leave New York on the California steamer. If you see him, tell him I was wrong, and that I will die if he does not come back. Tell him—tell him—that."

"Never mind, mum," said Buffle, leading her hastily toward the shanty, and talking with unusual rapidity. "I'll bring him back all right ef I find him; an' find him I will, ef he's on top of the ground."

They entered the cabin, and Buffle was rather astonished at the appearance of his own home. The men were gone, but on the bare logs, where Buffle usually reposed, they had spread their coats neatly, and covered them with a blanket which little Muggy usually wore.

The cards had disappeared, and in their place lay a very small fragment of looking-glass; the demijohn stood in its accustomed place, but against it leaned a large chip, on which was scrawled, in charcoal, the word *Worter*.

"Good," said Buffle, approvingly. "Now, mum, keep up yer heart. I tell yer I'll fetch him, an' any man at the Gulch ken tell yer thet lyin' ain't my gait."

Buffle slammed the door, called at two or three other shanties, and gave orders in a style befitting a feudal lord, and in ten minutes was on horseback, galloping furiously out on the trail to Green Flat.

The Green Flatites wondered at finding the great man among them, and treated him with the most painful civility. As he neither hung about the saloon, "got up" a game, nor provoked a horse-trade, it was immediately surmised that he was looking for some one, and each man searchingly questioned his trembling memory whether he had ever done Buffle an injury.

All preserved a respectful silence as Buffle walked from claim to claim, carefully scrutinizing many, and all breathed freer as they saw him and his horse disappear over the hill on the Sonora trail.

At Sonora he considered it wise to stay over Sunday—not to enjoy religious privileges, but because on Sunday sinners from all parts of the country round flocked into Sonora, to commune with the spirits, infernal rather than celestial, gathered there.

He made the tour of all the saloons, dashed eagerly at two or three men, with plain gold rings on left fore-fingers, disgustedly found them the wrong men beyond doubt, cursed them, and invited them to drink. Then he closely catechised all the barkeepers, who were the only reliable directories in that country; they were anxious to oblige him, but none could remember such a man. So Buffle took his horse, and sought his man elsewhere.

Meanwhile, Mrs. Berryn remained in camp, where she was cared for in a manner which called out her astonishment equally with her gratitude. Buffle was hardly well out of the Gulch when Mrs. Berryn heard a knock at the door; she opened it, and a man handed her a frying-pan, with the remark, "Buffle is cracked," and hastily disappeared.

In the morning she was awakened by a crash outside the door, and, on looking out, discovered a quantity of firewood ready cut; each morning thereafter found in the same place a fresh supply, which was usually decorated with offerings of different degrees of appropriateness—pieces of fresh meat, strings of dried ditto, blankets enough for a large hotel, little packages of gold dust, case knives and forks, cans of salt butter, and all sorts of provisions, in quantity.

Each man in camp fondly believed his own particular revolver was better than any other, and, as a natural consequence, the camp became almost peaceful, by reason of the number of pistols that were left in front of Mrs. Berryn's door. But she carefully left them alone, and when this was discovered the boys sorrowfully removed them.

Then old Griff, living up the Gulch, with a horrible bull-dog for companion, brought his darling animal down late one dark night, and tied him near the lady's residence, where he discoursed sweet sounds for two hours, until, to Mrs. Berryn's delight, he broke his chain, and returned to his old home.

Then Sandytop, the ace-thief, suddenly left camp. Many

were the surmises and bets on the subject; and on the third
day, when two men, one of whom believed he had gone to
steal a mule, and the other believed he had rolled into the
creek while drunk, were about to refer the whole matter to
pistols, they were surprised at seeing Sandytop stagger into
camp, under a large, unsightly bundle. The next day Mrs.
Berryn ate from crockery instead of tin, and had a china
wash-bowl and pitcher.

Little Muggy, who sold out his claim the day after Buffle
left, went to San Francisco, but reappeared in camp in a
few days, with a large bundle, a handsaw and a plane.
Some light was thrown on the contents of the bundle by
sundry scraps of linen, cotton, and very soft flannel, that
the wind occasionally blew from the direction of Mrs.
Berryn's abode; but why Muggy suddenly needed a very
large window in the only boarded side of his house; why
he never staked another claim and went to "washing;" why
his door always had to be unlocked from the inside before
any one could get in, instead of being ajar, as was the usual
custom with doors at Fat Pocket Gulch; why visitors
always found the floor strewn with shavings and blocks, but
were told to mind their business if they asked what he was
making; and why Uppercrust, an aristocratic young reprobate, who had been a doctor in the States, had suddenly
taken up his abode with Muggy, were mysteries unsolvable
by the united intellects of Fat Pocket Gulch.

It was finally suggested by some one, that, as Muggy
had often and fluently cursed the "rockers" used to wash
out dirt along the Gulch, it was likely enough he was
inventing a new one, and the ex-doctor, who, of course,
knew something about chemistry, was helping him to work
an amalgamator into it; a careful comparison of bets
showed this to be a fairly accepted opinion, and so the
matter rested.

Meanwhile, Buffle had been untiring in his search, as his
horse, could he have spoken, would have testified. Men
wondered what Berryn had done to Buffle, and odds of ten

to one that some undertaker would soon have reason to
bless Buffle were freely offered, but seldom taken. One
night Buffle's horse galloped into Deadlock Ridge, and the
rider, hailing the first man he met, inquired the way to the
saloon.

"I don't know," replied the man.

"Come, no foolin' thar," said Buffle, indignantly.

"I don't know, I tell you—I don't drink."

"Hang yer!" roared Buffle, in honest fury at what
seemed to him the most stupendous lie ever told by a
miner, "I'll teach yer to lie to me." And out came Buffle's
pistol.

The man saw his danger, and, springing at Buffle with
the agility of a cat, snatched the pistol and threw it on the
ground; in an instant Buffle's hand had firmly grasped the
man by his shirt-collar, and, the horse taking fright, Buffle,
a second later, found in his hand a torn piece of red flannel,
a chain, and a locket, while the man lay on the ground.

"At last!" exclaimed Buffle, convinced that he had found
his man ; but his emotions were quickly cooled by the man
in the road, who, jumping from the ground, picked up
Buffle's pistol, cocked and aimed it, and spoke in a grating
voice, as if through set teeth :

"Give back that locket this second, or, as God lives, I'll
take it out of a dead man's hand."

The rapidity of human thought is never so beautifully
illustrated as when the owner of a human mind is serving
involuntarily as a target.

"My friend," said Buffle, "ef I've got anything uv
yourn, yer ken hev it on provin' property. We'll go to
whar that fust light is up above—I'll walk the hoss slow,
an' yer ken keep me covered with the pistol; ain't that
fair?"

"Be quick, then," said the man, excitedly; "start!"

The trip was not more than two minutes in length, but
it seemed a good hour to Buffle, whose acquaintanceship
with the delicacy of the trigger of his beloved pistol caused

his past life to pass in retrospect before him several times before they reached the light. The light proved to be in the saloon whose locality had provoked the quarrel. The saloon was full, the door was open, and there was a buzz of astonishment, which culminated in a volley of ejaculations, in which strength predominated over elegance, as a large man, followed closely by a small man with a cocked pistol, marched up to the bar.

"Gentlemen," said Buffle, "this feller sez I've got some uv his property, an' he's come here to prove it. Now, feller, wot's yer claim?"

"A chain and locket," said the man; "hang you, I see them in your hand now."

"Ennybody ken see a chain an' locket in my hand," said Buffle, "but that don't make it yourn."

"The locket contains the portrait of a lady, and the inscription 'Frances to Allan'—look quick, or I'll shoot!" said the little man, savagely.

Buffle opened it, and saw Mrs. Berryn's portrait.

"Mister, yer right," said he; "here's yer property, an' I'll apologize, er drink, er fight—er apologize, an' drink, an' fight, whichever is yer style. Fust, however, ef ye'll drop that pistol, I'll drink myself, considerin'—never mind. Denominate yer pizen, gentlemen," said he, as the audience crowded to the bar.

"Buffle," whispered the barkeeper, who knew the great man by sight, "he's a littler man than you."

"I know it, boss," replied Buffle, most brazenly. "He sez he don't drink."

"Never saw him *here* before—there, he's goin' out now," said the barkeeper.

Buffle turned and dashed through the crowd; all who held glasses quickly laid them down and followed.

"Stand back, the hull crowd uv yer," said Buffle; "this ain't no fight—me an' the gentleman got private bizness." And, laying his hand on Berryn's shoulder, he said, "What are yer doin' here, when yer know a lady like that?"

"Suffering hell for abusing heaven,'" replied Berryn, passionately.

"Then why don't yer go back?" inquired Buffle.

"Because I've got no money ; all luck has failed me ever since I left home—shipwreck, hunger, poverty——"

"Come back a minute," interrupted Buffle. I forgot to come down with the dust for the drinks. Now I tell yer what—I want yer to go back to my camp—I've got plenty uv gold, an' it's no good to me, only fur gamblin' an' drinkin'; yer welcome to enough uv it to git yerself home, an' git on yer feet when yer get thar."

Berryn looked doubtingly at him as they entered the saloon.

"P'r'aps somebody here ken tell this gentleman my name?" said Buffle.

"Buffle!" said several voices in chorus.

"Bully! Now, p'r'aps you same fellers ken tell him ef I'm a man uv my word?"

"You bet," responded the same chorus.

"An' now, p'r'aps some uv yer'll sell me a good hoss, pervidin' yer don't want him stole mighty sudden?"

Several men invited attention to their respective animals, tied near the door. Promptly selecting one, paying for it, and settling with the barkeeper, and mounting his own horse while Berryn mounted the new one, the two men galloped away, leaving the bystanders lost in astonishment, from which they only recovered after almost superhuman industry on the part of the barkeeper.

———

ONE evening, when the daily labors and household cares of the Fat Pocket Gulchites had ended, the residents of that quiet village were congregated, as usual, at the saloon. It was too early for gambling and fighting, and the boys chatted peacefully, pausing only a few times to drink "Here's her," which had become the standard toast of the Gulch. Conversation turned on Muggy's invention, and a few bets were exchanged, which showed the boys were not quite sure it was a rocker, after all. Suddenly Sandytop, who had been leaning against the door-frame, and, looking in the direction of Buffle's old cabin, ejaculated:

"'*Tis* a rocker, boys—it's a rocker, but—but not that kind."

The boys poured out the door, and saw an unusual procession approaching Mrs. Berryn's cabin; first came Uppercrust, the young ex-doctor, then an Irishwoman from a neighboring settlement, and then Muggy, bearing a baby's cradle, neatly made of pine boards. The doctor and woman went in, and Muggy, dropping the cradle, ran at full speed to the saloon, and up to the bar, the crowd following.

Muggy looked along the line, saw all the glasses were filled and in hand, and then, raising his own, exclaimed, "Here's her, boys!" and then went into a fully developed boo-hoo. And he was not alone; for once the boys watered their liquor, and purer water God never made.

It was some moments before shirt-sleeves ceased to officiate as handkerchiefs; but just as the boys commenced to look savagely at each other, as if threatening cold lead if any one suspected undue tenderness, Sandytop, who had returned to his post at the door to give ease to the stream which his sleeve could not staunch, again startled the crowd by staring earnestly toward the hill over which led the trail, and exclaiming, "Good God!"

There was another rush to the door, and there, galloping down the trail, was Buffle and another man. The boys stared at each other, but said nothing—their gift of swearing was not equal to the occasion.

Steadily they stared at the two men, until Buffle, reining back a little, pointed his pistol threateningly. They took the hint, and after they were all inside, Sandytop closed the door and the shutters of the unglazed windows.

"Thar's my shanty," said Buffle, as they neared it from one side; "that one with two bar'ls fur a chimley. You jest go right in. I'll be thar ez soon ez I put up the hosses."

As they reached the front, both men started at the sight of the cradle.

"Why, I didn't know you were a married man, Buffle?" said his companion.

"I—well—I—I—don't tell everythin'," stammered Buffle; and, catching the bridle of Berryn's horse the moment his rider had dismounted, Buffle dashed off to the saloon, and took numerous solitary drinks, at which no one took offense. Then he turned, nodded significantly toward the old shanty, and asked:

"How long since?"

"Not quite yit—yer got him here in time, Buffle," said Muggy.

"Thank the Lord!" said Buffle. His lips were very familiar with the name of the Lord, but they had never before used it in this sense."

Then, while several men were getting ready to ask Buffle where he found his man—Californians never ask questions in a hurry—there came from the direction of Buffle's shanty the sound of a subdued cry.

"Gentlemen," said the barkeeper, "there's no more drinking at this bar to-night until—until I say so."

No one murmured. No one swore. No one suggested a game. An old enemy of Buffle's happened in, but that worthy, instead of feeling for his pistol, quietly left the leaning-post, and bowed his enemy into it.

The boys stood and sat about, studied the cracks in the floor, the pattern of the shutters, contemplated the insides of their hats, and chewed tobacco as if their lives depended on it.

Buffle made frequent trips to the door, and looked out. Suddenly he closed the door, and had barely time to whisper, "No noise, now, or I'll shoot," when the doctor walked in. The crowd arose.

"It's all right," gentlemen," said the doctor—"as fine a boy as I ever saw."

"My treat for the rest of the evening, boys," said the

barkeeper, hurriedly crowding glasses and bottles on the bar. "Her," "Him," "Him, Junior," "Buffle," "Doc.," and "Old Rockershop," as some happily inspired miner dubbed little Muggy, were drunk successively.

The door opened again, and in walked Allan Berryn. Glancing quickly about, he soon distinguished Buffle. He grasped his hand, looked him steadily in the eye, and exclaimed:

"Buffle, you——"

He was a Harvard graduate, and a fine talker, was Allan Berryn, but, when he had spoken two words, he somehow forgot the remainder of the speech he had made up on his way over; his silence for two or three seconds seemed of hours to every man who looked on his face, so that it was a relief to all when he gave Buffle a mighty hug, and then precipitately retreated.

Buffle looked sheepish, and shook himself.

"That feller can outhug a grizzly," said he. "Boys," he continued, "that chap's been buckin' agin luck sence he's been in the diggin's, an' is clean busted. But his luck begun to turn this evening, an' here's what goes for keepin' the ball a-rollin'. Here's my ante;" saying which, he laid his old hat on the bar, took out his buckskin bag of gold-dust, and emptied it into the hat.

Bags came out of pockets all around, and were either entirely emptied, or had their contents largely diminished by knife-blades, which scooped out the precious dust, and dropped it into the hat.

"There," said Buffle, looking into the hat," "I reckon that'll kerry 'em back to their folks."

For a fortnight the saloon was as quiet as a well-ordered prayer-meeting, and it was solemnly decided that no fight with pistols should take place nearer than The Bend, which was, at least, a mile from where the new resident's cradle was located.

One pleasant, quiet evening, Buffle, who frequently passed an hour with Berryn on the latter's woodpile, was seen approaching the saloon with a very small bundle, which, nevertheless, occupied both his arms and all his attention.

"It, by thunder," said one. So it was ; a wee, pink-faced, blue-eyed, fuzzy-topped little thing, with one hand frantically clutching three hairs of Buffle's beard.

"See the little thing pull," said one.

"Is that all the nose they hev at fust?" asked another, seriously.

"Can't yer take them pipes out uv yer mouths when the baby's aroun'?" indignantly demanded another.

Little Muggy edged his way through the crowd, threw away his quid of tobacco, took the baby from Buffle, and kissed it a dozen times.

"I'm goin' home, fellers," said Muggy, finally. "I'm wanted by the lawyers for cuttin' a man that sassed me while I was shoe-makin'. But I'm a-goin' to see my young uns, even if all creation wants me."

"An' I'm a-goin', too," said Buffle. "I'm wanted pretty bad by some that's East, but I reckon I'm well enough hid by the har that's grow'd sence I wuz a boy, an' dug out from old Varmont. I've had a new taste uv decency lately, an' I'm goin' to see ef I can't stan' it for a stiddy diet. The chap over to the shanty sez he ken git me somethin' to do, an' ennythin's better'n gamblin', drinkin', and fightin'.

"It's agin the law to kerry shootin'-irons there, Buffle," suggested one.

"Yes, an' they got a new kind uv a law there, to keep a man from takin' his bitters," said another.

"Yes," said Buffle, "all that's mighty tough, but ef a feller's bound fur bed-rock, he might ez well git that all uv a sudden, ef he ken."

Buffle started toward the door, stopped as if he had something else to say, started again, hesitated, feigned indignation at the baby, flushed the least bit, opened the door, partly closed it again, squeezed himself out and displaying only the tip of his nose, roared :

"This baby's name is Allan Buffle Berryn — Allen
Buffle Berryn!" and then rushed at full speed to leave
the baby at home, while the boys clinked glasses me-
lodiously.

At the end of another fortnight there was a procession
formed at Fat Pocket Gulch; two horses, one wearing a
side-saddle, were brought to the door of Buffle's old house,
and Mrs. Berryn and her husband mounted them; they
were soon joined by Buffle and Muggy.

"THIS BABY'S NAME IS ALLAN BUFFLE BERRYN."

For months after there was mourning far and wide among
owners of mules and horses, for each Gulchite had been out
stealing, that he might ride with the escort which was to see
the Berryns safely to the crossing. An advance-guard was
sent ahead, and the party were about to start, when Buffle
suddenly dismounted and entered his old cabin; when he
reappeared, a cloud of smoke followed him.

"Thar," said he, a moment later, as flames were seen

bursting through the roof, "no galoot uv a miner don't live in that shanty after that.   Git."

Away galloped the party, the baby in the arms of its father.   The crossing was safely reached, and the stage had room for the whole party, and, after a hearty hand-shaking all around, the stage started.   Sandytop threw one of his only two shoes after it for luck.

As the stage was disappearing around a bend, a little way from the crossing, the back curtain was suddenly thrown up, a baby, backed by a white hat and yellow beard, was seen, and a familiar voice was heard to roar, "Allan *Buffle* Berryn."

"NICE place? I guess it is; ther hain't no such farm in *this* part of Illinoy, nor anywhere else that *I* knows on. Two-story house, and painted instead of being white-washed; blinds on the winders; no thirty-dollar horses in the barn, an' no old, unpainted wagons around; no deadened trees standin' aroun' in the corn-lot or the wheat-field—not a one. Good cribs to hold his corn, instead of leaving it on the stalk, or tuckin' it away in holler sycamore logs, good pump to h'ist his drinkin'-water with, good help to keep up with the work—why, ther hain't a man on Matalette's whole place that don't look smart enough to run a farm all alone by himself. And money—well, he don't ask no credit of no man: he just hauls out his money and pays up, as if he enjoyed gettin' rid of it. There's nobody like him in these parts, you can just bet your life."

The speaker was a Southern Illinoisan of twenty-five years ago, and his only auditor was a brother farmer.

Both worked hard and shook often (with ague) between the seed time and harvest, but neither had succeeded in amassing such comfortable results as had seemed to reward the efforts of their neighbor Matalette. For the listener had not heard half the story of Matalette's advantages. He was as good-natured, smart and hospitable as he was lucky. He indulged in the unusual extravagance of a hired cook; and the neighbors, though they, on principle, disapproved of such expenditure, never failed to appreciate the results of the said cook's labors.

Matalette had a sideboard, too, and the contents smelled and tasted very unlike the liquor which was sold at the only store in Bonpas Bottoms.

When young Lauquer, who was making a gallant fight against a stumpy quarter section, had his only horse lie down and die just as the second corn-plowing season came on, it was Matalette who supplied the money which bought the new horse.

When the inhabitants of the Bottoms wondered and talked and argued about the advisability of trying some new seed-wheat, which had the reputation of being very heavy, Matalette settled the whole question by ordering a large lot, and distributing it with his compliments.

Lastly—though the statement has not, strictly speaking, any agricultural bearing—Matalette had a daughter. There were plenty of daughters among the families in Bonpas Bottoms, and many of them were very estimable girls; but Helen Matalette was very different from any of them.

"Always knows just what to say and do," remarked Syle Conover, one day, at the store, where the male gossips of the neighborhood met to exchange views. "A fellow goes up to see Matalette—goes in his shirt-sleeves, not expectin' to see any women around—when who comes to the door but *her*. For a minute a fellow wishes he could fly, or sink; next minute he feels as if he'd been acquainted with her for a year. Hanged if I understand it, but she's the kind of gal I go in fur!"

The latter clause of Syle's speech fitly expressed the sentiments of all the young men in Bonpas Bottoms, as well as of many gentlemen not so young.

Old men—farmers with daughters of their own—would cheerfully forego the delights of either a prayer-meeting or a circus, and suddenly find some business to transact with Matalette, whenever there seemed a reasonable chance of seeing Helen; and such of them as had sons of a marriage-able age would express to those young men their entire willingness to be promoted to the rank of fathers-in-law.

There was just one unpleasant thing about the Matalettes, both father and daughter, and that was, the ease with which one could startle them.

It was rather chilling, until one knew Matalette well, to see him tremble and start violently on being merely slapped on the shoulder by some one whose approach he had not noticed; it was equally unpleasant for a newcomer, on suddenly confronting Helen, to see her turn pale, and look quickly and furtively about, as if preparing to run.

The editor of the *Bonpas Cornblade*, in a sonnet addressed to " H. M.," compared this action to that of a startled fawn ; but the public wondered whether Helen's father could possibly be excused in like manner, and whether the comparison could, with propriety, be extended so as to include the three hired men, who, curiously enough, were equally timorous at first acquaintance.

But this single fault of the Matalettes and their adherents was soon forgotten, for it did not require a long residence in Bonpas Bottoms to make the acquaintance of every person living in that favored section, and strangers—except such passengers as occasionally strolled ashore while the steamboat landed supplies for the store, or shipped the grain which Matalette was continually buying and sending to New Orleans—seldom found their way to Bonpas Bottoms.

The Matalettes sat at supper one evening, when there was heard a knock at the door. There was in an instant an unusual commotion about the table, at which sat the three hired men, with the host and his daughter—a commotion most extraordinary for a land in which neither Indians nor burglars were known.

Each of the hired men hastily clicked something under the table, while Helen turned pale, but quickly drew a small stiletto from a fold of her dress.

"Ready?" asked Matalette, in a low tone, as he took a candle from the table, and placed his unoccupied hand in his pocket.

"Yes," whispered each of the men, while Helen nodded.

"Who's there?" shouted Matalette, approaching the outer door.

"I—Asbury Crewne—the new circuit preacher," replied a voice. "I'm wet, cold and hungry—can you give me shelter, in the name of my Master?"

"Certainly!" cried Matalette, hastening to open the door, while the three hired men rapidly repocketed their pistols, and Helen gave vent to a sigh of relief.

They heard a heavy pack thrown on the floor, a hearty greeting from Matalette, and then they saw in the doorway a tall, straight young man, whose blue eyes, heavy, closely curling yellow hair and finely cut features made him extremely handsome, despite a solemn, puritanical look which not even a driving rain and a cold wind had been able to banish from his face.

There were many worthy young men in the Bonpas Bottoms, but none of them were at all so fine-looking as Asbury Crewne; so, at least, Helen seemed to think, for she looked at him steadily, except when he was looking at her. Of course, Crewne, being a preacher, took none but a spiritual interest in young ladies; but where a person's face seems to show forth the owner's whole soul, as was the case with Helen Matalette's, a minister of the Gospel is certainly justifiable in looking oft and long at it—nay, is even grossly culpable if he does not regard it with a lively and tender interest.

Such seemed to be the young divine's train of reasoning, and his consequent conclusion, for, from the time he exchanged his dripping clothing for a suit of Matalette's own, he addressed his conversation almost entirely to Helen. And Helen, who very seldom met, in the Bonpas Bottoms, gentlemen of taste and intelligence, seemed to be spending an unusually agreeable evening, if her radiant and expressive countenance might be trusted to tell the truth.

When the young preacher, according to the custom of his class and denomination, at that day, finally turned the course of conversation toward the one reputed object of his life, it was with a sigh which indicated, perhaps, how earnestly he regretted that the dominion of Satan in the world compelled him to withdraw his soul from such pure and unusual delights as had been his during that evening. And when, after offering a prayer with the family, Crewne followed Matalette to a chamber to rest, Helen bade him goodnight with a bright smile which mixed itself up inextricably with his private devotions, his thoughts and his plans for forthcoming sermons, and seriously curtailed his night's rest in addition.

In the morning it was found that his clothing was still wet, so, as it was absolutely necessary that he should go to fulfil an appointment, it was arranged that he should retain Matalette's clothing, and return within a few days for his own.

Then Matalette, learning that the young man was traveling his circuit on foot, insisted on lending him a horse, and on giving him money with which to purchase one.

It was a great sum of money—more than his salary for a year amounted to—and the young man's feelings almost overcame him as he tried to utter his thanks; but just then Helen made her first appearance during the morning, and from the instant she greeted Crewne all thoughts of gratitude seemed to escape his mind, unless, indeed, he suddenly determined to express his thanks through a third party. Such a supposition would have been fully warranted by the expressive looks he cast upon Helen's handsome face.

Had any member of the flock at Mount Pisgah Station seen these two young people during the moment or two which followed Helen's appearance, he would have sorrowfully but promptly dismissed from his mind any expectation of hearing the sermon which Crewne had promised to preach at Mount Pisgah that morning. But the young preacher was of no ordinary human pattern : with sorrow, yet determination, he bade Helen good-by, and though, as he rode away, he frequently turned his head, he never stopped his horse.

Down the road through the dense forest he went, trying, by reading his Bible as he rode, to get his mind in proper condition for a mighty effort at Mount Pisgah. He wasn't conscious of doing such a thing—he could honestly lay his hand on his heart and say he had'nt the slightest intention of doing anything of the kind, yet somehow his Bible opened at the Song of Solomon. For a moment he read, but for a moment only ; then he shut his lips tightly, and deliberately commenced reading the Book of Psalms.

He had fairly restored his mind to working shape, and was just whispering fervent thanks to the Lord, when a couple of horsemen galloped up to him. As he turned his head to see who they might be, he observed that each of them held a pistol in a very threatening manner. As he looked, however, the pistols dropped, and one of the riders indulged in a profane expression of disappointment.

" It's Matalette's clothes and horse, Jim," he said to his companion, " but it's the preacher's face.

" And you have been providentially deferred from committing a great crime !" exclaimed Crewne, with a reproving look. " Mr. Matalette took me in last night, wet, cold, and footsore ; this morning I departed, refreshed, clothed and mounted. To rob a man who is so lavish of——"

" Beg your pardon, parson," interrupted one of the men, "but you haven't got the right pig by the ear. We're not highwaymen. I'm the sheriff of this county, and Jim's a constable. And as for Matalette, he's a counterfeiter, and we're after him."

Crewne dropped his bridle-rein, and his lower jaw, as he exclaimed :

" Impossible !"

" 'Tis, eh ?" said the sheriff. " Well, we've examined several lots of money he's paid out lately, and there isn't a good bill among 'em."

Crewne mechanically put his hands in his pocket and drew forth the money Matalette had given him to buy a horse with. The sheriff snatched it.

"That's some of his stock?" said he, looking it rapidly over. *That* seems good enough."

"What will become of his poor daughter?" ejaculated the young preacher, with a vacant look.

"What, Helen?" queried the sheriff. "She's the best engraver of counterfeits there is in the whole West."

"Dreadful—dreadful!" exclaimed the young preacher, putting his hand over his eyes.

"Fact," replied the sheriff. "You parsons have got a big job to do 'fore this world's in the right shape, an' sheriffs and constables ain't needed. Wish you good luck at it, though 'twill be bad for trade. You'll keep mum 'bout this case, of course. We'll catch 'em in the act finally; then there won't be any danger about not getting a conviction, an' our reward, that's offered by the banks."

The sheriff and his assistant galloped on to the village they had been approaching when they overtook Crewne; but the young minister did not accompany them, although the village toward which they rode was the one in which he was to preach that morning.

Perhaps he needed more time and quietness in which to compose his sermon. If this supposition is correct, it may account for the fact that the members of the Mount Pisgah congregation pronounced his sermon that day, from the text, "All is vanity," one of his most powerful efforts.

In fact, old Mrs. Reets, who had for time immemorial entertained the probable angels who appeared at Mount Pisgah in ministerial guise, remarked that "preacher seemed all tuckered out by that talk; tuk his critter, an' left town 'fore the puddin' was done."

That same evening, the sheriff and his deputy, with several special assistants, rode from Mount Pisgah toward Matalette's section.

The night was dark, rainy and cloudy; the horses stumbled over roots and logs in the imperfectly made road; the low-hanging branches spitefully cut the faces of the riders, and brought several hats to grief, and snatched the sheriff's pipe out of his mouth.

And yet the sheriff seemed in excellent spirits. To be sure, he softly whistled the air of, " Jordan is a hard road to travel," which was the popular air twenty-five years ago, but there was a merry tone to his whistle. He stopped whistling suddenly, and remarked to the constable :

"Got notice to-day of another new counterfeit. Five hundred offered for arrest and conviction on *that*. Hope we can prove *that* on Matalette's gang. We can go out of politics, and run handsome farms of our own, if things go all right to-night. Don't know but I'd give my whole share, though, to whoever would arrest Helen. It's a dog's life, anyhow, this bein' a sheriff. I won't complain, however, if we get that gang to-night."

The party rode on until they were within a mile of Matalette's section, when they reined their horses into the woods, dismounted, left a man on watch, and approached the dwelling on foot.

Reaching the fence, the party halted, whispered together for a moment, and silently surrounded the house in different directions.

The sheriff removed his boots, walked noiselessly around the house, saw that he had a man at each door and window, and posted one at the cellar-door. Then the sheriff put on his boots, approached the front door, and knocked loudly.

There was no response. The light was streaming brightly from one of the windows, and the sheriff tried to look in, but the thick curtain prevented him. He knocked again, and louder, but still there was no response. Then he became uneasy. He was a brave man when he knew what was to be met, but now all sorts of uncomfortable suspicions crossed his mind ; the rascals might be up-stairs waiting for a quiet opportunity to shoot down at him, or they might be under the small stoop on which he stood, and preparing to fire up at him. They might be quietly burning their spurious money up-stairs, so as to destroy the evidence against them ; they might be in the cellar burying the plates.

The sheriff could endure the suspense no longer. Signaling to him two of his men, he, with a blow of a stick of wood, broke in the window-sash. As, immediately afterward, he tore aside the curtain, he and his assistance presented pistols and shouted :

" Surrender !"

No one was visible, and the sheriff only concealed his sheepish feelings by jumping into the room. His assistants followed him, and they searched the entire house without finding any one.

.They searched the cellar, the outhouses, and the barn, but encountered only the inquiring glances of the horses and cattle. Then they searched the house anew, hoping to find proof of the guilt of Matalette and his family ; but, excepting holes in the floor of a vacant room, they found nothing which might not be expected in a comfortable home.

Suddenly some one thought of the boats which Matalette kept at the mouth of the creek, and a detachment, headed by the sheriff, went hastily down to examine them.

The boats were gone—not even the tiniest canoe or most dilapidated skiff remained. It is grievous to relate—but truth is truth—that the sheriff, who was on Sundays a Sabbath-school superintendent, now lost his temper and swore frightfully. But no boats were conjured up by the sheriff's language, nor did his assistance succeed in finding any up the creek ; so the party returned to the house, and resorted to the illegal measure of helping themselves liberally to the contents of Matalette's sideboard.

Meanwhile a black mass, floating down the Wabash, about a dozen miles below the Bonpas's mouth, seemed the cause of some mysterious plunging and splashing in the river. Finally an aperture appeared in the black mass, and the light streamed out. Then the figure of a man appeared in the aperture, and all was dark again.

As the figure disappeared within the mass, three bearded

men, dressed like emigrants, looked up furtively, one yellow-haired man stared vacantly and sadly into the fire which illumed the cabin of the little trading boat, while Helen Matalette sprang forward and threw her arms about the figure's neck.

"It's all gone, Nell," said the man. "Presses and plates are where nobody will be likely to find them. The Wabash won't tell secrets."

"I'm so glad—*oh*, so glad!" cried the girl.

"It's a fortune thrown away," said one of the men, moodily.

"Yes, and a bad name, too," said she, with flashing eyes.

"We're beggars for life, anyhow," growled another of the men.

"Nonsense!" exclaimed Matalette. "Nell's right—if we're not tracked and caught, I'll never be sorry that we sunk the accursed business for ever. And, considering our narrow escape, and how it happened, I don't think we're very gentlemanly to sit here bemoaning our luck. Mr. Crewne," continued Matalette, crossing to the yellow-haired figure in front of the fire, "you've saved me—what can I give you?"

The young preacher recovered himself, and replied, briefly:

"Your soul."

Matalette winced, and, in a weak voice, asked:

"Anything else?"

Crewne looked toward Helen; Helen blushed, and looked a little frightened; Crewne blushed, too, and seemed to be clearing his throat; then, with a mighty effort, he said:

"Yes—Helen."

The counterfeiter looked at his daughter for an instant, and then failed to see her partly because something marred the clearness of his vision just then, and partly because Crewne, interpreting the father's silence as consent, took

possession of the reward he had named, and almost hid her
from her father's view.

Matalette's section was finally sold for taxes, and was
never reclaimed, but the excitement relating to its former
occupants was for years so great that the purchasers of the
estate found it worldly wisdom to dispense refreshments on
the ground.

As for Crewne—a few months after the occurrences
mentioned above there appeared, in the wilds of Missouri,
a young preacher with unusual zeal and a handsome wife.
And about the same time four men entered a quarter-section
of prairie-land near the young preacher's station, and
appeared then and evermore to be the most ardent and
faithful of the young man's admirers.

A STORY OF TEN MILE GULCH.

I.

THE horse which Mr. Tom Ruger rode kept the path, steep and rugged though it was, without any guidance from him, and its mate followed demurely. They were accustomed to it; and many a mile had they traversed in this way, taking turns at carrying their owner and master. Indeed, the trio seemed inseparable, and "as happy as Tom Ruger and his horses" was a phrase that was very often heard in every mining camp and settlement.

As for Mr. Tom Ruger himself, very little was known of him save what had been learned during the two years that he had sojourned among them. Where he came from never was known, nor asked but once by the same person. All that could be said of him might be summed up in the following statement :

"The finest-looking, the best-dressed, and the best-mannered man on the Pacific coast, and the best horseman."

These were the words of "mine host" at the Ten Mile House, and, as he was a gentleman whose word was as good as his paper, we will accept them as truth.

As Mr. Ruger rode down the mountain-side that beautiful Autumn day, dressed in the finest of broadcloth, with linen of the most immaculate whiteness, smoking what appeared to be a very good cigar, and humming to himself a fragment of some old song, he looked strangely out of place.

So thought Miss Fanny Borlan as she looked out of the stage-window, and caught her first glimpse of him just where his path intersected the stage-road; and she would have asked the driver about him, had he not been so near.

Mr. Ruger caught sight of her face about that time, and tossing away the cigar, he lifted his hat to her in the most approved style.

She acknowledged the salute by a bow, and when he rode up to the side of the stage, and made some casual remark about the fine weather, she did not choose to consider it out of the way to receive this advance toward a traveling acquaintance with seeming cordiality.

"Have you traveled far?" he asked.

"From the Atlantic coast, sir."

"The same journey that I intend to take some of these days, only that I hope to substitute the word Pacific at its termination. I hope you are near the end of your journey in this direction?"

"My destination is Ten Mile Gulch, I believe; but you have such horrid names out here."

"I presume they do appear somewhat queer to a stranger, but they nearly all have the merit of being appropriate. You stop at the settlement?"

"I do not know. My brother wrote to me to come to Ten Mile Gulch. Is it the name of a town?"

"Both of a village and a mining district, from which the village takes its name. Is your brother a miner?"

"Yes, sir."

"I presume he intended to meet you at the settlement. You will no doubt find him at the tavern; if not, I will tell him of your arrival, for my way leads through the mines."

"Thank you, sir. My brother's name is John Borlan."

"I am somewhat acquainted with him," said Mr. Ruger, "though in this region of strange names we call him Jack. My name is Thomas Ruger."

"Tom, in California style?" she asked, with a merry twinkle in her eye.

"Yes, Miss Borlan," he said, also smiling. "Tom Ruger is well known where Thomas Ruger never was heard of. And now I will bid you good-day, Miss Borlan, for I am in something of a hurry to reach the settlement. If I do not find Jack there, I will go on to the mines and tell him."

"Ah, Miss, you don't have such men as Tom Ruger out where you come from," said the driver, as Tom disappeared up the road. "And them nags of his'n can't be beat this side of the mountains. He makes a heap o' money with 'em."

"What! a horse-jockey?" exclaimed Miss Borlan.

"We don't call him that, miss. Some says he's a sportin' man, which ain't nothin' ag'in him, for the country's new, ye see. He's got heaps o' money anyway, and there ain't a camp nor a town on the coast that don't know Tom Ruger. Ah, ye don't have such men as Tommy. He'd be at home in a palace, now wouldn't he? And it's jest the same in a miner's shanty. Ye don't have such men as he. If he takes a likin' to anybody, he sticks to 'em through thick and thin ; but if he gits ag'in ye once, he's—the—very —deuce. Ah, ye don't have no such man out where you come from."

She did not care to dispute this point. In fact, after what she had seen and heard, she was inclined to believe that there was no such men as Tom Ruger out where she had come from ; so she made no reply ; and the driver, following out his train of thought, rattled on about Tom Ruger until they came in sight of Ten Mile Gulch, winding up his narrative with the sage, but rather unexpected, remark, that there weren't no such men as Tom Ruger out where she had come from.

II.

THE barroom at the Miners' Home might have been more crowded at some former period of its existence, but to have duplicated the two dozen faces and forms of the two dozen Ten Milers who were congregated there that beautiful Autumn afternoon would have been a hopeless task.

Ten Mile Gulch had turned out *en masse*, and those same Ten Milers were distinguished neither for their good looks, nor taste in dress, nor softness of heart or language, nor elegance of manners. Further than that we do not care to go at present.

But there was one face and one form absent. No more would the genial atmosphere of that barroom respond to the heavings of his broad chest, no more would the dignified concoctor of rare and villainous drinks pass him the whisky-straight. Alas! Bill Foster had passed in his checks, and gone the way of all Ten Milers.

And it was this fact that brought these diligent delvers after hidden treasure from their work, for Bill had not gone in the ordinary way. At night he was in the full enjoyment of health and a game of poker; in the morning they found him just outside the domicile of Jack Borlan, with a small puncture near the heart to tell how it was done. Such was life at Ten Mile Gulch.

Who made the puncture?

Circumstances pointed to Jack Borlan, and they escorted him down to the settlement. He stood by the bar conversing with the dispenser of liquid lightning. Two very calm-looking Ten Milers were within easy reach of Mr. Borlan; two more at the door, which was left temptingly open; two more at each window, and the remainder scattered about the room to suit themselves.

Mr. Bob Watson was the only one calm enough to enjoy a seat, and he was whittling away at the pine bench with such energy that a stranger might have concluded that whittling was his best hold. Not so, however; he whittled until he found a nail with the edge of his knife, and then varied his diversion by grasping the point of the blade between the thumb and first finger of his right hand, and throwing it at the left eye of a very flattering representation of Yankee Sullivan which graced the wall.

By a slight miscalculation of distance and elevation, the eye was unharmed, but the well-developed nose was more effectually ruined than its original ever was by the most scientific pugilist.

"Well, gentlemen, what shall we do with the prisoner?" asks Watson.

"We're waiting for *you*," said a tall Ten Miler, who had been a pleased witness of the knife-throwing and its results.

"Well, you need not," retorted Mr. Watson, as he made a fling at Yankee's other eye, and with very good success. "You know my sentiments, gentlemen. I was opposed to bringing the prisoner here. We might have fixed up the matter all at one time, and saved a heap of diggin'."

"It—might—have—done," said the tall Miler, doubtfully; "but I wouldn't like to see the two together. It would spoil all my enjoyment of the occasion."

"Bet yer ten to one ye don't swing him!" cried Watson, springing to his feet with sudden inspiration, and mounting the bench he had been whittling. "Twenty to one Jack Borlan don't choke this heat! Who takes me? who? who?"

No one seemed disposed to take him.

"Bosh! you Ten Milers are all babies. Now, if this had happened up at Quit Claim, Borlan would have had a beautiful tombstone over him long ago. What do *you* say, Borlan?"

The prisoner, thus addressed, cut short some remark he was making, and turned to Watson. "There have been cases where the prisoner had the benefit of a trial, Mr. Watson."

"Which is so, Mr. Borlan. Obliged to you fur reminding me. Let's have one, gentlemen. I'll be prosecuting attorney, if no one objects; now, who'll defend the prisoner at the bar?"

"I'll make a feeble attempt that way," was the reply that came from the doorway. All eyes turned, and recognized Tom Ruger.

"This is betwixt us Ten Milers," said Watson. "Borlan is guilty, and we're bound to hang him before sundown; but we want to do the fair thing, and give him the benefit of a trial. Who of you Ten Milers will defend him?"

"I told you *I* would defend Mr. Borlan," said Tom Ruger, as he removed his silk hat and wiped his broad forehead with the finest of silk handkerchiefs.

"I tell you we won't have any outsiders in this game," said Watson.

"I really dislike to contradict you, Mr. Watson," remarked Tom Ruger, as he very carefully readjusted his hat. "Very sorry, Mr. Watson, and I do hope you'll pardon me when I repeat that I will defend Mr. Borlan—*with—my—life!*"

This remark surprised no one more than Jack Borlan. He had never spoken to Mr. Ruger a dozen times in his life, and he could not account for such disinterestedness. However, there was not much time for conjecture, for Mr. Watson had taken offense.

"With your death, Tom Ruger, if you interfere!" cried Watson, jumping down from his elevation.

It did look that way; but Mr. Ruger had not strolled up and down that auriferous coast without acquiring some knowledge of the usual means of defense in that sunny clime, as well as some practice. It was quite warm for a moment; then Mr. Borlan, believing it to be his duty, as client, to aid his counsel in the defense, went in gladly.

Still it was quite warm; also somewhat smoky from the powder that had been burned; likewise noisy. Not so noisy, however, that Mr. Borlan could not hear his counsel say:

"Clear yourself, Borlan! My horses are down at the ford!"

Mr. Borlan followed the advice of his counsel, and Mr. Ruger followed Mr. Borlan. The Ten Milers—some of them —followed both counsel and client.

It was neck and heels until the horses were reached. After that the pursuers were left at a great disadvantage.

"I'll have his heart!" ejaculated Watson. Which heart

he meant we have no means of knowing. "Give me a horse! quick!"

They brought a mule.

"Wait here, every man of you!" Watson shouted back over the shaved tail of his substitute for a horse. "I'll bring him back, dead or alive, or my name ain't Watson!"

And over the way the stage had stopped, and Fanny Borlan had reached Ten Mile Gulch at last.

III.

A LITTLE after sunrise, the next morning, Mr. Tom Ruger might have been seen leisurely riding along the bridle-path between the mines and the settlement of Ten Mile Gulch. He was headed toward the village, and was nine and three-quarter miles nearer to it than the mines. He had found another good cigar somewhere, and was humming the self-same tune as on the previous afternoon; but the riderless horse was not with him.

As Mr. Ruger rode into the only street in the village, his approach was heralded, and the Ten Milers, who were waiting for Watson's return, filed out of the Miners' Home, and took stations in the street.

Mr. Ruger took note of this demonstration, and, with a very business-like air, examined the contents of his holsters. He also noticed that patched noses and heads, and canes and crutches, were the predominating features in the group of Ten Milers, with an occasional closed eye and a bandaged hand to vary the monotony.

Miss Fanny Borlan, from her window at the Ten Mile House, also noticed the dilapidated looks of the frequenters of the Miners' Home, and wondered if they kept a hospital there. Then she saw Mr. Ruger, and bowed and smiled as he drew up at her window.

"So you arrived all safe, Miss Borlan? How do you like the place?"

"Better than the inhabitants," she answered, with a

glance over the way. "Than those, I mean. Is it a hospital?"

"For the present I believe it is."

"And will be for some time to come, if they all stay till they're cured. But have you seen Jack?"

"Yes—last evening. He was very sorry that he could not wait for you, but it may be as well, however. He has gone down to San Francisco, and he will wait for you there. The stage leaves here in about two hours, and I advise you to take passage in it, if you are not too much fatigued."

"I'm not tired a bit, Mr. Ruger. I will go back. Thank you for the trouble you have taken."

"No trouble, Miss Borlan. Give my respects to Jack, and tell him I will be down in a week or two. Good-morning."

While talking, Mr. Ruger had about evenly divided his glances between the very beautiful face of Fanny Borlan and the somewhat expressive countenances of the Ten Milers. Not that he found anything to admire in their damaged physiognomies, but he never wholly ignored the presence of any one.

"Good-morning, gentlemen," he said, as he rode up in front of them.

"Not to *you*, Tom Ruger," spoke a tall Ten Miler—the only one, by-the-way, who had come out of the previous day's trial unscathed. "Not to you, Tom Ruger! Where's Borlan?"

"He's gone down the coast on business," said Ruger, " and may not be back for several months."

"We'll not wait for *him*," was the miner's reply.

At the same time he drew a revolver.

"You had *better* wait," said Ruger, also producing a revolver.

The Ten Miler paused, and looked around at his companions. They did not present a formidable array of fighting stock. In fact, they were the sorest-looking men that Ten Mile Gulch ever saw ; and as the unscathed surveyed them, he seemed to think he *had* better wait.

"YOU HAD BETTER WAIT," SAID RUGER, ALSO PRODUCING A REVOLVER.

149

"You'll wait for Mr. Borlan?" queried Ruger.

"I reckon we'd better," answered the unscathed.

"And while you are waiting, you had better take a cursory glance at Mr. Watson," suggested Ruger. "At the present time he is reposing in the shade of an acacia-bush, just back of the late lamented William Foster's rural habitation. Good-morning, gentlemen; and don't get impatient."

If Mr. Ruger had any fear of treachery, he did not exhibit it, for he never turned his head as he rode off toward the valley. Nor was there any danger; for beneath his suggestions about Mr. Watson the unscathed had detected a thing or two.

"I'm glad we waited," he said. "I begin to see a thing or two. Them as is able will follow me up the Gulch."

About half a score went with him. Mr. Watson was still enjoying the shade of the acacia-bush. In fact, he couldn't get away, which Mr. Ruger well knew.

"It's all up with me, Gulchers," whispered Watson. "Ruger was too many for me, and I ought to have known it. You'll find Bill Foster's dust in a flour-sack, in my cabin. My respects to Borlan when you see him, and tell him I beg his pardon for discommoding him. Give what dust is honestly mine to him. It's all I can do now. Good-by, boys. I'm jest played out; but take my advice and never buck against Tom Ruger. He's too many for any dozen chaps on the coast. I knew 'twas all up with me the minute Tom came in, for he can look right through a feller's heart. But never mind! It's too late to help it now. I staked everything I had against Foster's pile, and I'm beat, beat, beat!"

These were the last words Mr. Bob Watson ever spoke, as many a surviving Ten Miler will tell you, and they buried him in the spot where he died, without any beautiful stone to mark the place.

IV.

Miss Fanny Borlan found Jack awaiting her at San Francisco.

" What made you run away ?"

" Why, Fanny, didn't Tom tell you about it ?" queried Jack.

"Tom ? Oh, you mean Mr. Ruger. He only sent me down here."

" Just like him, Fan ; very few words he ever wastes. Ah, sister, we don't have such men out East."

" So the stage-driver told me," said Fanny, demurely.

"There, Fan, you're poking fun now. Wait till I get through. Only for Tom, you would have found me at Ten Mile Gulch, hanging by the neck to the limb of that tree just in front of the Home."

" Hanging, Jack ?"

" Hanging, Fan—lynched for a murder I never committed. Tom came along just in the nick of time, and—— Well, Fan, perhaps you saw some of the Ten Milers before you came away ?"

" Yes, Jack ; and there was only one whole nose in the lot, and I do believe that was out of joint. But, oh, Jack ! if they had taken your life !"

" Never mind now, sis. Tom was too many for 'em ; and here I am safe. We'll wait here till Tom comes down, for I've got one of his horses, which he thinks more of than he does of himself ; then for home, sis."

Mr. Tom Ruger went down, as he said he would, and remained with them several days. On the morning that they were to sail, Fanny said to Tom :

" I wish you were going with us, Mr. Ruger. We shall miss you very much. Won't you go ?"

Mr. Ruger was talking with Jack at the time, but he heard Fanny—he always heard what *she* said.

He did not reply at once, however, but said to Jack, in a low tone :

"Jack, you know what I *have* been—can I ever become worthy of her?"

And Jack answered, promptly : ·

"God bless you, Tom, you are worthy now!"

"Thank you, Jack—if you believe!"

Then he went over to Fanny.

"I will go," was all he said.

It was a great wonder to both Jack and his sister how Tom could have got ready for the journey on so short a notice ; but one day, more than a year afterward, Tom said to Jack :

"Old friend, I'm not what I was, I hope. Ever since I first saw Fanny on the road to Ten Mile Gulch, I have tried to live differently. I hope I am better, for she said last night that she would take me for better or worse."

And Jack wondered no more.

CAPTAIN SAM'S CHANGE.

"WELL, there's nothin' to do, but to hev faith, an' keep a-tryin'."

The speaker was old Mrs. Simmons, boarding-house keeper, and resident of a certain town on the Ohio River. The prime cause of her remark was Captain Sam Toppie, of the steamboat Queen Ann.

Captain Sam had stopped with Mrs. Simmons every time the Queen Ann laid up for repairs, and he was so genial, frank and manly, that he had found a warm spot in the good old lady's heart.

But one thing marred the otherwise perfect happiness of Mrs. Simmons when in Captain Sam's society, and that was what she styled his "lost condition." For Mrs. Simmons was a consistent, conscientious Methodist, while Captain Sam was—well, he was a Western steamboat captain.

This useful class of gentlemen are in high repute among shippers and barkeepers, and receive many handsome compliments from the daily papers along the line of the Western rivers; but, somehow, the religious Press is entirely silent about them, nor have we ever seen of any special mission having been sent to them.

Captain Sam was a good specimen of the fraternity—good-looking, good-natured, quick-witted, prompt, and faithful, as well as quick-tempered, profane, and perpetually thirsty. To carry a full load, put his boat through in time, and always drink up to his peg, were his cardinal principles, and he faithfully lived up to them.

154

Of the fair sex he was a most devoted admirer, and if he had not possessed a great deal of modesty, for a steamboat captain, he could have named two or three score of young women who thought almost as much of him as the worthy boarding-house keeper did.

Good Mrs. Simmons had, to use her own language, "kerried him before the Lord, and wrastled for him ;" but it was very evident, from Sam's walk and conversation, that his case had not yet been adjudicated according to Mrs. Simmons's liking.

He still had occasional difficulties with the hat-stand and stairway after coming home late at night; his breath, though generally odorous, seemed to grieve Mrs. Simmons's olfactories, and his conversation, as heard through his open door in Summer, was thickly seasoned with expressions far more Scriptural than reverential.

One Christmas, the old lady presented to the captain a handsome Bible, with his name stamped in large gilt letters on the cover. He was so delighted and so proud of his present, that he straightway wrapped it in many folds of paper to prevent its being soiled, and then stowed it neatly away in the Queen Ann's safe, for secure keeping.

When he told Mrs. Simmons what he had done, she sighed deeply ; but fully alive to the importance of the case, promised him a common one, not too good to read daily.

"Daily! Bless you, Mrs. Simmons! Why, I hardly have time to look in the paper, and see who's gone up, and who's gone down, and who's been beat."

"But your better part, cap'en ?" pleaded the old lady.

"I—I don't know, my good woman—hard to find it, I guess—the hull lot averages purty low."

"But, cap'en," she continued, "don't you feel your need of a change ?"

"Not from the Queen Ann, ma'am—she only needs bigger engines——"

"Change of heart, I mean, cap'en," interrupted Mrs. Simmons. "Don't you feel your need of religion ?"

"Ha! ha!" roared Captain Sam; "the idea of a steamboat captain with religion! Why, bless your dear, innocent, old soul, the fust time he wanted to wood up in a hurry, his religion would git, quicker'n lightnin'. The only steamboatman I ever knowed in the meetin'-house line went up for seven year for settin' fire to his own boat to git the insurance."

Mrs. Simmons could not recall at the moment the remembrance of any pious captain, so she ceased laboring with Captain Sam. But when he went out, she placed on his table a tract, entitled "The Furnace Seven Times Heated," which tract the captain considerately handed to his engineer, supposing it to be a circular on intensified caloric.

Year after year the captain laid up for repairs, and put up with Mrs. Simmons. Year after year he was jolly, genial, chilvalrous, generous, but—not what good Mrs. Simmons earnestly wanted him to be.

He would buy tickets to all the church fairs, give free passages to all preachers recommended by Mrs. Simmons, and on Sunday morning he would respectfully escort the old lady as far as the church-door.

On one occasion, when Mrs. Simmons's church building was struck by lightning, a deacon dropped in with a subscription-paper, while the captain was in. The generous steamboatman immediately put himself down for fifty dollars; and although he improved the occasion to condemn severely the meanness of certain holy people, and though his language seemed to create an atmosphere which must certainly melt the money—for those were specie days—Mrs. Simmons declared to herself that "he couldn't be fur from the kingdom when his heart was so little set on Mammon as that."

"He's too good for Satan—the Lord *must* hev him," thought the good old lady.

Once again the Queen Ann needed repairing, and again the captain found himself at his old boarding-place.

Good Mrs. Simmons surveyed him tenderly through her

glasses, and instantly saw there had something unusual happened. Could it be—oh! if it only *could* be—that he had put off the old man, which is sin! She longed to ask him, yet, with a woman's natural delicacy, she determined to find out without direct questioning.

" Good season, cap'en ?" she inquired.

"A No. 1, ma'am—positively first-class," replied the captain.

" Hed good health—no ager?" she continued.

"Never was better, my dear woman—healthy right to the top notch," he answered.

" It must be," said good Mrs. Simmons, to herself—" it can't be nothin' else. Bless the Lord !"

This pious sentiment she followed up by a hymn, whose irregularities of time and tune were fully atoned for by the spirit with which she sung. A knock at the door interrupted her.

" Come in!" she cried.

Captain Sam entered, and laid a good-sized, flat flask on the table, saying :

" I've just been unpackin', an' I found this ; p'r'aps you ken use it fur cookin'. It's no use to me ; I've sworn off drinkin'."

And before the astonished lady could say a word, he was gone.

But the good soul could endure the suspense no longer. She hurried to the door, and cried :

" Cap'en !"

"That's me," answered Captain Sam, returning.

" Cap'en," said Mrs. Simmons, in a voice in which solemnity aad excitement struggled for the mastery, " hez the Lord sent His angel unto you ?"

" He hez," replied the captain, in a very decided tone, and abruptly turned, and hurried to his own room.

" Bless the Lord, O my soul!" almost shouted Mrs. Simmons, in her ecstacy. " We musn't worry them that's weak in the faith, but I sha'n't be satisfied till I hear him tell his experience. Oh, *what* a blessed thing to relate at prayer-meetin' to-night !"

There was, indeed, a rattling of dry bones at the prayer-meeting that night, for it was the first time in the history of the church that the conversion of a steamboat captain had been reported.

On returning home from the meeting, additional proof awaited the happy old saint. The captain was in his room —in his room at nine o'clock in the evening! She had known the captain for years, but he had never before got in so early. There could be no doubt about it, though—there he was, softly whistling.

"I'd rather hear him whistlin' Windham or Boylston," thought Mrs. Simmons; "that tune don't fit any hymn *I* know. P'r'aps, though, they sing it in some of them churches up to Cincinnaty," she charitably continued.

"Cap'en," said she, at breakfast, next morning, when the other guests had departed, "is your mind at peace ?"

"Peace ?" echoed the captain—"peaceful as the Ohio at low water."

The captain's simile was not so Scriptural as the old lady could have desired, but she remembered that he was but a young convert, and that holy conversation was a matter of gradual attainment. So, simply and piously making the best of it, she fervently exclaimed :

"That it may ever be thus is my earnest prayer, cap'en."

"Amen to that," said Captain Sam, very heartily, upsetting the chair in his haste to get out of the room.

For several days Mrs. Simmons lived in a state of bliss unknown to boarding-house keepers, whose joys come only from a sense of provisions purchased cheaply and paying boarders secured.

From the kitchen, the dining-room, or wherever she was, issued sounds of praise and devotion, intoned to some familiar church melody. Scrubbing the kitchen-floor dampened not her ardor, and even the fateful washing-day produced no visible effects on her spirits. From over the bread-pan she sent exultant strains to echo through the house, and her fists vigorously marked time in the yielding dough. From the third-story window, as she hung out the bed-linen to air, her holy notes fell on the ears of passing teamsters, and caused them to cast wondering glances upward. What was the heat of the kitchen-stove to her, now that Captain Sam was insured against flames eternal? What, now, was even money, since Captain Sam had laid up his treasures above?

And the captain's presence, which had always comforted her, was now a perpetual blessing. Always pleasant, kind, and courteous, as of old, but oh, so different!

All the coal-scuttles and water-pails in the house might occupy the stairway at night, but the captain could safely thread his way among them.

No longer did she hurry past his door, with her fingers ready, at the slightest alarm, to act as compressers to her ears; no, the captain's language, though not exactly religious, was eminently proper.

He was at home so much evenings, that his lamp consumed more oil in a week than it used to in months; but the old lady cheerfully refilled it, and complained not that the captain's goodness was costly.

The captain brought home a book or two daily, and left them in his room, seeing which, his self-denying hostess carried up the two flights of stairs her own copies of "Clarke's Commentaries," "The Saints' Rest," "Joy's Exercises," and "Morning and Night Watches," and arranged them neatly on his table.

Finally, after a few days, Captain Sam seemed to have something to say—something which his usual power of speech was scarcely equal to. Mrs. Simmons gave him every opportunity.

At last, when he ejaculated, "Mrs. Simmons," just as she was carrying her beloved glass preserve-dish to its place in the parlor-closet, she was so excited that she dropped the brittle treasure, and uttered not a moan over the fragments.

"Mrs. Simmons, I've made up my mind to lead an entirely new life," said the captain, gravely.

"It's what I've been hopin' fur years an' years, cap'en," responded the happy old lady.

"Hev you, though? God bless your motherly old soul," said the captain, warmly. "Well, I've turned over a new leaf, and it don't git turned back again."

"That's right," said Mrs. Simmons, with a happy tear under each spectacle-glass. "Fight the good fight, cap'en."

"Just my little game," continued the captain. "'Tain't ev'ry day that a man ken find an angel willin' to look out fur him, Mrs. Simmons."

"An angel! Oh, cap'en, how richly blessed you hev been!" sobbed Mrs. Simmons. "Many's the one that hez prayed all their lives long for the comin' of a good sperrit to guide 'em."

"Well, I've got one, sure pop," continued Captain Sam; "and happy ain't any kind of a name fur what I be all the time now."

"Bless you!" said the good woman, wringing the captain's hand fervidly. "But you'll hev times of trouble an' doubt, off an' on."

"Is that so?" asked the captain, thoughtfully.

"Yes," continued Mrs. Simmons; "but don't be afeard; ev'ry thing'll come right in the end. I know—I've been through it all."

"That's so," said the captain, "you hev that. Well, now, would you mind interdoosin' me to your minister?"

"Mind!" said the good old lady. "I've been a-dyin' to do it ever since you come. I've told him about it, and he's ez glad fur you ez I am."

"Oh!" said the captain, looking a little confused, "you suspected it, did you?"

"From the very minute you fust kem," replied Mrs. Simmons; "I know the signs."

"Well," said the captain, "might ez well see him fust as last then, I reckon."

"I'll get ready right away," said Mrs. Simmons. And away she hurried, leaving the captain greatly puzzled.

The old lady put on her newest bombazine dress—all this happened ten years ago, ladies—and a hat to match.

Never before had these articles of dress been seen by the irreligious light of a weekday; the day seemed fully as holy as an ordinary Sabbath.

They attracted considerable attention, in their good clothes and solemn faces, and finally, as they stood on the parson's doorstep, two of the captain's own deckhands saw him, and straightway drank themselves into a state of beastly intoxication in trying to decide what the captain could want of a preacher.

The minister entered, cordially greeted Mrs. Simmons, and expressed his pleasure at forming the captain's acquaintance.

"Parson," said the captain, in trembling accents—"don't go away, Mrs. Simmons—parson, my good friend here tells me you know all about my case ; now the question is, how soon can you do the business?"

The reverend gentleman shivered a little at hearing the word "business" applied to holy things, but replied, in excellent temper :

"The next opportunity will occur on the first Sabbath of the coming month, and I shall be truly delighted to gather into our fold one whose many worthy qualities have been made known to us by our dearly beloved sister Simmons. And let me further remind you that there is joy in heaven over one sinner that repenteth, and that therefore——"

"Just so, parson," interrupted the captain, wincing a little, and looking exceedingly puzzled—"just so ; but ain't thar no day but Sunday for a man to be married——"

"Married !" ejaculated the minister, looking inquiringly at Mrs. Simmons.

"Married !" screamed the old lady, staring wildly at the captain—"married! Oh, what shall I do? I thought you'd

11

experienced a change! And I've told everybody about it!"

The captain burst into a laugh, which made the minister's chandeliers rattle, and the holy man himself, seeing through the mistake, heartily joined the captain.

But poor Mrs. Simmons burst into an agony of tears.

"My dear, good old friend," said the captain, tenderly putting his arm about her, "I'm very sorry you have been disappointed; but one thing at a time, you know. When you see my angel, you'll think I'm in a fair way to be an angel myself some day, I guess. Annie's her name—Annie May—an' I've named the boat after her. Don't take on so, an' I'll show you the old boat, new painted, an' the name Annie May stuck on wherever there's a chance."

But the good old woman only wrung her hands, and exclaimed:

"Thar's a lovely experience completely spiled—completely spiled!"

At length she was quieted and escorted home, and a few days afterward appeared, in smiles and the new bombazine, at the captain's wedding.

The bride, a motherless girl, speedily adopted Mrs. Simmons as mother, and made many happy hours for the old lady; but that venerable and pious person is frequently heard to say to herself, in periods of thoughtfulness:

"A lovely experience completely spiled!"

THE CAPTAIN BURST INTO A LAUGH, WHICH MADE THE MINISTER'S CHANDELIERS RATTLE.

MISS FEWNE'S LAST CONQUEST.

HOW many conquests Mabel Fewne had made since she had entered society no one was able to tell. Perhaps the conqueror herself kept some record of the havoc she had worked, but if she did, no one but herself ever saw it. Even·such of her rivals as were envious admitted that Miss Fewne's victims could be counted by dozens, while the men who came under the influence of that charming young lady were wont to compute their fellow-sufferers by the hundred. It mattered not where Miss Fewne spent her time : whether she enjoyed the season in New York or Washington, Baltimore or Boston, she found that climatic surroundings did not in the least change the conduct of men toward her. In what her attractions especially consisted, her critics and admirers were not all agreed. Palette, the artist, who was among her earliest victims, said she was the embodiment of all ideal harmonies; while old Coupon, who at sixty offered her himself and his property, declared in confidence to another unfortunate that what took him was her solid sense. At least one young man, who thought himself a poet, fell in love with her for what he called the golden foam of her hair ; a theological student went into pious ecstasy (and subsequent dejection) over the spiritual light of her eyes. The habitual pose of her pretty fingers accounted for the awkward attentions of at least a score of young men, and the piquancy of her manner attracted, to their certain detriment, all the professional beaus who met her. And yet, a clear-headed literary Bostonian declared

165

that she was better read than some of his distinguished
confreres; while a member of Congress excused himself for
monopolizing her for an entire half-hour, at an evening party,
by saying that Miss Fewne talked politics so sensibly, that
for the first time in his life he had learned how much he
himself knew. As for the ladies, some said any one could
get as much admiration as Mabel Fewne if they could dress
as expensively; others said she was so skillful a flirt that
no man could see through her wily ways; two or three
inclined to the theory of personal magnetism; while a few
brave women said that Mabel was so pretty and tasteful,
and modest and sensible and sweet, that men would be
idiots if they didn't fall in love with her at sight.

But one season came in which those who envied and
feared Mabel were left in peace, for that young lady determined to spend the Winter with her sister, who was the wife
of a military officer stationed at Smithton, in the Far West.
Smithton was a small town, but a pleasant one; it had a
railroad and mines; a government land office was established there, as was the State Government also; trading
was incessant, money was plenty, so men of wit and culture
came there to pay their respects to the almighty dollar; and
as there were nearly two-score of refined ladies in the town,
society was delightful to the fullest extent of its existence.
And Mabel Fewne enjoyed it intensely; the change of air
and of scene gave stimulus to her spirits and new grace to her
form and features, so that she soon had at her feet all the
unmarried men in Smithton, while many sober Benedicts
admired as much as they could safely do without transfer-
ring their allegiance.

Smithton was not inhabited exclusively by people of
energy and culture. New settlements, like all other things
new, powerfully attract incapables, and Smithton was no
excuse to the rule. In one portion of it, yclept "the End,"
were gathered many characters more odd than interesting.
Their local habitations seemed to be the liquor-shops which
fairly filled that portion of the town. About the doors of

these shops the "Enders" were most frequently seen. If one of them chanced to stray into the business street of the town, he seemed as greatly confused and troubled as a lost boy. In his own quarter, however, and among his own kind, the Ender displayed a composure which was simply superb. No one could pass through the End by daylight without seeing many of the inhabitants thereof leaning against fences, trees, buildings, and such other objects as could sustain without assistance the weight of the human frame. From these points of support the Enders would contemplate whatever was transpiring about them, with that immobility of countenance which characterizes the finished tourist and the North American Indian. There were occasions when these self-possessed beings assumed erect positions and manifested ordinary human interest. One of these was the breaking out of a fight between either men or animals; another was the passing of a lady of either handsome face or showy dress. So it happened that, when pretty, well-dressed Mabel Fewne was enjoying a drive with one of her admirers, there was quite a stir among such Enders as chanced to see her. The venders of the beverages for which the Enders spent most of their money noticed that, upon that particular afternoon, an unusual proportion of their customers stood at the bar with no assistance from the bar itself, that some spirit was manifest in their walk and conversation, and yet they were less than usual inclined to be quarrelsome. So great was the excitement caused by Miss Fewne's appearance, that one Ender was heard to ask another who she was—an exhibition of curiosity very unusual in that part of the town. Even more: One member of that apparently hopeless gang was known to wash his face and hands, purchase a suit of cheap—but new and clean—clothing, and take an eastern-bound train, presumably to appear among respectable people he had known during some earlier period of his existence.

On the evening of the next day a delightful little party was enjoyed by the well-to-do inhabitants of Smithton.

New as was the town, the parlors of Mrs. General Wader (her husband was something for the railway company) were handsomely furnished, the ladies were elaborately dressed, the gentlemen lacked not one of the funereal garments which men elsewhere wear to evening parties, and stupid people were noticeably rarer than, in similar social gatherings, in older communities. Mabel Fewne was there, and as human nature is the same at Smithton as in the East, she was the belle of the evening. She entered the room on the arm of her brother-in-law, and that warrior's height, breadth, bronzed countenance and severe uniform, made all the more striking the figure which, clad apparently in a pale blue cloud, edged with silver and crowned with gold, floated beside him. Men crowded about her at once, and the other ladies present had almost undisturbed opportunity in which to converse with each other.

At the End there was likewise a social gathering. The place was Drake's saloon, and the guests were self-invited. Their toilets, though unusual, scarcely require description, and a list of their diversions would not interest people of taste. Refreshments were as plentiful as at Mrs. Wader's, and, after the manner of refreshments everywhere, they caused a general unbending of spirits. Not all the effects were pleasing to contemplate. One of them was a pistol-shot, which, missing the man for whom it was intended, struck a person called Baggs, and remarkable only for general worthlessness. Baggs had a physical system of the conventional type, however, and the bullet caused some disarrangement so radical in its nature, that Baggs was soon stretched upon the floor of the saloon, with a face much whiter than he usually wore. The barkeeper poured out a glass of brandy, and passed it over the bar, but the wounded man declined it; he also rejected a box of pills which was proffered. An Ender, who claimed to have been a physician, stooped over the victim, felt his pulse, and remarked:

"Baggs, you're a goner."

"I know it," said Baggs; "and I want to be prayed for."

The barkeeper looked puzzled. He was a public-spirited man, whose heart and pocket were open to people in real trouble, but for prayers he had never been asked before, and, was entirely destitute of them. He felt relieved when one of his customers—a leaden-visaged man, with bulbous nose and a bad temper—advanced toward the wounded man, raised one hand, threw his head back a trifle, and exclaimed:

"Once in grace, always in grace. I've *been* there, I know. Let us pray."

The victim waived his hand impatiently, and faintly exclaimed:

"*You* won't do; somebody that's better acquainted with God than *you* are must do it."

"But, Baggs," reasoned the barkeeper, "perhaps he's been a preacher—you'd better not throw away a chance."

"Don't care if he has," whispered Baggs; "he don't look like any of the prayin' people mother used to know."

The would-be petitioner took his rebuff considerably to heart, and began, in a low and rapid voice, an argument with himself upon the duration of the state of grace. The Enders listened but indifferently, however; the dying man was more interesting to them than living questions, for he had no capacity for annoyance. The barkeeper scratched his head and pinched his brow, but, gaining no idea thereby, he asked:

"Do *you* know the right man, Baggs?"

"Not here, I don't," gasped the sufferer; "not the right *man.*"

The emphasis on the last word was not unheeded by the bystanders; they looked at each other with as much astonishment as Enders were capable of displaying, and thrust their hands deep into the pockets of their pantaloons, in token of their inability to handle the case. Baggs spoke again.

"I wish mother was here!" he said. *She'd* know just what to say and how to say it."

"She's too far away; leastways, I suppose she is," said the barkeeper.

"I know it," whispered the wounded man; "an' yet a woman——"

Baggs looked inquiringly, appealingly about him, but seemed unable to finish his sentence. His glance finally rested upon Brownie, a man as characteristic as himself, but at times displaying rather more heart than was common among Enders. Brownie obeyed the summons, and stooped beside Baggs. The bystanders noticed that there followed some whispering, at times shame-faced, and then in the agony of earnestness on the part of Baggs, and replied to by Brownie with averted face and eyes gazing into nowhere.

Finally Brownie arose with an un-Ender-like decision, and left the saloon. No one else said much, but there seemed to circulate an impression that Baggs was consuming more time than was customary at the End.

Very different was the scene in Mrs. Wader's parlor; instead of a dying man surrounded by uncouth beings, there stood a beautiful woman, radiant with health and animation; while about her stood a throng of well-dressed gentlemen, some of them handsome, all of them smart, and each one craving a smile, a word, or a look. Suddenly the pompous voice of General Wader arose:

"Most astonishing thing I ever heard of," said he. "An Ender has the impudence to ask to see Miss Fewne!"

"An Ender?" exclaimed the lady, her pretty lips parting with surprise.

"Yes, and he declares you could not have the heart to say no; if you knew his story."

"Is it possible, Miss Fewne," asked one admirer, "that your cruelty can have driven any one to have become an Ender?"

Mabel's eyes seemed to glance inward, and she made no reply. She honestly believed she had never knowingly encouraged a man to become her victim; yet she had heard of men doing very silly things when they thought themselves disappointed in love. She cast a look of timid inquiry at her host.

"Oh, perfectly safe, if you like," said the general. "The fellow is at the door, and several of our guests are in the hall."

Miss Fewne looked serious, and hurried to the door. She saw a man in shabby clothing and with unkempt beard and hair, yet with a not unpleasing expression.

"Madame," said he, "I'm a loafer, but I've been a gentleman, and I know better than to intrude without a good cause. The cause is a dying man. He's as rough and worthless as I am, but all the roughness has gone out of him, just now, and he's thinking about his mother and a sweetheart he used to have. He wants some one to pray for him— some one as unlike himself and his associates as possible. He cried for his mother—then he whispered to me that he had seen, here in Smithton, a lady that looked like an angel —seen her driving only to-day. He meant you. He isn't pretty; but, when a *dying* man says a lady is an angel, he means what he says."

Two or three moments later Miss Fewne, with a very pale face, and with her brother-in-law as escort, was following Brownie. The door of the saloon was thrown open, and when the Enders saw who was following Brownie they cowered and fell back as if a sheriff with his *posse* had appeared. The lady looked quickly about her, until her eye rested upon the figure of the wounded man; him she approached, and as she looked down her lip began to tremble.

"I didn't mean it," whispered Baggs, self-depreciation and pain striving for the possession of his face. "If I hadn't have been a-goin', I shouldn't have thought of such a thing, but dyin' takes away one's reg'lar senses. It's not my fault, ma'am, but when I thought about what mother used to say about heaven, *you* came into my mind. I felt as if I was insultin' you just by thinkin' about you—a feller such as me to be thinking about such a lady. I tried to see

mother an' Liz, my sweetheart that was, just as I've seen
'em when my eyes was shut, but I couldn't see nothin' but
you, the way you looked goin' along that road and makin'
the End look bright. I'd shoot myself for the imperdence
of the thing if I was goin' to get well again, but I ain't.
Ther needs to be a word said for me by somebody—somebody that don't chaw, nor drink, nor swear—somebody that
'll catch God's eye if He happens to be lookin' down—and
I never saw that kind of a person in Smithton till to-day."

Mabel stood speechless, with a tear in each eye.

"Don't, if you don't think best," continued Baggs. "I'd
rather go to—to t'other place than bother a lady. Don't
speak a word, if you don't want to ; but mebbe you'll *think*
the least thing? God *can't* refuse *you*. But if you think
t'other place is best for me, all right."

The fright, the sense of strangeness, were slowly departing from Mabel, and as she recovered herself her heart
seemed to come into her face and eyes.

"Ev'rybody about here is rough, or dirty, or mean, or
rich, or proud, or somethin'," continued the dying man, in
a thin yet earnest voice. "It's all as good as I deserve ;
but my heart's ached sometimes to look at somebody that
would keep me from b'leevin' that ev'rything was black an'
awful. And I've seen her. Can I just touch my finger to
your dress ? I've heard mother read how that somebody in
the Old Country was once made all right by just touchin'
the clothes Christ had on."

In his earnestness, the wretched man had raised himself
upon one elbow, and out of his face had departed every
expression but one of pitiful pleading. Still Mabel could
not speak ; but, bending slightly forward, she extended one
of her slender, dainty hands toward the one which Baggs
had raised in his appeal.

"White—shining—good—all right," he murmured. Then
all of Baggs which fell back upon the floor was clay.

*   *   *   *   *   *   *

With the prudence of a conqueror, who knows when the

full extent of his powers has been reached, Mabel Fewne married within six months. The happy man was not a new conquest, but an old victim, who was willfully pardoned with such skill, that he never doubted that his acceptance to favor was the result of the renewal of his homage.

RAINES is my name—Joseph Raines. I am a house-builder by profession, and as I do not often see my writings in print, except as prepaid advertisements, I consider this a good opportunity to say to the public in general that I can build as good a house for a given sum of money as any other builder, and that I am a square man to deal with. I am aware of the fact that both of these assertions have been made by many other persons about themselves; but to prove their trustworthiness when uttered by me, the public needs only to give me a trial. (In justice to other builders, I must admit they can use even this last statement of mine with perfect safety for the present, and with prospective profit if they get a contract to build a house.)

I suppose it will be considered very presumptuous in me to attempt to write a story, for, while some professions seem relatives of literature, I freely admit that there is no carpenter's tool which prepares one to handle a pen. To be sure, I have read some stories which, it seemed to me, could have been improved by the judicious use of a handsaw, had that extremely radical tool been able to work æsthetically as it does practically; and while I have read certain other stories, and essays, and poems, I have been tormented by an intense desire to apply to them a smoothing-plane, a pair of compasses, or a square, or even to so far interfere with their arrangement as to cut a window-hole or two, and an occasional ventilator. Still, admitting that the carpenter should stick to his bench—or to his office or carriage, if he is a master builder, as I am—I must yet insist that there are occasions when a man is absolutely compelled to handle tools to which he is not accustomed. Doctor Buzzle, my own revered pastor, established this principle firmly in my mind one day by means of a mild rebuke, administered on the occasion of my volunteering to repair some old chairs which had come down to him through several generations. The doctor was at work upon them himself, and although he seemed to regard the very chips and sawdust—even such as found a way into his eyes—with a reverent affection, he was certainly ruining good material in a shocking manner. But when I proffered my assistance, he replied :

"Thank you, Joseph ; but—they wouldn't be the same chairs if any one else touched them."

I feel similarly about the matter of my story—perhaps you will understand why as you read it.

When I had finished my apprenticeship, people seemed to like me, and some of our principal men advised me to stay at Bartley, my native village—it was so near the city, they said, and would soon fill up with city people, who would want villas and cottages built. So I staid, and between small jobs of repairing, and contracts to build fences, stables and carriage-houses, I managed to keep myself busy, and to save a little money after I had paid my bills.

One day it was understood that a gentleman from the city had bought a villa site overlooking the town, and intended to build very soon. I immediately wrote him a note, saying I would be glad to see his plans and make an estimate ; and in the course of time the plans were sent me, and I am happy to say that I under-estimated every one, even my own old employer.

Then the gentleman—Markson his name was—drove out to see me, and he put me through a severe course of questions, until I wondered if he was not some distinguished architect. But he wasn't—he was a shipping-merchant. It's certainly astonishing how smart some of those city fellows are about everything.

The upshot was, he gave me the contract, and a very pretty one it was: ten thousand three hundred and forty dollars. To be sure, he made me alter the specifications so that the sills should be of stuff ten inches square, instead of the thin stuff we usually use for the sills of balloon-frame houses, such as his was to be; and though the alteration would add quite a few dollars to the cost of materials, I did not dare to add a cent to my estimate, for fear of losing the contract. Besides—though, of course, I did not intend to do so dishonorable a thing—I knew that I could easily make up the difference by using cheap paint instead of good English lead for priming, or in either one of a dozen other ways; builders have such tricks, just as ministers and manufacturers and railroadmen do.

I felt considerably stuck up at getting Markson's house to build, and my friends said I had a perfect right to feel so, for no house so costly had been built at Bartley for several years.

So anxious were my friends that I should make a first-class job of it, that they all dropped in to discuss the plan with me, and to give me some advice, until—thanks to their thoughtful kindness—my head would have been in a muddle had the contemplated structure been a cheap barn instead of a costly villa.

But, by a careful review of the original plan every night after my friends departed, and a thoughtful study of it each morning before going to work, I succeeded in completing it according to the ideas of the only two persons really concerned—I refer to Mr. Markson and myself.

Admitting in advance that there is in the house-building business very little that teaches a man to be a literary critic, I must nevertheless say that many poets of ancient and modern times might have found the building of a house a far more inspiring theme than some upon which they have written, and even a more respectable one than certain others which some distinguished rhymers have unfortunately selected.

I have always wondered why, after Mr. Longfellow wrote "The Building of a Ship," some one did not exercise his muse upon a house. I never attempted poetry myself, except upon my first baby, and even *those* verses I transcribed with my left hand, so they might not betray me to the editor of the Bartley *Conservator*, to whom I sent them, and by whom they were published.

I say I never attempted poetry-writing save once; but sometimes when I am working on a house, and think of all that must transpire within it—of the precious ones who will escape, no matter how strongly I build the walls; of the destroyer who will get in, in spite of the improved locks I put on all my houses; of the darkness which cannot at times be dispelled, no matter how large the windows, nor how perfect the glass may be (I am very particular about the glass I put in); of the occasional joys which seem meet for heavenly mansions not built by contract; of the unseen heroisms greater than any that men have ever cheered, and the conquests in comparison with which the achievements of mighty kings are only as splintery hemlock to Georgia pine—when I think of all this, I am so lifted above all that is prosaic and matter-of-fact, that I am likely even to forget. that I am working by contract instead of by the day.

Besides, Markson's house was my first job on a residence, and it was a large one, and I was young, and full of what I fancied were original ideas of taste and effect; and as I was unmarried, and without any special lady friend, I was completely absorbed in Markson's house.

How it would look when it was finished; what views it would command; whether its architectural style was not rather subdued, considering the picturesque old hemlocks which stood near by; what particular shade of color would be effective alike to the distant observer and to those who stood close by when the light reached it only through the green of the hemlock; just what color and blending of slate to select, so the steep-pitched roof should not impart a sombre effect to the whole house; how much money I would

12

make on it (for this is a matter of utter uncertainty until
your work is done, and you know what you've paid out and
what you get); whether Markson could influence his friends
in my favor; what sort of a family he had, and whether they
were worthy of the extra pains I was taking on their house
—these and a thousand other wonderings and reveries kept
possession of my mind; while the natural pride and hope
and confidence of a young man turned to sweet music the
sound of saw and hammer and trowel, and even translated
the rustling of pine shavings with hopeful whispers.

The foundations had been laid, and the sills placed in
position, and I was expecting to go on with the work as
soon as Markson himself had inspected the sills—this, he
said, he wished to do before anything further was done; and,
so that he might not have any fault to find with them, I had
them sawn to order, and made half an inch larger each way,
so they couldn't possibly shrink before he could measure
them.

The night before he was to come up and examine them,
I was struck at the supper-table by the idea that perhaps,
from one of the western chamber-windows, there might be
seen the river which lay, between the hills, a couple of
miles beyond. As the moon was up and full, I could
not rest until I had ascertained whether I was right
or wrong; so I put a twenty-foot tapeline in my pocket, and
hurried off to the hill where the house was to stand.

Foundation three feet, height of parlor ceilings twelve
feet, allow for floors two feet more, made the chamber-floor
seventeen feet above the level of the ground.

Climbing one of the hemlocks which I thought must be
in line with the river and the window, I dropped my line
until I had unrolled seventeen feet, and then ascended until
the end of the line just touched the ground. I found I was
right in my supposition; and in the clear, mellow light of
the moon the river, the hills and valleys, woods, fields,
orchards, houses and rocks (the latter ugly enough by daylight, and utterly useless for building purposes) made a

picture which set me thinking of a great many exquisite things entirely out of the housebuilding line.

I might have stared till the moon went down, for when I've nothing else to do I dearly enjoy dreaming with my eyes open; but I heard a rustling in the leaves a little way off, and then I heard footsteps, and then, looking downward, I saw a man come up the path, and stop under the tree in which I was.

Of course I wondered what he wanted; I should have done so, even if I had had no business there myself; but under the circumstances, I became very much excited.

Who could it be? Perhaps some rival builder, come to take revenge by setting my lumber afire! I would go down and reason with him. But, wait a moment; if he *has* come for that purpose, he may make things uncomfortable for me before I reach the ground. And if he sets the lumber afire, and it catches the tree I am in, as it will certainly do, I will be——

There is no knowing what sort of a quandary I might not have got into if the man had not stepped out into the moonlight, and up on the sills, and shown himself to be —Mr. Markson.

"Well," I thought, "you *are* the most particular man I ever knew—and the most anxious! I don't know, though—it's natural enough; if *I* can't keep away from this house, it's not strange that *he* should want to see all of it he can. It's natural enough, and it does him credit."

But Mr. Markson's next action was neither natural nor to his credit. He took off his traveling shawl, and disclosed a carpenter's brace; this and the shawl he laid on the ground, and then he examined the sills at the corners, where they were joined.

They were only half joined, as we say in the trade—that is, the ends of each piece of timber were sawn half through and the partially detached portions cut out, so that the ends lapped over each other.

Well, Mr. Markson hastily stacked up bricks and boards

to the height of the foundation, and then made a similar
stack at the other end of the foundation-wall, and then he
rolled one of the sills over on these two supports, so it was
bottom side up.   Then he fitted a bit—a good wide one, an
inch and a quarter, at least, I should say—to the brace, and
then commenced boring a hole in the sill.

I was astonished, but not too much so to be angry. That
piece of timber was mine ; Mr. Markson had not paid me a
cent yet, and was not to do so until the next morning, after
examining the foundations and sills.

I had heard of such tricks before ; my old employer had
had men secretly injure a building, so as to claim it was not
built according to contract when the money came due, but
none of them did it so early in the course of the business.

Within a few seconds my opinion of Mr. Markson's
smartness altered greatly, and so did my opinion of human
nature in general. I would have sadly, but promptly sold out
my contract with Mr. Markson for the price of a ticket for
the West, and I should have taken the first train.

As he bored that hole I could see just how all the other
builders in town would look when I had to take the law on
Markson, and how all my friends would come and tell me I
ought to have insisted on a payment in advance.

But, after several sorrowful moments had elapsed, I
commenced to think, and I soon made up my mind what I
would do. I would *not* descend from the tree while he was
there—I have too much respect for my person to put it at
the mercy of an ill-disposed individual. But as soon as he
left the place, I would hasten to the ground, follow him, and
demand an explanation. He might be armed, but I was,
too—there were hard characters at Bartley, and they knew
my pocket-book was sometimes full.

Hole after hole that man bored ; he made one join
another until he had a string of them ten inches long, or
thereabouts ; then he began another string, right beside the
first, and then another.

I saw that his bit went but six or seven inches deep, so

HE KNELT ON THE GROUND BESIDES THE SILL, AND I COULD SEE THAT HE
WAS PRAYING.

that it did not pierce the sill, and I could almost believe him in league with some rival builder to ruin my reputation by turning over, next morning, a log apparently sound, and showing it to be full of holes.

I didn't feel any better-natured, either, when I noticed that he had carefully put a newspaper under where he was boring to catch all the chips, and destroy any idea of the mischief having been done wilfully and on the spot; but I determined I would follow him, and secure that paper of chips as evidence.

Suddenly he stopped boring, and took a chisel from somewhere about his clothes, and he soon chiseled that honeycombed spot into. a single hole, about five inches by ten, and six or seven inches deep.

It slowly dawned over me that perhaps his purpose wasn't malicious, after all; and by the time I had reasoned the matter he helped me to a conclusion by taking from his pocket a little flat package, which he put into the hole.

It looked as if it might be papers, or something the size of folded papers; but it was wrapped in something yellow and shiny—oil skin, probably, to keep it from the damp. Then he drove a few little nails inside the holes to keep the package from falling out when the sill was turned over; and then he did something which I never saw mixed with carpenter-work in my life—he stooped and kissed the package as it lay in the hole, and then he knelt on the ground beside the sill, and I could see by his face upturned in the moonlight, showing his closed eyes and moving lips, that he was praying.

Up to that moment I had been curious to know what was in that package; but after what I saw then, I never thought of it without wanting to utter a small prayer myself, though I never could decide what would be the appropriate thing to say, seeing I knew none of the circumstances. I am very particular not to give recommendations except where I am very sure the person I recommend is all right.

Well, Markson disappeared a moment or two after, first

carefully replacing the sill, and carrying away the chips, and I got out of my tree, forgetting all about the view I had discovered; and the unexpected scene I had looked at ran in my mind so constantly that, during the night, I dreamed that Markson stood in the hemlock-tree, with a gigantic brace and bit, and bored holes in the hills beside the river, while I kneeled in the second story window-frame, and kissed my contract with Markson, and prayed that I might make a hundred thousand dollars out of it. It is perfectly astonishing what things a sensible man will sometimes dream.

Next morning I arrived at the building a few minutes before seven, and found Markson there before me. He expressed himself satisfied with everything, and paid me then and there a thousand dollars, which was due on acceptance of the work as far as then completed.

He hung around all day while we put up the post and studding—probably to see that the sill was not turned over and his secret disclosed; and it was with this idea that I set the studding first on his particular sill. By night we had the frame so near up, that there was no possibility of the sill being moved; and then Markson went away.

He came up often, after that, to see how his house was getting along. Each time he came he would saunter around to that particular sill, and when I noticed that he did this, I made some excuse to call the men away from that side of the house.

Sometimes he brought his family with him, and I scarcely knew whether to be glad or sorry; for, while his daughter, a handsome, strong, bright, honest, golden-haired girl of fifteen or sixteen, always affected me as if she was a streak of sunshine, and made me hope I should some day have a daughter like her, his wife always affected me unpleasantly.

I am not a good physiognomist, but I notice most people resemble animals of some sort, and when I decide on what animal it is, in any particular case, I judge the person accordingly.

Now, Mrs. Markson—who was evidently her husband's second wife, for she was too young to be Helen's mother— was rather handsome and extremely elegant, but neither manners nor dress could hide a certain tigerish expression which was always in her face. It was generally inactive, but it was never absent, and the rapidity with which it awoke once or twice when she disapproved something which was done or said, made me understand why Mr. Markson, who always seemed pleasant and genial with any one else, was quite silent and guarded when his wife was with him.

Pretty soon the people of Bartley knew all about the Marksons. How people learn all about other people is more than I can explain. *I* never have a chance to know all about my neighbors, for I am kept busy in looking to myself; but if all the energy that is devoted to other people's business in Bartley were expended on house-building, trade would soon be so dull that I should be longing for a mansion in the skies.

Everybody in Bartley knew that Helen Markson's mother, who was very beautiful and lovable, had died years before, and that her stepmother had been Mrs. Markson only two or three years ; that the second Mrs. Markson had married for money, and that her husband was afraid of her, and would run away from her if it wasn't for Helen ; that Mrs. Markson sometimes got angry, and then she raved like mad, and that it was wearing Mr. Markson's life away ; for he was a tender-hearted man, in spite of his smartness. Some even declared that Markson had willed her all his property, and insured his life heavily for her besides, and that if he died before Helen was married, Helen would be a beggar.

But none of these things had anything to do with my contract. I worked away and had good weather, so I lost no time, and at the end of five months I had finished the house, been paid for it, had paid my bills, and made a clear two thousand dollars on the job. I could have made a thousand more, without any one being the wiser for it, but I don't build houses in that way—the public will greatly oblige me by cutting this out. This money gave me a handsome business start, and having had no serious losses, nor any houses thrown back upon my hands—(for I always make it a point to do a little better than I promise, so folks can't find fault)—I am now quite well off, and building houses on my own account, to sell ; while some of my competitors, who started before I did, have been through bankruptcy, while some have been too poor to do even that.

A few years after building Markson's house, I went with a Southern friend into a black-walnut speculation. We bought land in the Southwest, cut the timber, got it to market, and made a handsome profit, I am glad to say. This business took me away from home, and kept me for months, but, as I was still without family ties, I did not suffer much during my absence. · Still the old village seemed to take on a kind of motherly air as the stage, with me in it, rattled into town, and I was just dropping into a pleasant little reverie, when a carriage, which I recognized as Markson's, dashed down the road, met us, and stopped, while the coachman shouted :

" Raines's foreman says the old man's coming home to-day."

He meant me.

" Reckon his head was purty level," replied the stage-driver, tossing his head backward toward me.

" Mr. Raines," said the coachman, recognizing me, " Mr. Markson is awful sick—like to die any minute—an' he wants to see you right away—wishes you wouldn't wait for anything."

What to make of it I didn't know, and said so, upon which the stage-driver rather pettishly suggested that 'twouldn't take long to find out if I got behind Markson's team ; and, as I agreed with him, I changed conveyances, and was soon at Markson's house.

Helen met me at the door, and led me immediately to Markson's chamber. The distance from the door of his

room to the side of his bed couldn't have been more than
twenty feet, yet, in passing over it, it seemed to me that I
imagined at least fifty reasons why the sick man had sent
for me, but not one of the fifty was either sensible or satisfactory.

I was even foolish enough to imagine Markson's conscience was troubled, and that he was going to pay me some
money which he justly owed me, whereas he had paid me
every cent, according to contract.

We reached his bedside before I had determined what it
could be. Helen took his hand, and said :

"Father, here is Mr. Raines."

Markson, who was lying motionless, with his face to the
wall, turned quickly over and grasped my hand and beckoned me closer. I put my head down, and he whispered :

"I'm glad you've come; I want to ask you a favor—a
dying man's last request. You're an honest man (N. B.—
People intending to build will please make a note of this.—
J. R.), I am sure, and I want you to help me do justice. You
have seen my wife; she can be a tiger when she wants to.
She married me for money; she thinks the will I made some
time ago, leaving everything to her, is my last. But it is
not. I've deceived her, for the sake of peace. I made one
since, leaving the bulk of my property to Helen; it came
to me through her dear mother. I know nobody to trust it
with. Mrs. Markson can wrap almost any one around her
finger when she tries, and——"

His breath began to fail, and the entrance of his wife did
not seem to strengthen him any ; but he finally regained it,
and continued :

"She will try it with *you;* but you are cool as well as
honest, I believe. I meant to tell Helen where the will was
the day after I put it there ; but she was so young—it seemed
dreadful to let her know how cowardly her father was—how
he feared her. Get it—get a good lawyer—see she has her
rights. I put it—no one could suspect where—I put it—
in—the——"

His breath failed him entirely, and he fixed his eyes on mine with an agonized expression which makes me shiver whenever I think of it. Suddenly his strange operation with that sill, of which I had not thought for a long time, came into my mind, and I whispered, quickly:

"In the sill of the house?"

His expression instantly changed to a very happy one, and yet he looked wonderstruck, which was natural enough.

"I saw you put it there," said I. "But," I continued, fearing the dying man might suspect me of spying, and so fear he had mistaken my character—"but I did not mean to—— I was on the ground when you came there that evening; and when I saw what you were doing, I could not move for fear of disturbing you. I know where to find it, and I can swear you put it there."

Markson closed his eyes, and never opened them again; and his last act, before going out of the world, was to give my hand a squeeze, which, under the circumstances, I could not help believing was an honest one.

As his hand relaxed, I felt that I had better give place to those who had a right to it, so I quietly retired. Helen fell on her knees by his bedside, but Mrs. Markson followed me out of the room.

"Mr. Raines," said she, with a very pleasant smile for a woman widowed but a moment before, "what did my dear husband want?"

Now, I am an honest man and a Church-member—and I was one then, and believed in truth and straightforwardness just as much as I do now—but, somehow, when such a person speaks to me, I feel as if I were all of a sudden a velvet-pawed cat myself. So I answered, with the straightest of faces:

"Only to see to one of the sills of the house, ma'am, and he made me solemnly swear to do it right away. He was an extraordinary man, ma'am, to think of the good of his family up to the last moment."

"Ah, yes, dear man!" said she, with a sigh which her

face plainly showed came from nowhere deeper than her lips. "I hope it won't take long, though," she continued, "for I can't endure noise in the house."

"Not more than an hour," I replied.

"Oh, I'm glad to hear it!" said she. "Perhaps, then, you might do it while we are at the funeral, day after to-morrow? We will be gone at least two hours."

"Easily, ma'am," said I, with my heart in my mouth at the idea of managing the matter so soon, and having the papers for Helen as soon as, in any sort of decency, Mrs. Markson would be likely to have the old will read.

For the rest of the day I was so absent-minded to everything except this business of Markson's that my acquaintances remarked that, considering how long I had been gone, I didn't seem very glad to see any one.

Finally I went to old Judge Bardlow, who was as true as steel, and told him the whole story, and he advised me to get the papers, and give them to him to examine. So, on the day of the funeral, I entered the house with a mallet and a mortizing chisel, and within fifteen minutes I had in my pocket the package Markson had put in the sill years before, and was hurrying to the judge's office.

He informed me that Mrs. Markson's lawyer, from the city, had called on him that very morning, and invited him to be present at the reading of the will in the afternoon, so he would be able to put things in proper shape at once.

I was more nervous all that day than I ever was in waiting to hear from an estimate. It was none of my business, to be sure ; but I longed to see Mrs. Markson punished for the mischief which I and every one else believed she had done her husband ; and I longed to see Helen, whom every one liked, triumph over her stepmother, who, still young and gay, was awfully jealous of Helen's beauty and general attractiveness.

Finally the long day wore away, and an hour or two after the carriages returned from the funeral, the city lawyer called for the judge, and, at the judge's suggestion, they both called for me.

We found Mrs. Markson and Helen, with some of Mrs.
Markson's relatives—Helen had not one in the world—in
the parlor, Mrs. Markson looking extremely pretty in her
neat-fitting suit of black, and Helen looking extremely dis-
consolate.

The judge, in a courtly, old-fashioned way, but with a
good deal of heart for all that, expressed his sympathy for
Helen, and I tried to say a kind word to her myself. To be
sure, it was all praise of her father, whom I really respected
very highly (aside from my having had my first contract
from him), but she was large-hearted enough to like it all
the better for that. I was still speaking to her when Mrs.
Markson's lawyer announced that he would read the last
will and testament of the deceased ; so, when she sat down
on a 'sofa, I took a seat beside her.

The document was very brief. He left Helen the interest of twenty thousand dollars a year, the same to cease if
she married ; all the rest of the property he left to his wife.
As the lawyer concluded, Helen's face put on an expression
of wonder and grief, succeeded by one of utter loneliness ;
while from Mrs. Markson's eyes there flashed an exultant
look that had so much of malignity in it that it made me
understand the nature of Satan a great deal more clearly
than any sermon ever made me do. Poor Helen tried to
meet it with fearlessness and dignity, but she seemed to feel
as if even her father had abandoned her, and she dropped
her head and burst into tears.

I know it wasn't the thing to do before company, but I
took her hand and called her a poor girl, and begged her to
keep a good heart, and trust that her father loved her truly,
and that her wrongs would be righted at the proper time.

Being kind to my fellow-creatures is the biggest part of
my religion, for it's the part of religion I understand best ;
but even if I had been a heathen, I couldn't have helped
wishing well to a noble, handsome woman like Helen Markson. I tried to speak in a very low tone, but Mrs. Markson
seemed to understand what I said, for she favored me with
a look more malevolent than any I had ever received *from*

my most impecunious debtor; the natural effect was to wake up all the old Adam there was in *me*, and to make me long for what was coming.

"May I ask the date of that will?" asked Judge Bardlow.

"Certainly, sir," replied Mrs. Markson's lawyer, handing the document to the judge. The judge looked at the date, handed the will back to the lawyer, and drew from his pocket an envelope.

"Here is a will made by Mr. Markson," said the judge, "and dated three months later."

Mrs. Markson started; her eyes flashed with a sort of fire which I hope I may never see again, and she caught her lower lip up between her teeth. The judge read the document as calmly as if it had been a mere supervisor's notice, whereas it was different to the first will in every respect, for it gave to Helen all of his property, of every description, on condition that she paid to Mrs. Markson yearly the interest of twenty thousand dollars until death or marriage, "this being the amount," as the will said, "that she assured me would be amply sufficient for my daughter under like circumstances."

As the judge ceased reading, and folded the document, Mrs. Markson sprang at him as if she were a wild beast.

"Give it to me!" she screamed—hissed, rather; "'tis a vile, hateful forgery!"

"Madame," said the judge, hastily putting the will in his pocket, and taking off his glasses, "that is a matter which the law wisely provides shall not be decided by interested parties. When I present it for probate——"

"I'll *break* it!" interrupted Mrs. Markson, glaring, as my family cat does when a mouse is too quick for her.

Mrs. Markson's lawyer asked permission to look at the newer will, which the judge granted. He looked carefully at the signature of Markson and the witnesses, and returned the document with a sigh.

"Don't attempt it, madame—no use," said he. "I know all the signatures; seen them a hundred times. I'm sorry, very—affects *my* pocket some, for it cuts some of my prospective fees, but—*that* will can't be broken."

Mrs. Markson turned, looked at Helen a second, and then dashed at her, as if "to scatter, tear and slay," as the old funeral hymn says. Helen stumbled and cowered a little toward me, seeing which I—how on earth I came to do it I don't know—put my arm around her, and looked indignantly at Mrs. Markson.

"You treacherous hussy!" said Mrs. Markson, stamping her foot—"you scheming little minx! I could kill you! I could tear you to pieces! I could drink your very heart's blood—I could——"

What else she could do she was prevented from telling, for she fell into a fit, and was carried out rigid and foaming at the mouth.

I am generally sorry to see even wicked people suffer, but I wasn't a bit sorry to see Mrs. Markson; for, while she was talking, poor Helen trembled so violently that it seemed to me she would be scared to death if her cruel stepmother talked much longer.

Two hours later Mrs. Markson, with all her relatives and personal effects, left the house, and six months afterward Mrs. Markson entrapped some other rich man into marrying her. She never tried to break Marston's will.

As Helen was utterly ignorant of the existence of this new will until she heard it read, the judge explained to her where it came from; and as she was naturally anxious for all the particulars of its discovery, the judge sent me to her to tell her the whole story. So I dressed myself and drove down—for, though still under thirty, I was well off, and drove my own span—and told her of my interview with her father, on his deathbed, as well as of the scene on the night he hid the will.

As I told the latter part of the story a reverent, loving, self-forgetful look came into her face, and made her seem to me like an angel. As for myself, the recalling of the incident, now that I knew its sequel, prevented my keeping my eyes dry. I felt a little ashamed of myself and hurried away, but her look while I spoke of her father, and her trembling form in my arms while Mrs. Markson raved at her, were constantly in my mind, and muddled a great many important estimates. They finally troubled me so that I drove down again and had a long and serious talk with Helen.

What we said, though perfectly proper and sensible, might not be interesting in print, so I omit it. I will say, however, that my longing—when I first saw Helen as a little girl—for a daughter just like her, has been fulfilled so exactly, that I have named her Helen Markson Raines, after her mother; and if she is not as much comfort to me as I supposed she would be, it is no fault of hers, but rather because the love of her mother makes me, twenty years after the incidents of this story occurred, so constantly happy, that I need the affection of no one else.

ON a certain day in November, 1850, there meandered into the new mining camp of Painter Bar, State of California, an individual who was instantly pronounced, all voices concurring, the ugliest man in the camp. The adjective ugly was applied to the man's physiognomy alone; but time soon gave the word, as applied to him, a far wider significance. In fact, the word was not at all equal to the requirements made of it, and this was probably what influenced the prefixing of numerous adjectives, sacred and profane, to this little word of four letters.

The individual in question stated that he came from " no whar in pu'tiklar," and the savage, furtive glance that shot from his hyena-like eyes seemed to plainly indicate why the land of his origin was so indefinitely located. A badly broken nose failed to soften the expression of his eyes, a long, prominent, dull-red scar divided one of his cheeks, his mustache was not heavy enough to hide a hideous hare-lip; while a ragged beard, and a head of stiff, bristly red hair, formed a setting which intensified rather than embellished the peculiarities we have noted.

The first settlers, who seemed quite venerable and dignified, now that the camp was nearly a fortnight old, were in the habit of extending hospitality to all newcomers until these latter could build huts for themselves; but no one hastened to invite this beauty to partake of cracker, pork and lodging-place, and he finally betook himself to the southerly side of a large rock, against which he placed a few boughs to break the wind.

The morning after his arrival, certain men missed provisions, and the ugly man was suspected; but so depressing, as one miner mildly put it, was his aspect when even looked at inquiringly, that the bravest of the boys found excuse for not asking questions of the suspected man.

"Ain't got no chum," suggested Bozen, an ex-sailor, one day, after the crowd had done considerable staring at this unpleasant object; "ain't got no chum, and's lonesome— needs cheerin' up." So Bozen philanthropically staked a new claim near the stranger, apart from the main party. The next morning found him back on his old claim, and volunteering to every one the information that "stranger's a grump—a reg'lar grump." From that time forth "Grump" was the only name by which the man was known.

Time rolled on, and in the course of a month Painter Bar was mentioned as an old camp. It had its mining rules, its saloon, blacksmith-shop, and faro-bank, like the proudest camp on the Run, and one could find there colonels, judges, doctors, and squires by the dozen, besides one deacon and a dominie or two.

Still, the old inhabitants kept an open eye for newcomers, and displayed an open-hearted friendliness from whose example certain Eastern cities might profit.

But on one particular afternoon, the estimable reception committee were put to their wit's end. They were enjoying their *otium cum dignitate* on a rude bench in front of the saloon, when some one called attention to an unfamiliar form which leaned against a stunted tree a few rods off.

It was of a short, loose-jointed young man, who seemed so thin and lean, that Black Tom ventured the opinion that "that feller had better hold tight to the groun', ter keep from fallen' upards." His eyes were colorless, his nose was enormous, his mouth hung wide open and then shut with a twitch, as if its owner were eating flies, his chin seemed to have been entirely forgotten, and his thin hair was in color somewhere between sand and mud.

As he leaned against the tree he afforded a fine opportunity for the study of acute and obtuse angles. His neck, shoulders, elbows, wrists, back, knees and feet all described angles, and even the toes of his shocking boots deflected from the horizontal in a most decided manner.

"Somebody ort to go say somethin' to him," said the colonel, who was recognized as leader by the miners.

"Fact, colonel," replied one of the men; "but what's a feller to say to sich a meanderin' bone-yard ez that? Might ask him, fur perliteness sake, to take fust pick uv lots in a new buryin' ground; but then Perkins died last week, yur know."

"Say *somethin'*, somebody," commanded the colonel, and as he spoke his eyes alighted on Slim Sam, who obediently stepped out to greet the newcomer.

"Mister," said Sam, producing a plug of tobacco, "hev a chaw?"

"I don't use tobacco," languidly replied the man, and his answer was so unexpected that Sam precipitately retired.

Then Black Tom advanced, and pleasantly asked:

"What's yer fav'rit game, stranger?"

"Blind man's buff," replied the stranger.

"What's that?" inquired Tom, blushing with shame at being compelled to display ignorance about games; "anything like going it blind at poker?"

"Poker?—I don't know what that is," replied the youth.

"He's from the country," said the colonel, compassionately, "an' hesn't hed the right schoolin'. P'r'aps," continued the colonel, "he'd enjoy the cockfight at the saloon to-night—these country boys are pretty well up on roosters. Ask him, Tom."

Tom put the question, and the party, in deep disgust, heard the man reply:

"No, thank you; I think it's cruel to make the poor birds hurt each other."

"Look here," said the good-natured Bozen, "the poor lubber's all gone in amidships—see how flat his breadbasket is. I say, messmate," continued Bozen, with a roar, and a jerk of his thumb over his shoulder, "come and splice the main-brace."

"No, thank you," answered the unreasonable stranger; "I don't drink."

The boys looked incredulously at each other, while the colonel arose and paced the front of the saloon two or three times, looking greatly puzzled. He finally stopped and said:

"The mizzable rat isn't fit to be out uv doors, an' needs takin' keer ov. Come here, feller," called the colonel; "be kinder sociable—don't stand there a gawpin' at us ez ef we wuz a menagerie."

The youth approached slowly, stared through the crowd, and finally asked:

"Is there any one here from Pawkin Centre?"

No one responded.

"Some men went out to Californy from Pawkin Centre, and I didn't know but some of 'em was here. I come from ther' myself—my name's Mix," the youth continued.

"Meanin' no disrespect to your dad," said the colonel, "Mr. Mix, Senior, ortn't to hev let you come out here—you ain't strong enough—you'll git fever 'n ager 'fore you've washed dirt half a day."

"I ain't got no dad," replied the stranger; "leastways he ran away ten years ago, an' mother had a powerful hard time since, a-bringin' up the young uns, an' we thought I might help along a big sight if I was out here."

The colonel was not what in the States would be called a prayer-meeting man, but he looked steadily at the young man, and inwardly breathed a very earnest "God have mercy on you all." Then he came back to the more immediate present, and, looking about, asked:

"Who's got sleepin'-room for this young man?"

"I hev," quickly answered Grump, who had approached, unnoticed, while the newcomer was being interviewed.

Every one started, and Grump's countenance did not

gather amiability as he sneakingly noticed the general distrust.

"Yer needn't glare like that," said he, savagely; "I sed it, an' I mean it. Come along, youngster—it's about the time I generally fry my pork."

And the two beauties walked away together, while the crowd stared in speechless astonishment.

"He won't make much out uv that boy, that's one comfort," said Black Tom, who had partially recovered from his wonder. "You ken bet yer eye-teeth that his pockets wouldn't pan out five dollars."

"Then what does he want uv him?" queried Slim Sam.

"Somethin' mean an' underhand, for certain," said the colonel, "and the boy must be purtected. And I hereby app'int this whole crowd to keep an eye on Grump, an' see he don't make a slave of the boy, an' don't rob him of dust. An' I reckon I'll take one of yer with me, an' keep watch of the old rascal to-night. I don't trust him wuth a durn."

That night the boys at the saloon wrinkled their brows like unto an impecunious Committee of Ways and Means, as they vainly endeavored to surmise why Grump could want that young man as a lodger. Men who pursued wittling as an aid to reason made pecks of chips and shavings, and were no nearer a solution than when they began.

There were a number of games played, but so great was the absentmindedness of the players, that several hardened scamps indulged in some most unscrupulous "stocking" of the cards without detection. But even one of these, after having dealt himself both bowers and the king, besides two aces, suddenly imagined he had discovered Grump's motive, and so earnest was he in exposing that nefarious wretch, that one of his opponents changed hands with him. Even the barkeeper mixed the bottles badly, and on one occasion, just as the boys were raising their glasses, he metaphorically dashed the cup from their lips by a violent, "I tell you what," and an unsatisfactory theory. Finally the colonel arose.

"Boys," said he, in the tone of a man whose mind is settled, " 'tain't 'cos the youngster looked like lively comp'ny, fur he didn't. 'Taint 'cos Grump wanted to do him a good turn, fur 'tain't his style.   Cons'kently, thar's sumthin' wrong.   Tom, I reckon I take *you* along."

And Tom and the colonel departed.

During the month which had elapsed since his advent, Grump had managed to build him a hut of the usual mining pattern, and the colonel and Tom stealthily examined its walls, front and rear, until they found crevices which would admit the muzzle of a revolver, should it be necessary. Then they applied their eyes to the same cracks, and saw the youth asleep on a pile of dead grass, with Grump's knapsack for a pillow, and one of Grump's blankets over him.   Grump himself was sitting on a fragment of stone, staring into the fire, with his face in his hands.

He sat so long that the worthy colonel began to feel indignant; to sit in a cramped position on the outside of a house, for the sake of abused human nature, was an action more praiseworthy than comfortable, and the colonel began to feel personally aggrieved at Grump's delay.   Besides, the colonel was growing thirsty.

Suddenly Grump arose, looked down at the sleeping youth, and then knelt beside him.   The colonel briskly brought his pistol to bear on him, and with great satisfaction noted that Tom's muzzle occupied a crack in the front walls, and that he himself was out of range.

A slight tremor seemed to run through the sleeper; "and no wonder," said the colonel, when he recounted the adventure to the boys; " anybody'd shiver to hev *that* catamount glarin' at him."

Grump arose, and softly went to a corner which was hidden by the chimney.

" Gone for his knife, I'll bet," whispered the colonel to himself.   "I hope Tom don't spile my mad by firin' fust."

Grump returned to view; but instead of a knife, he bore another blanket, which he gently spread over his sleeping guest, then he lay down beside Mix with a log of wood for a pillow.

The colonel withdrew his pistol, and softly muttered to himself a dozen or two enormous oaths; then he arose, straightened out his cramped legs, and started to find Tom. That worthy had started on a similar errand, and on meeting, the two stared at each other in the moonlight as blankly as a couple of well-preserved mummies.

"S'pose the boys 'll believe us?" whispered the colonel.

"We ken bring 'em down to see the show themselves, ef they don't," replied Tom.

The colonel's report was productive of the choicest assortment of ejaculations that had been heard in camp since Natchez, the leader of the Vinegar Gulch Boys, joined the Church and commenced preaching.

The good-natured Bozen was for drinking Grump's health at once, but the colonel demurred. So did Slim Sam.

"He's goin' to make him work on sheers, or some hocus-pocusin' arrangement, an' he can't afford to hev him git sick. That's what his kindness amounts to," said Sam.

"Ur go fur his gratitude—and dust, when he gets any," suggested another, and no one repelled the insinuation.

It was evident, however, that there was but little chance of either inquest or funeral from Grump's, and the crowd finally dispersed with the confirmed assurance that there would be one steady cause of excitement for some time to come.

Next morning young Mix staked a claim adjoining Grump. The colonel led him aside, bound him to secrecy, and told him that there was a far richer dirt further down the stream. The young man pointed toward the hut, and replied :

"He sed 'twas payin' dirt, an' I ort to take his advice, seein' he giv me a pick an' shovel an' pan—sed he'd hev to git new ones anyhow."

"Thunder!" ejaculated the colonel, more puzzled than

ever, knowing well how a miner will cling as long as possible to tools with which he is acquainted.

"Jest wait till that boy gets a bag of dust," said a miner, when the colonel had narrated the second wonder. "The express agent 'll be here next week to git what fellers wants to send to their folks—the boy'll want to send some to his'n —his bag 'll be missin' 'bout then—jist wait, and ef my words don't come true, call me greaser."

The colonel pondered over the prophecy, and finally determined on another vigil outside Grump's hut.

Meanwhile, Grump's Pet, as Mix had been nicknamed, afforded the camp a great deal of amusement. He was not at all reserved, and was easily drawn out on the subject of his protector, of whom he spoke in terms of unmeasured praise.

"By the piper that played before Moses," said one of the boys one day, "ef half that boy sez is true, some day Grump 'll hev wings sprout through his shirt, an' 'll be sittin' on the sharp edge uv a cloud an' playin' onto a harp, jist like the other angels."

As for Grump himself, he improved so much that suspicion was half disarmed when one looked at him; nevertheless the colonel deemed it prudent to watch the Pet's landlord on the night preceding the express day.

The colonel timed himself by counting the games of old sledge that were played. At the end of the sixth game after dark he made his way to Grump's hut and quietly located himself at the same crack as before.

The Pet and his friend were both lying down, but by the light of the fire the colonel could see the eyes of the former were closed, while those of the latter were wide open. The moments flew by, and still the two men remained in the same positions, the Pet apparently fast asleep, and Grump wide awake.

The interior of a miner's hut, though displaying great originality of design, and ingenious artistic effects, becomes after a time rather a tiresome object of contemplation. The colonel found it so, and he relieved his strained eyes by an occasional amateur astronomical observation. On turning his head, with a yawn, from one of these, he saw inside the hut a state of affairs which caused him to feel hurriedly for his pistol.

Grump had risen upon one elbow, and was stealthily feeling with his other hand under the Pet's head.

"Ha !" thought the colonel ; "right at last."

Slowly Grump's hand emerged from beneath the Pet's head, and with it came a leather bag containing gold dust.

The colonel drew a perfect bead on Grump's temple.

"I'll jest wait till you're stowin' that away, my golden-haired beauty," said the colonel, within himself, "an' then we'll see what cold lead's got to say about it."

Grump untied the bag, set it upon his own pillow, drew forth his own pouch, and untied it ; the colonel's aim remained true to its unconscious mark.

"Ef that's the game," continued the colonel, to himself, "I reckon the proper time to play my trump is just when you're a-pourin' from his bag into your'n. It 'll be ez good's a theatre, to bring the boys up to see how 'twas done. Lord ! I wish he'd hurry up !"

Grump placed a hand upon each bag, and the colonel felt for his trigger. Grump's left hand opened wide the mouth of Pet's bag, and his right hand raised his own ; in a moment he had poured out all his own gold into Pet's bag, tied it, and replaced it under Pet's head.

The colonel retired quietly for a hundred yards, or more, then he started for the saloon like a man inspired by a three-days' thirst. As he entered the saloon the crowd arose.

"Any feller ken say I lie," meekly spoke the colonel, "an' I won't shoot. *I* wouldn't believe it ef I hedn't seen it with my own eyes. Grump's poured all his gold into the Pet's pouch !"

The whole party, in chorus, condemned their optical organs to supernatural warmth ; some, more energetic than the rest, signified that the operation should extend to their lungs and lives. But the doubter of the party again spoke :

"Mind yer," said he, "to-morrow he'll be complainin' that the Pet stole it, an' then he'll claim all in the Pet's pouch."

The colonel looked doubtful ; several voices expressed dissent; Bozen, reviving his proposition to drink to Grump, found opinion about equally balanced, but conservative. It was agreed, however, that all the boys should "hang around" the express agent next day, and should, if Grump made the Pet any trouble, dispose of him promptly, and give the Pet a clear title to all of Grump's rights and properties.

The agent came, and one by one the boys deposited their dust, saw it weighed, and took their receipts. Presently there was a stir near the door, and Grump and Pet entered. Pet's gold was weighed, his mother's name given, and a receipt tendered.

"Thinks he's goin' to hev conviction in writin'," whispered the doubter to the colonel.

But the agent finished his business, took the stage, and departed. Grump started to the door to see the last of it. The doubter was there before him, and saw a big tear in the corner of each of Grump's eyes.

*   *   *   *   *   *   *

A few days after Grump went to Placerville for a new pick for the Pet—the old one was too heavy for a light man, Grump said. Pet himself felt rather lonesome working on his neighbor's claim, so he sauntered down the creek, and got a kind word from almost every man. His ridiculous anatomy had escaped the grave so long, he was so industrious and so inoffensive, that the boys began to have a sort of affection for the boy who had come so far to "help the folks."

Finally, some weak miner, unable to hold the open secret any longer, told the Pet about Grump's operation in dust. Great was the astonishment of the young man, and puzzling miners gained sympathy from the weak eyes and open mouth

of the Pet as he meandered homeward, evidently as much at
a loss as themselves.

Unlucky was the spirit which prompted Grump in the
selection of his claim! It was just beyond a small bend
which the Run made, and was, therefore, out of sight of the
claims of the other men belonging to the camp. And it came
to pass that while Pet was standing on his own claim, leaning on his spade, and puzzling his feeble brain, there came
down the Run the great Broady, chief of the Jolly Grasshoppers, who were working several miles above.

Mr. Broady had found a nugget a few days before, and,
in his exultation, had ceased work and become a regular
member of the bar. A week's industrious drinking developed in him that peculiar amiability and humanity which
is characteristic of cheap whisky, and as Pet was small, ugly,
and alone, Broady commenced working off on him his own
superfluous energy.

Poor Pet's resistance only increased the fury of Broady,
and the family at Pawkin Centre seemed in imminent danger
of being supported by the town, when suddenly a pair of
enormous stubby hands seized Broady by the throat, and
a harsh voice, which Pet joyfully recognized as Grump's, exclaimed :

"Let him go, or I'll tear yer into mince-meat, curse
yer !"

The chief of the Jolly Grasshoppers was not in the habit
of obeying orders, but Grump's hands imparted to his command considerable moral force.

No sooner, however, had Broady extricated himself from
Grump's grasp than he drew his revolver and fired. Grump
fell, and the chief of the Jolly Grasshoppers, his injured
dignity made whole, walked peacefully away.

The sound of the shot brought up all the boys from
below.

"They've fit !" gasped the doubter, catching his breath
as he ran, " an' the boy—boy's hed to—lay him out.

It seemed as if the doubter might be right, for the boys

found Grump lying on the ground bleeding badly, and the Pet on his hands and knees.

"How did it come 'bout?" asked the colonel of Pet.

"Broady done it," replied Grump, in a hoarse whisper; "he pounded the boy, and I tackled him—then he fired."

The doubter went around and raised the dying man's head. Pet seemed collecting all his energies for some great effort; finally he asked :

"What made you pour your dust into my pouch?"

"'Cause," whispered the dying man, putting one arm about Pet's neck, and drawing him closer, "'cause I'm yer dad; give this to yer mar," and on Pet's homely face the ugliest man at Painter Bar put the first token of human affection ever displayed in that neighborhood.

The arm relaxed its grasp and fell loosely, and the red eyes closed. The experienced colonel gazed into the up-turned face, and gently said :

"Pet, yer an orphan."

Reverently the boys carried the dead man into his own hut. Several men dug a grave beside that of Perkins, while the colonel and doubter acted as undertakers, the latter donating his only white shirt for a shroud.

This duty done, they went to the saloon, and the doubter called up the crowd. The glasses filled, the doubter raised his own, and exclaimed :

"Boys, here's corpse—corpse is the best-looking man in camp."

And so he was. For the first time in his wretched life his soul had reached his face, and the Judge mercifully took him while he was yet in His own image.

The body was placed in a rude coffin, and borne to the grave on a litter of spades, followed by every man in camp, the colonel supporting the only family mourner. Each man threw a shovelful of dirt upon the coffin before the filling began. As the last of the surface of the coffin disappeared from view, Pet raised a loud cry and wept bitterly, at which operation he was joined by the whole party.

WARDELOW'S BOY.

NEW Boston has once been the most promising of the growing cities of the West, according to some New York gentleman who constituted a land improvement company, distributed handsome maps gratis, and courted susceptible Eastern editors. Its water-power was unrivaled; ground for all desirable public buildings, and for a handsome park with ready-grown trees and a natural lake, had been securely provided for by the terms of the company's charter; building material abounded; the water was good; the soil of unequaled fertility; while the company, with admirable forethought, had a well-stocked store on the ground, and had made arrangements to send to the town a skillful physician and a popular preacher.

A reasonable number of colonists found their way to the ground in the pleasant Spring time, and, in spite of sundry local peculiarities not mentioned in the company's circular, they might have remained, had not a mighty freshet, in June, driven them away, and even saved some of them the trouble of moving their houses.

When, however, most of the residences floated down the river, some of them bearing their owners on their roofs, such of the inhabitants as had money left the promised land for ever; while the others made themselves such homes as they could in the nearest settlements which were above water, and fraternized with the natives through the medium of that common bond of sympathy in the Western lowlands, the ague.

Only a single one of the original inhabitants remained, and he, although he might have chosen the best of the abandoned houses for his residence, or even the elegant but deserted "company's store," continued to inhabit the cabin he had built upon his arrival. The solid business men of the neighboring town of Mount Pisgah, situated upon a bluff, voted him a fool whenever his name was mentioned; but the wives of these same men, when they chanced to see old Wardelow passing by, with the wistful face he always wore, looked after him tenderly, and never lost an opportunity to speak to him kindly. When they met at tea-parties, or quilting-bees, or sewing-societies, or in other gatherings exclusively feminine, there were not a few of them who had the courage to say that the world would be better if more men were like old Wardelow.

For love seemed the sole motive of old Wardelow's life. The cemetery which the thoughtful projectors of New Boston had presented to the inhabitants had for its only occupant the wife of old Wardelow; and she had been conveyed thereto by a husband who was both young and handsome. The freshet which had, soon afterward, swept the town, had carried with it Wardelow's only child, a boy of seven years, who had been playing in a boat which he, in some way, unloosed.

From that day the father had found no trace of his child, yet he never ceased hoping for his return. Every steamboat captain on the river knew the old man, and the roughest of them had cheerfuly replied in the affirmative when asked if they wouldn't bring up a small boy who might some day come on board, report himself as Stevie Wardelow, and ask to be taken to New Boston.

Almost every steamboat man, from captain and pilot down to fireman and roustabout, carried and posted Wardelow's circulars wherever they went—up Red River, the Yazoo, the White, the Arkansas, the Missouri, and all the smaller tributaries of the Mississippi.

New Boston had long been dropped from the list of post-towns, but every cross-road for miles around had a fingerboard showing the direction and telling the distance to New Boston. Upon a tall cottonwood-tree on the river-bank, and nearly in front of Wardelow's residence, was an immense signboard bearing the name of "New Boston Landing," and on the other side of the river, at a ferry-staging belonging to a crossing whose other terminus was a mile further down the river, was a sign which informed travelers that persons wishing to go to New Boston would find a skiff marked "Wardelow" tied near the staging.

The old man never went to Mount Pisgah for stores, or up the river to fish, or even into his own cornfield and garden, without affixing to his door a placard telling where he had gone and when he would return.

When he went to the cemetery, which he frequently did, a statement to that effect, and a plan showing the route to and through the cemetery, was always appended to his door, and, as he could never clearly imagine his boy as having passed the childhood in which he had last seen him, all the signboards, placards, and circulars were in large capital letters.

Even when the river overflowed its banks, which it did nearly every Spring, the old man did not leave his house. He would not have another story built upon it, as he was advised to do, lest Stevie might fail to recognize it on his return; but, after careful study, he had the house raised until the foundation was above high-water mark, and then had the ground made higher, but sloped so gradually that the boy could not notice the change.

When one after another of the city's "plots," upon which deserted houses stood, were sold for default in payment of taxes, old Wardelow bought them himself—they always went for a song, and the old man preferred to own them, lest some one else might destroy the ruins, and thus make the place unfamiliar to the returning wanderer.

Of friends he had almost none. Although he was intelligent, industrious, ingenious, and owned a library which passed for quite a large one in those days and in the new West, he cared to talk on only one subject, and as that was

THE OLD MAN NEVER LEFT HIS HOUSE WITHOUT AFFIXING TO HIS DOOR A PLACARD
TELLING WHERE HE HAD GONE AND WHEN HE WOULD RETURN.

of no particular interest to other people, and became, in the course of time, extremely stale to those who did not like it, the people of Mount Pisgah and the adjoining country did not spend more time upon old Wardelow than was required by the necessities of business.

There were a few exceptions to this rule. Old Mrs. Perry, who passed for a saint, and whose life did not belie her reputation, used to drive her old pony up to New Boston about once a month, carrying some home-made delicacy with her, and chatting sympathetically for an hour or two.

Among the Mount Pisgah merchants there was one—who had never had a child of his own—who always pressed the old man's hand warmly, and admitted the possibility of whatever new hope Wardelow might express.

The pastors of the several churches at Mount Pisgah, however much they disagreed on doctrinal points, were in perfect accord as to the beauty of a character which was so completely under the control of a noble principle that had no promise of money in it ; most of them, therefore, paid the old man professional visits, from which they generally returned with more benefit than they had conferred.

Time had rolled on as usual, in spite of Wardelow's great sorrow. The Mexican war was just breaking out when New Boston was settled, and Wardelow's hair was black, and Mount Pisgah was a little cluster of log huts ; but when Lincoln was elected, Wardelow had been gray and called old for nearly ten years, and Mount Pisgah had quite a number of two-story residences and brick stores, and was a county town, with court-house and jail all complete.

None of the railway lines projected toward and through Mount Pisgah had been completed, however, nor had the town telegraphic communication with anywhere; so, compared with localities enjoying the higher benefits of civilization, Mount Pisgah and its surroundings constituted quite a paradise for horse-thieves.

There were still sparsely settled places, too, which needed the ministrations of the Methodist circuit-rider.

The young man who had been sent by the Southern Illinois Conference to preach the Word on the Mount Pisgah circuit was great-hearted and impetuous, and tremendously in earnest in all that he did or said; but, like all such men, he paid the penalty of being in advance of his day and generation by suffering some terrible fits of depression over the small results of his labor.

And so, following the example of most of his predecessors on the Mount Pisgah circuit, he paid many a visit to old Wardelow, to learn strength from this perfect example of patient faith.

As the circuit-rider left the old man one evening, and sought his faithful horse in the deserted barn in which he had tied him, he was somewhat astonished to find the horse unloosed, and another man quietly leading him away.

Courage and decision being among the qualities which are natural to the successful circuit-rider, he sprang at the thief and knocked him down. The operator in horse-flesh speedily regained his feet, however, and as he closed with the preacher the latter saw, under the starlight, the gleam of a knife.

Commending himself to the Lord, he made such vigorous efforts for the safety of his body that, within two or three moments, he had the thief face downward on the ground, his own knee on the thief's back, one hand upon the thief's neck, and in his other hand the thief's knife. Then the circuit-rider delivered a short address.

"My sinful friend," said he, "when two men get into such a scrape as this, and one of them is in your line of business, one or the other will have to die, and I don't propose to be the one. I haven't finished the work which the Master has given me to do. If you've any dying messages to send to anybody, I give you my word as a preacher that they shall be delivered, but you must speak quick. What's your name?"

"I'll give you five hundred dollars to let me off—you may holler for help and tie my hand, and——"

"No use—speak quick," hissed the preacher—"what's your name?"

"Stephen Wardelow," gasped the thief.

"What!" roared the preacher, loosening his grasp, but instantly tightening it again.

"Stephen Wardelow," replied the thief. "But I haven't got any messages to send to anybody. I haven't a relative in the world, and nobody would care if I was dead. I might as well go now as any time. Hit square when yo *do* let me have it—that's all!"

"Where's your parents?" asked the preacher.

"Dead, I reckon," the thief answered. "Leastways, I know mother is, and dad lived in a fever an' aguerish place, an' I s'pose he's gone, too, before this."

"Where did he live?"

"I don't know—some new settlement somewheres in Illinois. I got lost in the river when I was a little boy, an' was picked up by a tradin'-boat an' sold for a nearly-white nigger—I s'pose I *was* pretty dark."

There was a silence; the captive lay perfectly quiet, as if expecting the fatal blow. Suddenly a voice was heard:

"Not wishin' to interfere in a fair fight—it's me, parson, Sheriff Peters—not wishin' to interfere in a fair fight, I've been a-lookin' on here, where I'd tracked the thief myself, and would have grabbed him if you hadn't been about half a minute ahead of me. And if you want to know my honest opinion—my professional opinion—it's just this : There was stuff for a splendid sheriff spiled when you went a-preachin'. How you'd get along when it come to collectin' taxes, I don't know, never havin' been at any meetin' where you took up a collection; but when it come to an arrest, you'd be just chain-lightning ground down to a pint. The pris'ner's yours, and so's all the rewards that's offered for him, though they're not offered for a man of the name *he* gives. But honest, now, don't you think there's a chance of mitigatin' circumstances in his case? Let's talk it over—I'll help you tie him so he can't slip you."

The sheriff lighted a pocket-lantern and placed it in a window-frame behind him, then he tied the prisoner's feet and legs in several places, tied his hands behind his back, sat him upon the ground with his face toward the door, cocked a pistol, and then beckoned the preacher toward a corner. The sheriff opened his pocketbook and took out a paper, whispering as he did so:

"I've carried this as a sort of a curiosity, but it may come in handy now. Let's see—confound it!—the poor old fellow is describing the child just as it was fifteen years ago. Oh, here's a point or two!—'brown eyes, black hair'—oh, bully! here's the best thing yet!—'first joint of the left fore-finger gone.'"

The sheriff snatched the light, and both men hastened to examine the prisoner's hand. After a single glance their eyes met and each set of optics inquired of the other.

At length the sheriff remarked:

"He's *your* pris'ner."

The circuit-rider flushed and then turned pale. He took the lantern from the sheriff, turned the light full on the prisoner's face, and said:

"Prisoner, suppose you were to find that your father was alive?"

The horse-thief replied with a piercing glance, which was full of wonder, but said not a word. A moment or two passed, and the preacher said:

"Suppose you were to find that your father was alive, and had searched everywhere for *you*, and that he thought of nothing but you, and was all the time hoping for your return—that he had grown old before his time, all because of his longing and sorrow for you?" The thief dropped his eyes, then his face twitched; at last he burst out crying. "Your father *is* alive; he isn't far from this cabin; he's very sick; I've just left him. Nothing but the sight of you will do him any good; but I think so much of him that I'd rather kill you this instant than let him know what business you've been in."

"Them's my sentiments, too," remarked the sheriff.

"Let me see him!" exclaimed the prisoner, clasping and raising his manacled hands, while his face filled with an earnestness which was literally terrible—"let me see him, if it's only for a few minutes! You needn't be afraid that *I'll* tell him what I am, and *you* won't be mean enough to do it, if I don't try to run away. Have mercy on me! You don't know what it is to never have had anybody to love you, and then suddenly to find that there *is* some one that wants you!"

The preacher turned to the officer and said:

"I'm a law-abiding citizen, sheriff."

And the sheriff replied:

"He's *your* pris'ner."

"Then suppose I let him go, on his promise to stick to his father for the rest of his life!"

"He s your pris'ner," repeated the sheriff.

"Suppose, then, I were to insist upon your taking him into custody."

"Why, then," said the sheriff, speaking like a man in the depths of meditation, "I would let him go myself, and—and I'd have to shoot *you* to save my reputation as a faithful officer."

The preacher made a peculiar face. The prisoner exclaimed:

"Hurry, you brutes!"

The preacher said, at last:

'Let him loose."

The sheriff removed the handcuffs, dived into his own pocket, brought out a pocket-comb and glass, and handed them to the thief; then he placed the lantern in front of him, and said:

"Fix yourself up a little. Your hat's a miz'able one—I'll swap with you. You've got to make up some cock-and-bull story now, for the old man'll want to know everything. You might say you'd been a sheriff down South somewhere since you got away from the feller that owned you."

The preacher paused over a knot in one of the cords on the prisoner's legs, and said:

"Say you were a circuit-rider—that's more near the literal truth."

The sheriff seemed to demur somewhat, and he said, at length:

"Without meanin' any disrespect, parson, don't you think 'twould tickle the old man and the citizens more to think he'd been a sheriff? They wouldn't dare to ask him so many questions then, either. And it might be onhandy for him if he was asked to preach, while a smart horse-thief has naturally got some of the p'ints of a real sheriff about him."

"You insist upon it that he's my prisoner," said the preacher, tugging away at his knot, "and I insist upon the circuit-rider story. And," continued the young man, with one mighty pull at the knot, "he's *got* to be a circuit-rider, and I'm going to make one of him. Do you hear that, young man? I'm the man that's setting you free and giving you to your father!"

"You can make anything you please out of me," said the prisoner. "Only hurry!"

"As you say, parson," remarked the sheriff, with admirable meekness; "he's *your* prisoner, but I *could* make a splendid deputy out of him if you'd let him take my advice. And I'd agree to work for his nomination for my place when my term runs out. Think of what he might get to be!—there *has* sheriffs gone to the Legislature, and I've heard of one that went to Congress."

"Circuit-riders get higher than that, sometimes," said the preacher, leading his prisoner toward old Wardelow's cabin; "they get as high as heaven!"

"Oh!" remarked the sheriff, and gave up the contest.

Both men accompanied the prisoner toward his father's house. The preacher began to deliver some cautionary remarks, but the young man burst from him, threw open the door, and shouted:

"Father!"

The old man started from his bed, shaded his eyes, and exclaimed:

"Stevie!"

The father and son embraced, seeing which the sheriff proved that even sheriffs are human by snatching the circuit-rider in his arms and giving him a mighty hug.

* * * * * * *

The father recovered and lived happily. The son and the preacher fulfilled their respective promises, and the sheriff, always, on meeting either of them, so abounded in genial winks and effusive handshakings, that he nearly lost his next election by being suspected of having become religious himself.

"LUCK? Why, I never seed anything like it! Yer might give him the sweepin's of a saloon to wash, an' he'd pan out a nugget ev'ry time—do it ez shure as shootin'!"

This rather emphatic speech proceeded one day from the lips of Cairo Jake, an industrious washer of the golden sands of California; but it was evident to all intelligent observers that even language so strong as to seem almost figurative did not fully express Cairo Jake's conviction, for he shook his head so positively that his hat fell off into the stream, which found a level only an inch or two below Jacob's boot-tops, and he stamped his right foot so vigorously as to endanger his equilibrium.

"Well," sighed a discontented miner from New Jersey, "Providence knows His own bizness best, I s'pose; but I could have found him a feller that could have made a darn sight better use of his good luck—ef he'd had any—than Tom Chafflin. *He* don't know nothin' 'bout the worth of money—never seed him drunk in my life, an' he don't seem to get no fun out of keerds."

"Providence 'll hev a season's job a-satisfyin' *you*, old Redbank," replied Cairo Jake; "but it's all-fired queer, for all that. Ef a feller could only learn how he done it, 'twouldn't seem so funny; but he don't seem to have no way in p'tickler about him that a feller ken find out."

"Fact," said Redbank, with a solemn groan. "I've studied his face—why, ef I'd studied half ez hard at school

I'd be a president, or missionary, or somethin' now—but I
don't make it out. Once I 'llowed 'twas cos he didn't keer,
an' was kind o' reckless—sort o' went it blind. So *I* tried it
on a-playin' monte."

"Well, how did it work?" asked the gentleman from Cairo.

"Work?" echoed the Jerseyman, with the air of an unsuccessful candidate musing over the "saddest words of
thought or pen;" "I started with thirteen ounces, an' in
twenty minutes I was borryin' the price of a drink from the
dealer. *That's* how it worked."

Certain other miners looked sorrowful; it was evident
that they, too, had been reckless, and had trusted to luck,
and that in a place where gold-digging and gambling were
the only two means of proving the correctness of their theory,
it was not difficult to imagine by which one they were disappointed.

"Long an' short of it's jest this," resumed Cairo Jake,
straightening himself for a moment, and picking some coarse
gravel from his pan, "Tom Chafflin's always in luck. His
claim pays better'n anybody else's; he always gets the lucky
number at a raffle, his shovel don't never break, an' his
chimbly ain't always catchin' a-fire. He's gone down to
'Frisco now, an' I'll bet a dozen ounces that jest cos he's
aboard, the' old boat 'll go down an' back without runnin'
aground a solitary durned time."

No one took up Cairo Jake's bet, so that it was evident
he uttered the general sentiment of the mining camp of
Quicksilver Bar.

Every man, in the temporary silence which followed
Jake's summary, again bent industriously over his pan, until
the scene suggested an amateur water-cure establishment returning thanks for basins of gruel, when suddenly the whole
line was startled into suspension of labor by the appearance
of London George, who was waving his hat with one hand and
a red silk handkerchief with the other, while with his left foot
he was performing certain *pas* not necessary to successful
pedestrianism.

"Quicksilver Bar hain't up to snuff—oh, no! Ain't a catchin' up with 'Frisco—not at all! Little Chestnut don't know how to run a saloon, an' make other shops weep—not in the least—not at all—oh, no!"

"Eh?" inquired half a dozen.

"Don't b'leeve me if you don't want to, but just bet against it 'fore you go to see—that's all!" continued London George, fanning himself with his hat.

"George," said Judge Baggs, with considerable asperity, "ef you *are* an Englishman, try to speak your native tongue, an' explain what you mean by actin' ez ef you'd jes' broke out of a lunatic 'sylum. Speak quick, or I'll fine you drinks for the crowd."

"Just as lieve you would," said the unabashed Briton, "seein'—seein' Chestnut's got a female—a woman—a lady cashier—there! Guess them San Francisco saloons ain't the only ones that knows what's what—not any!"

"I don't b'leeve a word of it," said the judge, washing his hands rather hastily; "but I'll jest see for myself."

Cairo Jake looked thoughtfully on the retreating form of the judge, and remarked:

"He'll feel ashamed of hisself when he gits thar an' finds he'll hev to drink alone. Reckon I'll go up, jest to keep him from feelin' bad."

Several others seemed impressed by the same idea, and moved quite briskly in the direction of Chestnut's saloon.

The judge, protected by his age and a pair of green spectacles, boldly entered, while his followers dispersed themselves sheepishly just outside the open door, past which they marched and re-marched as industriously as a lot of special sentries.

There was no doubt about it. Chestnut had installed a lady at the end of the bar, and as, between breakfast and dinner, there was but little business done at the saloon, the lady was amusing herself by weighing corks and pebbles in the tiny scales which were to weigh the metallic equivalent for refreshments.

The judge contemplated the arrangements with considerable satisfaction, and immediately called up all thirsty souls present.

Those outside the door entered with the caution of veterans in an enemy's country, and with a bashfulness that was painful to contemplate. They stood before the bar, they glanced cautiously to the right, and gently inclined their heads backward, until only a line of eyes and noses were visible from the cashier's desk.

Then the judge raised his green glasses a moment, and smiled benignantly on the new cashier as he raised his liquor aloft; then he turned to his party, and they drank the toast as solemnly as if they were the soldiers of Miles Standish fortifying the inner man against fear of the Pequods. Then they separated into small groups, and conversed gravely on subjects in which they had not the slightest interest, while each one pretended not to look toward the cashier, and each one saw what the others were earnestly striving to do.

But when the judge settled the score, and chatted for several minutes with the receiver of treasure, and the lady—young, and rather pretty, and quite pleasant and modest and business-like—laughed merrily at something the judge said, an idea gradually dawned upon the bystanders, and within a few moments the boys feverishly awaited their chances to treat the crowd, for the sole purpose of having an excuse to speak to the new cashier, and to stand within three feet of her for about the space of a minute.

Great was the excitement on the Creek when the party returned, and testified to the entire accuracy of London George's report.

Every one went to the saloon that night—there _had_ been some games arranged to take place at certain huts, but they were postponed by mutual consent.

Even the Dominie—an ex-preacher, who had never yet set foot upon the profane floor of the saloon—appeared there that evening in search of some one so exceeding hard to find that the Dominie was compelled to make several tours of all the tables and benches in the room.

Chestnut himself, when questioned, said she had come by the way of the Isthmus with her father and mother, who had both died of the Chagres fever before reaching San Francisco—that some friends of her family and his had been trying to get her something to do in 'Frisco, and that he had engaged her at an ounce a day ; and, furthermore, that he would be greatly obliged if the boys at Quicksilver wouldn't marry her before she had worked out her passage-money from 'Frisco, which he had advanced. But the boys at Quicksilver were not so thoughtful of Chestnut's interests as they might have been. They began to buy blacking and neckties and white shirts, and to patronize the barber.

No one had any opportunity for love-making, for the lady's working hours were all spent in public, and in a business which caused frequent interruptions of even the most agreeable conversation.

It soon became understood that certain men had proposed and been declined, and betting on who would finally capture the lady was the most popular excitement in camp.

Cool-headed betting men watched closely the countenance of Sunrise (as some effusive miner had named the new cashier) as each man approached to pay in his coin or dust, and though they were intensely disgusted by its revelations, they unhesitatingly offered two to one that Dominie would be the fortunate man.

To be sure, she saw less of the Dominie than of any one else, for, though he did not drink, or pay for the liquor consumed by any one else, he occasionally came in to get a large coin changed, and then it was noticed that Sunrise regarded him with a sort of earnestness which she never exhibited toward any one else.

"Too bad !" sighed Cairo Jake. "Somebody ort to tell her that he's only a preacher, an' she'll only throw herself away ef she takes him. Ef any stranger wuz to insult her, Dominie wouldn't be man 'nuff to draw on him."

"Beats thunder, though!" sighed Redbank, "how them preachers kin take folks in. Thar's Chestnut himself, *he's* took with Dominie—'stead of orderin' him out, he talks with him an' her just ez ef he'd as lieve get rid of her as not."

"Boat's a-comin'!" shouted Cairo Jake, looking toward

TOM WALKED RAPIDLY TO THE CASHIER'S DESK, AND GAVE SUNRISE SEVERAL HEARTY KISSES.

the place, half a mile below, where the creek emptied into the river. "See her smoke? Like 'nuff Tom Chafflin's on board. He wuz a-goin' to try to come back by the first boat, an' of course he's done it—jest his luck. Ef he'd only come

sooner, somebody besides the preacher would hev got her—
you kin just bet your bottom ounce on it. Let's go down an'
see ef he's got any news."

Several miners dropped tools and pans, and followed Jake
to the landing, and gave a hearty welcome to Tom Chafflin.

He certainly looked like anything but a lucky man; he
was good-looking, and seemed smart, but his face wore a
dismal expression, which seemed decidedly out of place on
the countenance of a habitually lucky man.

"Things hain't gone right, Tom?" asked Cairo Jake.

"Never went worse," declared Tom, gloomily. "Guess
I'll sell out, an' try my luck somewheres else."

"*Ef* you'd only come a little sooner!" sighed Jake, "you'd
hev hed a chance that would hev made ev'rything seem to go
right till Judgment Day. I'll show yer."

Jake opened the saloon-door, and there sat Sunrise, as
bright, modest, and pleasant-looking as ever.

With the air of a man who has conferred a great benefit,
and is calmly awaiting his rightful reward, Jake turned to
Tom; but his expression speedily changed to one of hopeless wonder, and then to one of delight, as Tom Chafflin
walked rapidly up to the cashier's desk, pushed the Dominie
one side and the little scales the other, and gave Sunrise several very hearty kisses, to which the lady didn't make the
slightest objection—in fact, she blushed deeply, and seemed
very happy.

"That's what I went to 'Frisco to look for," explained
Tom, to the staring bystander, "but I couldn't find out a
word about her."

"Don't wonder yer looked glum, then," said Cairo Jake;
"but—but it's jest your luck!"

"Dominie here was going down to hurry you back,"
said Sunrise; "but——"

"But we'll give him a different job now, my dear," said
Tom, completing the sentence.

And they did.

OLD TWITCHETT'S TREASURE.

OLD TWITCHETT was in a very bad way. He must have been in a bad way, for Crockey, the extremely mean storekeeper at Bender, had given up his own bed to Twitchett, and when Crockey was moved with sympathy for any one, it was a sure sign that the object of his commiseration was going to soon stake a perpetual claim in a distant land, whose very streets, we are told, are of precious metal, and whose walls and gates are of rare and beautiful stones.

It was Twitchett's own fault, the boys said, with much sorrowful profanity. When they abandoned Black Peter Gulch to the Chinese, and located at Bender, Twitchett should have come along with the crowd, instead of staying there by himself, in such an unsociable way. Perhaps he preferred the society of rattlesnakes and horned toads to that of high-toned, civilized beings—there was no accounting for tastes—but then he should have remembered that all the rattlesnakes in the valley couldn't have raised a single dose of quinine between them, and that the most sociable horned toad in the world, and the most obliging one, couldn't fry a sick man's pork, or make his coffee.

But, then, Twitchett was queer, they agreed—he always was queer. He kept himself so much apart from the crowd, that until to-night, when the boys were excited about him, few had ever noticed that he was a white-haired, delicate

225

young man, instead of a decrepit old one, and that the
twitching of his lips was rather touching than comical.

At any rate it was good for Twitchett that two old residents of Black Peter Gulch had, ignorant of the abandon-
ment of the camp, revisited it, and accidentally found him
insensible, yet alive, on the floor of his hut. They had
taken turns in carrying him—for he was wasted and light—
until they reached Crockey's store, and when they laid him
down, while they should drink, the proprietor of the establishment (so said a pessimist in the camp), seeing that his
presence, while he lived, and until he was buried, would attract trade and increase the demand for drinks, insisted on
putting Twitchett between the proprietary blankets.

Twitchett had rallied a little, thanks to some of Crockey's
best brandy, but it was evident to those who saw him that
when he left Crockey's he would be entirely unconscious of
the fact. Suddenly Twitchett seemed to realize as much himself, and to imagine that his exit might be made very soon,
for he asked for the men who brought him in, and motioned
to them to kneel beside him.

"I'm very grateful, boys, for your kindness—I wish I
could reward you; but haven't got anything—I've got
nothing at all. The only treasure I had I buried—buried it
in the hut, when I thought I was going to die alone—I
didn't want those heathens to touch it. I put it in a can—I
wish you'd git it, and—it's a dying man's last request—take
it—and——"

If Twitchett finished his remark, it was heard only by
auditors in some locality yet unvisited by Sam Baker and
Boylston Smith, who still knelt beside the dead man's face,
and with averted eyes listened for the remainder of Twitchett's last sentence.

Slowly they comprehended that Twitchett was in a condition which, according to a faithful proverb, effectually
precluded the telling of tales; then they gazed solemnly
into each other's faces, and each man placed his dexter fore-
finger upon his lips. Then Boylston Smith whispered:

" Virtue is its own reward—hey, Sam ?"

" You bet," whispered Mr. Baker, in reply. " It's on the square now, between us ?"

" Square as a die," whispered Boylston.

" When'll we go for it ?" asked Sam Baker.

" Can't go till after the fun'ril," virtuously whispered Boylston. " 'Twould be mighty ungrateful to go back on the corpse that's made our fortunes."

" Fact," remarked Mr. Baker, holding near the nostrils of Old Twitchett a pocket-mirror he had been polishing on his sleeve. After a few seconds he examined the mirror, and whispered :

" Nary a sign—might's well tell the boys."

The announcement of Twitchett's death was the signal for an animated discussion and considerable betting. How much dust he had washed, and what he had done with it, seeing that he neither drank nor gambled, was the sole theme of discussion. There was no debate on the deceased's religious evidences—no distribution of black crape—no tearful beating down of the undertaker ; these accessories of a civilized deathbed were all scornfully disregarded by the bearded men who had feelingly drank to Twitchett's good luck in whatever world he had gone to. But when it came to deceased's gold—his money—the bystanders exhibited an interest which was one of those touches of nature which certifies the universal kinship.

Each man knew all about Twitchett's money, though no two agreed. He had hid it—he had been unlucky, and had not found much—he had slyly sent it home—he had wasted it by sending it East for lottery tickets which always drew blanks—he had been supporting a benevolent institution. Old Deacon Baggs mildly suggested that perhaps he only washed out such gold as he actually needed to purchase eatables with, but the boys smiled derisively—they didn't like to laugh at the deacon's gray hairs, but he *was* queer.

Old Twitchett was buried, and Sam Baker and Boylston Smith reverently uncovered with the rest of the boys, while

Deacon Baggs made an extempore prayer. But for the remainder of the day Old Twitchett's administrators foamed restlessly about, and watched each other narrowly, and listened to the conversation of every group of men who seemed to be talking with any spirit; they kept a sharp eye on the trail to Black Peter Gulch, lest some unscrupulous miner should suspect the truth and constitute himself sole legatee.

But when the shades of evening had gathered, and a few round drinks had stimulated the citizens to more spirited discussion, Sam and Boylston strode rapidly out on the Black Peter Gulch trail, to obtain the reward of virtue.

"He didn't say what kind of a can it was," remarked Mr. Baker, after the outskirts of Bender had been left behind.

"Just what I thought," replied Boylston; "pity he couldn't hev lasted long enough for us to hev asked him. But I've been a-workin' some sums about different kinds of cans—I learned how from Phipps, this afternoon—he's been to college, an' his head's cram-full of sech puzzlin' things. It took multiplyin' with four figures to git the answer, but I couldn't take a peaceful drink till I knowed somethin' 'bout how the find would pan out."

"Well?" inquired Mr. Baker, anathematizing a stone over which he had just stumbled.

"Well," replied Boylston, stopping in an exasperating manner to light his pipe, "the smallest can a-goin' is a half-pound powder-can, and that'll hold over two thousand dollars worth—even *that* wouldn't be bad for a single night's work—eh?"

"Just so," responded Mr. Baker; "then there's oyster-cans an' meat-cans."

"Yes," said Boylston, " an' the smallest of 'em's good fur ten thousand, ef it's full. An' when yer come to five-pound powders—why, one of them would make two fellers rich!"

They passed quickly and quietly through Greenhorn's

Bar. The diggings at the Bar were very rich, and experienced poker-players, such as were Twitchett's executors, had made snug little sums in a single night out of the innocent countrymen who had located at the Bar; but what were the chances of the most brilliant game to the splendid certainty which lay before them?

They reached Black Peter Gulch and found Twitchett's hut still unoccupied, save by a solitary rattlesnake, whose warning scared them not. Mr. Baker carefully covered the single window with his coat, and then Boylston lit a candle and examined the clay floor. There were several little depressions in its surface, and in each of these Boylston vigorously drove his pick, while Mr. Baker stood outside alternately looking out for would-be disturbers, and looking in through a crack in the door to see that his partner should not, in case he found the can, absentmindedly spill some of the contents into his own pocket before he made a formal division.

Boylston stopped a moment for breath, leaned on his pick, stroked his yellow beard thoughtfully, and offered to bet that it would be an oyster-can. Mr. Baker whispered through the crack that he would take that bet, and make it an ounce.

Boylston again bent to the labor, which, while it wearied his body, seemed to excite his imagination, for he paused long enough to bet that it would be a five-pound powder-can, and Mr. Baker, again willing to fortify himself against possible loss, accepted the bet in ounces.

Suddenly Boylston's pick brought to light something yellow and round—something the size of an oyster-can, and wrapped in a piece of oilskin.

"You've won *one* bet," whispered Mr. Baker, who was inside before the yellow package had ceased rolling across the floor.

"Not ef *this* is it," growled Boylston; "it don't weigh more'n ounce can, wrapper and all. Might's well see what 'tis, though."

The two men approached the candle, hastily tore off the oilskin, and carefully shook the contents from the can. The contents proved to be a small package, labeled: *"My only treasures."*

Boylston mentioned the name of the arch-adversary of souls, while Mr. Baker, with a well-directed blow of his heel, reduced the can from a cylindrical form to one not easily described by any geometric term.

Unwrapping the package, Mr. Baker discovered a picture-case, which, when opened, disclosed the features of a handsome young lady; while from the wrappings fell a small envelope, which seemed distended in the middle.

"Gold in that, mebbe," suggested Boylston, picking it up and opening it. It *was* gold ; fine, yellow, and brilliant, but not the sort of gold the dead man's friends were seeking, for it was a ringlet of hair.

Sadly Mr. Baker put on his coat, careless of the light which streamed through the window; slowly and sorely they wended their way homeward; wrathfully they bemoaned their wasted time, as they passed by the auriferous slumberers of Greenhorn's Bar; depressing was the general nature of their conversation. Yet they were human in spite of their disappointment, for, as old Deacon Baggs, who was an early riser, strolled out in the gray dawn for a quiet season of meditation, he saw Boylston Smith filling up a little hole he had made on top of Old Twitchett's grave, and putting the dirt down very tenderly with his hands.

THE mining-camp of Tough Case, though small, had its excitements, as well as did many camps of half a dozen saloon-power; and on the first day of November, 1850, it was convulsed by the crisis of by far the greatest excitement it had ever enjoyed.

It was not a lucky " find," for some of the largest nuggets in the State had been taken out at Tough Case. It was not a grand spree, for *all* sprees at Tough Case were grand, and they took place every Sunday. It was not a fight, for when the average of fully-developed fights fell below one a fortnight, some patriotic citizen would improvise one, that the honor of his village should not suffer.

No; all these promoters of delicious and refreshing tumult were as nothing to the agitation which, commencing three months before, had increased and taken firmer hold of all hearts at Tough Case, until to-day it had reached its culmination.

Blizzer's wife had come out, and was to reach camp by that day's boat.

Since Blizzer had first announced his expectation, every man in camp had been secretly preparing for the event ; but to-day all secrecy was at an end, and white shirts, standing collars, new pants, black hats, polished boots, combs, brushes and razors, and even hair-oil and white handkerchiefs, so transformed the tremulous miners, that a smart detective would have been puzzled in looking for any particular citizen of Tough Case.

Even old Hatchetjaw, whose nickname correctly indicated the moral import of his countenance, sheepishly gave Moosoo, the old Frenchman, an ounce of gold-dust for an hour's labor bestowed on Hatchetjaw's self-asserting red hair.

Bets as to what she looked like were numerous; and, as no one had the slightest knowledge on the subject, experienced bettists made handsome fortunes in betting against every description which was backed by money. For each man had so long pondered over the subject, that his ideal portrait seemed to him absolutely correct; and an amateur phrenologist, who had carefully studied Blizzer's cranium and the usually accepted laws of affinity, consistently bet his last ounce, his pistol, hut, frying-pan, blankets, and even a pack of cards in a tolerable state of preservation.

Sailors, collegemen, Pikes, farmers, clerks, loafers, and sentimentalists, stood in front of Sim Ripson's store, and stared their eyes into watery redness in vain attempts to hurry the boat.

A bet of drinks for the crowd, lost by the non-arrival of the boat on time, was just being paid, when Sim Ripson, whose bar-window commanded the river, exclaimed:

" She's comin' !"

Many were the heeltaps left in glasses as the crowd hurried to the door; numerous were the stealthy glances bestowed on shirt-cuffs and finger-nails and boot-legs. Crosstree, a dandyish young sailor, hung back to regard himself in a small fragment of looking-glass he carried in his pocket, but was rebuked for his vanity by stumbling over the door-sill—an operation which finally resulted in his nose being laid up in ordinary.

The little steamer neared the landing, whistled shrilly, snorted defiantly, buried her nose in the muddy bank in front of the store, and shoved out a plank.

Several red-shirted strangers got off, but no one noticed them; at any other time, so large an addition to the population of Tough Case would have justified an extra spree.

Sundry barrels were rolled out, but not even old Guzzle

inspected the brand; barrels and bags of onions and pota-
toes were stacked on the bank, but though the camp was
sadly in need of vegetables, no one expressed becoming exultation.

All eyes were fixed on the steamer-end of the gang-plank,
and every heart beat wildly as Blizzer appeared, leading a
figure displaying only the top of a big bonnet and a blanket-
shawl hanging on one arm.

They stepped on the gang-plank, they reached the
shore, and then the figure raised its head and dropped the
shawl.

"Thunder!" ejaculated Fourteenth Street, and immediately retired and drank himself into a deplorable condition.

The remaining observers dispersed respectfully; but the
reckless manner in which they wandered through mud-pud-
dles and climbed over barrels and potato-sacks, indicated
plainly that their disappointment had been severe.

After another liquid bet had been paid, and while sleeves
but lately tenderly protected were carelessly drying damp
mustaches, an old miner remarked:

"Reckon that's why he left the States;" and the emphatic "You bet!" which followed his words showed that
the Tough Caseites were unanimous on the subject of Mrs.
Blizzer.

For she was short and fat, and had a pug nose, and a
cast in one eye; her forehead was low and square, and her
hair was of a color which seemed "fugitive," as the paper-
makers say. Her hands were large and pudgy, her feet
afforded broad foundations for the structure above them, and
her gait was not suggestive of any popular style. Besides,
she seemed ten years older than her husband, who was not
yet thirty.

For several days boots were allowed to grow rusty and
chins unshaven, as the boys gradually drank and worked
themselves into a dumb forgetfulness of their lately cherished
ideals.

But one evening, during a temporary lull in the conversation at Sim Ripson's, old Uncle Ben, ex-deacon of a New Hampshire church, lifted up his voice, and remarked :

"'Pears to me Blizzer's beginnin' to look scrumptious. He used to be the shabbiest man in camp."

Through the open door the boys saw Blizzer carrying a pail of water; and though water-carrying in the American manner is not an especially graceful performance, Blizzer cer-tainly looked unusually neat.

Palette, who had spoiled many canvases and paint-brushes in the East, attentively studdied Blizzer in detail, and found his hair was combed, his shirt buttoned at the collar, and his trowsers lacking the California soil which always adorns the seat and knees of orthodox mining panta-loons.

"It's her as did it," said Pat Fadden ; " an' 'tain't all she's done. Fhat d'ye tink she did dhis mornin' ?   I was a-fixin' me pork, jist as ivery other bye in camp allers does it, an' jist then who should come along but hersilf. I tuk off me pork, and comminced me breakfast, when sez she to me, sez she, ' Ye don't ate it widout gravy, do ye ?' ' Gravy, is it?' sez I. Nobody iver heard of gravy here,' sez I. ' Thin it's toime,' sez she, an' she poured off the fat, an' crumbled a bit of cracker in the pan, an' put in some wather, an' whin I thought the ould thing 'ud blow up for the shteam it made, she poured the gravy on me plate—yes, she did."

There were but a few men at Tough Case who were not willing to have their daily fare improved, and as Mrs. Bliz-zer did not make a tour of instruction, the boys made it con-venient to stand near Mrs. Blizzer's own fire, and see the mysteries of cooking.

As a natural consequence, Sim Ripson began to have in-quiries for articles which he had never heard of, much less sold, and he found a hurried trip to 'Frisco was an actual business necessity.

As several miners took their departure, after one of these culinary lessons, Arkansas Bill, with a mysterious air, took Fourteenth Street aside.

"Forty," said he, in a most appealing tone, "ken *you* see what 'twas about? She kep' a-lookin' at my left han' a'l the time, ez ef she thort there wuz somethin' the matter with it. Mebbe she thort I was tuckin' biscuits up my sleeves, like keerds in a live game. *Ken* you see any thin' the matter with that paw ?"

The aristocratic young reprobate gave the hand a critical glance, and replied :

"Perhaps she thought you didn't know what buttons and buttonholes were made for."

" Thunder !" exclaimed the miner, with an expression of countenance which Archimedes might have worn when he made his famous discovery.

From that day forward the gentleman from Arkansas instituted a rigid buttonhole inspection before venturing from his hut, besides purchasing a share in a new clothes-broom.

" 'Pears to me I don't see Blizzer playin' keerds with you fellers ez much ez he wuz," remarked Uncle Ben one evening at the store.

"No," said Flipp, the champion euchre-player, with a sad face and a strong oath. " He used to lose his ounces like a man. But t'other night I knocked at his door, and asked him to come down an' hev a han'. He didn't say nothin', but *she* up an' sed he'd stopped playin'. I reely tuk it to be my duty to argy with her, an' show her how tough it wuz to cut off a feller's enjoyment ; but she sed 'twas too high-priced fur the fun it fetched."

"That ain't the wust, nuther," said Topjack Flipp's usual partner. " There wuz Arkansas Bill an' Jerry Miller, thet used to be ez fond of ther little game ez anybody. Now, ev'ry night they go up thar to Blizzer's, an' jest do nothin' but sit aroun' an' talk. It's enough to make a marble statoo cuss to see good men spiled that way."

"Somethin' 'stonishin' 'bout what comes of it, though," resumed the deacon. " 'Twas only yestiddy thet Bill was kerryin' a bucket of dirt to the crick, an' jest ez he got there his foot slipped in, an' he went kerslosh. Knowin' Bill's language on sech occasions ain't what a church-member ort to hear, I was makin' it convenient to leave, when along come *her*, an' he choked off ez suddin ez a feller on the gallers."

Day by day the boys dug dirt, and carried it to the creek, and washed out the precious gold; day by day the denizens of Tough Case worked as many hours and as industriously as men anywhere. But no Tough Caseite was so wicked as to work on Sunday.

Sunday at Tough Case commenced at sunset on Saturday, after the good old Puritan fashion, and lasted through until working-time on Monday morning. But beyond this matter of time the Puritan parallel could not be pursued, for on Sunday was transacted all the irregular business of the week; on Sunday was done all the hard drinking and heavy gambling; and on Sunday were settled such personal difficulties as were superior to the limited time and low liquor-pressure of the week.

The evening sun of the first Saturday of Mrs. Blizzer's residence at Tough Case considered 'his day's work done, and retired under the snowy coverlets the Sierras lent him. The tired miners gladly dropped pick, shovel, and pan, but bedclothing was an article which at that moment they scorned to consider; there was important business and entertainment, which would postpone sleep for many hours.

The express would be along in the morning, and no prudent man could sleep peaceably until he had deposited his gold dust in the company's strong box. Then there were two or three old feuds which *might* come to a head—they always *did* on Sunday. And above all, Redwing, a man with enormous red whiskers, had been threatening all week to have back the money Flipp had won from him on the preceding Sunday, and Redwing had been very lucky in his claim all week, and the two men were very nearly matched, and were magnificent players, so the game promised to last many hours, and afford handsome opportunities for outside betting.

Sim Ripson understood his business. By sunset he had all his bottles freshly filled, and all his empty boxes distributed about the room for seats, and twice as many candles lighted as usual, and the card-tables reinforced by some upturned barrels.   He also had a neat little woodpile under the bar, to serve as a barricade against stray shots.

The boys dropped in pleasantly, two or three at a time, and drank merrily with each other ; and the two or three who were not drinking men sauntered in to compare notes with the others.

There were no aristocrats or paupers at Tough Case, nor any cliques ; whatever the men were at home, here they were equal, and Sim Ripson's was the general gathering-place for everybody.

But in the course of two or three hours there was a perceptible change of the general tone at Sim Ripson's—it was so every Saturday night, or Sunday morning.   Old Hatchetjaw said it was because Sim Ripson's liquor wasn't good ; Moosoo, the Frenchman, maintained it was due to the absence of chivalrous spirit ; Crosstree, the sailor, said it was always so with landsmen ; Fourteenth Street privately confided to several that 'twas because there was no good blood in camp ; the amateur phrenologist ascribed it to an undue cerebral circulation ; and Uncle Ben, the deacon, insisted upon it that the fiend, personally, was the disturbing element.

Probably all of them were right, for it seemed impossible that the Sunday excitements at Sim Ripsons's could proceed from any single cause—their proportions were too magnificent.

Drinking, singing, swearing, gambling, and fighting, the Tough Caseites made night so hideous that Uncle Ben spent half the night in earnest prayer for these misguided men, and the remainder of it in trying to make up his mind to start for home.

But by far the greater number of the boys, on that particular night, surrounded the table at which sat Redwing and Flip.   Both were playing their best, and as honestly as each was compelled to do by his adversary's watchfulness.

Each had several times accused the other of cheating; each had his revolver at his right hand ; and the crowd about them had the double pleasure of betting on the game and on which would shoot first.

Suddenly Redwing arose, as Flipp played an ace on his adversary's last card, and raked the dust toward himself.

"Yer tuk that ace out of yer sleeve—I seed yer do it. Give me back my ounces," said Redwing.

" It's a lie !" roared the great Flipp, springing to his feet, and seizing Redwing's pistol-arm.

The weapon fell, and both men clutched like tigers. Sim Ripson leaped over the bar and separated them.

"No rasslin' here !" said he.   " When gentlemen gits too mad to hold in, an' shoots at sight, I hev to stan' it, but rasslin's vulgar—you'll hev to go out o' doors to do it."

" I'll hev it out with him with pistols, then !" cried Redwing, picking up his weapon.

"'Greed !" roared Flip, whose pistol lay on the table. " We'll do it cross the crick, at daylight.

" It's daylight now," said Sim Ripson, hurriedly, after looking out of his window at the end of the bar.

He was a good storekeeper, was Sim Ripson, and he knew how to mix drinks, but he had an unconquerable aversion to washing blood stains out of the floor.

The two gamblers rushed out of the door, pistols in hand, and the crowd followed, each man talking at the top of his voice, and betting on the chances of the combatants.

Suddenly, above all the noise, they heard a cracked soprano voice singing with some unauthorized flatting and sharping :

> " Another six days' work is done,
> Another Sabbath is begun.
> Return, my soul, enjoy thy rest,
> Improve the day thy God has blessed."

Redwing stopped, and dropped his head to one side, as

if expecting more; Flipp stopped; everybody did. Arkan-
saš Bill, whose good habits had been laid aside late Saturday afternoon, exclaimed:

"Well, I'll be blowed!"

Bill didn't mean anything of the sort, but the tone in
which he said it expressed precisely the feeling of the crowd.
The voice was again heard:

> "Oh, that our thoughts and thanks may rise,
> As grateful incense to the skies;
> And draw from heaven that sweet repose
> Which none but he that feels it knows."

Redwing turned abruptly on his heel.

"Keep the ounces," said he. "Ther's an old woman to
hum that thinks a sight o' me—I reckon, myself, I'm good
fur somethin' besides fillin' a hole in the ground."

That night Sim Ripson complained that it had been the
poorest Sunday he had ever had at Tough Case; the boys
drank, but it was a sort of nerveless, unbusinesslike way
that Sim Ripson greatly regretted; and very few bets were
settled in Sim Ripson's principal stock in trade.

When Sim finally learned the cause of his trouble, he
promptly announced his intention of converting Mrs. Blizzer to common sense, and as he had argued Uncle Ben, first
into a perfect frenzy and then into silence, the crowd considered Mrs. Blizzer's faith doomed.

Monday morning, bright and early, as men with aching
heads were taking their morning bitters, Mrs. Blizzer appeared at Sim Ripson's store, and purchased a bar of soap.

"Boys heard ye singin' yesterday," said Sim.

"Yes?" inquired Mrs. Blizzer.

"Yes—all of 'em delighted," said Sim, gallantly. "But
ye don't believe in no sich stuff, I s'pose, do ye?"

"What stuff?" asked Mrs. Blizzer.

"Why, 'bout heaven an' hell, an' the Bible, an' all them
things. Do ye know what the Greek fur hell meant? An'
do ye know the Bible's all the time contradictin' itself?" I
can show ye——"

"I tell you what I *do* know, Mr. Ripson," said the woman;
"I know some things in my heart that no mortal bein' never
told me, an' they couldn't be skeered out by all the diction-
aries an' commentators a-goin; that's what I know."

And Mrs. Blizzer departed, while the astonished theologian sheepishly admitted that he owed drinks to the crowd.

While the ex-deacon, Uncle Ben, was trying to determine to go home, he found quite a pretty nugget that settled his mind, and he announced that same night, at the
store, that all his mining property was for sale, as he was
going back East.

"I'll go with you, Uncle Ben," said Fourteenth Street.

The crowd was astounded; men of Fourteenth Street's
calibre seldom had pluck enough to go to the mines, and
their getting away, or their doing *any* thing that required
manliness, was of still more unfrequent occurrence.

"I know it," said the young man, translating the glances
which met his eye. "You fellows think I don't amount to
much, anyway. Perhaps I don't. I came out here because
I fell out with a girl I thought I loved. She acted like a
fool, and I made up my mind *all* women were fools. But
that wife of Blizzer's has shown me more about true
womanliness than all the girls I ever knew, and I'm going
back to try it over again."

One morning a small crowd of early drinkers at Sim
Ripson's dropped their glasses, yet did not go briskly out
to work as usual. In fact, they even hung aloof, in a most
ungentlemanly manner, from Jerry Miller, who had just
stood treat, and both these departures from the usual custom indicated that something unusual was the matter.
Finally, Topjack remarked:

"He's a stranger, an' typhus is a bad thing to hev aroun',
but *somethin'* 'ort to be done for him. 'Taint the thing to
ax fur volunteers, fur it's danger without no chance of pleas-
in' excitement. We might throw keerds aroun', one to each
feller in the camp, and him as gets ace of spades is to tend
to the poor cuss."

"I think Jerry ought to go himself," argued Flipp.

"He's been exposed already, by lookin' in to the feller's shanty, an's prob'bly hurt ez bad as he's goin' to be."

"*I* might go," said Sim Ripson, who, in his character of barkeeper, had to sustain a reputation for bravery and public spirit, "but 'twouldn't do to shut up the store, ye know, an' specially the bar—nobody'd stan' it."

"Needn't trouble yerselves," said Arkansas Bill, who had entered during the conversation; "*she's* thar."

"Thunder!" exclaimed Topjack, frowning, and then looking sheepish.

"Yes," continued Bill; "she stopped me ez I wuz comin' along, an' sed she'd jist heerd of it, an' was a-goin'. I tol' her ther' wuz men enough in camp to look out fur him, but she said she reckoned she could do it best. Wants some things from 'Frisco, though, an' I'm a-goin' for 'em."

And Arkansas Bill departed, while the men at Sim Ripson's sneaked guiltily down to the creek.

For many days the boys hung about the camp's single street every morning, unwilling to go to work until they had seen Mrs. Blizzer appear in front of the sick man's hut. The boys took turns at carrying water, making fires, and serving Mrs. Blizzer generally, and even paid handsomely for the chance.

One morning Mrs. Blizzer failed to appear at the usual hour. The boys walked about nervously—they smoked many pipes, and took hurried drinks, and yet she did not appear. The boys looked suggestingly at her husband, and he himself appeared to be anxious; but being one of the shiftless kind, he found anxiety far easier than action.

Suddenly Arkansas Bill remarked, "I can't stan' it any longer," and walked rapidly toward the sick man's hut, and knocked lightly on the door, and looked in. There lay the sick man, his eyes partly open, and on the ground, apparently asleep, and with a very purple face, lay Mrs. Blizzer.

"Do somethin' for her," gasped the sick man; "give her a chance, for God's sake. I don't know how long I've been here, but I kind o' woke up las' night ez ef I'd been

16

asleep; she wuz a-standin' lookin' in my eyes, an' hed a han' on my cheek. 'I b'lieve it's turned,' sez she, still a-lookin'. After a bit she sez: 'It's turned sure,' an' all of a sudden she tumbled. I couldn't holler—I wish to God I could."

Arkansas Bill opened the door, and called Blizzer, and

ARKANSAS BILL KNOCKED LIGHTLY ON THE DOOR, AND LOOKED IN. THERE LAY THE SICK MAN, HIS EYES PARTLY OPEN, AND ON THE GROUND, APPARENTLY ASLEEP, AND WITH PURPLE FACE, LAY MRS. BLIZZER.

the crowd followed Blizzer, though at a respectful distance. In a moment Blizzer reappeared with his wife, no longer fat, in his arms, and Arkansas Bill hurried on to open Blizzer's door. The crowd halted, and didn't know what to do, until Moosoo, the little Frenchman, lifted his hat, upon which every man promptly uncovered his head

A moment later Arkansas Bill was on Sim Ripson's horse, and galloping off for a doctor, and Sim Ripson, who had always threatened sudden death to any one touching his beloved animal, saw him, and refrained even from profanity. The doctor came, and the boys crowded the door to hear what he had to say.

"Hum!" said the doctor, a rough miner himself, "new arrival—been fat—worn out—rainy season just coming on—not much chance. No business to come to California—ought to have had sense enough to stay home."

"Look a' here, doctor," said Arkansas Bill, indignantly; "she's got this way a-nussin' a feller—stranger, too—that ev'ry *man* in camp wuz afeard to go nigh."

"Is that so?" asked the doctor, in a tone considerably softened; "then she shall get well, if my whole time and attention can bring it about."

The sick woman lay in a burning fever for days, and the boys industriously drank her health, and bet heavy odds on her recovery. No singing was allowed anywhere in camp, and when an old feud broke out afresh between two miners, and they drew their pistols, a committee was appointed to conduct them at least two miles from camp, before allowing them to shoot.

The Sundays were allowed to pass in the commonplace quietness peculiar to the rest of the week, and men who were unable to forego their regular weekly spree were compelled to emigrate. Sim Ripson, though admitting that the change was decidedly injurious to his business, declared that he would cheerfully be ruined in business rather than have that woman disturbed; he was ever heard to say that, though of course there was no such place as heaven, there *ought* to be, for such women.

One evening, as the crowd were quietly drinking and betting, Arkansas Bill suddenly opened the door of the store, and cried: "She's mendin'! The fever's broke—'sh-h!"

"My treat, boys," said Sim Ripson, hurrying glasses and favorite bottles on the bar.

The boys were just clinking glasses with Blizzer himself, who, during his wife's absence and illness, had drifted
back to the store, when Arkansas Bill again opened the
door.

"She's a-sinkin', all of a sudden!" he gasped.   "Blizzer,
yer wanted."

The two men hurried away, and the crowd poured out
of the store. By the light of a fire in front of the hut in
which the sick woman lay, they saw Blizzer enter, and
Arkansas Bill remain outside the hut, near the door.

The boys stood on one foot, put their hands into their
pockets and took them out again, snapped their fingers, and
looked at each other, as if they wanted to talk about something that they couldn't. Suddenly the doctor emerged
from the hut, and said something to Arkansas Bill, and the
boys saw Arkansas Bill put both hands up to his face.
Then the boys knew that their sympathy could help Blizzer's wife no longer.

Slowly the crowd re-entered the store, and mechanically
picked up the yet untasted glasses. Sim Ripson filled a
glass for himself, looked a second at the crowd, and dropping
his eyes, raised them again, looked as if he had something
to say, looked intently into his glass, as if espying some
irregularity, looked up again, and exclaimed :

"Boys, it's no use—mebbe ther's no hell—mebbe the
Bible contradicts itself, but—but ther *is* a heaven, or such
folks would never git their just dues. Here's to Blizzer's
wife, the best man in camp, an' may the Lord send us somebody like her !"

In silence, and with uncovered heads, was the toast
drank ; and for many days did the boys mourn for her
whose advent brought them such disappointment.

A BOARDING-HOUSE ROMANCE.

I KEEP a boarding-house.

If any fair proportion of my readers were likely to be members of my own profession, I should expect the above announcement to call forth more sympathetic handkerchiefs than have waved in unison for many a day. But I don't expect anything of the sort; I know my business too well to suppose for a moment that any boarding-house proprietor, no matter how full her rooms, or how good pay her boarders are, ever finds time to read a story. Even if they did, they'd be so lost in wonder at one of themselves finding time to *write* a story, that they'd forget the whole plot and point of the thing.

I can't help it, though—I *must* tell about poor dear Mrs. Perry, even if I run the risk of cook's overdoing the beef, so that Mr. Bluff, who is English, and the best of pay, can't get the rare cut he loves so well. Mrs. Perry's story has run in my head so long, that it has made me forget to take change from the grocer at least once to my knowledge, and even made me lose a good boarder, by showing a room before the bed was made up. They say that poets get things out of their heads by writing them down, and I don't know why boarding-house keepers can't do the same thing.

It's about three months since Mrs. Perry came here to board. I'm very sure about the time, and it was the day I was to pay my quarter's rent, and to-morrow will be quarter-day again; thank the Lord I've got the money ready.

I *didn't* have the money ready then, though, and the landlord left his temper behind him, instead of a receipt,

245

and I was just having a little cry in my apron, and asking the Lord *why* it was that a poor lone woman who was working her finger-ends off should have such a hard time, when the door-bell rang.

"That's the landlord again. *I* know his ways, the mean wretch!" said I to myself, hastily rubbing my eyes dry, and making up before the mirror in the hat-tree as fierce a face as I could. Then I snatched open the door, and tried to make believe my heart *wasn't* in my mouth.

But the landlord wasn't there, and I've always been a little sorry, for I was looking so savage, that a wee little woman, who *was* at the door, trembled all over, and started to go down the steps.

"Don't go, ma'am," I said, very quickly, with the best smile I could put on (and I think I've been long enough in the business to give the right kind of a smile to a person that looks like a new boarder). "Don't go—I thought it was—I thought it was—somebody else that rang. Come in, do."

She looked as if I was doing her a great honor, and I thought that looked like poor pay, but I was too glad at not seeing the landlord just 'then to care if I did lose *one* week's board; besides, she didn't look as if she *could* eat much.

"I see you advertise a small bedroom to let," said she, looking appealing-like, as if she was going to beat me down on the strength of being poor. "How much is it a week?"

"Eight dollars," said I, rather shortly. Seven dollars was all I expected to get, but I put on one, so as to be beaten down without losing anything. "I can get eight from a single gentleman, the only objection being that he wants to keep a dog in the back yard." ·

"Oh, I'll pay it," said she, quickly taking out her pocket-book. "I'll take it for six weeks, anyhow."

I never felt so ashamed of myself in my life. I made up my mind to read a penitential passage of Scripture as soon as I closed the bargain with her, but, remembering the Book says to be reconciled to your brother before laying your gift on the altar, I says, quick as I could, for fear that if I thought over it again I couldn't be honest :

"You shall have it for seven, my dear madame, if you're going to stay so long, and I'll do your washing without extra charge."

This last I said to punish myself for suspecting an innocent little lady.

"Oh, thank you—thank you *very* much," said she, and then she began to cry.

I knew *that* wasn't for effect, for we were already agreed on terms, and she had her pocketbook open showing more money that *I* ever have at a time, unless it's rent-day.

She tried to stop crying by burying her face in her hands, and it made her look so much smaller and *so* pitiful that I picked her right up, as if she was a baby, and kissed her. Then she cried harder, and I—a woman over forty, too—couldn't find anything better to do than to cry with her.

I knew her whole story within five minutes—knew it perfectly well before I'd fairly shown her the room and got it aired.

They were from the West, and had been married about a year. She hadn't a relative in the world, but *his* folks had friends in Philadelphia, so he'd got a place as clerk in a big clothing factory, at twelve hundred dollars a year. They'd been keeping house, just as cozy as could be in four rooms, and were as happy as anybody in the world, when one night he didn't come home.

She was almost frantic about him all night long, and first thing in the morning she was at the factory. She waited until all the clerks got there, but George—his name was George Perry—didn't come. The proprietor was a good-hearted man, and went with her to the police-office, and they telegraphed all over the city ; but there didn't seem to be any such man found dead or drunk, or arrested for anything.

She hadn't heard a word from him since. Her husband's

family's friends were rich—the stuck up brutes!—but they
seemed to be annoyed by her coming so often to ask if there
wasn't any other way of looking for him, so she, like the
modest, frightened little thing she was, staid away from
them. Then somebody told her that New York was the
place everybody went to, so she sold all her furniture and
pawned almost all her clothes, and came to New York with
about fifty dollars in her pocket.

"What I'll do when that's gone I don't know," said she,
commencing to cry again, "unless I find George. I won't
live on *you*, though, ma'am," she said, lifting her face up
quickly out of her handkerchief; "I won't, indeed. I'll go to
the poorhouse first. But——"

Then she cried worse than before, and I cried, too, and
took her in my arms, and called her a poor little thing, and
told her she shouldn't go to any poorhouse, but should stay
with me and be my daughter.

I don't know how I came to say it, for, goodness knows,
I find it hard enough to keep out of the poorhouse myself,
but I did say it, and I meant it, too.

Her things were all in a little valise, and she soon had
the room to rights, and when I went up again in a few minutes
to carry her a cup of tea, she pointed to her husband's picture which she had hung on the wall, and asked me if I didn't
think he was very handsome.

I said yes, but I'm glad she looked at the tea instead of
me, for I believe she'd seen by my face that I didn't like her
George. The fact is, men look very differently to their
wives or sweethearts than they do to older people and to
boarding-house keepers. There was nothing vicious about
George Perry's face, but if he'd been a boarder of mine, I'd
have insisted on my board promptly—not for fear of his
trying to cheat me, but because if he saw anything else he
wanted, he'd spend his money without thinking of what he
owed.

I felt so certain that he'd got into some mischief or
trouble, and was afraid or ashamed to come back to his wife,

that I risked the price of three ribs of prime roasting beef
in the following "Personal" advertisement:

"GEORGE P.—Your wife don't know anything about it,
and is dying to see you. Answer through Personals."

But no answer came, and his wife grew more and more
poorly, and I couldn't help seeing what was the matter with
her. Then her money ran out, and she talked of going away,
but I wouldn't hear of it. I just took her to my own room,
which was the back parlor, and told her she wasn't to think
again of going away; that she was to be my daughter, and I
would be her mother, until she found George again.

I was afraid, for _her_ sake, that it meant we were to be
with each other for ever, for there was no sign of George.

She wrote to his family in the West, but _they_ hadn't
heard anything from him or about him, and they took pains
not to invite her there, or even to say anything about giving
her a helping hand.

There was only one thing left to do, and that was to
pray, and pray I _did_, more constantly and earnestly than I
ever did before, although, the good Lord knows there _have_
been times, about quarter-day, when I haven't kept much
peace before the Throne.

Finally, one day Mrs. Perry was taken unusually bad,
and the doctor had to be sent for in a hurry. We were in
her room—the doctor and Mrs. Perry and I—I was endeavoring to comfort and strengthen the poor thing, when the servant knocked, and said a lady and gentleman had come to
look at rooms.

I didn't _dare_ to lose boarders, for I'd had three empty
rooms for a month, so I hurried into the parlor. I was
almost knocked down for a second, for the gentleman was
George Perry, and no mistake, if the picture his wife had
was to be trusted.

In a second more I was cooler and clearer-headed than
I ever was in my life before. I felt more like an angel of
the Lord than a boarding-house keeper.

"Kate,' said I, to the servant "show the lady all the rooms."

Kate stared, for I'd never trusted her, or any other girl, with such important work, and she knew it. She went though, followed by the lady, who, though she seemed a weak, silly sort of thing, I *hated* with all my might. Then I turned quickly, and said :

"Don't you want a room for your wife, too, George Perry?"

He stared at me a moment, and then turned pale and looked confused. Then he tried to rally himself, and he said :

"You seem to know me, ma'am."

"Yes," said I; "and I know Mrs. Perry, too; and if ever a woman needed her husband she does *now*, even if her husband *is* a rascal."

He tried to be angry, but he couldn't. He walked up and down the room once or twice, his face twitching all the time, and then he said, a word or two at a time :

"I wish I could—poor girl!—God forgive me!—what *can* I do?—I wish I was dead!"

"You wouldn't be any use to *any*body then but the Evil One, George Perry, and you're not ready to see *him* just yet," said I.

Just then there came a low, long groan from the back-room, and at the same time some one came into the parlor. I was too excited to notice who it was; and George Perry, when he heard the groan, stopped short and exclaimed:

"Good God! who's that?"

"Your wife," said I, almost ready to scream, I was so wrought up.

He hid his face in his hands, and trembled all over.

There was half a minute's silence—it seemed half an hour—and then we heard a long, thin wail from a voice that hadn't ever been heard on earth before.

"What's that?" said Perry, in a hoarse whisper, his eyes almost starting out of his head, and hands thrown up.

"Your baby—just born," said I. "Will you take rooms for your family *now*, George Perry?" I asked.

"*I* sha'n't stand in the way," said a voice behind me.

I turned around quickly, just in time to see, with her eyes full of tears, the woman who had come with George go out the door and shut the hall-door behind her.

"Thank God!" said George, dropping on his knees.

"Amen!" said I, hurrying out of the parlor and locking the door behind me.

I thought if he wanted to pray while on his knees he shouldn't be disturbed, while if he should suddenly be tempted to follow his late companion, *I* shouldn't be held at the Judgment day for any share of the guilt.

I found the doctor bustling about, getting ready to go, and Mrs. Perry looking very peaceful and happy, with a little bundle hugged up close to her.

"I guess the Lord will bring him *now*," said Mrs. Perry, "if it's only to see his little boy."

"Like enough, my dear," said I, thanking the Lord for opening the question, for my wits were all gone by this time, and I hadn't any more idea of what to do than the man in the moon; "but," said I, "He won't bring him till you're well, and able to bear the excitement."

"Oh, I could bear it any time now," said she, very calmly, "It would seem just as natural as could be to have him come in and kiss me, and see his baby and bless it."

"Would it?" I asked, with my heart all in a dance. "Well, trust the Lord to do just what's right."

I hurried out and opened the parlor-door. There stood George Perry, changed so I hardly knew him. He seemed years older; his thick lips seemed to have suddenly grown thin, and were pressed tightly together, and there was such an appealing look from his eyes.

"Be very careful now," I whispered, "and you may see them. She expects you, and don't imagine anything has gone wrong."

I took him into the room, and she looked up with a face like what I hope the angels have. I didn't see anything more, for my eyes filled up all of a sudden, so I hurried upstairs into an empty room, and spent half an hour crying and thanking the Lord.

There was a pretty to-do at the dinner table that day. I'd intended to have *souffle* for desert, and I always make my own *souffles;* but I forgot everything but the Perrys, and the boarders grumbled awfully. I didn't care, though; I was too happy to feel abused.

I don't know how George Perry explained his absence to his wife; perhaps he hasn't done it at all. But I know she seems to be the happiest woman alive, and that *he* don't seem to care for anything in the world but his wife and baby.

As to the woman who came with him to look at a room, I haven't seen her since; but if she happens to read this story, she may have the consolation of knowing that there's an old woman who remembers her one good deed, and prays for her often and earnestly.

WHAT the colonel's business was nobody knew, nor did any one care, particularly. He purchased for cash only, and he never grumbled at the price of anything that he wanted; who could ask more than that?

Curious people occasionally wondered how, when it had been fully two years since the colonel, with every one else, abandoned Duck Creek to the Chinese, he managed to spend money freely, and to lose considerable at cards and horse-races. In fact, the keeper of that one of the two Challenge Hill saloons which the colonel did not patronize was once heard to absentmindedly wonder whether the colonel hadn't a money-mill somewhere, where he turned out double-eagles and "slugs" (the Coast name for fifty-dollar gold-pieces).

When so important a personage as a barkeeper indulged publicly in an idea, the inhabitants of Challenge Hill, like good Californians everywhere, considered themselves in duty bound to give it grave consideration; so, for a few days, certain industrious professional gentlemen, who won money of the colonel, carefully weighed some of the brightest pieces and tested them with acids, and tasted them and sawed them in two, and retried them and melted them up, and had the lumps assayed.

The result was a complete vindication of the colonel, and a loss of considerable custom to the indiscreet bar-keeper.

The colonel was as good-natured a man as had ever been

253

known at Challenge Hill, but, being mortal, the colonel had
his occasional times of despondency, and one of them
occurred after a series of races, in which he had staked his
all on his own bay mare Tipsie, and had lost.

Looking reproachfully at his beloved animal failed to heal
the aching void of his pockets, and drinking deeply, swearing eloquently and glaring defiantly at all mankind, were
equally unproductive of coin.

The boys at the saloon sympathized most feelingly with
the colonel; they were unceasing in their invitations to
drink, and they even exhibited considerable Christian for-
bearance when the colonel savagely dissented with every
one who advanced any proposition, no matter how incon-
trovertible.

But unappreciated sympathy grows decidedly tiresome
to the giver, and it was with a feeling of relief that the
boys saw the colonel stride out of the saloon, mount Tipsie,
and gallop furiously away.

Riding on horseback has always been considered an excellent sort of exercise, and fast riding is universally admitted to be one of the most healthful and delightful means
of exhilaration in the world.

But when a man is so absorbed in his exercise that he
will not stop to speak to a friend; and when his exhilaration
is so complete that he turns his eyes from well-meaning
thumbs pointing significantly into doorways through which
a man has often passed while seeking bracing influences, it
is but natural that people should express some wonder.

The colonel was well known at Toddy Flat, Lone Hand,
Blazers, Murderer's Bar, and several other villages through
which he passed, and as no one had been seen to precede
him, betting men were soon offering odds that the colonel
was running away from somebody.

Strictly speaking they were wrong, but they won all
the money that had been staked against them; for within
half an hour's time there passed over the same road an
anxious-looking individual, who reined up in front of the

principal saloon of each place, and asked if the colonel had passed.

Had the gallant colonel known that he was followed, and by whom, there would have been an extra election held at the latter place very shortly after, for the colonel's pursuer was no other than the constable of Challenge Hill, and for constables and all other officers of the law the colonel possessed hatred of unspeakable intensity.

On galloped the colonel, following the stage-road, which threaded the old mining camps on Duck Creek; but suddenly he turned abruptly out of the road, and urged his horse through the young pines and bushes, which grew thickly by the road, while the constable galloped rapidly on to the next camp.

There seemed to be no path through the thicket into which the colonel had turned, but Tipsie walked between trees and bushes as if they were but the familiar objects of her own stable-yard.

Suddenly a voice from the bushes shouted:

"What's up?"

"Business—*that's* what," replied the colonel.

"It's time," replied the voice, and its owner—a bearded six-footer—emerged from the bushes, and stroked Tipsie's nose with the freedom of an old acquaintance. "We hain't had a nip sence last night, an' thar' ain't a cracker or a handful of flour in the shanty. The old gal go back on yer?"

"Yes," replied the colonel, ruefully—lost ev'ry blasted race. 'Twasn't *her* fault, bless her—she done her level best. Ev'rybody to home?"

"You bet," said the man. "All ben a-prayin' for yer to turn up with the rocks, an' somethin' with more color than spring water. Come on."

The man led the way, and Tipsie and the colonel followed, and the trio suddenly found themselves before a small log hut, in front of which sat three solemn, disconsolate-looking individuals, who looked appealingly at the colonel.

"Mac'll tell yer how 'twas, fellers," said the colonel, meekly, "while I picket the mare."

The colonel was absent but a very few moments, but when he returned each of the four men was attired in pistols and knives, while Mac was distributing some dominoes, made from a rather dirty flour-bag.

"'Tain't so late as all that, is it?" inquired the colonel.

"Better be an hour ahead than miss it this '*ere* night," said one of the four. "I ain't been so thirsty sence I come round the Horn, in '50, an' we run short of water. *Somebody*'ll get hurt ef thar' ain't no bitters on the old concern— they will, or my name ain't Perkins."

"Don't count yer chickings 'fore they're hetched, Perky," said one of the party, as he adjusted his domino under the rim of his hat. "'S'posin' ther' shud be too many for us?"

"Stiddy, Cranks!" remonstrated the colonel. "Nobody ever gets along ef they 'low 'emselves to be skeered."

"Fact," chimed in the smallest and thinnest man of the party. "The Bible says somethin' mighty hot 'bout that. I disremember dzackly how it goes; but I've heerd Parson Buzzy, down in Maine, preach a rippin' old sermon from that text many a time. The old man never thort what a comfort them sermons wus a-goin' to be to a road-agent, though. That time we stopped Slim Mike's stage, an' he didn't hev no more manners than to draw on me, them sermons wus a perfec' blessin' to me—the thought uv 'em cleared my head ez quick ez a cocktail. An'——"

"I don't want to disturb Logroller's pious yarn," interrupted the colonel; "but ez it's Old Black that's drivin' today instid of Slim Mike, an' ez Old Black ollers makes his time, hedn't we better vamose?"

The door of the shanty was hastily closed, and the men filed through the thicket until near the road, when they marched rapidly on parallel lines with it. After about half an hour, Perkins, who was leading, halted, and wiped his perspiring brow with his shirt-sleeve.

"Fur enough from home now," said he. "'Tain't no use bein' a gentleman ef yer hev to work *too* hard."

"Safe enough, I reckon," replied the colonel. "We'll do the usual; I'll halt 'em, Logroller'll tend .to the driver, Cranks takes the boot, an' Mac an' Perk takes right an' left. An'—I know it's tough—but consid'rin' how everlastin' eternally hard up we are, I reckon we'll have to ask contributions from the ladies, too, ef ther's any aboard—eh, boy?"

"Reckon so," replied Logroller, with a chuckle that seemed to inspire even his black domino with a merry wrinkle or two. "What's the use of women's rights ef they don't ever hev a chance of exercisin' 'em? Hevin' ther purses borrowed 'ud show 'em the hull doctrine in a bran-new light."

"They're treacherous critters, women is," remarked Cranks; "some of 'em might put a knife into a feller while he was 'pologizin'."

"Ef *you're* afeard of 'em," said Perkins, "you ken go back an' clean up the shanty."

"Reminds me of what the Bible sez," said Logroller; "'there's a lion on the trail; I'll be chawed up, sez the lazy galoot,' ur words to that effect."

"Come, come boys," interposed the colonel; "don't mix religion an' bizness. They don't mix no more than—— Hello, thar's the crack of Old Black's whip! Pick yer bushes—quick! All jump when I whistle!"

Each man secreted himself near the roadside. The stage came swinging along handsomely; the inside passengers were laughing heartily about something, and Old Black was just giving a delicate touch to the flank of the off leader, when the colonel gave a shrill, quick whistle, and the five men sprang into the road.

The horses stopped as suddenly as if it was a matter of common occurrence, Old Black dropped his reins, crossed his legs, and stared into the sky, and the passengers all put out their heads with a rapidity equaled only by that with
17

which they withdrew them as they saw the dominoes and
revolvers of the road-agents.

"Seems to be something the matter, gentlemen," said
the colonel, blandly, as he opened the door. "Won't you
please git out? Don't trouble yourselves to draw, cos my
friend here's got his weapon cocked, an' his fingers is rather
nervous. Ain't got a han'kercher, hev yer?" asked the
colonel of the first passenger who descended from the
stage. "Hev? Well, now, that's lucky. Jest put yer
hands behind yer, please—so—that's it." And the unfortunate man was securely bound in an instant.

The remaining passengers were treated with similar
courtesy, and then the colonel and his friends examined the
pockets of the captives. Old Black remained unmolested,
for who ever heard of a stage-driver having money?

"Boys," said the colonel, calling his brother agents
aside, and comparing receipts, "'tain't much of a haul; but
there's only one woman, an' she's old enough to be a feller's
grandmother. Better let her alone, eh?"

"Like enough she'll pan out more'n all the rest of the
stage put together," growled Cranks, carefully testing the
thickness of case of a gold watch. "Jest like the low-lived
deceitfulness of some folks, to hire an old woman to kerry
ther money so it 'ud go safe. Mebbe what she's got hain't
nothin' to some folks thet's got hosses thet ken win 'em
money at races, but——"

The colonel abruptly ended the conversation, and approached the stage. The colonel was very chivalrous, but
Cranks's sarcastic reference to Tipsie needed avenging, and
as he could not consistently with business arrangements
put an end to Cranks, the old lady would have to suffer.

"I beg your parding, ma'am," said the colonel, raising
his hat politely with one hand, while he reopened the
coach-door with the other, "but we're a-takin' up a collection fur some very deservin' object. We *wuz* a-goin' to
make the gentlemen fork over the hull amount, but ez they
hain't got enough, we'll hev to bother *you*."

The old lady trembled, and felt for her pocketbook, and raised her vail. The colonel looked into her face, slammed the stage-door, and, sitting down on the hub of one of the wheels, stared vacantly into space.

"Nothin'?" queried Perkins, in a whisper, and with a face full of genuine sympathy.

"No—yes," said the colonel, dreamily. "That is, untie

'em and let the stage go ahead," he continued, springing to his feet. "*I'll* hurry back to the cabin."

And the colonel dashed into the bushes, and left his followers so paralyzed with astonishment, that Old Black afterward remarked that, "ef ther'd ben anybody to hold the hosses, he could hev cleaned out the hull crowd with his whip."

The passengers, now relieved of their weapons, were un-bound, and allowed to re-enter the stage, and the door was slammed, upon which Old Black picked up his reins as coolly as if he had merely laid them down at the station while horses were being changed; then he cracked his whip, and the stage rolled off, while the colonel's party has-tened back to their hut, fondly inspecting as they went cer-tain flasks they had obtained while transacting their busi-ness with the occupants of the stage.

Great was the surprise of the road-agents as they en-tered their hut, for there stood the colonel in a clean white shirt, and in a suit of clothing made up from the limited spare wardrobes of the other members of the gang.

But the suspicious Cranks speedily subordinated his wonder to his prudence, as, laying on the table a watch, two pistols, a pocket-book, and a heavy purse, he ex-claimed:

"Come, colonel, bizness before pleasure; let's divide an' scatter. Ef anybody should hear 'bout it, an' find our trail, an' ketch us with the traps in our possession, they might——"

"Divide yerselves!" said the colonel, with abruptness and a great oath. "*I* don't want none of it."

"Colonel," said Perkins, removing his own domino, and looking anxiously into the leader's face, "be you sick? Here's some bully brandy I found in one of the passengers' pockets."

"I hain't nothin'," replied the colonel. "I'm a-goin', an' I'm a-retirin' from *this* bizness for ever."

"Ain't a-goin' to turn evidence?" cried Cranks, grasping the pistol on the table.

"I'm a-goin' to make a lead-mine of *you* ef you don't take that back!" roared the colonel, with a bound, which caused Cranks to drop his pistol, and retire precipitately backward, apologizing as he went. "I'm goin' to tend to my own bizness, and that's enough to keep *any* man busy. Somebody lend me fifty, till I see him again?"

Perkins pressed the money into the colonel's hand, and within two minutes the colonel was on Tipsie's back, and galloping on in the direction the stage had taken. He overtook it, he passed it, and still he galloped on.

The people at Mud Gulch knew the colonel well, and made it a rule never to be astonished at anything he did; but they made an exception to the rule when the colonel canvassed the principal bar-rooms for men who wished to purchase a horse; and when a gambler, who was flush, obtained Tipsie in exchange for twenty slugs—only a thousand dollars, when the colonel had always said that there wasn't gold enough on top of the ground to buy her—Mud Gulch experienced a decided sensation.

One or two enterprising persons speedily discovered that the colonel was not in a communicative mood, so every one retired to his favorite saloon, and bet according to his own opinion of the colonel's motives and actions.

But when the colonel, after remaining in a barber-shop for half an hour, emerged with his face clean shaven and his hair neatly trimmed and parted, betting was so wild that a cool-headed sporting man speedily made a fortune by betting against every theory that was advanced.

Then the colonel made a tour of the stores, and fitted himself to a new suit of clothes, carefully eschewing all of the generous patterns and pronounced colors so dear to the average miner. He bought a new hat, put on a pair of boots, and pruned his finger-nails, and, stranger than all, he mildly but firmly declined all invitations to drink.

As the colonel stood in the door of the principal saloon, where the stage always stopped, the Challenge Hill constable was seen to approach the colonel, and tap him on the shoulder, upon which all men who had bet that the colonel was dodging somebody claimed the stakes. But those who stood near the colonel heard the constable say:

"Colonel, I take it all back, an' I own up fair an' square. When I seed you git out of Challenge Hill, it come to me all of a sudden that you might be in the road-agent business, so I followed you—duty, you know. But after I seed you sell Tipsie, I knowed I was on the wrong trail. I wouldn't suspect you now if all the stages in the State was robbed ; an' I'll give you satisfaction any way you want it."

"It's all right," said the colonel, with a smile. The constable afterward said that nobody had any idea of how curiously the colonel smiled when his beard was off. "Give this fifty to Jim Perkins fust time yer see him? I'm leavin' the State."

Suddenly the stage pulled up at the door with a crash, and the male passengers hurried into the saloon, in a state of utter indignation and impecuniosity.

The story of the robbery attracted everybody, and during the excitement the colonel slipped quietly out, and opened the door of the stage. The old lady started, and cried :

" George !"

And the colonel, jumping into the stage, and putting his arms tenderly about the trembling form of the old lady, exclaimed :

"Mother !"

THE OLD LADY CRIED, "GEORGE!" AND THE COLONEL EXCLAIMED, "MOTHER!"

THE HARDHACK MISTAKE.

EXCITEMENT ? The venerable Deacon Twinkham, the oldest inhabitant, said there had not been such an excitement at Hardhack since the meeting-house steeple blew down in a terrible equinoctial, forty-seven years before.

And who could wonder ?

Even a larger town than Hardhack would have experienced unusual agitation at seeing one of its own boys, who had a few years before gone away poor, slender and twenty, come back with broad shoulders, a full beard, and a pocketful of money, dug out of the ugly hills of Nevada.

But even the return of Nathan Brown, in so unusual a condition for a Hardhackian to be found in, was not the fullness of Hardhack's excitement, for Nathan had brought with him Tom Crewne and Harry Faxton, two friends he had made during his absence, and both of them broadshouldered, full-bearded, and auriferous as Nathan himself.

No wonder the store at Hardhack was all the while crowded with those who knew all about Nathan, or wanted to—no wonder that "Seen 'm ?" was the passing form of salutation for days.

The news spread like wildfire, and industrious farmers deliberately took a day, drove to town, and stood patiently on the door-steps of the store until they had seen one or more of the wonderful men.

The good Deacon Twinkham himself, who had, at a late prayer-meeting, stated that "his feet already felt the

splashin' of Jordan's waves," temporarily withdrew his aged
limbs from the rugged banks famed in song, and caused
them to bear him industriously up and down the Ridge
Road, past Nathan's mother's house, until he saw all three
of the bearded Crœsuses seat themselves on the piazza to
smoke.   Then he departed, his good face affording an excellent study for a "Simeon in the Temple."

Even the peaceful influences of the Sabbath were unable
to restore tranquillity to Hardhack.

On Sunday morning the meeting-house was fuller than
it had been since the funeral services of the last pastor.   At
each squeak of the door, every head was quickly turned ;
and when, in the middle of the first hymn, the three ex-
miners filed decorously in, the staring organist held one
chord of "Windham" so long that the breath of the congregation was entirely exhausted.

The very pulpit itself succombed to the popular excitement ; and the Reverend Abednego Choker, after reading of
the treasures of Solomon's Temple, and of the glories of the
New Testament, for the first and second lessons, preached
from Isaiah xlvi. 6 : "They lavish gold out of the bag and
weigh silver in the balance.".

But all this excitement was as nothing compared with
the tumult which agitated the tender hearts of the maidens
at Hardhack.

Young, old, handsome, plain, smart and stupid, until now
few of them had dared to hope for a change of name ; for,
while they possessed as many mental and personal charms
as girls in general, all the enterprising boys of Hardhack
had departed from their birthplace in search of the lucre
which Hardhack's barren hills and lean meadows failed to
supply, and the cause of their going was equally a preven-
tive of the coming of others to fill their places.

But now—oh, hope !—here were three young men, good-
looking, rich, and—if the other two were fit companions for
the well-born and bred Nathan—all safe custodians for
tender hearts.

Few girls were there in Hardhack who did not determine, in their innermost hearts, to strive as hard as Yankee wit and maiden modesty would allow for one of those tempting prizes.

Nor were they unaided. Rich and respectable sons-in-law are scarce enough the world over, so it was no wonder that all the parents of marriageable daughters strove to make Hardhack pleasant for the young men.

Fathers read up on Nevada, and cultivated the three ex-miners; mothers ransacked cook-books and old trunks; Ladies' Companions were industriously searched for pleasing patterns; crimping-irons and curling-tongs were extemporized, and the demand for ribbons and trimmings became so great that the storekeeper hurried to the city for a fresh supply.

Then began that season of mad hilarity and reckless dissipation, which seemed almost a dream to the actors themselves, and to which patriotic Hardhackians have since referred to with feelings like those of the devout Jew as he recalls the glorious deeds of his forefathers, or of the modern Roman as, from the crumbling arches of the Coliseum, he conjures up the mighty shade of the Cæsarian period.

The fragrant bohea flowed as freely as champagne would have done in a less pious locality; ethereal sponge-cakes and transparent currant-jellies became too common to excite comment; the surrounding country was heavily drawn upon for fatted calves, chickens and turkeys, and mince-pies were so plenty, that observing children wondered if the Governor had not decreed a whole year of special Thanksgiving.

Bravely the three great catches accepted every invitation, and, though it was a very unusual addition to his regular duties, the Reverend Abednego Choker faithfully attended all the evening festivities, to the end that they might be decorously closed with prayer, as had from time immemorial been the custom of Hardhack.

And the causes of all these efforts on the part of Hard-hack society enjoyed themselves intensely. Young men of respectable inclinations, who have lived for several years in a society composed principally of scoundrels, and modified only by the occasional presence of an honest miner or a respectable mule-driver, would have considered as Elysium a place far less proper and agreeable than Hardhack. In fact, the trio was so delighted, that its eligibility soon became diminished in quantity.

Faxton, at one of the first parties, made an unconditional surrender to a queenly damsel, while Nathan, having found his old schoolday sweetheart still unmarried, whispered something in her ear (probably the secret of some rare cosmetic), which filled her cheeks with roses from that time forth.

But Crewne, the handsomest and most brilliant of the three, still remained, and over him the fight was far more intense than in the opening of the campaign, when weapons were either rusty or untried, and the chances of success were seemingly more numerous.

But to designate any particular lady as surest of success seemed impossible. Even Nathan and Faxton, when besought for an opinion by the two ladies who now claimed their innermost thoughts, could only say that no one but Crewne knew, and perhaps even *he* didn't.

Crewne was a very odd boy, they said—excellent company, the best of good fellows, the staunchest of friends, and the very soul of honor; but there were some things about him they never *could* understand. In fact, he was something like that sum of all impossibilities, a schoolgirl's hero.   •

"But, Harry," said the prospective Mrs. Faxton, with rather an angry pout for a Church-member in full communion, "just see what splendid girls are dying for him! I'm sure there are no nicer girls anywhere than in Hardhack, and he needn't be so stuck up——"

"My dear," interrupted Faxton, "I say it with fear and

trembling, but perhaps Crewne don't want to be in love at all."

An indignant flash of doubt went over the lady's face.

"Just notice him at a party," continued Faxton. "He seems to distribute his attentions with exact equality among all the ladies present, as if he were trying to discourage the idea that he was a marrying man."

"Well," said the lady, still indignant, "I think you might ask him and settle the matter."

"Excuse me, my dear," replied Faxton. "I have seen others manifest an interest in Crewne's affairs, and the result was discouraging. I'd rather not try the experiment."

A few mornings later Mrs. Leekins, who took the place of a newspaper at Hardhack, was seen hurrying from house to house on her own street, and such housekeepers as saw her instantly discovered that errands must be made to houses directly in Mrs. Leekins's route.

Mrs. Leekins's story was soon told. Crewne had suddenly gone to the city, first purchasing the cottage which Deacon Twinkham had built several years before for a son who had never come back from sea.

Crewne had hired old Mrs. Bruff to put the cottage to rights, and to arrange the carpets and furniture, which he was to forward immediately. But who was to be mistress of the cottage Mrs. Leekins was unable to tell, or even to guess.

The clerks at the store had been thoroughly pumped; but while they admitted that one young lady had purchased an unusual quantity of inserting, another had ordered a dress pattern of gray empress cloth, which was that year the fashionable material and color for traveling dresses.

Old Mrs. Bruff had received unusual consideration and unlimited tea, but even the most systematic question failed to elicit from her anything satisfactory.

At any rate, it was certain that Crewne was absent from Hardhack, and it was evident that *he* had decided who was to be the lady of the cottage, so the season of festivity was brought to an abrupt close, and the digestions of Hardhack were snatched from ruin.

From kitchen-windows were now wafted odors of boiled corned beef and stewed apples, instead of the fragrance of delicate preserves and delicious turkey.

Young ladies, when they met in the street, greeted each other with a shade less of cordiality than usual, and fathers and mothers in Israel cast into each other's eyes searching and suspicious glances.

One afternoon, when the pious matrons of Hardhack were gathering at the pastor's residence to take part in the regular weekly mothers' prayer-meeting, the mail-coach rolled into town, and Mrs. Leekins, who was sitting by the window, as she always did, exclaimed:

"He's come back—there he is—on the seat with the driver!"

Every one hurried to the window, and saw that Mrs. Leekins had spoken truly, for there sat Crewne with a pleasant smile on his face, while on top of the stage were several large trunks marked C.

"Must have got a handsome fit-out," suggested Mrs. Leekins.

The stage stopped at the door of Crewne's new cottage, and Crewne got out. The pastor entered the parlor to open the meeting, and was selecting a hymn, when Mrs. Leekins startled the meeting by ejaculating:

"Lands alive!"

The meeting was demoralized; the sisters hastened to the window, and the good pastor, laying down his hymn-book, followed in time to see Crewne helping out a well-dressed and apparently young and handsome lady.

"Hardhack girls not good 'nough for him, it seems!" sneered Mrs. Leekins.

A resigned and sympathetic sigh broke from the motherly lips present, then Mrs. Leekins cried:

"Gracious sakes! married a widder with children!"

It certainly seemed that she told the truth, for Crewne

THE SISTERS HASTENED TO THE WINDOW.

lifted out two children, the youngest of whom seemed not more than three years old.

The gazers abruptly left the window, and the general tone of the meeting was that of melancholy resignation.

*　　*　　*　　*　　*　　*　　*

"Why didn't he ever say he was a married man?" asked the prospective Mrs. Faxton, of her lover, that evening.

"Partly because he is too much of a gentleman to talk of his own affairs," replied Faxton; "but principally because there had been, as he told me this afternoon, an unfortunate quarrel between them, which drove him to the mines. A few days ago he heard from her, for the first time in three years, and they've patched up matters, and are very happy."

"Well," said the lady, with considerable decision, "Hardhack will never forgive him."

"Hardhack did, however, for Crewne and his two friends drew about them a few of their old comrades, who took unto themselves wives from the people about them, and made of Hardhack one of the pleasantest villages in the State.

THE CARMI CHUMS.

THE Carmi Chums was the name they went by all along the river. Most other roustabouts had each a name of his own; so had the Carmi Chums for that matter, but the men themselves were never mentioned individually—always collectively.

No steamboat captain who wanted only a single man ever attempted to hire half of the Carmi Chums at a time—as easy would it have been to have hired half of the Siamese Twins. No steamboat mate who knew them ever attempted to "tell off" the Chums into different watches, and any mate who, not knowing them, committed this blunder, and adhered to it after explanation was made, was sure to be two men short immediately after leaving the steamer's next landing.

There seemed no possible way of separating them; they never fell out with each other in the natural course of events; they never fought when drunk, as other friendly roustabouts sometimes did, for the Carmi Chums never got drunk; there never sprang up any coolness between them because of love for the same lady, for they did not seem to care at all for female society, unless they happened to meet some old lady whom one might love as a mother rather than as a sweetheart.

Even professional busybodies, from whose presence roustabouts are no freer than Church-members, were unable to provoke the Carmi Chums even to suspicion, and those of them who attempted it too persistently were likely to have a difficulty with the slighter of the Chums.

This man, who was called Black, because of the color of his hair, was apparently forty years of age, and of very ordinary appearance, except when an occasional furtive, frightened look came into his face and attracted attention.

His companion, called Red, because his hair was of the hue of the carrots, and because it was occasionally necessary to distinguish him from his friend, seemed of about the same age and degree of ordinaries as Black, but was rather stouter, more cheery, and, to use the favorite roustabout simile, held his head closer to the current.

He seemed, when Black was absent-minded (as he generally was while off duty), to be the leading spirit of the couple, and to be tenderly alive to all of his partner's needs ; but observing roustabouts noticed that when freight was being moved, or wood taken on board, Black was always where he could keep an eye on his chum, and where he could demand instant reparation from any wretch who trod upon Red's toes, or who, with a shoulder-load of wood, grazed Red's head, or touched Red with a box or barrel.

Next to neighborly wonder as to the existence of the friendship between the Chums, roustabouts with whom the couple sailed concerned themselves most with the cause of the bond between them. Their searches after first causes were no more successful, however, than those of the naturalists who are endeavoring to ascertain who laid the cosmic egg.

They gave out that they came from Carmi, so, once or twice, when captains with whom the Chums were engaged determined to seek a cargo up the Wabash, upon which river Carmi was located, inquisitive roustabouts became light-hearted. But, alas, for the vanity of human hopes! when the boat reached Carmi the Chums could not be found, nor could any inhabitant of Carmi identify them by the descriptions which were given by inquiring friends.

At length they became known, in their collective capa-

city, as one of the institutions of the river. Captains knew
them as well as they knew Natchez or Piankishaw Bend,
and showed them to distinguished passengers as regularly
as they showed General Zach. Taylor's plantation, or the
scene of the Grand Gulf "cave," where a square mile of
Louisiana dropped into the river one night. Captains
rather cultivated them, in fact, although it was a difficult
bit of business, for roustabouts who wouldn't say "thank
you" for a glass of French brandy, or a genuine, old-fashioned "plantation cigar," seemed destitute of ᴜrdinary
handles of which a steamboat captain could take hold.

Lady passengers took considerable notice of them, and
were more successful than any one else at drawing them
into conversation. The linguistic accomplishments of the
Chums were not numerous, but it did one good to see Black
lose his scared, furtive look when a lady addressed him,
and to see the affectionate deference with which he appealed
to Red, until that worthy was drawn into the conversation.
When Black succeeded in this latter-named operation, he
would, by insensible stages, draw himself away, and give
himself up to enthusiastic admiration of his partner, or,
apparently, of his conversational ability.

The Spring of 1869 found the Chums in the crew of the
Bennett, "the peerless floating palace of the Mississippi,"
as she was called by those newspapers whose reporters had
the freedom of the *Bennett's* bar ; and the same season saw
the *Bennett* staggering down the Mississippi with so heavy
a load of sacked corn, that the gunwales amidships were
fairly under water.

The river was very low, so the *Bennett* kept carefully in
the channel ; but the channel of the great muddy ditch which
drains half the Union is as fickle as disappointed lovers
declare women to be, and it has no more respect for great
steamer-loads of corn than Goliath had for David.

A little Ohio river-boat, bound upward, had reported
the sudden disappearance of a woodyard a little way above
Milliken's Bend, where the channel hugged the shore, and

with the woodyard there had disappeared an enormous sycamore-tree, which had for years served as a tying-post for steamers.

As live sycamores are about as disinclined to float as bars of lead are, the captain and pilot of the *Bennett* were somewhat concerned—for the sake of the corn—to know the exact location of the tree.

Half a mile from the spot it became evident, even to the passengers clustered forward on the cabin-deck, that the sycamore had remained quite near to its old home, for a long, rough ripple was seen directly across the line of the channel.

Then arose the question as to how much water was on top of the tree, and whether any bar had had time to accumulate.

The steamer was stopped, the engines were ·reversed and worked by hand to keep the *Bennett* from drifting downstream, a boat was lowered and manned, the Chums forming part of her crew, and the second officer went down to take soundings ; while the passengers, to whom even so small a cause for excitement was a godsend, crowded the rail and stared.

The boat shot rapidly down stream, headed for the shore-end of the ripple. She seemed almost into the boiling mud in front of her when the passengers on the steamer heard the mate in the boat shout : "Back all !"

The motion of the oars changed in an instant, but a little too late, for, a heavy root of the fallen giant, just covered by the water, caught the little craft, and caused it to career so violently that one man was thrown into the water. As she righted, another man went in.

"Confound it !" growled the captain, who was leaning out of the pilot-house window. I hope they can swim. Still, 'tain't as bad as it would be if we had any more cargo to take aboard."

"It's the Chums," remarked the pilot, who had brought a glass to bear upon the boat.

"Thunder!" exclaimed the captain, striking a bell. "Below there! Lower away another boat—lively!" Then, turning to the passengers, he exclaimed: "Nobody on the river'd forgive me if I lost the Chums. 'Twould be as bad as Barnum losing the giraffe."

The occupants of the first boat were evidently of the captain's own mind, for they were eagerly peering over her side, and into the water.

Suddenly the pilot dropped his glass, extemporized a trumpet with both hands, and shouted:

"Forrard—forrard! One of 'em's up!" Then he put his mouth to the speaking-tube, and screamed to the engineer: "Let her drop down a little, Billy!"

The sounding party headed toward a black speck, apparently a hundred yards below them, and the great steamer slowly drifted down-stream. The speck moved toward shore, and the boat, rapidly shortening distance, seemed to scrape the bank with her port oars.

"Safe enough now, I guess!" exclaimed Judge Turner, of one of the Southern Illinois circuits.

The Judge had been interrupted in telling a story when the accident occurred, and was in a hurry to resume.

"As I was saying," said he, "he hardly looked like a professional horse-thief. He was little and quiet, and had always worked away steadily at his trade. I believed him when he said 'twas his first offense, and that he did it to raise money to bury his child; and I was going to give him an easy sentence, and ask the .Governor to pardon him. The laws have to be executed, you know, but there's no law against mercy being practiced afterward. Well, the sheriff was bringing him from jail to hear the verdict and the sentence, when the short man, with red hair, knocked the sheriff down, and off galloped that precious couple for the Wabash. I saw the entire——"

"The deuce!" interrupted the pilot, again dropping his glass.

The Judge glared angrily; the passengers saw, across

the shortened distance, one of the Chums holding by a root to the bank, and trying to support the other, whose shirt hung in rags, and who seemed exhausted.

"Which one's hurt?" asked the captain. "Give me the glass."

But the pilot had left the house and taken the glass with him.

The Judge continued:

"I saw the whole transaction through the window. I was so close that I saw the sheriff's assailant's very eyes. I'd know that fellow's face if I saw it in Africa."

"Why, they're *both* hurt!" exclaimed the captain. "They've thrown a coat over one, and they're crowdin' around the other. What the—— They're comin' back without 'em — need whisky to bring 'em to, I suppose. Why didn't I send whisky down by the other boat? There's an awful amount of time being wasted here. What's the matter, Mr. Bell?" shouted the captain, as the boat approached the steamer.

"Both dead!" replied the officer.

"Both? Now, ladies and gentlemen," exclaimed the captain, turning toward the passengers, who were crowded forward just below him, "I want to know if that isn't a streak of the meanest kind of luck? Both the Chums gone! Why, I won't be able to hold up my head in New Orleans. How came it that just those two fellows were knocked out?"

"Red tumbled out, and Black jumped in after him," replied the officer. "Red must have been caught in an eddy and tangled in the old tree's roots—clothes torn almost off —head caved in. Black must have burst a blood-vessel— his face looked like a copper pan when he reached shore, and he just groaned and dropped."

The captain was sorry, so sorry that he sent a waiter for brandy. But the captain was human—business was business—the rain was falling, and a big log was across the boat's bow; so he shouted:

"Hurry up and bury 'em, then. You ought to have let the second boat's crew gone on with that, and you have gone back to your soundings. They *was* the Chums, to be sure, but now they're only dead roustabouts. Below there! Pass out a couple of shovels!"

"Perhaps some ladies would go down with the boat, captain—and a preacher, too, if there's one aboard," remarked the mate, with an earnest but very mysterious expression.

"Why, what in thunder does the fellow mean?" soliloquized the captain, audibly. "Women—and a preacher—for dead roustabouts? What do you mean, Mr. Bell?"

"Red's a woman," briefly responded the mate.

The passengers all started—the captain brought his hands together with a tremendous clap, and exclaimed:

"Murder will out! But who'd have thought *I* was to be the man to find out the secret of the Carmi Chums? Guess I'll be the biggest man on the New Orleans levee, after all. Yes, certainly—of course some ladies'll go—and a preacher, too, if there's such a man aboard. Hold up, though—we'll *all* go. Take your soundings, quick, and we'll drop the steamer just below the point, and tie up. I wonder if there's a preacher aboard?"

No one responded for the moment; then the Judge spoke.

"Before I went into the law I was the regularly settled pastor of a Presbyterian Church," said he. "I'm decidedly rusty now, but a little time will enable me to prepare myself properly. Excuse me, ladies and gentlemen."

The sounding-boat pulled away, and the Judge retired to his stateroom. The ladies, with very pale faces, gathered in a group and whispered earnestly with each other; then ensued visits to each other's staterooms, and the final regathering of the ladies with two or three bundles. The soundings were taken, and, as the steamer dropped downstream, men were seen cutting a path down the rather steep clay bank. The captain put his hands to his mouth and shouted:

Dig only *one* grave—make it wide enough for two."

And all the passengers nodded assent and satisfaction.

Time had been short since the news reached the steamer, but the *Bennett's* carpenter, who was himself a married man, had made a plain coffin by the time the boat tied up, and another by the time the grave was dug. The first one was put upon a long handbarrow, over which the captain had previously spread a tablecloth, and, followed by the ladies, was deposited by the side of the body of Red. Half an hour later, the men placed Black in the other coffin, removed both to the side of the grave, and signalled the boat.

"Now, ladies and gentlemen," said the captain.

The Judge appeared with a very solemn face, his coat buttoned tight to his throat, and the party started. Colonel May, of Missouri, who read Voltaire and didn't believe in anything, maliciously took the Judge's arm, and remarked:

"You didn't finish your story, Judge."

The Judge frowned reprovingly.

"But, really," persisted the colonel, "I don't want curiosity to divert my mind from the solemn services about to take place. Do tell me if they ever caught the rascals."

"They never did," replied the Judge. "The sheriff hunted and advertised, but he could never hear a word of either of them. But I'd know either one of them at sight. Sh—h——here we are at the grave."

The passengers, officers, and crew gathered about the grave. The Judge removed his hat, and, as the captain uncovered the faces of the dead, commenced:

"'I am the resurrection and the life'—Why, there's the horse-thief now, colonel! I beg your pardon, ladies and gentlemen. 'He that believeth in——'"

Just then the Judge's eye fell upon the dead woman's face, and he screamed:

"And there's the sheriff's assailant!"

LITTLE GUZZY.

BOWERTON was a very quiet place. It had no factories, mills, or mines, or other special inducements to offer people looking for new localities; and as it was not on a railroad line, nor even on an important post-road, it gained but few new inhabitants.

Even of travelers Bowerton saw very few. An occasional enterprising peddler or venturesome thief found his way to the town, and took away such cash as came in their way while pursuing their respective callings; but peddlers were not considered exactly trustworthy as news-bearers, while house-breakers, when detained long enough to be questioned, were not in that communicative frame of mind which is essential to one who would interest the general public.

When, therefore, the mail-coach one day brought to Bowerton an old lady and a young one, who appeared to be mother and daughter, excitement ran high.

The proprietor of the Bowerton House, who was his own clerk, hostler, and table-waiter, was for a day or two the most popular man in town; even the three pastors of the trio of churches of Bowerton did not consider it beneath their dignity to join the little groups which were continually to be seen about the person of the landlord, and listening to the meagre intelligence he was able to give.

The old lady was quite feeble, he said, and the daughter was very affectionate and very handsome. He didn't know where they were going, but they registered themselves from Boston. Name was Wyett—young lady's name was Helen.

He hoped they wouldn't leave for a long time—travelers weren't any too plenty at Bowerton, and landlords found it hard work to scratch along. Talked about locating at Bowerton if they could find a suitable cottage. Wished 'em well, but hoped they'd take their time, and not be in a hurry to leave the Bowerton House, where—if *he* did say it as shouldn't —they found good rooms and good board at the lowest living price.

The Wyetts finally found a suitable cottage, and soon afterward they began to receive heavy packages and boxes from the nearest railway station.

Then it was that the responsible gossips of Bowerton were worked nearly to death, but each one was sustained by a fine professional pride which enabled them to pass creditably through the most exciting period.

For years they had skillfully pried into each other's private affairs, but then they had some starting-place, some clue ; now, alas ! there was not in all Bowerton a single person who had emigrated from Boston, where the Wyetts had lived. Worse still, there was not a single Bowertonian who had a Boston correspondent.

To be sure, one of the Bowerton pastors had occasional letters from a missionary board, whose headquarters were at the Hub, but not even the most touching appeals from members of his flock could induce him to write the board concerning the newcomers.

But Bowerton was not to be balked in its striving after accurate intelligence.

From Squire Brown, who leased Mrs. Wyett a cottage, it was learned that Mrs. Wyett had made payment by check on an excellent Boston bank. The poor but respectable female who washed the floors of the cottage informed the public that the whole first floor was to be carpeted with Brussels.

The postmaster's clerk ascertained and stated that Mrs. Wyett received *two* religious papers per week, whereas no one else in Bowerton took more than one.

The grocer said that Mrs. Wyett was, by jingo, the sort of person *he* liked to trade with—wouldn't have anything that wasn't the very best.

The man who helped to do the unpacking was willing to take oath that among the books were a full set of Barnes, Notes, and two sets of commentaries, while Mrs. Battle, who lived in the house next to the cottage, and who was suddenly, on hearing the crashing of crockery next door, moved to neighborly kindness to the extent of carrying in a nice hot pie to the newcomers, declared that, as she hoped to be saved, there wasn't a bit of crockery in that house which wasn't pure china.

Bowerton asked no more. Brussels carpets, religious tendencies, a bank account, the ability to live on the best that the market afforded, and to eat it from china, and china only—why, either one of these qualifications was a voucher of respectability, and any two of them constituted a patent of aristocracy of the Bowerton standard.

Bowerton opened its doors, and heartily welcomed Mrs. and Miss Wyett.

It is grievous to relate, but the coming of the estimable people was the cause of considerable trouble in Bowerton.

Bowerton, like all other places, contained lovers, and some of the young men were not so blinded by the charms of their own particular lady friends as to be oblivious to the beauty of Miss Wyett.

She was extremely modest and retiring, but she was also unusually handsome and graceful, and she had an expression which the young men of Bowerton could not understand, but which they greatly admired.

It was useless for plain girls to say that they couldn't see anything remarkable about Miss Wyett; it was equally unavailing for good-looking girls to caution their gallants against too much of friendly regard even for a person of whose antecedents they really knew scarcely anything.

Even casting chilling looks at Miss Wyett when they met her failed to make that unoffending young lady any less attractive to the young men of Bowerton, and critical analysis of Miss Wyett's style of dressing only provoked manly comparisons, which were as exasperating as they were unartistic.

Finally Jack Whiffer, who was of a first family, and was a store-clerk besides, proposed to Miss Wyett and was declined ; then the young ladies of Bowerton thought that perhaps Helen Wyett had some sense after all.

Then young Baggs, son of a deceased Congressman, wished to make Miss Wyett mistress of the Baggs mansion and sharer of the Baggs money, but his offer was rejected.

Upon learning this fact, the maidens of Bowerton pronounced Helen a noble-spirited girl to refuse to take Baggs away from the dear, abused woman who had been engaged to him for a long time.

Several other young men had been seen approaching the Wyett cottage in the full glory of broadcloth and hair-oil, and were noticeably depressed in spirits for days afterward, and the native ladies of marriageable age were correspondingly elated when they heard of it.

When at last the one unmarried minister of Bowerton, who had been the desire of many hearts, manfully admitted that he had proposed and been rejected, and that Miss Wyett had informed him that she was already engaged, all the Bowerton girls declared that Helen Wyett was a darling old thing, and that it was perfectly shameful that she couldn't be let alone.

After thus proving that their own hearts were in the right place, all the Bowerton girls asked each other who the lucky man could be.

Of course he couldn't be a Bowerton man, for Miss Wyett was seldom seen in company with *any* gentleman. He must be a Boston man—he was probably very literary—Boston men always were.

Besides, if he was at all fit for her, he must certainly be very handsome.

Suddenly Miss Wyett became the rage among the Bowerton girls. Blushingly and gushingly they told her of their own loves, and they showed her their lovers, or pictures of those gentlemen.

Miss Wyett listened, smiled and sympathized, but when they sat silently expectant of similar confidences, they were disappointed, and when they endeavored to learn even the slightest particular of Helen Wyett's love, she changed the subject of conversation so quickly and decidedly that they had not the courage to renew the attempt.

But while most Bowertonians despaired of learning much more about the Wyetts, and especially about Helen's lover, there was one who had resolved not only to know the favored man, but to do him some frightful injury, and that was little Guzzy.

Though Guzzy's frame was small, his soul was immense, and Helen's failure to comprehend Guzzy's greatness when he laid it all at her feet had made Guzzy extremely bilious and gloomy.

Many a night, when Guzzy's soul and body should have been taking their rest, they roamed in company up and down the quiet street on which the Wyetts' cottage was located, and Guzzy's eyes, instead of being fixed on sweet pictures in dreamland, gazed vigilantly in the direction of Mrs. Wyett's gate.

He did not meditate inflicting personal violence on the hated wretch who had snatched away Helen from his hopes —no, personal violence could produce suffering but feeble compared with that under which the victim would writhe as Guzzy poured forth the torrent of scornful invective which he had compiled from the memories of his bilious brain and the pages of his "Webster Unabridged."

At length there came a time when most men would have despaired.

Love is warm, but what warmth is proof against the chilling blasts and pelting rains of the equinoctial storm?

But then it was that the fervor of little Guzzy's soul showed itself; for, wrapped in the folds of a waterproof overcoat, he paced his accustomed beat with the calmness of a faithful policeman.

And he had his reward.

As one night he stood unseen against the black background of a high wall, opposite the residence of Mrs. Wyett, he heard the gate—*her* gate—creak on its hinges.

It could be no ordinary visitor, for it was after nine o'clock —it must be *he.*

Ha! the lights were out! He would be disappointed, the villain! Now was the time, while his heart would be bleeding with sorrow, to wither him with reproaches. To be sure, he seemed a large man, while Guzzy was very small, but Guzzy believed his own thin legs to be faithful in an emergency.

The unknown man knocked softly at the front-door, then he seemed to tap at several of the windows.

Suddenly he raised one of the windows, and Guzzy, who had not until then suspected that he had been watching a house-breaker, sped away like the wind and alarmed the solitary constable of Bowerton.

That functionary requested Guzzy to notify Squire Jones, justice of the peace, that there was business ahead, and then hastened away himself.

Guzzy labored industriously for some moments, for Squire Jones was very old, and very cautious, and very stupid; but he was at last fully aroused, and then Guzzy had an opportunity to reflect on the greatness which would be his when Bowerton knew of his meritorious action.

And Helen Wyett—what would be her shame and contrition when she learned that the man whose love she had rejected had become the preserver of her peace of mind and her portable personal property?

He could not exult over *her,* for that would be unchivalrous; but would not her own conscience reproach her bitterly?

Perhaps she would burst into tears in the court-room, and thank him effusively and publicly! Guzzy's soul swelled at the thought, and he rapidly composed a reply appropriate to such an occasion. Suddenly Guzzy heard footsteps approaching, and voices in earnest altercation.

Guzzy hastened into the squire's office, and struck an attitude befitting the importance of a principal witness.

An instant later the constable entered, followed by two smart-looking men, who had between them a third man, securely handcuffed.

The prisoner was a very handsome, intelligent-looking young man, except for a pair of restless, over-bright eyes.

"There's a difference of opinion 'bout who the prisoner belongs to," said the constable, addressing the squire; and we agreed to leave the matter to you. When I reached the house, these gentlemen already had him in hand, and they claim he's an escaped convict, and that they've tracked him from the prison right straight to Bowerton."

The prisoner gave the officers a very wicked look, while these officials produced their warrants and handed them to the justice for inspection.

Guzzy seemed to himself to grow big with accumulating importance.

"The officers seem to be duly authorized," said the squire, after a long and minute examination of their papers; "but they should identify the prisoner as the escaped convict for whom they are searching."

"Here's a description," said one of the officers, "in an advertisement: 'Escaped from the Penitentiary, on the —th instant, William Beigh, *alias* Bay Billy, *alias* Handsome; age, twenty-eight; height, five feet ten; complexion dark, hair black, eyes dark brown, mole on left cheek; general appearance handsome, manly, and intelligent. A skillful and dangerous burglar. Sentenced in 1866 to five years' imprisonment—two years yet to serve.' That," continued the officer, "describes him to a dot; and, if there's any further doubt, look here!"

As he spoke, he unclasped a cloak which the prisoner wore, and disclosed the striped uniform of the prison.

"There seems no reasonable doubt in this case, and the prisoner will have to go back to prison," said the justice. "But I must detain him until I ascertain whether he has stolen anything from Mrs. Wyett's residence. In case he has done so, we can prosecute at the expiration of his term."

The prisoner seemed almost convulsed with rage, though of a sort which one of the officers whispered to the other ho did not exactly understand.

Guzzy eyed him resentfully, and glared at the officers with considerable disfavor.

Guzzy was a law-abiding man, but to have an expected triumph belittled and postponed because of foreign interference was enough to blind almost *any* man's judicial eyesight.

"Well," said one of the officers, "put him in the lock-up' and investigate in the morning; we won't want to start until then, after the tramp he's given us. Oh, Bay Billy, you're a smart one—no mistake about that. Why in thunder don't you use your smartness in the right way?—there's more money in business than in cracking cribs."

"Besides the moral advantage," added the squire, who was deacon as well, and who, now that he had concluded his official duties, was not adverse to laying down the higher law.

"Just so," exclaimed the officer; "and for his family's sake, too. Why, would you believe it, judge? they say Billy has one of the finest wives in the commonwealth—handsome, well-educated, religious, rich, and of good family. Of course she didn't know what his profession was when she married him."

Again the prisoner seemed convulsed with that strange rage which the officer did not understand. But the officers were tired, and they were too familiar with the disapprobation of prisoners to be seriously affected by it; so, after an appointment by the squire, and a final glare of indignation from little Guzzy, they started, under the constable's guidance, to the lock-up.

18

Suddenly the door was thrown open, and there appeared, with uncovered head, streaming hair, weeping yet eager eyes, and mud-splashed garments, Helen Wyett.

"WE MAY AS WELL FINISH THIS CASE TO-NIGHT, IF MISS WYETT IS PREPARED TO TESTIFY," SAID THE JUDGE.

Every one started, the officers stared, the squire looked a degree or two less stupid, and hastened to button his dressing-gown; the restless eyes of the convict fell on

Helen's beautiful face, and were restless no longer; while
little Guzzy assumed a dignified pose, which did not seem
at all consistent with his confused and shamefaced countenance.

"We may as well finish this case to-night, if Miss Wyett
is prepared to testify," said the squire, at length. "Have
you lost anything, Miss Wyett?"

"No," said Helen; "but I have found my dearest treasure—my own husband!"

And putting her arms around the convict's neck, she
kissed him, and then, dropping her head upon his shoulder,
she sobbed violently.

The squire was startled into complete wakefulness, and
as the moral aspect of the scene presented itself to him, he
groaned :

"Onequally yoked with an onbeliever."

The officers looked as if they were depraved yet remorse-
ful convicts themselves, while little Guzzy's diminutive di-
mensions seemed to contract perceptibly.

At length the convict quieted his wife, and persuaded
her to return to her home, with a promise from the officers
that she should see him in the morning.

Then the officers escorted the prisoner to the jail, and
Guzzy sneaked quietly out, while the squire retired to his
slumbers, with the firm conviction that if Solomon had been
a justice of the peace at Bowerton, his denial of the newness
of anything under the sun would never have been made.

Now, the jail at Bowerton, like everything else in the
town, was decidedly antiquated, and consisted simply of a
thickly-walled room in a building which contained several
offices and living apartments.

It was as extensive a jail as Bowerton needed, and was
fully strong enough to hold the few drunken and quarrelsome people who were occasionally lodged in it.

But Beigh, *alias* Bay Billy, *alias* Handsome, was no ordinary and vulgar jail-bird, the officers told him, and, that he
and they might sleep securely, they considered it advisable
to carefully iron his hands.

A couple of hours rolled away, and left Beigh still sitting moody and silent on the single bedstead in the Bowerton jail.

Suddenly the train of his thoughts was interrupted by a low "stt—stt" from the one little, high, grated window of the jail."

The prisoner looked up quickly, and saw the shadow of a man's head outside the grating.

"Hello!" whispered Beigh, hurrying under the window.

"Are you alone?" inquired the shadow.

"Yes," replied the prisoner.

"All right, then," whispered the voice. "There *are* secrets which no vulgar ears should hear. My name is Guzzy. I have been in love with your wife. I hadn't any idea she was married; but I've brought you my apology."

"I'll forgive you," whispered the criminal; but——"

"'Tain't that kind of apology," whispered Guzzy. "It's a steel one—a tool—one of those things that gunsmiths shorten gun-barrels with. If they can saw a rifle-barrel in two in five minutes, you ought to get out of here inside of an hour."

"Not quite," whispered Beigh. "My hands and feet are ironed."

"Then I'll do the job myself," whispered Guzzy, as he applied the tool to one of the bars; for it will be daylight within two hours."

The unaccustomed labor—for Guzzy was a bookkeeper—made his arms ache severely, but still he sawed away.

He wondered what his employer would say should he be found out, but still he sawed.

Visions of the uplifted hands and horror-struck countenances of his brother Church-members came before his eyes, and the effect of his example upon his Sunday-school class, should he be discovered, tormented his soul; but neither of these influences affected his saw.

Bar after bar disappeared, and when Guzzy finally stopped to rest, Beigh saw a small square of black sky, unobstructed by any bars whatever.

"Now," whispered Guzzy, "I'll drop in a small box you can stand on, so you can put your hands out and let me file off your irons. I brought a file or two, thinking they might come handy."

Five minutes later the convict, his hands unbound, crawled through the window, and was helped to the ground by Guzzy.

Seizing the file from the little bookkeeper, Beigh commenced freeing his feet. Suddenly he stopped and whispered:

"You'd better go now. I can take care of myself, but if those cursed officers should take a notion to look around, it would go hard with *you*. Run, God bless you, run!"

But little Guzzy straightened himself and folded his arms.

The convict rasped away rapidly, and finally dropped the file and the fragments of the last fetter. Then he seized little Guzzy's hand.

"My friend," said he, "criminal though I am, I am man enough to appreciate your manliness and honor. I think I am smart enough to keep myself free, now I am out of jail. But, if ever you want a friend, tell Helen, *she* will know where I am, and I will serve you, no matter what the risk and pain."

"Thank you," said Guzzy; "but the only favor I'll ever ask of you might as well be named now, and you ought to be able to do it without risk or pain either. It's only this: be an honest man, for Helen's sake."

Beigh dropped his head.

"There *are* men who would die daily for the sake of making her happy, but you've put it out of their power, seeing you've married her," continued Guzzy. "*I'm* nothing to her, and can't be, but for her sake to-night I've broken open the gunsmith's shop, broken a jail, and "—here he stooped, and picked up a bundle—" robbed my own employer's store of a suit of clothes for you, so you mayn't be caught again in those prison stripes. If I've made myself a criminal for her sake: can't her husband be an honest man for the same reason ?"

The convict wrung the hand of his preserver. He seemed to be trying to speak, but to have some great obstruction in his throat.

Suddenly a bright light shone on the two men, and a voice was heard exclaiming, in low but very ferocious tones:

"Do it, you scoundrel, or I'll put a bullet through your head !"

Both men looked up to the window of the cell, and saw a bull's-eye lantern, the muzzle of a pistol, and the face of the Bowerton constable.

The constable's right eye, the sights of his pistol and the breast of the convict were on the same visual line.

Without altering his position or that of his weapon, the constable whispered :

"I've had you covered for the last ten minutes. I only held in to find out who was helping you ; but I heard too much for *my* credit as a faithful officer. Now, what are you going to do ?"

"Turn over a new leaf," said the convict, bursting into tears.

"Then get out," whispered the officer, "and be lively, too—it's almost daybreak."

"I'll tell you what to do," said little Guzzy, when the constable hurriedly whispered :

"Wait until *I* get out of hearing."

*   *   *   *   *   *   *

The excitement which possessed Bowerton the next morning, when the events of the previous night were made public, was beyond the descriptive powers of the best linguists in the village.

Helen Wyett a burglar's wife !

At first the Bowertonians scarcely knew whether it would be proper to recognize her at all, and before they were able to arrive at a conclusion the intelligence of the convict's escape, the breaking open of the gunsmith's shop, the finding of the front door of Cashing's store ajar, and the discovery by Cashing that at least one suit of valuable clothing had been taken, came upon the astonished villagers and rendered them incapable of reason, and of every other mental attribute except wonder.

That the prisoner had an accomplice seemed certain, and some suspicious souls suggested that the prisoner's wife *might* have been the person ; but as one of the officers declared he had watched her house all night for fear of some such attempt, that theory was abandoned.

Under the guidance of the constable, who zealously assisted them in every possible manner, the officers searched every house in Bowerton that might seem likely to afford a hiding-place, and then departed on what they considered the prisoner's most likely route.

For some days Helen Wyett gave the Bowertonians no occasion to modify their conduct toward her, for she kept herself constantly out of sight.

When, however, she did appear in the street again, she met only the kindest looks and salutations, for the venerable Squire Jones had talked incessantly in praise of her courage and affection, and the Squire's fellow-townsmen knew that when their principal magistrate was affected to tenderness and mercy, it was from causes which would have simply overwhelmed any ordinary mortal.

It was months before Bowerton gossip descended again to its normal level; for a few weeks after the escape of Baigh, little Guzzy, who had never been supposed to have unusual credit, and whose family certainly hadn't any money, left his employer and started an opposition store.

Next to small scandal, finance was the favorite burden of conversation at Bowerton, so the source of Guzzy's sudden prosperity was so industriously sought and surmised that the gossips were soon at needles' points about it.

Then it was suddenly noised abroad that Mrs. Baggs, Sr., who knew everybody, had given Guzzy a letter of introduction to the Governor of the State.

Bowerton was simply confounded. What *could* he want? The Governor had very few appointments at his disposal, and none of them were fit for Guzzy, except those for which Guzzy was not fit.

Even the local politicians became excited, and both sides consulted Guzzy.

Finally, when Guzzy started for the State capital, and Helen Wyett, as people still called her, accompanied him, the people of Bowerton put on countenances of hopeless resignation, and of a mute expectation which nothing could astonish.

It might be an elopement—it might be that they were going as missionaries; but no one expressed a positive opinion, and every one expressed a perfect willingness to believe anything that was supported by even a shadow of proof.

Their mute agony was suddenly ended, for within forty-eight hours Guzzy and his traveling companion returned.

The latter seemed unusually happy for the wife of a convict, while the former went straight to Squire Jones and the constable's.

Half an hour later all Bowerton knew that William Beigh, *alias* Bay Billy, *alias* Handsome, had received a full and free pardon from the Governor.

The next day Bowerton saw a tall, handsome stranger, with downcast eyes, walk rapidly through the principal street and disappear behind Mrs. Wyett's gate.

A day later, and Bowerton was electrified by the intelligence that the ex-burglar had been installed as a clerk in Guzzy's store.

People said that it was a shame—that nobody knew how soon Beigh might take to his old tricks again. Nevertheless, they crowded to Guzzy's store, to look at him, until shrewd people began to wonder whether Guzzy hadn't really taken Beigh as a sort of advertisement to draw trade.

A few months later, however, they changed their opinions, for the constable, after the expiration of his term of office, and while under the influence of a glass too much, related the whole history of the night of Beigh's first arrival at Bowerton.

The Bowertonians were law-abiding people; but, somehow, Guzzy's customers increased from that very day, and his prosperity did not decline even after " Guzzy & Beigh " was the sign over the door of the store which had been built and stocked with Mrs. Wyett's money.

A ROMANCE OF HAPPY REST.

HAPPY REST is a village whose name has never appeared in gazetteer or census report. This remark should not cause any depreciation of the faithfulness of public and private statisticians, for Happy Rest belonged to a class of settlements which sprang up about as suddenly as did Jonah's Gourd, and, after a short existence, disappeared so quickly that the last inhabitant generally found himself alone before he knew that anything unusual was going on.

When the soil of Happy Rest supported nothing more artificial than a broken wagon wheel, left behind by some emigrants going overland to California, a deserter from a fort near by discovered that the soil was auriferous.

His statement to that effect, made in a bar-room in the first town he reached thereafter, led to his being invited to drink, which operation resulted in certain supplementary statements and drinks.

Within three hours every man within five miles of that barroom knew that the most paying dirt on the continent had been discovered not far away, and three hours later a large body of gold-hunters, guided by the deserter, were *en route* for the auriferous locality; while a storekeeper and a liquor-dealer, with their respective stocks-in-trade, followed closely after.

The ground was found; it proved to be tolerably rich; tents went up, underground residences were burrowed, and the grateful miners ordered the barkeeper to give unlimited credit to the locality's discoverer. The barkeeper obeyed the order, and the ex-warrior speedily met his death in a short but glorious contest with John Barleycorn.

There was no available lumber from which to construct a coffin, and the storekeeper had no large boxes; but as the liquor-seller had already emptied two barrels, these were taken, neatly joined in the centre, and made to contain the remains of the founder of the hamlet. The method of his death and origin of his coffin led a spirituous miner to suggest that he rested happily, and from this remark the name of the town was elaborated.

Of course, no ladies accompanied the expedition. Men who went West for gold did not take their families with them, as a rule, and the settlers of new mining towns were all of the masculine gender.

When a town had attained to the dignity of a hotel, members of the gentler sex occasionally appeared, but— with the exception of an occasional washerwoman—their influence was decidedly the reverse of that usually attrib- uted to woman's society.

For the privileges of their society, men fought with pis- tols and knives, and bought of them disgrace and sorrow for gold. But at first Happy Rest was unblessed and un- cursed by the presence of any one who did not wear pan- taloons.

On the fifth day of its existence, however, when the ar- rival of an express agent indicated that Capital had for- mally acknowledged the existence of Happy Rest, there was an unusual commotion in the never-quiet village.

An important rumor had spread among the tents and gopher-holes, and, one after another, the citizens visited the saloon, took the barkeeper mysteriously aside, and, with faces denoting the greatest concern, whispered earnestly to him. The barkeeper felt his importance as the sole cus- todian of all the village news, but he replied with affability to all questions:

"Well, yes; there *hed* a lady come; come by the same stage as the express agent. What kind?—Well, he really couldn't say—some might think one way, an' some another.

He thought she was a real lady, though she wouldn't 'low anything to be sent her from the bar, and she hedn't brought no baggage. Thought so—*knowed* she was a lady —in fact, would bet drinks for the crowd on it. 'Cos why? —'Cos nobody heerd her cuss or seed her laugh. H'd bet three to two she was a lady—*might* bet two to one, ef he got his dander up on the subject. Then, on t'other hand, she'd axed for Major Axel, and the major, ez everybody know'd, was—well, he wasn't 'xactly a saint. Besides, as the major hedn't come to Happy Rest, nohow, it looked ez if he was dodgin' her for somethin'. Where was she stopping?—up to Old Psalmsinger's. Old Psalm hed turned himself out of house an' home, and bought her a new tea-kettle to boot. If anybody know'd anybody that wanted to take three to two, send him along."

A few men called to bet, and bets were exchanged all over the camp, but most of the excitement centred about the storekeeper's.

Argonauts, pioneers, heroes, or whatever else the early gold-seekers were, they were likewise mortal men, so they competed vigorously for the few blacking-brushes, boxes of blacking, looking-glasses, pocket-combs and neckties which the store contained. They bought toilet-soap, and borrowed razors ; and when they had improved their personal appearance to the fullest possible extent, they stood aimlessly about, like unemployed workmen in the market-place. Each one, however, took up a position which should rake the only entrance to old Psalmsinger's tent.

Suddenly, two or three scores of men struck various attitudes, as if to be photographed, and exclaimed in unison :

" There she is !"

From the tent of old Psalmsinger there had emerged the only member of the gentler sex who had reached Happy Rest.

For only a moment she stood still and looked about her, as if uncertain which way to go ; but before she had taken a step, old Psalmsinger raised his voice, and said :

"I thort it last night, when I only seed her in the moonlight, but I *know* it now—she's a lady, an' no mistake. Ef I was a bettin' man, I'd bet all my dust on it, an' my farm to hum besides!"

A number of men immediately announced that they would bet, in the speaker's place, to any amount, and in almost any odds. For, though old Psalm, by reason of non-participation in any of the drinks, fights, or games with which the camp refreshed itself, was considered a mere nonentity, it was generally admitted that men of his style could tell a lady or a preacher at sight.

The gentle unknown finally started toward the largest group of men, seeing which, several smaller groups massed themselves on the larger with alacrity.

As she neared them, the men could see that she was plainly dressed, but that every article of attire was not only neat but tasteful, and that she had enough grace of form and carriage to display everything to advantage. A few steps nearer, and she displayed a set of sad but refined features, marred only by an irresolute, purposeless mouth.

Then an ex-reporter from New York turned suddenly to a graceless young scamp who had once been a regular ornament to Broadway, and exclaimed :

"Louise Mattray, isn't it?"

"'Tis, by thunder!" replied the young man. "I knew I'd seen her somewhere. Wonder what she's doing here?"

The reporter shrugged his shoulders.

"Some wild-goose speculation, I suppose. Smart and gritty—if *I* had her stick I shouldn't be here—but she always slips up—can't keep all her wires well in hand. Was an advertising agent when I left the East—picked up a good many ads, too, and made folks treat her respectfully, when they'd have kicked a man out of doors if he'd come on the same errand."

"Say she's been asking for Axel," remarked the young man.

"That so!" queried the reporter, wrinkling his brow,

and hurrying through his mental notebook. "Oh, yes—there was some talk about them at one time. Some said they were married—*she* said so, but she never took his name. She had a handsome son, that looked like her and the major, but she didn't know how to manage him—went to the dogs, or worse, before he was eighteen."

"Axell here?" asked the young man.

"No," replied the reporter; "and 'twouldn't do her any good if he was. The major's stylish and good-looking, and plays a brilliant game, but he hasn't any more heart than is absolutely necessary to his circulation. Besides, his——"

The reporter was interrupted by a heavy hand falling on his shoulder, and found, on turning, that the hand belonged to "The General."

The general was not a military man, but his title had been conferred in recognition of the fact that he was a born leader. Wherever he went the general assumed the reins of government, and his administration had always been popular as well as judicious.

But at this particular moment the general seemed to feel unequal to what was evidently his duty, and he, like a skillful general, sought a properly qualified assistant, and the reporter seemed to him to be just the man he wanted.

"Spidertracks," said the general, with an air in which authority and supplication were equally prominent, "you've told an awful sight of lies in your time. Don't deny it, now—nobody that ever reads the papers will b'leeve you. Now's yer chance to put yer gift of gab to a respectable use. The lady's bothered, and wants to say somethin' or ask somethin', and she'll understand your lingo better'n mine. Fire away now, lively!"

The ex-shorthand-writer seemed complimented by the general's address, and stepping forward and raising the remains of what had once been a hat, said:

"Can I serve you in any way, madame?"

The lady glanced at him quickly and searchingly, and then, seeming assured of the reporter's honesty, replied:

"I am looking for an old acquaintance of mine—one Major Axell."

"He is not in camp, ma'am," said Spidertracks. "He was at Rum Valley a few days ago, when our party was organized to come here."

"I was there yesterday," said the lady, looking greatly disappointed, "and was told he started for here a day or two before."

"Some mistake, ma'am, I assure you," replied Spidertracks. "I should have known of his arrival if he had come. I'm an old newspaper man, ma'am, and can't get out of the habit of getting the news."

The lady turned away, but seemed irresolute. The reporter followed her.

"If you will return to Rum Valley, ma'am, I'll find the major for you, if he is hereabouts," said he. "You will be more comfortable there, and I will be more likely than you to find him."

The lady hesitated for a moment longer; then she drew from her pocket a diary, wrote a line or two on one of its leaves, tore it out and handed it to the reporter.

"I will accept your offer, and be very grateful for it, for I do not bear this mountain traveling very well. If you find him, give him this scrawl and tell him where I am—that will be sufficient."

"Trust me to find him, ma'am," replied Spidertracks. "And as the stage is just starting, and there won't be another for a week, allow me to see you into it. Any baggage?"

"Only a small hand-bag in the tent," said she.

They hurried off together, Spidertracks found the bag, and five minutes later was bowing and waving his old hat to the cloud of dust which the departing stage left behind it. But when even the dust itself had disappeard, he drew from his pocket the paper the fair passenger had given him.

"'Tain't sealed," said he, reasoning with himself, "so

there can't be any secrets in it. Let's see—hello! 'Ernest is somewhere in this country ; I wish to see you about *him* —and about nothing else.' Whew-w-w! What splendid material for a column, if there was only a live paper in this infernal country! Looking for that young scamp, eh? There *is* something to her, and I'll help her if I can. Wonder if I'd recognize him if I saw him again? I *ought* to, if he looks as much like his parents as he used to do. 'Twould do my soul good to make the poor woman smile once ; but it's an outrageous shame there's no good daily paper here to work the whole thing up in. With the chase, and fighting, and murder that *may* come of it, 'twould make the leading sensation for a week !"

The agonized reporter clasped his hands behind him and walked slowly back to where he had left the crowd. Most of the citizens had, on seeing the lady depart, taken a drink as a partial antidote to dejection, and strolled away to their respective claims, regardless of the occasional mud which threatened the polish on their boots ; but two or three gentlemen of irascible tempers and judicial minds lingered, to decide whether Spidertracks had not, by the act of seeing the lady to the stage, made himself an accessory to her departure, and consequently a fit subject for challenge by every disappointed man in camp.

The reporter was in the midst of a very able and voluble defense, when the attention of his hearers seemed distracted by something on the trail by which the original settlers had entered the village.

Spidertracks himself looked, shaded his eyes, indulged in certain disconnected fragments of profanity, and finally exclaimed :

Axell himself, by the white coat of Horace Greeley! Wonder who he's got with him ! They seem to be having a difficulty about something !"

The gentlemen who had arraigned Spidertracks allowed him to be acquitted by default. Far better to them was a fight near by than the most interesting lady afar off.

They stuck their hands into their pockets, and stared intently. Finally one of them, in a tone of disgusted resignation, remarked:

"Axell ought to be ashamed of hisself; he's draggin' along a little feller not half the size *he* is. Blamed if he ain't got his match, though; the little feller's jest doin' some gellorious chawin' an' diggin'.'"

The excitement finally overcame the inertia of the party, and each man started deliberately to meet the major and his captive. Spidertracks, faithful to his profession, kept well in advance of the others. Suddenly he exclaimed to himself:

"Good Lord! don't they know each other? The major didn't wear that beard when in New York; but the boy—he's just the same scamp, in spite of his dirt and rags. If *she* were to see them now—but, pshaw! 'twould all fall flat —no live paper to take hold of the matter and work it up."

"There, curse your treacherous heart!" roared the major, as he gave his prisoner a push which threw him into the reporter's arms. "Now we're in a civilized community, and you'll have a chance of learning the opinions of gentlemen on such irregularities. Tried to kill me, gentlemen, upon my honor!—did it after I had shared my eatables and pocket-pistol with him, too. Did it to get my dust. Got me at a disadvantage for a moment, and made a formal demand for the dust, and backed his request with a pistol—my own pistol, gentlemen! I've only just reached here ; I don't yet know who's here, but I imagine there's public spirit enough to discourage treachery. Will some one see to him while I take something?"

Spidertracks drew his revolver, mildly touched the young man on the shoulder, and remarked :

"Come on."

The ex-knight of the pencil bowed his prisoner into an abandoned gopher-hole (*i. e.*, an artificial cave,) cocked his revolver, and then stretched himself on the ground and devoted himself to staring at the unfortunate youth. To a

20

student of human nature Ernest Mattray was curious, fascinating, and repulsive. Short, slight, handsome, delicate, nervous, unscrupulous, selfish, effeminate, dishonest, and cruel, he was an excellent specimen of what city life could make of a boy with no father and an irresolute mother.

The reporter, who had many a time studied faces in the Tombs, felt almost as if at his old vocation again as he gazed into the restless eyes and sullen features of the prisoner.

Meanwhile Happy Rest was becoming excited. There had been some little fighting done since the settlement of the place, but as there had been no previous attempt at highway robbery and murder made in the vicinity, the prisoner was an object of considerable interest.

In fact, the major told so spirited a story, that most of the inhabitants strolled up, one after another, to look at the innovator, while that individual himself, with the modesty which seems inseparable from true greatness, retired to the most secluded of the three apartments into which the cave was divided, and declined all the attentions which were thrust upon him.

The afternoon had faded almost into evening, when a decrepit figure, in a black dress and bonnet, approached the cave, and gave Spidertracks a new element for the thrilling report he had composed and mentally rearranged during his few hours of duty as jailer.

"Beats the dickens," muttered the reporter to himself, "how these Sisters of Charity always know when a tough case has been caught. Natural enough in New York. But where did *she* come from? Who told her? Cross, beads, and all. Hello! Oh, Louise Mattray, you're a deep one; but it's a pity your black robe isn't quite long enough to hide the very tasty dress you wore this morning? Queer dodge, too—wonder what it means? Wonder if she's caught sight of the major, and don't want to be recognized?"

The figure approached.

"May I see the prisoner?" she asked.

"No one has a better right, Mrs. Mattray," said the guardian of the cave, with a triumphant smile, while the poor woman started and trembled. "Don't be frightened—no one is going to hurt you. Heard all about it, I suppose? —know who just missed being the victim?"

"Yes," said the unhappy woman, entering the cave.

When she emerged it was growing quite dark. She passed the reporter with head and vail down, and whispered:

"Thank you."

"Don't mention it," said the reporter, quickly. "Going to stay until you see how things go with him?"

She shook her head and passed on.

The sky grew darker. The reporter almost wished it might grow so dark that the prisoner could escape unperceived, or so quickly that a random shot could not find him. There were strange noises in camp.

The storekeeper, who never traveled except by daylight, was apparently harnessing his mules to the wagon—he was moving the wagon itself to the extreme left of the camp, where there was nothing to haul but wood, and even that was still standing in the shape of fine old trees.

There seemed to be an unusual clearness in the air, for Spidertracks distinctly heard the buzz of some earnest conversation. There seemed strange shadows floating in the air—a strange sense of something moving toward him—something almost shapeless, yet tangible—something that approached him—that gave him a sense of insecurity and then of alarm. Suddenly the indefinable something uttered a yell, and resolved itself into a party of miners, led by the gallant and aggrieved major himself, who shouted:

"Lynch the scoundrel, boys—that's the only thing to do!"

The excited reporter sprang to his feet in an agony of genuine humanity and suppressed itemizing, and screamed:

"Major, wait a minute—you'll be sorry if you don't!"

But the gallant major had been at the bar for two or

three hours, preparing himself for this valorous deed, and
the courage he had there imbibed knew not how to brook
delay—not until the crowd had reached the mouth of the
cave and found it dark, and had heard one unduly prudent
miner suggest that it might be well to have a light, so as to
dodge being sliced in the dark.

"Bring a light quick, then," shouted the major. "*I'll*
drag him out when it comes; he knows *my* grip, curse him!"

A bunch of dried grass was hastily lighted and thrown
into the cave, and the major rapidly followed it, while as
many miners as could crowd in after him hastened to do so.
They found the major, with white face and trembling limbs,
standing in front of the lady for whose sake they had done
so much elaborate dressing in the morning, and who they
had afterwards wrathfully seen departing in the stage.

The major rallied, turned around, and said:

"There's some mistake here, gentlemen. Won't you
have the kindness to leave us alone?"

Slowly—very slowly—the crowd withdrew. It seemed to
them that, in the nature of things, the lady ought to have it
out with the major with pistols or knives for disturbing her,
and that they, who were in all the sadness of disappointment at failure of a well-planned independent execution,
ought to see the end of the whole affair. But a beseeching
look from the lady herself finally cleared the cave, and the
major exclaimed:

"Louise, what does this mean?"

"It means," said the lady, with most perfect composure,
" that, thanks to a worthless father and a bad bringing-up
by an incapable mother, Ernest has found his way into this
country. I came to find him, and I found him in this hole,
to which his affectionate father brought him to-day. It is
about as well, I imagine, that I helped him to escape, seeing
to what further kind attentions you had reserved him."

"Please don't be so icy, Louise," begged the major.
"He attempted to rob and kill me, the young rascal; besides,
I had not the faintest idea of who he was."

"Perhaps," said the lady, still very calm, "you will tell me from whom he inherited the virtues which prompted his peculiar actions towards you ? His *mother* has always earned her livelihood honorably."

"Louise," said the major, with a humility which would have astonished his acquaintance, "won't you have the kindness to reserve your sarcasm until I am better able to bear it ? You probably think I have no heart—I acknowledge I have thought as much myself—but *something* is making me feel very weak and tender just now."

The lady looked critically at him for a moment, and then burst into tears.

"Oh, God !" she sobbed, "what else is there in store for this poor, miserable, injured life of mine ?"

"Restitution," whispered the major softly—"if you will let me make it, or try to make it."

The weeping woman looked up inquiringly, and said only the words :

"And she ?"

"My first wife ?" answered the major. "Dead—*really* dead, Louise, as I hope to be saved. She died several years ago, and I longed to do you justice then, but the memory of our parting was too much for my cowardly soul. If you will take me as I am, Louise, I will, as long as I live, remember the past, and try to atone for it."

She put her hand in his, and they left the gopher-hole together. As they disappeared in the outer darkness, there emerged from one of the compartments of the cave an individual whose features were indistinguishable in the darkness, but who was heard to emphatically exclaim :

"If I had the dust, I'd start a live daily here, just to tell the whole story ; though the way he got out didn't do *me* any particular credit."

*　　*　　*　　*　　*　　*　　*

For days the residents of Happy Rest used all available mental stimulants to aid them in solving the mystery of the major and the wonderful lady ; but, as the mental stimulants aforesaid were all spirituous, the results were more deplorable than satisfactory. But when, a few days later, the couple took the stage for Rum Valley, the enterprising Spidertracks took an outside passage, and at the end of the route had his persistency rewarded by seeing, in the Bangup House, a Sister of Charity tenderly embrace the major's fair charge, start at the sight of the major, and then, after some whispering by the happy mother, sullenly ex tend a hand, which the major grasped heartily, and over which there dropped something which, though a drop of water, was not a rain-drop. Then did Spidertracks return to the home of his adoption, and lavish the stores of his memory; and for days his name was famous, and his liquor was paid for by admiring auditors.

TWO POWERFUL ARGUMENTS.

"GOT him?"

"You bet!"

The questioner looked pleased, yet not as if his pleasure engendered any mental excitement. The man who answered spoke in an ordinary, careless tone, and with unmoved countenance, as if he were merely signifying the employment of an additional workman, or the purchase of a desirable rooster.

Yet the subject of the brief conversation repeated above was no other than Bill Bowney, the most industrious and successful of the horse-thieves and "road-agents" that honored the southern portion of California with their presence.

Nor did Bowney restrict himself to the duty of redistributing the property of other people. Perhaps he belonged to that class of political economists which considers superfluous population an evil; perhaps he was a religious enthusiast, and ardently longed that all mankind should speedily see the pearly gates of the New Jerusalem.

Be his motives what they might, it is certain that when an unarmed man met Bowney, entered into a discussion with him, and lived verbally to report the same, he was looked upon with considerably more interest than a newly-made Congressman or a ten-thousand-acre farmer was able to inspire.

The two men whose conversation we have recorded
311

studied the ears of their own horses for several minutes, after which the first spe.ker asked :

"How did you do it ?"

"Well," replied the other man, "ther' wasn't anything p'tickler 'bout it. Me an' him wuzn't acquainted, so he didn't suspect me. But I know'd his face—he wuz p'inted out to me once, durin' the gold-rush to Kern River, an' I never forgot him. I wuz on a road I never traveled before—goin' to see an old greaser, ownin' a mighty pretty piece of ground I wanted—when all of a sudden I come on a cabin, an' thar stood Bill in front of it, a-smokin'. I axed him fur a light, an' when he came up to give it to me, I grabbed him by the shirt-collar an' dug the spur into the mare. 'Twus kind of a mean trick, imposin' on hospitality that-a-way ; but 'twuz Bowney, you know. He hollered, an' I let him walk in front, but I kep' him covered with the revolver till I met some fellers, that tied him good an' tight. 'Twuzn't.excitin' wurth a durn—that is, ixcep' when his wife—I s'pose 'twuz —hollered, then I a'most wished I'd let him go."

"Sheriff got him ?" inquired the first speaker.

"Well, no," returned the captor. · "Sheriff an' judge mean well, I s'pose ; but they're slow—mighty slow. Besides, he's got friends, an' they might be too much fur the sheriff some night. We tuk him to the Broad Oak, an' we thought we'd ax the neighbors over thar to-night, to talk it over. Be thar ?"

"You bet !" replied the first speaker. "And I'll bring my friends ; nothing like having plenty of witnesses in important legal cases."

"Jus' so," responded the other. "Well, here's till then ;" and the two men separated.

The Broad Oak was one of those magnificent trees which are found occasionally through Southern California, singly or dispersed in handsome natural parks.

The specimen which had so impressed people as to gain a special name for itself was not only noted for its size, but because it had occasionally been selected as the handiest place in which Judge Lynch could hold his court without fear of molestation by rival tribunals.

Bill Bowney, under favorable circumstances, appeared to be a very homely, lazy, sneaking sort of an invidual; but Bill Bowney, covered with dust, his eyes bloodshot, his clothes torn, and his hands and feet tightly bound, had not a single attractive feature about him.

He stared earnestly up into the noble tree under whose shadow he lay ; but his glances were not of admiration— they seemed, rather, to be resting on two or three fragments of rope which remained on one of the lower limbs, and to express sentiments of the most utter loathing and disgust.

The afternoon wore away, and the moon shone brilliantly down from the cloudless sky.

The tramp of a horse was heard at a distance, but rapidly growing more distinct, and soon Bowney's captor galloped up to the tree.

Then another horse was heard, then others, and soon ten or a dozen men were gathered together.

Each man, after dismounting, walked up to where the captive lay, and gave him a searching look, and then they joined those who had already preceded them, and who were quietly chatting about wheat, cattle, trees—everything but the prisoner.

Suddenly one of the party separated himself from the others, and exclaimed :

" Gentlemen, there don't seem to be anybody else a-comin' —we might as well 'tend to bizness. I move that Major Burkess takes the chair, if there's no objections."

No objections were made, and Major Burkess—a slight, peaceable, gentlemanly-looking man—stepped out of the crowd, and said :

" You all know the object of this meeting, gentlemen. The first thing in order is to prove the identity of the prisoner."

" Needn't trouble yourself 'bout that," growled the prisoner. " I'm Bill Bowney ; an' yer too cowardly to untie me, though ther *be* a dozen uv yer."

" The prisoner admits he is Bill Bowney," continued the major, " but of course no gentleman will take offense at his remarks. Has any one any charge to make against him ?"

" Charges ?" cried an excitable farmer. " Didn't I catch him untying my horse, an' ridin' off on him from Budley's? Didn't I tell him to drop that anamile, an' didn't he purty near drop *me* instead ? Charges ?—here's the charge !" concluded the farmer, pointing significantly to a scar on his own temple.

"Pity I didn't draw a better bead !" growled the prisoner. " The hoss only fetched two ounces."

" Prisoner admits stealing Mr. Barke's horse, and firing on Mr. Barke. Any further evidence ?"

" Rather, drawled an angular gentleman. " I was goin' up the valley by the stage, an' all of a sudden the driver stopped where there wasn't no station. There was fellers had hold of the leaders, an' there was pistols p'inted at the driver an' folks in general. Then our money an' watches was took, an' the feller that took mine had a cross-cut scar on the back of his hand—right hand ; maybe somebody'll look at Bill's."

The prisoner was carried into the moonlight, and the back of his right hand was examined by the major. The prisoner was again placed under the tree.

" The cut's there, as described," said the major. " Anything else ?"

" Ther's this much," said another. " I busted up flat, you all know, on account of the dry season, last year, an' I hadn't nothin' left but my hoss. Bill Bowney knowed it as well's anybody else, yet he come and stole that hoss. It pawed like thunder, an' woke me up—fur 'twas night, an' light as 'tis now—an' I seed Bowney a-ridin' him off. 'Twas a sneakin', mean, cowardly trick."

The prisoner hung his head ; he would plead guilty to theft and attempt to kill, and defy his captors to do their worst ; but when meanness and cowardice were proved against him, he seemed ashamed of himself.

"Prisoner virtually admits the charge," said the major, looking critically at Bowney.

"Gentlemen," said Caney, late of Texas, "what's the use of wastin' time this way? Everybody knows that Bowney's been at the bottom of all the deviltry that's been done in the county this three year. Highway robbery's a hangin' offense in Texas an' every other well-regilated State; so's hoss-stealin', an' so's shootin' a man in the back, an' yit Bowney's done ev'ry one of 'em over an' over agin. Ev'rybody knows what we come here fur, else what's the reason ev'ry man's got a nice little coil o' rope on his saddle fur? The longer the bizness is put off, the harder it'll be to do. I move we string him up instanter."

"Second the motion!" exclaimed some one.

"I move we give him a chance to save himself," said a quiet farmer from New England. "When he's in the road-agent business, he has a crowd to help him. Now, 'twould do us more good to clean *them* out than him alone, so let's give him a chance to leave the State if he'll tell who his confederates are. Somebody'll have to take care of him, of course, till we can catch them, and make sure of it."

"'Twon't cost the somebody much, then," said the prisoner, firmly; "an' I'd give a cool thousand for a shot at any low-lived coyote that 'ud ax me to do sich an ungentlemanly thing."

"Spoke like a man," said Caney, of Texas. "I hope ye'll die easy for that, Bill."

"The original motion prevails," said the major; "all in favor will say ay."

A decided "ay" broke from the party.

"Whoever has the tallest horse will please lead him up and unsaddle him," said the major, after a slight pause. "The witnesses will take the prisoner in charge."

A horse was brought under the limb, with the fragments of rope upon it, and the witnesses, one of them bearing a piece of rope, approached the prisoner.

The silence was terrible, and the feelings of all present

were greatly relieved when Bill Bowney—placed on the horse, and seeing the rope hauled taught and fastened to a bough by a man in the tree—broke into a frenzy of cursing, and displayed the defiant courage peculiar to an animal at bay.

"Has the prisoner anything to say?" asked the major, as Bowney stopped for breath.

"Better own up, and save yourself and reform, and help rid the world of those other scoundrels," pleaded the New Englander.

"Don't yer do it, Bill—don't yer do it!" cried Caney, of Texas. "Stick to yer friends, an' die like a man!"

"That's me!" said the prisoner, directing a special volley of curses at the New Englander. "It's ben said here that I wuz sneakin' an' cowardly; ther's *one* way of givin' that feller the lie—hurry up an' do it!"

"When I raise my hand," said the major, "lead the horse away; and may the Lord have mercy on your soul, Bowney!"

"Amen!" fervently exclaimed the New Englander.

Again there was a moment of terrible silence, and when a gentle wind swept over the wild oats and through the tree, there seemed to sound on the air a sigh and a shudder.

Suddenly all the horses started and pricked up their ears.

"Somebody's comin'!" whispered one of the party. "Sheriff's got wind of the arrangements, maybe!"

"Comes from the wrong direction," cried Caney, of Texas, quickly. "It's somebody on foot—an' tired—an' light-footed —ther's two or three—dunno what kind o' bein's they *ken* be. Thunder an' lightnin'!"

Caney's concluding remark was inspired by the sudden appearance of a woman, who rushed into the shadow of the tree, stopped, looked wildly about for a moment, and then threw herself against the prisoner's feet, and uttered a low, pitiful cry.

There was a low murmur from the crowd, and the major cried:

"Take him down; give him fifteen minutes with his wife, and see she doesn't untie him."

The man in the tree loosened the rope, Bowney was lifted off and placed on the ground again, and the woman

"TAKE HIM DOWN; GIVE HIM FIFTEEN MINUTES WITH HIS WIFE."

threw herself on the ground beside him, caressed his ugly face, and wailed pitifully. The judge and jury fidgeted about restlessly. Still the horses stood on the alert, and soon three came through the oats—three children, all crying.

As they saw the men they became dumb, and stood mute and frightened, staring at their parents.

They were not pretty—they were not even interesting. Mother and children were alike—unwashed, uncombed, shoeless, and clothed in dirty, faded calico. The children were all girls—the oldest not more than ten years old, and the youngest scarce five. None of them pleaded for the prisoner, but still the woman wailed and moaned, and the children stood staring in dumb piteousness.

The major stood quietly gazing at the face of his watch. There was not in Southern California a more honest man than Major Burkess; yet the minute-hand of his watch had not indicated more than one-half of fifteen minutes, when he exclaimed:

"Time's up!"

The men approached the prisoner—the woman threw her arms around him, and cried:

"My husband! Oh, God!"

"Madam," said the major, "your husband's life is in his own hands. He can save himself by giving the names of his confederates and leaving the State."

"I'll tell you who they are?" cried the woman.

"God curse yer if yer do!" hissed Bowney from between his teeth.

"Better let him be, madam," argued Caney, of Texas. He'd better die like a man than go back on his friends. Might tell us which of 'em was man enough to fetch you and the young uns here? We'll try to be easy on him when we ketch him."

"None of 'em," sobbed the woman. "We walked, an' I took turns totin' the young uns. My husband! Oh, God! my husband!"

"Beg yer pardon, ma'am," said Bowney's captor, "but nobody can't b'leeve that; it's nigh onto twenty mile."

"I'd ha' done it ef it had been fifty," cried the woman, angrily, "when *he* wuz in trouble. Oh, God! Oh, God! Don't yer b'leeve it? Then look here!" She picked up the smallest child as she spoke, and in the dim light the men saw that its little feet were torn and bleeding. "'Twas their blood or his'n," cried the woman, rapidly, " an' I didn't know how to choose between 'em. God hev mercy on me! I'm nigh crazy !"

Caney, of Texas, took the child from its mother and carried it to where the moonlight was unobstructed. He looked carefully at its feet, and then shouted :

" Bring the prisoner out here."

Two men carried Bowney to where Caney was standing, and the whole party, with the woman and remaining children, followed.

" Bill," said Caney, " I ain't a askin' yer to go back on yer friends, but them is—look at 'em."

And Caney held the child's feet before the father's eyes, while the woman threw her arms around his neck, and the two older children crept up to the prisoner, and laid their faces against his legs.

" They're a-talkin' to yer, Bill," resumed Caney, of Texas, " an' they're the convincenist talkers I ever seed."

The desperado turned his eyes away ; but Caney moved the child so its bleeding feet were still before its father's eyes.

The remaining men all retired beneath the shadow of the tree, for the tender little feet were talking to them, too, and they were ashamed of the results.

Suddenly Bowney uttered a deep groan.

" 'Tain't no use a-tryin'," said he, in a resigned tone. " Everybody'll be down on me, an' after all I've done, too ! But yer ken hev their names, curse yer !"

The woman went into hysterics ; the children cried ; Caney, of Texas, ejaculated, " Bully !" and then kissed the poor little bruised feet.

The New Englander fervently exclaimed, " Thank God !"

" I'll answer fur him till we get 'em," said Caney, after the major had written down the names Bowney gave him ; " an'," continued Caney, " somebody git the rest of these young uns an' ther mother to my cabin powerful quick. Good Lord, don't I jist wish they wuz boys ! I'd-adopt the hull family."

The court informally adjourned *sine die*, but had so many meetings afterward at the same place to dispose of Bowney's accomplices, that his freedom was considered fairly purchased, and he and his family were located a good way from the scenes of his most noted exploits.

MR. PUTCHETT'S LOVE.

JUST after two o'clock, on a July afternoon, Mr. Putchett
mounted several steps of the Sub-Treasury in Wall
Street, and gazed inquiringly up and down the street.
To the sentimental observer Mr. Putchett's action, in
taking the position we have indicated, may have seemed to
signify that Mr. Putchett was of an aspiring disposition, and
that in ascending the steps he exemplified his desire to get
above the curbstone whose name was used as a qualifying
adjective whenever Mr. Putchett was mentioned as a broker.
Those persons, however, who enjoyed the honor of Mr.
Putchett's acquaintance immediately understood that the
operator in question was in funds that day, and that he had
taken the position from which he could most easily announce his moneyed condition to all who might desire
assistance from him.

It was rather late in the day for business, and certain
persons who had until that hour been unsuccessful in obtaining the accommodations desired were not at all particular whether their demands were satisfied in a handsome
office, or under the only roof that can be enjoyed free of rent.

There came to Mr. Putchett oddly-clothed members of
his own profession, and offered for sale securities whose
numbers Mr. Putchett compared with those on a list of
bonds stolen; men who deposited with him small articles
of personal property—principally jewelry—as collaterals on
small loans at short time and usurious rates; men who
stood before him on the sidewalk, caught his eye, summoned

him by a slight motion of the head, and disappeared around the corner, whither Mr. Putchett followed them only to promptly transact business and hurry back to his business-stand.

In fact, Mr. Putchett was very busy, and as in his case business invariably indicated profit, it was not wonderful that his rather unattractive face lightened and expressed its owner's satisfaction at the amount of business he was doing. Suddenly, however, there attacked Mr. Putchett the fate which, in its peculiarity of visiting people in their happiest hours, has been bemoaned by poets of genuine and doubtful inspiration, from the days of the sweet singer of Israel unto those of that sweet singer of Erin, whose recital of experience with young gazelles illustrates the remorselessness of the fate alluded to.

Plainly speaking, Mr. Putchett went suddenly under a cloud, for during one of his dashes around the corner after a man who had signaled him, and at the same time commenced to remove a ring from his finger, a small, dirty boy handed Mr. Putchett a soiled card, on which was penciled:

"Bayle is after you, about that diamond."

Despite the fact that Mr. Putchett had not been shaved for some days, and had apparently neglected the duty of facial ablution for quite as long a time, he turned pale and looked quickly behind him and [across the street; then muttering "Just my luck!" and a few other words more desponding than polite in nature, he hurried to the Post-Office, where he penciled and dispatched a few postal-cards, signed in initials only, announcing an unexpected and temporary absence. Then, still looking carefully and often at the faces in sight, he entered a newspaper office and consulted a railway directory. He seemed in doubt, as he rapidly turned the leaves; and when he reached the time-table of a certain road running near and parallel to the seaside, the change in his countenance indicated that he had learned the whereabouts of a city of refuge.

An hour later Mr. Putchett, having to bid no family

good-by, to care for no securities save those stowed away in his capacious pockets, and freed from the annoyance of baggage by reason of the fact that he had on his back the only outer garments that he owned, was rapidly leaving New York on a train, which he had carefully assured himself did not carry the dreaded Bayle.

Once fairly started, Mr. Putchett in some measure recovered his spirits. He introduced himself to a brakeman by means of a cigar, and questioned him until he satisfied himself that the place to which he had purchased a ticket was indeed unknown to the world, being far from the city, several miles from the railroad, and on a beach where boats could not safely land. He also learned that it was not a fashionable Summer resort, and that a few farmhouses (whose occupants took Summer boarders) and an unsuccessful hotel were the only buildings in the place.

Arrived at his destination, Mr. Putchett registered at the hotel and paid the week's board which the landlord, after a critical survey of his new patron, demanded in advance.

Then the exiled operator tilted a chair in the barroom, lit an execrable cigar, and, instead of expressing sentiments of gratitude appropriate to the occasion, gave way to profane condemnations of the bad fortune which had compelled him to abandon his business.

He hungrily examined the faces of the few fishermen of the neighboring bay who came in to drink and smoke, but no one of them seemed likely to need money—certainly no one of them seemed to have acceptable collaterals about his person or clothing. On the contrary, these men, while each one threw Mr. Putchett a stare of greater or less magnitude, let the financier alone so completely that he was conscious of a severe wound in his self-esteem.

It was a strange experience, and at first it angered him so that he strode up to the bar, ordered a glass of best brandy, and defiantly drank alone; but neither the strength of the liquor nor the intensity of his anger prevented him from soon feeling decidedly lonely.

At the cheap hotel at which he lodged when in New York there was no one who loved him or even feared him, but there were a few men of his own kind who had, for purposes of mutual recreation, tabooed business transactions with each other, and among these he found a grim sort of enjoyment—of companionship, at least. Here, however, he was so utterly alone as to be almost frightened, and the murmuring and moaning of the surf on the beach near the hotel added to his loneliness a sense of terror.

Almost overcome by dismal forebodings, Mr. Putchett hurried out of the hotel and toward the beach. Once upon the sands, he felt better; the few people who were there were strangers, of course, but they were women and children; and if the expression of those who noticed him was wondering, it was inoffensive—at times even pitying; and Mr. Putchett was in a humor to gratefully accept even pity.

Soon the sun fell, and the people straggled toward their respective boarding-houses, and Mr. Putchett, to fight off loneliness as long as possible, rose from the bench on which he had been sitting and followed the party up the beach.

He had supposed himself the last person that left the beach, but in a moment or two he heard a childish voice shouting:

"Mister, mister! I guess you've lost something!"

Mr. Putchett turned quickly, and saw a little girl, six or seven years of age, running toward him. In one hand she held a small pail and wooden shovel, and in the other something bright, which was too large for her little hand to cover.

She reached the broker's side, turned up a bright, healthy face, opened her hand and displayed a watch, and said:

"It was right there on the bench where you were sitting. I couldn't think what it was, it shone so."

Mr. Putchett at first looked suspiciously at the child, for he had at one period of his life labored industriously in the business of dropping bogus pocketbooks and watches,

MR. PUTCHETT'S NEW FRIEND.

and obtaining rewards from persons claiming to be their owners.

Examining the watch which the child handed him, however, he recognized it as one upon which he had lent twenty dollars earlier in the day.

First prudently replacing the watch in the pocket of his pantaloons, so as to avoid any complication while settling with the finder, he handed the child a quarter.

" Oh, no, thank you," said she, hastily; " mamma gives me money whenever I need it."

The experienced operator immediately placed the fractional currency where it might not tempt the child to change her mind. Then he studied her face with considerable curiosity, and asked :

" Do you live here ?"

" Oh, no," she replied; " we're only spending the Summer here. We live in New York."

Mr. Putchett opened his eyes, whistled, and remarked:

" It's very funny."

" Why, I don't think so," said the child, very innocently. " Lots of people that board here come from New York. Don't you want to see my well? I dug the deepest well of anybody to-day. Just come and see—it's only a few steps from here."

Mechanically, as one struggling with a problem above his comprehension, the financier followed the child, and gazed into a hole, perhaps a foot and a half deep, on the beach.

" That's my well," said she, "and that one next it is Frank's. Nellie's is way up there. I guess hers *would* have been the biggest, but a wave came up and spoiled it."

Mr. Putchett looked from the well into the face of its little digger, and was suddenly conscious of an insane desire to drink some of the water. He took the child's pail, dipped some water, and was carrying it to his lips, when the child spoiled what was probably the first sentimental feeling of Mr. Putchett's life by hastily exclaiming :

" You mustn't drink that—it's salty !"

The sentimentalist sorrowfully put the bitter draught away, and the child rattled on :

"If you're down here to-morrow, I'll show you where we find scallop-shells ; maybe you can find some with pink and yellow spots on them. *I've* got some. If you don't find any, I'll give you one."

"Thank you," said her companion.

Just then some one shouted " Alice !" and the child exclaiming, "Mamma's calling me ; good-by," hurried away, while the broker walked slowly toward the hotel with an expression of countenance which would have hidden him from his oldest acquaintance.

Mr. Putchett spent the evening on the piazza instead of in the barroom, and he neither smoked nor drank. Before retiring he contracted with the colored cook to shave him in the morning, and to black his boots; and he visited the single store of the neighborhood and purchased a shirt, some collars, and a cravat.

When in the morning he was duly shaved, dressed and brushed, he critically surveyed himself in the glass, and seemed quite dissatisfied. He moved from the glass, spread a newspaper on the table, and put into it the contents of his capacious pockets. A second examination before the glass seemed more satisfactory in result, thus indicating that to the eye of Mr. Putchett his well-stuffed pockets had been unsightly in effect.

The paper and its contents he gave the landlord to deposit in the hotel safe ; then he ate a hurried, scanty breakfast, and again sought the bench on the beach.

No one was in sight, for it was scarcely breakfast-time at the boarding-houses; so he looked for little Alice's well, and mourned to find that the tide had not even left any sign of its location.

Then he seated himself on the bench again, contemplating his boots, looked up the road, stared out to sea, and then looked up the road again, tried to decipher some of the names carved on the bench, walked backward and forward, looking up the road at each turn he made, and in every way indicated the unpleasant effect of hope deferred.

Finally, however, after two hours of fruitless search, Mr. Putchett's eyes were rewarded by the sight of little Alice approaching the beach with a bathing-party. He at first hurried forward to meet her, but he was restrained by a sentiment found alike in curbstone-brokers and in charming young ladies—a feeling that it is not well to give one's self away without first being sufficiently solicited to do so.

He noticed, with a mingled pleasure and uneasiness, that little Alice did not at first recognize him, so greatly had his toilet altered his general appearance.

Even after he made himself known, he was compelled to submit to further delay, for the party had come to the beach to bathe, and little Alice must bathe, too.

She emerged from a bathing-house in a garb very odd to the eyes of Mr. Putchett, but one which did not at all change that gentleman's opinion of the wearer. She ran into the water, was thrown down by the surf, she was swallowed by some big waves and dived through others, and all the while the veteran operator watched her with a solicitude, which, despite his anxiety for her safety, gave him a sensation as delightful as it was strange.

The bath ended, Alice rejoined Mr. Putchett and conducted him to the spot where the wonderful shells with pink and yellow spots were found. The new shell-seeker was disgusted when the child shouted "Come along!" to several other children, and was correspondingly delighted when they said, in substance, that shells were not so attractive as once they were.

Mr. Putchett's researches in conchology were not particularly successful, for while he manfully moved about in the uncomfortable and ungraceful position peculiar to shell-seekers, he looked rather at the healthy, honest, eager little face near him than at the beach itself.

Suddenly, however, Mr. Putchett's opinion of shells

underwent a radical change, for the child, straightening herself and taking something from her pocket, exclaimed :

"Oh, dear, somebody's picked up all the pretty ones. I thought,may be, there mightn't be any here, so I brought you one; just see what pretty pink and yellow spots there are on it."

Mr. Putchett looked, and there came into his face the first flush of color that had been there—except in anger—for years. He had occasionally received presents from business acquaintances, but he had correctly looked at them as having been forwarded as investments, so they awakened feelings of suspicion rather than of pleasure.

But at little Alice's shell he looked long and earnestly, and when he put it into his pocket he looked for two or three moments far away, and yet at nothing in particular.

"Do you have a nice boarding-house?" asked Alice, as they sauntered along the beach, stopping occasionally to pick up pebbles and to dig wells.

"Not very," said Mr. Putchett, the sanded barroom and his own rather dismal chamber coming to his mind.

"You ought to board where we do," said Alice, enthusiastically. "We have *heaps* of fun. Have you got a barn ?"

Mr. Putchett confessed that he did not know.

"Oh, we've got a splendid one!" exclaimed the child. "There's stalls, and a granary, and a carriage-house and *two* lofts in it. We put out hay to the horses, and they eat it right out of our hands—aren't afraid a bit. Then we get into the granary, and bury ourselves all up in the oats, so only our heads stick out. The lofts are just *lovely :* one's full of hay and the other's full of wheat, and we chew the wheat, and make gum of it. The hay-stalks are real nice and sweet to chew, too. They only cut the hay last week, and we all rode in on the wagon—one, two, three, four—seven of us. Then we've got two croquet sets, and the boys make us whistles and squalks."

"Squalks ?" interrogated the broker.

"Yes; they're split quills, and you blow in them. . They don't make very pretty music, but it's ever so funny. We've got two big swings and a hammock, too."

"Is the house very full ?" asked Mr. Putchett.

"Not so very," replied the child. "If you come there to board, I'll make Frank teach you how to make whistles."

That afternoon Mr. Putchett took the train for New York, from which city he returned the next morning with quite a well-filled trunk. It was afterward stated by a person who had closely observed the capitalist's movements during his trip, that he had gone into a first-class clothier's and demanded suits of the best material and latest cut, regardless of cost, and that he had pursued the same singular coarse at a gent's furnishing store, and a fashionable jeweler's.

Certain it is that on the morning of Mr. Putchett's return a gentleman very well dressed, though seemingly ill at ease in his clothing, called at Mrs. Brown's boarding-house, and engaged a room, and that the younger ladies pronounced him very stylish and the older ones thought him very odd. But as he never intruded, spoke only when spoken to, and devoted himself earnestly and entirely to the task of amusing the children, the boarders all admitted that he was very good-hearted.

Among Alice's numerous confidences, during her second stroll with Mr. Putchett, was information as to the date of her seventh birthday, now very near at hand. When the day arrived, her adorer arose unusually early, and spent an impatient hour or two awaiting Alice's appearance. As she bade him good-morning, he threw about her neck a chain, to which was attached an exquisite little watch ; then, while the delighted child was astonishing her parents and the other boarders, Mr. Putchett betook himself to the barn in a state of abject sheepishness. He did not appear again until summoned by the breakfast-bell, and even then he sat with a very red face, and with eyes directed at his plate only. The child's mother remonstrated against so much money being squandered on a child, and attempted to return the watch, but he seemed so distressed at the idea that the lady dropped the subject.

For a fortnight, Mr. Putchett remained at the boarding-house, and grew daily in the estimation of every one. From being thought queer and strange, he gradually gained the reputation of being the best-hearted, most guileless, most considerate man alive. He was the faithful squire of all the ladies, both young and old, and was adored by all the children. His conversational powers—except on matters of business—were not great, but his very ignorance on all general topics, and the humility born of that ignorance, gave to his manners a deference which was more gratifying to most ladies than brilliant loquacity would have been. He even helped little Alice to study a Sunday-school lesson, and the experience was so entirely new to him, that he became more deeply interested than the little learner herself. He went to church on Sunday, and was probably the most attentive listener the rather prosy old pastor had.

Of course he bathed—everybody did. A stout rope was stretched from a post on the shore to a buoy in deep water where it was anchored, and back and forth on this rope capered every day twenty or thirty hideously dressed but very happy people, among whom might always be seen Mr. Putchett with a child on his shoulder.

One day the waves seemed to viciously break near the shore, and the bathers all followed the rope out to where there were swells instead of breakers. Mr. Putchett was there, of course, with little Alice. He seemed perfectly enamored of the water, and delighted in venturing as far to the sea as the rope would allow, and there ride on the swells, and go through all other ridiculously happy antics peculiar to ocean-lovers who cannot swim.

Suddenly Mr. Putchett's hand seemed to receive a shock, and he felt himself sinking lower than usual, while above the noise of the surf and the confusion of voices he heard some one roar:

HE THREW UP HIS HAND AS A SIGNAL THAT THE LINE SHOULD BE DRAWN IN.

"The rope has broken—scramble ashore!"

The startled man pulled frantically at the piece of rope in his hand, but found to his horror that it offered no assistance ; it was evident that the break was between him and the shore. He kicked and paddled rapidly, but seemed to make no headway, and while Alice, realizing the danger, commenced to cry piteously, Mr. Putchett plainly saw on the shore the child's mother in an apparent frenzy of excitement and terror.

The few men present—mostly boarding-house keepers and also ex-sailors and fishermen—hastened with a piece of the broken rope to drag down a fishing-boat which lay on the sand beyond reach of the tide. Meanwhile a boy found a fishing-line, to the end of which a stone was fastened and thrown toward the imperiled couple.

Mr. Putchett snatched at the line and caught it, and in an instant half a dozen women pulled upon it, only to have it break almost inside Mr. Putchett's hands. Again it was thrown, and again the frightened broker caught it. This time he wound it about Alice's arm, put the end into her hand, kissed her forehead, said, " Good-by, little angel, God bless you," and threw up his hand as a signal that the line should be drawn in. In less than a minute little Alice was in her mother's arms, but when the line was ready to be thrown again, Mr. Putchett was not visible.

By this time the boat was at the water's edge, and four men—two of whom were familiar with rowing—sat at the oars, while two of the old fishermen stood by to launch the boat at the proper instant. Suddenly they shot it into the water, but the clumsy dip of an oar turned it broadside to the wave, and in an instant it was thrown, waterlogged, upon the beach. Several precious moments were spent in righting the boat and bailing out the water, after which the boat was safely launched, the fishermen sprang to the oars, and in a moment or two were abreast the buoy.

Mr. Putchett was not to be seen—even had he reached the buoy it could not have supported him, for it was but a small stick of wood. One of the boarders—he who had swamped the boat—dived several times, and finally there came to the surface a confused mass of humanity which separated into the forms of the diver and the broker.

A few strokes of the oars beached the boat, and old "Captain" Redding, who had spent his Winters at a government life-saving station, picked up Mr. Putchett, carried him up to the dry sand, laid him face downward, raised his head a little, and shouted :

"Somebody stand between him and the sun so's to shade his head! Slap his hands, one man to each hand. Scrape up some of that hot, dry sand, and pile it on his feet and legs. Everybody else stand off and give him air."

The captain's orders were promptly obeyed, and there the women and children, some of them weeping, and all of them pale and silent, stood in a group in front of the bathing-house and looked up.

"Somebody run to the hotel for brandy," shouted the captain.

"Here's brandy," said a strange voice, "and I've got a hundred dollars for you if you bring him to life."

Every one looked at the speaker, and seemed rather to dislike what they saw. He was a smart-looking man, but his face seemed very cold and forbidding; he stood apart, with arms folded, and seemed regardless of the looks fastened upon him. Finally Mrs. Blough, one of the most successful and irrepressible gossips in the neighborhood, approached him and asked him if he was a relative of Mr. Putchett's.

"No, ma'am," replied the man, with unmoved countenance. "I'm an officer with a warrant for his arrest, on suspicion of receiving stolen goods. I've searched his traps at the hotel and boarding-house this morning, but can't find what I'm looking for. It's been traced to him, though—has he shown any of you ladies a large diamond?"

"No," said Mrs. Blough, quite tartly, "and none of us would have believed it of him, either.'

"I suppose not," said the officer, his face softening a little. "I've seen plenty of such cases before, though. Besides, it isn't my first call on Putchett—not by several."

Mrs. Blough walked indignantly away, but, true to her nature, she quickly repeated her news to her neighbors.

"He's coming to!" shouted the captain, turning Mr. Putchett on his back and attempting to provoke respiration. The officer was by his side in a moment. Mr. Putchett's eyes had closed naturally, the captain said, and his lips had moved. Suddenly the stranger laid a hand on the collar of the insensible man, and disclosed a cord about his neck.

"Captain," said the officer, in a voice very low, but hurried and trembling with excitement, "Putchett's had a very narrow escape, and I hate to trouble him, but I must do my duty. There's been a five thousand dollar diamond traced to him. He advanced money on it, knowing it was stolen. I've searched his property and can't find it, but I'll bet a thousand it's on that string around his neck—that's Putchett all over. Now, you let me take it, and I'll let him alone ; nobody else need know what's happened. He seems to have behaved himself here, judging by the good opinion folks have of him, and he deserves to have a chance which he won't get if I take him to jail."

The women had comprehended, from the look of the stranger and the captain, that something unusual was going on, and they had crowded nearer and nearer, until they heard the officer's last words.

"You're a dreadful, hateful man!" exclaimed little Alice.

The officer winced.

"Hush, daughter," said Alice's mother ; then she said: "Let him take it, captain ; it's too awful to think of a man's going right to prison from the gates of death."

The officer did not wait for further permission, but hastily opened the bathing-dress of the still insensible figure.

22

Suddenly the officer started back with an oath, and the people saw, fastened to a string and lying over Mr. Putchett's heart, a small scallop-shell, variegated with pink and yellow spots.

"It's one I gave him when I first came here, because he couldn't find any," sobbed little Alice.

The officer, seeming suddenly to imagine that the gem might be secreted in the hollow of the shell, snatched at it and turned it over. Mr. Putchett's arm suddenly. moved; his hand grasped the shell and carried it toward his lips; his eyes opened for a moment and fell upon the officer, at the sight of whom Mr. Putchett shivered and closed his eyes again.

"That chill's a bad sign," muttered the captain.

Mr. Putchett's eyes opened once more, and sought little Alice ; his face broke into a faint smile, and she stooped and kissed him. The smile on his face grew brighter for an instant, then he closed his eyes and quietly carried the case up to a Court of Final Appeals, before which the officer showed no desire to give evidence.

Mr. Putchett was buried the next day, and most of the people in the neighborhood were invited to the funeral. The story went rapidly about the neighborhood, and in consequence there were present at the funeral a number of uninvited persons : among these were the cook, bar-keeper and hostler of the hotel, who stood uncomfortably a little way from the house until the procession started, when they followed at a respectful distance in the rear.

When the grave was reached, those who dug it—who were also of those who carried the bier—were surprised to find the bottom of the coffin-box strewn and hidden with wild flowers and scraps of evergreen.

The service of the Church of England was read, and as the words, "Ashes to ashes ; dust to dust," were repeated, a bouquet of wild flowers was tossed over the heads of the mourners and into the grave. Mrs. Blough, though deeply affected by the services, looked quickly back to see who was the giver, and saw the officer (who had not been seen before that day) with such an embarrassed countenance as to leave no room for doubt. He left before daylight next morning, to catch a very early train : but persons passing the old graveyard that day beheld on Putchett's grave a handsome bush of white roses, which bush old Mrs. Gale, living near the hotel, declared was a darling pot-plant which had been purchased of her on the previous evening by an ill-favored man who declared he *must* have it, no matter how much he paid for it.

THE MEANEST MAN AT BLUGSEY'S.

TO MINERS, whose gold-fever had not reached a ridiculous degree of heat, Blugsey's was certainly a very satisfactory location. The dirt was rich, the river ran dry, there was plenty of standing-room on the banks, which were devoid of rocks, the storekeeper dealt strictly on the square, and the saloon contained a pleasing variety of consolatory fluids, which were dispensed by Stumpy Flukes, ex-sailor, and as hearty a fellow as any one would ask to see.

All thieves and claim-jumpers had been shot as fast as discovered, and the men who remained had taken each other's measures with such accuracy, that genuine fights were about as unfrequent as prayer-meetings.

The miners dug and washed, ate, drank, swore and gambled with that delightful freedom which exists only in localities where society is established on a firm and well-settled basis.

Such being the condition of affairs at Blugsey's, it seemed rather strange one morning, hours after breakfast, to see, sprinkled in every direction, a great number of idle picks, shovels and pans; in fact, the only mining implements in use that morning were those handled by a single miner, who was digging and carrying and washing dirt with an industry which seemed to indicate that he was working as a substitute for each and every man in the camp.

He was anything but a type of gold-hunters in general; he was short and thin, and slight and stooping, and greatly round-shouldered ; his eyes were of a painfully uncertain gray, and one of them displayed a cast which was his only striking feature; his nose had started as a very retiring nose, but had changed its mind half-way down; his lips were thin, and seemed to yearn for a close acquaintance with his large ears ; his face was sallow and thin, and thickly seamed, and his chin appeared to be only one of Nature's hasty afterthoughts. Long, thin gray hair hung about his face, and imparted the only relief to the monotonous dinginess of his features and clothing.

Such being the appearance of the man, it was scarcely natural to expect that miners in general would regard him as a special ornament to the profession.

In fact, he had been dubbed "Old Scrabblegrab" on the second day of his occupancy of Claim No. 32, and such of his neighbors as possessed the gift of tongues had, after more intimate acquaintance with him, expressed themselves doubtful of the ability of language to properly embody Scrabblegrab's character in a single name.

The principal trouble was, that they were unable to make anything at all of his character; there was nothing about him which they could understand, so they first suspected him, and then hated him violently, after the usual manner of society toward the incomprehensible.

And on the particular morning which saw Scrabblegrab the only worker at Blugsey's, the remaining miners were assembled in solemn conclave at Stumpy Fluke's saloon, to determine what was to be done with the detested man.

The scene was certainly an impressive one; for such quiet had not been known at the saloon since the few moments which intervened between the time, weeks before, when Broadhorn Jerry gave the lie to Captain Greed, and the captain, whose pistol happened to be unloaded, was ready to proceed to business.

The average miner, when sober, possesses a degree of composure and gravity which would be admirable even in a judge of ripe experience, and miners, assembled as a deliberative body, can display a dignity which would drive a venerable Senator or a British M. P. to the uttermost extreme of envy.

On the occasion mentioned above, the miners ranged themselves near the unoccupied walls, and leaned at various graceful and awkward angles. Boston Ben, who was by natural right the ruler of the camp, took the chair—that is, he leaned against the centre of the bar. On the other side of the bar leaned Stumpy Flukes, displaying that degree of conscious importance which was only becoming to a man who, by virtue of his position, was sole and perpetual secretary and recorder to all stated meetings at Blugsey's.

Boston Ben glanced around the room, and then collectively announced the presence of a quorum, the formal organization of the meeting, and its readiness for deliberation, by quietly remarking :

"Blaze away !"

Immediately one of the leaners regained the perpendicular, departed a pace from the wall, rolled his tobacco neatly into one cheek, and remarked :

"We've stood it long enough—the bottom's clean out of the pan, Mr. Chairman. Scrabblegrab's declined bitters from half the fellers in camp, an' though his gray old topknot's kept 'em from takin' satisfaction in the usual manner, they don't feel no better 'bout it than they did."

The speaker subsided into his section of wall, composed himself into his own especial angles, and looked like a man who had fully discharged a conscientious duty.

From the opposite wall there appeared another speaker, who indignantly remarked :

"Goin' back on bitters ain't a toothful to what he's done. There's young Curly, that went last week. That boy played his hand in a style that would take the conceit clean out uv an angeL But all to onct Curly took to lookin' flaxed, an' the judge here overheard Scrabblegrab askin' Curly what he thort his mother'd say ef she knew he was makin' his money that way ? The boy took on wuss an' wuss, an' now he's vamosed. Don't b'lieve me ef yer don't want ter, fellers—here's the judge hisself."

The judge briskly advanced his spectacles, which had gained him his title, and said :

"True ez gospel; and when I asked him ef he wasn't ashamed of himself fur takin' away the boy's comfort, he said No, an' that I d be a more decent man ef I'd give up keards myself."

"He's alive yit!" said the first speaker, in a tone half of inquiry and half of reproof.

"I know it," said the judge, hastening to explain. "I'd lent my pepperbox to Mose when he went to 'Frisco, an' the old man's too little fur a man uv my size to hit."

The judge looked anxiously about until he felt assured his explanation had been generally accepted. Then he continued :

"What's he good fur, anyhow? He can't sing a song, except somethin' about 'Tejus an' tasteless hours,' that nobody ever heard before, an' don't want to agin; he don't drink, he don't play keards, he don't even cuss when he tumbles into the river. Ev'ry man's got his p'ints, an' ef he hain't got no good uns, he's sure to have bad uns. Ef he'd only show 'em out, there might be somethin' honest about it; but when a feller jist eats an' sleeps an' works, an' never shows any uv the tastes uv a gentleman, ther's somethin' wrong."

"I don't wish him any harm," said a tall, good-natured fellow, who succeeded the judge; "but the feller's looks is agin the reputation uv the place. In a camp like this here one, whar society's first-class—no greasers nur pigtails nur loafers—it ain't the thing to hev anybody around that looks like a corkscrew that's been fed on green apples and watered with vinegar—it's discouragin' to gentlemen that might hev a notion of stakin' a claim, fur the sake uv enjoyin' our social advantages."

"N-none uv yer hev got to the wust uv it yit," remarked another. "The old cuss is too fond uv his dust. Billy

Banks seen him a-buyin' pork up to the store, an' he handled his pouch ez ef 'twas eggs instid of gold dust—poured it out as keerful ez yer please, an' even scraped up a little bit he spilt. Now, when I wuz a little rat, an' went to Sunday-school, they used to keep a-waggin' at me 'bout evil communication a-corruptin' o' good manners. That's what *he'll* do—fust thing yer know, *other* fellers'll begin to be stingy, an' think gold dust wuz made to save instid uv to buy drinks an' play keards fur. *That's* what it'll come to."

"Beggin' ev'rybody's pardon," interposed a deserter from the army, "but these here perceedin's is irreg'lar. 'Tai'nt the square thing to take evidence till the pris'ner's in court."

Boston Ben immediately detailed a special officer to summon Old Scrabblegrab, declared a recess of five minutes, and invited the boys to drink with him.

Those who took sugar in theirs had the cup dashed from their lips just as they were draining the delicious dregs, for the officer and culprit appeared, and the chairman rapped the assembly to order.

Boston Ben had been an interested attendant at certain law-courts in the States, so in the calm consciousness of his acquaintance with legal procedure he rapidly arraigned Scrabblegrab.

"Scrabblegrab, you're complained uv for goin' back on bitters, coaxin' Curly to give up keards, thus spoilin' his fun, an' knockin' appreciatin' observers out of their amusement; uv insultin' the judge, uv not cussin' when you stumble into the river, uv not havin' any good p'ints, an' not showin' yer bad ones; uv bein' a set-back on the tone uv the place—lookin' like a green-apple-fed, vinegar-watered corkscrew, or words to that effect; an', finally, in savin' yer money. What hev you got to say agin' sentence bein' passed on yer?"

The old man flushed as the chairman proceeded, and when the indictment reached its end, he replied, in a tone which indicated anything but respect for the court:

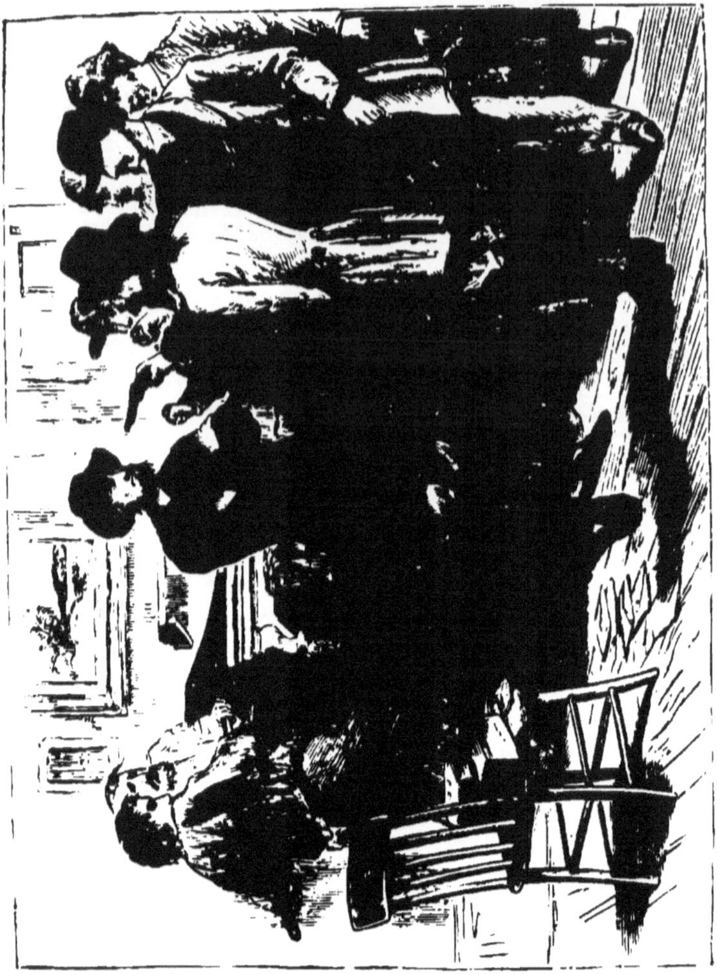

"I DON'T GENERALLY SHOOT TILL THE OTHER FELLER DRAWS."

"I've got just this to say, that I paid my way here, I've asked no odds of any man sence I've ben here, an' that anybody that takes pains to meddle with my affairs is an impudent scoundrel!"

Saying which, the old man turned to go, while the court was paralyzed into silence.

But Tom Dosser, a new arrival, and a famous shot, now stepped in front of the old man.

"I ax yer parding," said Tom, in the blandest of tones, "but, uv course, yer didn't mean me when yer mentioned impudent scoundrels?"

"Yes, I did—I meant you, and ev'rybody like yer," replied the old man.

Tom's hand moved toward his pistol. The chairman expeditiously got out of range. Stumpy Flukes promptly retired to the extreme end of the bar, and groaned audibly.

The old man *was* in the wrong; but, then, wasn't it *too* mean, when blood was so hard to get out, that these difficulties *always* took place just after he'd got the floor clean?

"I don't generally shoot till the other feller draws," explained Tom Dosser, while each man in the room wept with emotion as they realized they had lived to see Tom's skill displayed before their very eyes—"I don't generally shoot till the other feller draws ; but you'd better be spry. I usually make a little allowance for age, but——"

Tom's further explanations were indefinitely delayed by an abnormal contraction of his trachea, the same being induced by the old man's right hand, while his left seized the unhappy Thomas by his waist-belt, and a second later the dead shot of Blugsey's was tossed into the middle of the floor, somewhat as a sheaf of oats is tossed by a practiced hand.

"Anybody else?" inquired the old man. "Ill back Vermont bone an' muscle agin' the hull passel of ye, even if I *be* a deacon. 'The angel of the Lord encampeth round about them that fear him.'"

"The angel needn't hurry hisself," said Tom Dosser,

picking himself up, one joint at a time. "Ef that's the crowd yer travelin' with, and they've got a grip anything like yourn, I don't want nothin' to do with 'em."

Boston Ben looked excited, and roared:

"This court's adjourned *sine.die.*"

Then he rushed up to the newly announced deacon, caught him firmly by the right hand, slapped him heartily between the shoulders, and inquired, rather indignantly:

"Say, old Angelchum, why didn't you ever let folks know yer style, instead uv trottin' 'round like a melancholy clam with his shells shut up tight? That's what this crowd wants to know! Now yev opened down to bed-rock, we'll git English Sam from Sonora, an' git up the tallest kind uv a rasslin' match."

"Not unless English Sam meddles with my business, you won't," replied the deacon, quickly. "I've got enough to do fightin' speretual foes."

"Oh," said Boston Ben, "we'll manage it so the church folks needn't think 'twas a set-up job. We'll put Sam up to botherin' yer, and yer can tackle him at sight. Then——"

"Excuse me, Boston," interrupted Tom Dosser, "but yer don't hit the mark. I'm from Vermont myself, an' deacons there don't fight for the fun of it, whatever they may do in the village *you* hail from." Then, turning to the old man, Tom asked: "What part uv the old State be ye from, deacon, an' what fetched ye out?"

"From nigh Rutland," replied the deacon, "I hed a nice little place thar, an' wuz doin' well. But the young one's eyes is bad. None uv the doctors thereabouts could do anythin' fur 'em. Took her to Boston; nobody thar could do anythin'—said some of the European doctors were the only ones that could do the job safely. Costs money goin' to Europe an' payin' doctors—I couldn't make it to hum in twenty year; so I come here."

"Only child?" inquired Tom Dosser, while the boys crowded about the two Vermonters, and got up a low buzz of sympathetic conversation.

The old man heard it all, and to his lonesome and home-sick soul it was so sweet and comforting, that it melted his natural reserve, and made him anxious to unbosom himself to some one. So he answered Tom:

"Only child of my only darter."

"Father dead?" inquired Tom Dosser.

"Better be," replied the deacon, bitterly. "He left her soon after they were married."

"Mean skunk!" said Tom, sympathetically.

"I want to judge as I'd *be* judged," replied the deacon; "but I feel ez ef I couldn't call that man bad enough names. Hesby was ez good a gal ez ever lived, but she went to visit some uv our folks at Burlington, an' fust thing I know'd she writ me she'd met this chap, and they'd been married, an' wanted us to forgive her; but he was so good, an' she loved him so dearly."

"Good for the gal," said Tom, and a murmur of appro-bation ran through the crowd.

"Of course, we forgave her. We'd hev done it ef she married Satan himself," continued the deacon. "But we begged her to bring her husband up home, an' let us look at him. Whatever was good enough for *her* to love was good enough for us, and we meant to try to love Hesby's hus-band."

"Done yer credit, deacon, too," declared Tom, and again the crowd uttered a confirmatory murmur. "Ef some folks—deacons, too—wuz ez good—But go ahead, deac'n."

"Next thing we heard from her, he had gone to the place he was raised in; but a friend of his, who went with him, came back, an' let out he'd got tight, an' been arrested. She writ him right off, beggin' him to come home, and go with her up to our place, where he could be out of temptation an' where she'd love him dearer than ever."

"Pure gold, by thunder!" ejaculated Tom, while a low "You bet," was heard all over the room.

Tom's eyes were in such a condition that he thought the deacon's were misty, and the deacon noticed the same pecu-liarities about Tom.

"She never got a word from him," continued the deacon ; "but one of her own came back, addressed in his writing."

"The infernal scoundrel !" growled Tom, while from the rest of the boys escaped epithets which caused the deacon, indignant as he was, to shiver with horror.

"She was nearly crazy, an' started to find him, but nobody knowed where he was. The postmaster said he'd come to the office ev'ry day for a fortnight, askin' for a letter, so he must hev got hers."

"Ef all women had such stuff in 'em," sighed Tom, "there'll be one fool less in California. 'Xcuse me, deac'n."

"She never gev up hopin' he'd come back," said the deacon, in accents that seemed to indicate labored breath " an' it sometimes seems ez ef such faith 'd be rewarded by the Lord some time or other. She teaches Pet—that's her child—to talk about her papa, an' to kiss his pictur ; an' when she an' Pet goes to sleep, his pictur's on the pillar beween 'em."

"An' the idee that any feller could be mean enough to go back on such a woman ! Deacon, I'd track him right through the world, an' just tell him what you've told us. Ef *that* didn't fetch him, I'd consider it a Christian duty an' privilege to put a hole through him."

"I couldn't do that," replied the deacon, "even ef I was a man uv blood ; fur Hesby loves him, an' he's Pet's dad; Besides, his pictur looks like a decent young chap—ain't got no hair on his face, an' looks more like an innercent boy than anythin' else. Hesby thinks Pet looks like him, an' I couldn't touch nobody looking like Pet. Mebbe you'd like to see her pictur," continued the deacon, drawing from his pocket an ambrotype, which he opened and handed Tom.

"Looks sweet ez a posy," said Tom, regarding it tenderly. "Them little lips uv hern look jest like a rose when it don't know whether to open a little further or not."

The deacon looked pleased, and extracted another picture, and remarked, as he handed it to Tom :

"That's Pet's mother."

THE DEACON LOOKED PLEASED, AND EXTRACTED ANOTHER PICTURE, AND
REMARKED, AS HE HANDED IT TO TOM, "THAT'S PET'S MOTHER." TOM
TOOK IT, LOOKED AT IT, AND SCREAMED, "MY WIFE!"

Tom took it, looked at it, and screamed :

"*My wife!*"

He threw himself on the floor, and cried as only a big-hearted man *can* cry.

The deacon gazed wildly about, and gasped:

"What's his name?—tell me quick !"

"Tom Dosser!" answered a dozen or more.

"That's him! Bless the Lord !" cried the deacon, and finding a seat, dropped into it, and buried his face in his hands.

For several moments there was a magnificent attempt at silence, but it utterly failed. The boys saw that the deacon and Tom were working a very large claim, and to the best of their ability they assisted.

Stumpy Flukes, under the friendly shelter of the bar, was able to fully express his feelings through his eyelids, but the remainder of the party, by taking turns at staring out the windows, and contemplating the bottles behind the bar, managed to delude themselves into the belief that their eyes were invisible. Finally, Tom arose. "Deacon—boys," he said, "I never got that letter. I wus afeard she'd hear about my scrape, so I wrote her all about it, ez soon ez I got sober, an' begged her to forgive me. An' I waited an' hoped an' prayed for an answer, till I growed desperate, an' came out here."

"She never heerd from you, Thomas," sighed the deacon.

"Deac'n," said Tom, "do you s'pose I'd hev kerried this for years "—here he drew out a small miniature of his wife—"ef I hadn'; loved her? Yes, an' this too," continued Tom, producing a thin package, wrapped in oilskin. "There's the only two letters I ever got from her, an', just 'cos her hand writ 'em, I've had 'em just where I took 'em from for four years. I got 'em at Albany, 'fore I got on that cussed tare, an' they was both so sweet an' wifely, that I've never dared to read 'em since, fur fear that thinkin' on what I'd lost would make me even wuss than I am. But I

ain't afeard now," said Tom, eagerly tearing off the oilskin,
and disclosing two envelopes.

He opened one, took out the letter, opened it with trembling hands, stared blankly at it, and handed it to the deacon.

"Thar's my letter now—I got 'em in the wrong envelope!"

"Thomas," said the deacon, "the best thing you can do.
is to deliver that letter yourself. An' don't let any grass
grow under your feet, ef you ken help it."

"I'm goin' by the first hoss I ken steal," said Tom.

"An' tell her I'll be along ez soon as I pan out enough,"
continued the deacon.

"An' tell her," said Boston Ben, "that the gov'nor won't
be much behind you. Tell her that when the crowd found
out how game the old man was, and what was on his mind,
that the court was so ashamed of hisself that he passed
around the hat for Pet's benefit, and"—here Boston Ben
thoughtfully weighed the hat in his hands—"and that the
apology's heavy enough to do Europe a dozen times; I know
it, for I've had to travel myself occasionally."

Here he deposited the venerable tile with its precious
contents on the floor in front of the deacon. The old man
looked at it, and his eyes filled afresh, as he exclaimed:

"God bless you! I wish I could do something for you
in return."

"Don't mention it," said Boston Ben, "unless—you—
You *couldn't* make up your mind to a match with English
Sam, could you?"

"Come, boys," interrupted Stumpy Flukes; "its my treat
—name your medicine—fill high—all charged?—now then
—bottom up, to 'The meanest man at Blugsey's'!"

"That *did* mean *you*, deacon!" exclaimed Tom; "but I
claim it myself now, so—so I won't drink it."

The remainder of the crowd clashed glasses, while Tom
and his father-in-law bowed profoundly. Then the whole
crowd went out to steal horses for the two men, and had

them on the trail within an hour. As they rode off, Stumpy Flukes remarked :

"There's a splendid shot ruined for life."

"Yes," said Boston Ben, with a deep sigh struggling out of his manly bosom, "an' a bully rassler, too. The Church has got a good deal to answer fur, fur sp'ilin' that man's chances."

OF the several pillars of the Church at Pawkin Centre, Deacon Barker was by all odds the strongest. His orthodoxy was the admiration of the entire congregation, and the terror of all the ministers within easy driving distance of the Deacon's native village. He it was who had argued the late pastor of the Pawkin Centre Church into that state of disquietude which had carried him, through a few days of delirious fever, into the Church triumphant; and it was also Deacon Barker whose questions at the examination of seekers for the ex-pastor's shoes had cast such consternation into divinity-schools, far and near, that soon it was very hard to find a candidate for ministerial honors at Pawkin Centre.

Nor was his faith made manifest by words alone. Be the weather what it might, the Deacon was always in his pew, both morning and evening, in time to join in the first hymn, and on every Thursday night, at a quarter past seven in winter, and a quarter before eight in summer, the good Deacon's cane and shoes could be heard coming solemnly down the aisle, bringing to the prayer-meeting the champion of orthodoxy. Nor did the holy air of the prayer-meeting even one single evening fail to vibrate to the voice of the Deacon, as he made, in scriptural language, humble confessions and tearful pleadings before the throne, or — still strictly scriptural in expression—he warned and exhorted the impenitent. The contribution-box always received his sixpence as long as specie payment lasted, and the smallest fractional currency note thereafter; and to each of the regular annual offerings to the missionary cause, the Bible cause, and kindred Christian enterprises, the Deacon regularly contributed his dollar and his prayers. The Deacon could quote scripture in a manner which put Biblical professors to the blush, and every principle of his creed so bristled with texts, confirmatory, sustentive and aggressive, that doubters were rebuked and free-thinkers were speedily reduced to speechless humility or rage. But the unregenerate, and even some who professed righteousness, declared that more fondly than to any other scriptural passage did the good Deacon cling to the injunction, "Make to yourselves friends of the mammon of unrighteousness." Meekly insisting that he was only a steward of the Lord, he put out his Lord's money that he might receive it again with usury, and so successful had he been that almost all mortgages held on property near Pawkin Centre were in the hands of the good Deacon, and few were the foreclosure sales in which he was not the seller.

The new pastor at Pawkin Centre, like good pastors everywhere, had tortured himself into many a headache over the perplexing question, "How are we to reach the impenitent in our midst!" The said impenitent were, with but few exceptions, industrious, honest, respectable, law-abiding people, and the worthy pastor, as fully impregnated with Yankee-thrift as with piety, shuddered to think of the waste of souls that was constantly threatening. At length, like many another pastor, he called a meeting of the brethren, to prayerfully consider this momentous question. The Deacon came, of course, and so did all the other pillars, and many of them presented their views. Brother Grave thought the final doom of the impenitent should be more forcibly presented; Deacon Struggs had an abiding conviction that it was the Man of Sin holding dominion in their hearts that kept these people away from the means of grace; Deacon Ponder mildly suggested that the object might perhaps be attained if those within the fold maintained a more godly walk and conversation, but he was promptly though covertly rebuked by the good Deacon Barker, who reminded the brethren that "it is the *Spirit* that quickeneth"; Brother Flite, who hadn't any money, thought the Church ought to build a "working-man's chapel," but this idea was promptly and vigorously combated by all men of property in the congregation. By this time the usual closing hour had arrived, and after a benediction the faithful dispersed, each with about the ideas he brought to the meeting.

Early next morning the good Deacon Barker, with his mind half full of the state of the unconverted, and half of his unfinished cow-shed, took his stick and hobbled about the village in search of a carpenter to finish the incomplete structure. There was Moggs, but Moggs had been busy all the season, and it would be just like him to want full price for a day's work. Stubb was idle, but Stubb was slow. Augur—Augur used liquor, and the Deacon had long ago firmly resolved that not a cent of *his* money, if he could help it, should ever go for the accursed stuff. But there was Hay—he hadn't seen him at work for a long time—perhaps he would be anxious enough for work to do it cheaply.

The Deacon knocked at Hay's door, and Hay himself shouted:

"Come in."

"How are ye, George," said the Deacon, looking hastily about the room, and delightfully determining, from the patient face of sad-eyed Mrs. Hay and the scanty furnishing of the yet uncleared breakfast-table, that he had been providentially guided to the right spot. "How's times with ye?"

"Not very good, Deac'n," replied Hay. "Nothin' much doin' in town."

"Money's awful sceerce," groaned the Deacon.

"Dreadful," responded George, devoutly thanking the Lord that he owed the Deacon nothing.

"Got much to do this winter?" asked the Deacon.

"Not by a d—day's job—not a single day," sorrowfully replied Hay.

The Deacon's pious ear had been shocked by the young man's imperfectly concealed profanity, and for an instant he thought of administering a rebuke, but the charms of prospective cheap labor lured the good man from the path of rectitude.

"I'm fixin' my cow-shed—might p'raps give ye a job on't. 'Spose ye'd do it cheap, seein' how dull ev'ry thin' is?"

The sad eyes of Mrs. Hay grew bright in an instant. Her husband's heart jumped up, but he knew to whom he was talking, so he said, as calmly as possible:

"Three dollars is reg'lar pay."

The Deacon immediately straightened up as if to go.

"Too much," said he; "I'd better hire a common lab'rer at a dollar 'n a half, an' boss him myself. It's only a cow-shed, ye know."

"Guess, though, ye won't want the nails druv no less p'ticler, will ye, Deac'n?" inquired Hay. "But I tell yer what I'll do—I'll throw off fifty cents a day."

"Two dollars ort to be enough, George," resumed the Deacon. "Carpenterin's pooty work, an' takes a sight of headpiece sometimes, but there's no intellec' required to work on a cow-shed. Say two dollars, an' come along."

The carpenter thought bitterly of what a little way the usual three dollars went, and of how much would have to be done with what he could get out of the cow-shed, but the idea of losing even that was too horrible to be endured, so he hastily replied:

"Two an' a quarter, an' I'm your man."

"Well," said the Deacon, "it's a powerful price to pay for work on a cow-shed, but I s'pose I mus' stan' it. Hurry up; thar's the mill-whistle blowin' seven."

Hay snatched his tools, kissed a couple of thankful tears out of his wife's eyes, and was soon busy on the cow-shed, with the Deacon looking on.

23

"George," said the Deacon suddenly, causing the carpenter to stop his hammer in mid-air, "think it over agen, an' say two dollars."

Hay gave the good Deacon a withering glance, and for a few moments the force of suppressed profanity caused his hammer to bang with unusual vigor, while the owner of the cow-shed rubbed his hands in ecstasy at the industry of his *employe.*

The air was bracing, the Winter sun shone brilliantly, the Deacon's breakfast was digesting fairly, and his mind had not yet freed itself from the influences of the Sabbath. Besides, he had secured a good workman at a low price, and all these influences combined to put the Deacon in a pleasant frame of mind. He rambled through his mind for a text which would piously express his condition, and texts brought back Sunday, and Sunday reminded him of the meeting of the night before. And here was one of those very men before him—a good man in many respects, though he *was* higher-priced than he should be. How was the cause of the Master to be prospered if His servants made no effort? Then there came to the Deacon's mind the passage, " —— he which converteth the sinner from the error of his way shall save a soul from death, and shall hide a multitude of sins." What particular sins of his own needed hiding the Deacon did not find it convenient to remember just then, but he meekly admitted to himself and the Lord that he had them, in a general way. Then, with that directness and grace which were characteristic of him, the Deacon solemnly said :

"George, what is to be the sinner's doom ?"

"I dunno," replied George, his wrath still warm ; "'pears to me you've left that bizness till pretty late in life, Deac'n !"

"Don't trifle with sacrid subjec's, George," said the Deacon, still very solemn, and with a suspicion of annoyance in his voice. "The wicked shall be cast into hell, with—"

"They can't kerry their cow-sheds with 'em, neither," interrupted George, consolingly.

"Come, George," said the good Deacon, in an appealing tone, "remember the apostle says, 'Suffer the word of exhortation.'"

"'Xcuse me, Deac'n, but one sufferin' at a time; I ain't through sufferin' at bein' beaten down yet. How about deac'ns not being 'given to filthy lucre?'"

The good Deacon was pained, and he was almost out of patience with the apostle for writing things which came so handy to the lips of the unregenerate. He commenced an industrious search for a text which should completely annihilate the impious carpenter, when that individual interrupted him with :

"Out with it, Deac'n—ye had a meetin' las' night to see what was to be done with the impenitent. I was there— that is, I sot on a stool jest outside the door, an' I heerd all 'twas said. Ye didn't agree on nothin'—mebbe ye'v fixed it up sence. Any how, ye'v sot me down fur one of the impenitent, an' yer goin' fur me. Well——"

"Go on nailin'," interrupted the economical Deacon, a little testily; the noise don't disturb me; I can hear ye."

"Well, what way am I so much wickeder 'n you be—you an' t'other folks at the meetin'-house?" asked Hay.

"George, I never saw ye in God's house in my life," replied the Deacon.

"Well, s'pose ye hevn't—is God so small He can't be nowheres 'xcept in your little meetin'-house? How about His seein' folks in their closets?"

"George," said the Deacon, "ef yer a prayin' man, why don't ye jine yerself unto the Lord's people?"

"Why? 'Cos the Lord's people, as you call 'em, don't want me. S'pose I was to come to the meetin'-house in these clothes—the only ones I've got—d'ye s'pose any of the Lord's people 'd open a pew-door to me? An' spose my wife an' children, dressed no better 'n I be,'but as good 's I can afford, was with me, how d'ye s'pose I'd feel?"

"Pride goeth before a fall, an' a haughty sperit before," groaned the Deacon, when the carpenter again interrupted.

"I'd feel as ef the the people of God was a gang of in-sultin' hypocrites, an' ez ef I didn't ever want to see 'em again. Ef that kind o' pride's sinful, the devil's a saint. Ef there's anythin' wrong about a man's feelin' so about himself and them God give him, God's to blame for it him-self; but seein' it's the same feelin' that makes folks keep 'emselves strait in all other matters, I'll keep on thinkin' it's right."

"But the preveleges of the Gospel, George," remon-strated the Deacon.

"Don't you s'pose I know what they're wuth?" con-tinued the carpenter. "Haven't I hung around in front of the meetin'-house Summer nights, when the winders was open, jest to listen to the singin' and what else I could hear? Hezn't my wife ben with me there many a time, and hevn't both of us prayed an' groaned an' cried in our hearts, not only 'cos we couldn't join in it all ourselves, but 'cos we couldn't send the children either, without their learnin' to hate religion 'fore they fairly know'd what 'twas? Haven't I sneaked in to the vestibule Winter nights, an' sot just where I did last night, an' heard what I'd 'a liked my wife and children to hear, an' prayed for the time to come when the self-app'inted elect shouldn't offend the little ones? An' after sittin' there last night, an' comin' home and tellin' my wife how folks was concerned about us, an' our rejoicin' together in the hope that some day our children could hev the chances we're shut out of now, who should come along this mornin' but one of those same holy people, and Jewed me down on pay that the Lord knows is hard enough to live on."

The Deacon *had* a heart, and he knew the nature of self-respect as well as men generally. His mind ran entirely outside of texts for a few minutes, and then, with a sigh for the probable expense, he remarked:

"Reckon Flite's notion was right, after all—ther' ort to be a workin'-man's chapel."

"Ort?" responded Hay; "who d'ye s'pose 'd go to it?

Nobody? Ye can rent us second-class houses, an' sell us second-hand clothin', and the cheapest cuts o' meat, but when it comes to cheap religion—nobody knows its value better 'n we do. We don't want to go into yer parlors on carpets and furniture we don't know how to use, an' we don't expect to be asked into society where our talk an' manners might make some better eddicated people laugh. But when it comes to religion—God knows nobody needs an' deserves the very best article more 'n we do."

The Deacon was a reasonable man, and being old, was beginning to try to look fairly at matters upon which he expected soon to be very thoroughly examined. The indignant protest of the carpenter had, he feared, a great deal of reason, and yet—God's people deserved to hold their position, if, as usual, the argument ended where it began. So he asked, rather triumphantly:

" What *is* to be done, then?"

" Reform God's people themselves," replied the carpenter, to the horror of the pious old man. "When the right hand of fellowship is reached out to the front, instead of stuck behind the back when a poor man comes along, there'll be plenty that'll be glad to take it. Reform yer own people, Deac'n. 'Fore yer pick out of our eyes the motes we'll be glad enough to get rid of, ye can get a fine lot of heavy lumber out of yer own."

Soldiers of the Cross, no more than any other soldiers, should stand still and be peppered when unable to reply; at least so thought the Deacon, and he prudently withdrew.

Reform God's people themselves! The Deacon was too old a boy to tell tales out of school, but he knew well enough there was room for reform. Of course there was—weren't we all poor sinners?—when we would do good wasn't evil ever present with us?—what business had other sinners to complain, when they weren't, at least, any better? Besides, suppose he were to try to reform the ways of Brother Graves and Deacon Struggs and others he had in his mind

—would they rest until they had attempted to reform *him?*
And who was to know just what quantity and quality of
reform was necessary? "Be not carried about with divers
and strange doctrines." The matter was too great for his
comprehension, so he obeyed the injunction, "Commit thy
way unto the Lord."

But the Lord relegated the entire matter to the Deacon.
Hay did a full day's work, the Deacon made a neat little
sum by recovering on an old judgment he had bought for a
mere song, and the Deacon's red cow made an addition to
the family in the calf-pen; yet the Deacon was far from
comfortable. The idea that certain people must stay away
from God's house until God's people were reformed, seemed
to the Deacon's really human heart something terrible. If
they *would* be so proud—and yet, people who would stand
outside the meeting-house and listen, and pray and weep
because their children were as badly off as they, could
scarcely be very proud. He knew there couldn't be many
such, else this out-of-door congregation would be noticed—
there certainly wasn't a full congregation of modest me-
chanics in the vestibule of which Hay spoke, and yet, who
could tell how many more were anxious and troubled on
the subject of their eternal welfare.

What a pity it was that those working-men who wished
to repair to the sanctuary could not have steady work and
full pay! If he had only known all this early in the morning, he did not know but he might have hired him at three
dollars; though, really, was a man to blame for doing his
best in the labor market? "Ye cannot serve God and mammon." Gracious! he could almost declare he heard the
excited carpenter's voice delivering that text. What *had*
brought that text into his head just now?—he had never
thought of it before.

The Deacon rolled and tossed on his bed, and the subject of his conversation with the carpenter tormented him
so he could not sleep. Of one thing he was certain, and
that was that the reform of the Church at Pawkin Centre

was not to be relied on in an extremity, and was not such hungering and thirsting after righteousness an extreme case?—had he ever really known many such! If 'Hay only had means, the problem would afford its own solution. The good Deacon solemnly declared to himself that if Hay could give good security, he (the Deacon) would try to lend him the money.

But even this (to the Deacon) extraordinary concession was unproductive of sleep. "He that giveth to the poor lendeth to the Lord." There! he could hear that indignant carpenter again. What an unsatisfactory passage that was, to be sure! If it would only read the other way—it didn't seem a bit business-like the way it stood. And yet, as the Deacon questioned himself there in the dark, he was forced to admit that he had a very small balance—even of loans— to his credit in the hands of the Lord. He had never lent to the Lord except in his usual business manner—as small a loan as would be accepted, on as extensive collaterals as he could exact. Oh, why did people ever forsake the simple raiment of their forefathers, and robe themselves in garments grievous in price, and stumbling-blocks in the path of their fellow-men?

But sleep failed even to follow this pious reflection. Suppose—only suppose, of course—that he were to give— lend, that is—lend Hay money enough to dress his family fit for church—think what a terrible lot of money it would take! A common neat suit for a man would cost at least thirty dollars, an overcoat nearly twice as much; a suit cloak, and other necessities for his wife would amount to as much more, and the children—oh, the thing couldn't be done for less than two hundred and fifty dollars. Of course, it was entirely out of the question—he had only wondered what it *would* cost—that was all.

Still no sleep. He wished he hadn't spoken with Hay about his soul—next time he would mind his own business. He wished he hadn't employed Hay. He wished the meeting for consideration of the needs of the impenitent had never taken place. " No man can come to me except the Father which sent me draw him "—he wished he had remembered that passage, and quoted it at the meeting —it was no light matter to interfere with the Almighty's plans.

"Blessed are the merciful, for they shall obtain mercy." Hah! *Could* that carpenter be in the room, disarranging his train of thought with such—such—tantalizing texts ! They had kept him awake, and at his time of life a restless night was a serious matter. Suppose——

Very early the next morning the village doctor, returning from a patient's bedside, met the Deacon with a face which suggested to him (the doctor was pious and imaginative) "Abraham on Mount Moriah." The village butcher, more practical, hailed the good man, and informed him he was in time for a fine steak, but the Deacon shook his head in agony, and passed on. He neared the carpenter's house, stopped, tottered, and looked over his shoulder as if intending to run; at length he made his way behind the house, where Hay was chopping firewood. The carpenter saw him and turned pale—he feared the Deacon had found cheaper labor, and had come to give him warning.

"George," said the Deacon, " I've been doin' a heap of thinkin' 'bout what we talked of yesterday. I've come to say that if you like I'll lend you three hundred dollars fur as long as ye'v a mind to, without note, security or int'rest; you to spend as much of it ez ye need to dress you an' yer hull fam'ly in Sunday clothes, and to put the balance in the Savin's Bank, at interest, to go on doin' the same with when necessary. An' all of ye to go to church when ye feel so disposed. An' ef nobody else's pew-door opens, yer allus welcome to mine. And may the Lord " the Deacon finished the sentence to himself—"have mercy on my soul." Then he said, aloud:

"That's all."

The carpenter, at the beginning of the Deacon's speech, had dropped his axe, to the imminent danger of one of his feet. As the Deacon continued, the carpenter dropped his head to one side, raised one eye-brow inquiringly, and awaited the conditions. But when the Deacon said "That's all," George Hay seized the Deacon's hard old hand, gave it a grasp which brought agonized tears to the eyes of its venerable owner, and exclaimed :

" Deacon, God's people are reformin' ! "

The Deacon staggered a little—he had not thought of it in that light before.

"Deacon, that money 'll do more good than all the prayin' ye ever done. 'Xcuse me—I must tell Mary," and the carpenter dashed into the house. Had Mrs. Hay respected the dramatic proprieties, she would have made the Deacon a neat speech; but the truth is, she regarded him from behind the window-blind, and wiped her eyes with the corner of her apron; seeing which the Deacon abruptly started for home, making less use of his cane than he had done in any day for years.

It is grievous to relate, but truth is mighty—that within a fortnight the good Deacon repented of his generous action at least fifty times. He would die in the poor-house if he were so extravagant again. Three hundred dollars was more than the cow-shed—lumber, shingles, nails, labor and all—would cost. Suppose Hay should take the money and go West ? Suppose he should take to drinking, and spend it all for liquor! One suspicion after another tortured the poor man until he grew thin and nervous. But on the second Sunday, having satisfied himself that Hay was in town, sober, the day before, that he had been to the city and brought back bundles, and that he (the Deacon) had seldom been in the street without meeting one of Hay's children with a paper of hooks and eyes or a spool of thread, the Deacon stationed himself in one of his own front windows, and brought his spectacles to bear on Hay's door, a little distance off. The first bell had rung, apparently, hours before, yet no one appeared—could it be that he had basely sneaked to the city at night and pawned everything? No—

the door opened—there they came. It couldn't be—yes, it
was—well, he never imagined Hay and his wife were so fine
a-looking couple. They came nearer, and the Deacon, forgetting his cane, hobbled hurriedly to church, entered his
pew, and left the door wide open. He waited long, it seemed to him, but they did not come. He looked around impatiently, and there, O, joy and wonder!—the president of
the Pawkin Savings' Institution had invited the whole family into his pew! Just then the congregation rose to sing
the hymn commencing :

> " From all that dwell below the skies
>   Let the Creator's praise arise" ;

and the Deacon, in his excitement, distanced the choir, and
the organ, and the congregation, and almost brought the
entire musical service to a standstill.

The Deacon had intended to watch closely for Hays' conversion, but something wonderful prevented—it was reported everywhere that the Deacon himself had been converted,
and all who now saw the Deacon fully believed the report.
He was even heard to say that as there seemed to be some
doubt as to whether faith or works was the saving virtue,
he intended thereafter to practice both. He no longer
mentions the poor-house as his prospective dwelling, but is
heard to say that in his Father's house there are many
mansions, and that he is laying up his treasure in heaven
as fast as possible, and hopes he may get it all on the way
there before his heart is called for. At the post-office, the
tin-shop and the rum-shop the Deacon's conversion is constantly discussed, and men of all degrees now express a belief in the mighty power of the Spirit from on high. Other
moneyed men have been smitten and changed, and the pastor of the Pawkin Centre Church daily thanks the Lord for
such a revival as he never heard of before.

JOE GATTER'S LIFE INSURANCE.

GOOD? He was the model boy of Bungfield. While his idle school-mates were flying kites and playing marbles, the prudent Joseph was trading Sunday-school tickets for strawberries and eggs, which he converted into currency of the republic. As he grew up, and his old school-mates purchased cravats and hair-oil at Squire Tackey's store, it was the industrious Joseph who stood behind the counter, wrapped up their purchases, and took their money. When the same boys stood on the street-corners and cast sheep's eyes at the girls, the business-like Joseph stood in the store-door and contemplated these same boys with eyes such as a hungry cat casts upon a brood of young birds who he expects to eat when they grow older. Joe never wasted any time at parties; he never wore fine clothing; he never drank nor smoked; in short, Joe was so industrious that by the time he reached his majority he had a thousand dollars in the bank, and not a solitary virtue in his heart.

For Joe's money good Squire Tackey had an earnest longing, and soon had it to his own credit; while the sign over the store-door read "Tackey & Gatter." Then the Squire wanted Joe's soul, too, and so earnest was he that Joe soon found it necessary to remonstrate with his partner.

"'Twont do, Squire," said he; "religion's all very well in its place, but when a man loses the sale of a dozen eggs, profit seven cents, because his partner is talking religion with him so hard that a customer gets tired of waiting and goes somewhere else, then religion's out of place."

"The human soul's of more cons'kence than many eggs, Joseph," argued the Squire.

"That's just it," replied Joe; "money don't hit the value of the soul any way, and there's no use trying to mix 'em. And while we're talking, don't you think we might be mixing some of the settlings of the molasses barrel with the brown sugar?—'twill make it weigh better."

The Squire sighed, but he could not help admitting that Joe was as good a partner as a man could want.

In one of Joe's leisure moments it struck him that if he were to die, nobody would lose a cent by the operation. The idea was too exasperating, and soon the local agents of noted insurance companies ceased to enjoy that tranquility which is characteristic of business men in the country. Within a fortnight two of the agents were arraigned before their respective churches for profane brawling, while Joe had squeezed certain agents into dividing commissions to the lowest unit of divisibility, and had several policies in the safe at the store.

The Squire, his partner, was agent for the Pantagonian Mutual, and endured his full share of the general agony Joe had caused. But when he had handed Joe a policy and receipt, and taken the money, and counted it twice, and seen to it carefully that all the bills were good, the good Squire took his revenge.

"Joseph," said he, "you ain't through with insurance yet—you need to insure your soul against risk in the next · world, and there's only one Agent that does it."

The junior partner stretched himself on the counter and groaned. He knew the Squire was right—he had heard that same story from every minister he had ever heard. Joe was so agitated that he charged at twelve and a half cents some calico he had sold at fifteen.

Only one Agent! But the shrewd Joseph rejoiced to think that those who represented the Great Agent differed greatly in the conditions of the insurance, and that some made more favorable terms than others, and that if he could get the ministers thoroughly interested in him, he would have a good opportunity for comparing rates. The good men all wanted Joe, for he was a rising young man, and could, if the Spirit moved him, make handsome subscriptions to good purposes. So, in their zeal, they soon regarded each other with jealous eyes, and reduced their respective creeds to gossamer thinness. They agreed about grace being free, and Joe accepted that much promptly, as he did *anything* which could be had without price. But Joe was a practical man, and though he found fault with none of the doctrines talked at him, he yet hesitated to attach himself to any particular congregation. He finally ascertained that the Reverend Barzillai Driftwood's church had no debt, and that its contributions to missions and other religious purposes were very small, so Joe allowed himself to be gathered into the fine assortment of crooked sticks which the Reverend Barzillai Driftwood was reserving unto the day of burning.

Great was the rejoicing of the congregation at Joe's saving act, and sincere was the sorrow of the other churches, who knew their own creeds were less shaky. But in the saloon and on the street Joe's religious act was discussed exclusively on its merits, and the results were such as only special spiritual labor would remove. For no special change was noticeable in Joe; on Sunday he abjured the world, but on Monday he made things uncomfortable for the Widow Macnilty, whose husband had died in the debt of Tackey & Gatter. A customer bought some gingham, on Joe's assurance that the colors were fast, but the first washday failed to confirm Joe's statement. The proprietor of the stage line between Bungfield and Cleopas Valley traded horses with Joe, and was afterward heard mentioning his new property in language far more scriptural than proper.

Still, Joe was a church-member, and that was a patent of respectability. And as he gained years, and building lots, and horses, and commenced discounting notes, his respectability grew and waxed great in the minds of the

practical people of Bungfield. Even good women, real
mothers in Israel, could not help thinking, as they sorrowed
over the sand in the bottoms of their coffee-cups, and grew
wrathful at "runney" flour bought for "A 1 Superfine" of
Tackey & Gatter, that Joe would make a valuable husband.
So thought some of the ladies of Bungfield, and as young
ladies who can endure the idea of such a man for perpetual
partner can also signify their opinions, Joe began to comprehend that he was in active demand. He regarded the
matter as he would a sudden demand for any commodity of
trade, and by skillfully manipulating the market he was
soon enabled to choose from a full supply.

Thenceforward Joe was as happy as a man of his nature
could be. All his investments were paying well : the store
was prosperous, he was successful in all his trading enterprises, he had purchased, at fearful shaves, scores of perfectly good notes, he realized on loans interest which would
cause a usury law to shrivel and crack, his insurance policies
brought him fair dividends, and his wife kept house with
economy and thrift. But the church—the church seemed
an unmitigated drag. Joe attended all the church meetings
—determined to get the worth of the money he was compelled to contribute to the current expenses—he had himself
appointed treasurer, so he could get the use of the church
money ; but the interest, even at the rates Joe generally
obtained, did not balance the amount of his contribution.

Joe worried over the matter until he became very
peevish, yet he came no nearer a business-like adjustment
of receipts and expenditures. One day when his venerable
partner presented him a certificate of dividend from the
Pantagonian Mutual, Joe remarked :

"Never got any dividends on that other insurance you
put me up to taking, partner—that 'gainst fire risks in the
next world, you know. 'Twill be tough if there's any mistake—church does take a sight of money."

"Joseph," said the Squire, in a sorrowful tone, "I've
always been afeard they didn't look enough into your evi-

dences when they took you into that church. How can a man expect to escape on the day of wrath if he's all the time grumbling at the cost of his salvation? Mistake? If you don't know in your heart the truth of what you profess, there's mighty little hope for you, church or no church."

"Know in my heart!" cried Joe. "That's a pretty kind of security. Is that what I've been paying church dues for? Better have known it in my heart in the first place, and saved the money. What's the use, of believing all these knotty points, if they don't make a sure thing for a man?"

"If your belief don't make you any better or happier, Joseph," rejoined the Squire, "you'd better look again and see if you've got a good hold of it; those that's got a clear title don't find their investment as slow in making returns, while those that find fault are generally the ones that's made a mistake."

Poor Joe! He thought he had settled this whole matter; but now, if his partner was right, he was worse off than if he had n't begun. He believed in justification by faith; now, was n't his faith strong—first class, he might say? To be sure of being safe, had n't he believed everything that *all* the ministers had insisted upon as essential? And what *was* faith, if it was n't believing? He would ask his partner; the old man had got him into this scrape—now he must see him through.

"Squire," said he, "is n't faith the same thing as believing?"

"Well, said the Squire, adjusting his glasses, and taking from the desk the little Testament upon which he administered oaths, "that depends on how you believe. Here's a verse on the subject: 'Thou believest in God; thou doest well; the devils also believe, and tremble.'"

Ugh! Joe shivered. He was n't an aristocrat, but would *any* one fancy such companionship as the Squire referred to?

"Here, said the Squire, turning the leaves, "is another passage bearin' on the subject. 'O, generation of vipers,

who hath warned you to flee from the wrath to come?
Bring forth, therefore, *fruits* meet for repentance.' "

Vipers! Joe uncomfortably wondered who else the
Squire was going to introduce into the brotherhood of the
faith.

"Now, see what it says in another place," continued the
Squire, "Not every one that saith unto Me Lord, Lord, shall
enter into the kingdom of heaven, but he that doeth the
will of my Father which is in heaven."

"Yes," said Joe, grateful for hearing of no more horrible
believers, "but what *is* his will but believing on him?
Don't the Bible say that they that believe shall be
saved?"

"Joseph," said the Squire, "when you believed in my
store, you put in your time and money there. When you
believed in hoss-tradin' you devoted yourself to practicing
it. When you believed life insurance was a good thing, you
took out policies and paid for them, though you *have* complained of the Patagonian dividends. Now, if you do
believe in God, what have you done to prove it?"

"I've paid over a hundred dollars a year church dues,"
said Joe, wrathfully, "not counting subscriptions to a bell
and a new organ."

"That wasn't for God, Joseph," said the Squire; " 'twas
all for you. God never'll thank you for running an asylum
for paupers fit to work. You'll find in the twenty-fifth
chapter of Matthew a description of those that's going into
the kingdom of heaven—they're the people that give food
and clothing to the needy, and that visit the sick and prisoners, while those that don't do these things *don't* go in, to
put it mildly. He don't say a word about belief there,
Joseph; for He knows that giving away property don't
happen till a man's belief is pretty strong."

Joe felt troubled. Could it really be that his eternal insurance was going to cost more money? Joe thought
enviously of Colonel Bung, President of the Bungfield Railroad Co.—the Colonel didn't believe in anything; so he

saved all his money, and Joe wished he had some of the Colonel's courage.

Joe's meditations were interrupted by the entrance of Sam Ottrey, a poor fellow who owed Joe some money. Joe had lent Sam a hundred dollars, discounted ten per cent. for ninety days, and secured by a chattel mortgage on Sam's horse and wagon. But Sam had been sick during most of the ninety days, and when he went to Joe to beg a few days of grace, that exemplary business man insisted upon immediate payment.

It was easy to see by Sam's hopeless eye and strained features that he had not come to pay—he was staring ruin in the face, and felt as uncomfortable as if the amount were millions instead of a horse and wagon, his only means of support. As for Joe, he had got that hundred dollars and horse and wagon mixed up in the oddest way with what he and his partner had been talking about. It was utterly un-business-like—he knew it—he tried to make business business, and religion religion, but, try as he might, he could not succeed. Joe thought briskly; he determined to try an experiment.

"Sam," said he, "got the money?"

"No," Sam replied; "luck's agin me—I've got to stand it, I suppose."

"Sam," said Joe, "I'll give you all the time you need, at legal interest."

Sam was not such a young man as sentimental people would select to try good deeds upon. But he was human, and loved his wife and children, and the sudden relief he felt caused him to look at Joe in a manner which made Joe find a couple of entire strangers in his own eyes. He hurried into the little office, and when his partner looked up inquiringly, Joe replied:

"I've got a dividend, Squire—one of those we were talking about."

"How's that?" asked the old man, while Joe commenced writing rapidly.

"I'll show you," said Joe, handing the Squire the paper on which he has just put in writing his promise to Sam.

"Joseph," said the Squire, after reading the paper several times, to assure himself that his eyes did not deceive him, "it beats the widow's mites; she gave the Lord all she had, but you've given Him more than you ever had in all your life until to-day."

Joe handed Sam the paper, and it was to the teamster the strongest evidence of Christianity he had ever seen in Bungfield. He had known of some hard cases turning from the saloon and joining the church, but none of these things were so wonderful as this action of Joe Gatter's. Sam told the story, in strict confidence, to each of his friends, and the good seed was thus sown in soil that it had never reached before.

It would be pleasant to relate that Joe forthwith ceased shaving notes and selling antiquated grease for butter, and that he devoted the rest of his days and money to good deeds, but it wouldn't be true. Those of our readers who have always consistently acted according to their own light and knowledge are, of course, entitled to throw stones at Joe Gatter; but most of us know to our sorrow why he didn't always act according to the good promptings he received. Our only remaining duty is to say that when, thereafter, Joe's dividends came seldom, he knew who to blame.

THE TEMPERANCE MEETING AT BACKLEY.

LOUD and long rang the single church-bell at Backley, but its industry was entirely unnecessary, for the single church at Backley was already full from the altar to the doors, and the window-sills and altar-steps were crowded with children. The Backleyites had been before to the regular yearly temperance meetings, and knew too well the relative merits of sitting and standing to wait until called by the bell. Of course no one could afford to be absent, for entertainments were entirely infrequent at Backley; the populace was too small to support a course of lectures, and too moral to give any encouragement to circuses and minstrel troupes, but a temperance meeting was both moral and cheap, and the children might all be taken without extra cost.

For months all the young men and maidens at Backley had been practising the choruses of the songs which the Temperance Glee Club at a neighboring town was to sing at the meeting. For weeks had large posters, printed in the reddest of ink, announced to the surrounding country that the parent society would send to Backley, for this especial occasion, one of its most brilliant orators, and although the pastor made the statement (in the smallest possible type) that at the close of the entertainment a collection would be taken to defray expenses of the lecturer, the sorrowing ones took comfort in the fact that certain fractional currency represented but a small amount of money.

The bell ceased ringing, and the crowd at the door

attempted to squeeze into the aisles; the Backley Cornet Quartette played a stirring air; Squire Breet called the meeting to order, and was himself elected permanent Chairman; the Reverend Mr. Genial prayed earnestly that intemperance might cease to reign; the Glee Club sang several songs, with rousing choruses; a pretended drunkard and a cold water advocate (both pupils of the Backley High School), delivered a dialogue in which the pretended drunkard was handled severely; a tableau of "The Drunkard's Home" was given; and then the parent society's brilliant orator took the platform.

The orator was certainly very well informed, logical and convincing, besides being quite witty. He proved to the satisfaction of all present that alcohol was not nutritious; that it awakened a general and unhealthy physical excitement; and that it hardened the tissues of the brain. He proved by reports of analyses, that adulteration, and with harmful materials, was largely practiced. He quoted from reports of police, prison and almshouse authorities, to prove his statement that alcohol made most of our criminals. He unrolled a formidable array of statistics, and showed how many loaves of bread could be bought with the money expended in the United States for intoxicating liquors; how many comfortable houses the same money would build; how many schools it would support; and how soon it would pay the National Debt.

Then he drew a moving picture of the sorrow of the drunkard's family and the awfulness of the drunkard's death, and sat down amid a perfect thunder of applause.

The faithful beamed upon each other with glowing and expressive countenances; the Cornet Quartette played "Don't you go, Tommy"; the smallest young lady sang "Father, dear father, come Home with me Now"; and then Squire Breet, the Chairman, announced that the meeting was open for remarks.

A derisive laugh from some of the half-grown boys, and a titter from some of the misses, attracted the attention of the audience, and looking round they saw Joe Digg standing up in a pew near the door.

"Put him out!" "It's a shame!" "Disgraceful!" were some of the cries which were heard in the room.

"Mr. Digg is a citizen of Backley," said the Chairman, rapping vigorously to call the audience to order, "and though not a member of the Association, he is entitled to a hearing."

"Thank you, Mr. Chairman," said Joe Digg, when quiet was restored; "your words are the first respectful ones I've ever heard in Backley, an' I do assure you I appreciate 'em. But I want the audience to understand I ain't drunk—I haven't had a cent for two days, an' nobody's treated me."

By this time the audience was very quiet, but in a delicious fever of excitement. A drunkard speaking right out in a temperance meeting!—they had never heard of such a thing in their lives. Verily, Backley was going to add one to the roll of modest villages made famous by unusual occurrences.

"I 'spose, Mr. Chairman," continued Joe Digg, "that the pint of temp'rance meetin's is to stop drunkenness, an' as I'm about the only fully developed drunkard in town, I'm most likely to know what this meetin's 'mounted to."

Squire Breet inclined his head slightly, as if to admit the correctness of Joe Digg's position.

"I believe ev'ry word the gentleman has said," continued the drunkard, "and "—here he paused long enough to let an excitable member exclaim " Bless the Lord!" and burst into tears—" and he could have put it all a good deal stronger without stretchin' the truth. An' the sorrer of a drunkard's home can be talked about 'till the Dictionary runs dry, an' then ye don't know nothin' 'bout it. But hain't none of ye ever laughed 'bout lockin' the stable door after the hoss is stolen? That's just what this temp'rance meetin' an' all the others comes to."

A general and rather indignant murmur of dissent ran through the audience.

"Ye don't believe it," continued Joe Digg, "but I've been a drunkard, an' I'm one yet, an' ye all got sense enough to understan' that I ort to know best about it."

"Will the gentleman have the kindness to explain?" asked the lecturer.

"I'm a comin' to it, sir, ef my head 'll see me through," replied the drunkard. "You folks all b'leeve that its lovin' liquor that makes men drink it; now, 'taint no sech thing. I never had a chance to taste fancy drinks, but I know that every kind of liquor *I* ever got hold of was more like medi-cine than anything nice."

"Then what *do* they drink for?" demanded the excitable member.

"I'll tell you," said Joe, "if you'll have a little patience. I have to do it in my own way, for I ain't used to public speakin'. You all know who I am. My father was a church-member, an' so was mother. Father done day's work, fur a dollar'n a quarter a day. How much firewood an' clothes an' food d'ye suppose that money could pay for? We had to eat what come cheapest, an' when some of the women here wuz a sittin' comfortable o' nights, a knittin' an' sewin' an' readin', mother wuz hangin' aroun' the butchershop, tryin' to beat the butcher down on the scraps that wasn't good enough for you folks. Soon as we young 'uns was big enough to do anything we wuz put to work. I've worked for men in this room twelve an' fourteen hours a day. I don't blame 'em—they didn't mean nothin' out of the way—they worked just as long 'emselves, an' so did their boys. But they allers had somethin' inside to keep 'em up, an' I didn't. Does anybody wonder that when I harvested with some men that kep' liquor in the field, an' found how it helped me along, that I took it, an' thought 'twas a reg'lar God's-blessin'? An' when I foun' 'twas a-hurtin' me, how was I to go to work an' giv' it up, when it stood me in-stead of the eatables I didn't have, an' never had, neither?"

"You should hev prayed," cried old Deacon Towser, springing to his feet; "prayed long an' earnest."

THE TEMPERANCE MEETING.

385

"Deacon," said Joe Digg, "I've heerd of your dyspepsy for nigh on to twenty year; did prayin' ever comfort your stomach?"

The whole audience indulged in a profane laugh, and the good deacon was suddenly hauled down by his wife. The drunkard continued:

"There's lots of jest sech folks, here in Backley, an' ev'ry where's else—people that don't get half fed, an' do get worked half to death. Nobody *means* to 'buse 'em, but they do hev a hard time of it, an' whisky's the best friend they've got."

"I work my men from sunrise to sunset in summer, myself," said Deacon Towser, jumping up again, "an' I'm the first man in the field, an' the last man to quit. But I don't drink no liquor, an' my boys don't, neither."

"But ye don't start in the mornin' with hungry little faces a hauntin' ye—ye don't take the dry crusts to the field for yer own dinner, an' leave the meat an' butter at home for the wife an' young 'uns. An' ye go home without bein' afeard to see a half-fed wife draggin' herself aroun' among a lot of puny young 'uns that don't know what's the matter with 'em. Jesus Christ hissef broke down when it come to the cross, deac'n, an' poor human bein's sometimes reaches a pint where they can't stan' no more, an' when its wife an' children that brings it on, it gits a man awful."

"The gentleman is right, I have no doubt," said the Chairman, "so far as a limited class is concerned, but of course no such line of argument applies to the majority of cases. There are plenty of well-fed, healthy, and lazy young men hanging about the tavern in this very village."

"I know it," said Joe Digg, "an' I want to talk about them too. I don't wan't to take up all the time of this meetin', but you'll all 'low I know more 'bout that tavern than any body else does. Ther' is lots of young men a hanging aroun' it, an' why—'cos it's made pleasant for 'em, an' it's the only place in town that is. I've been a faithful attendant at that tavern for nigh onto twenty year, an' I never knowed a hanger-on there that had a comfortable home of his own. Some of them that don't hev to go to bed hungry hev scoldin' or squabblin' parents, an' they can't go a visitin'. an' hear fine music, an' see nice things of every sort to take their minds off, as some young men in this meetin' house can. But the tavern is allus comfortable, an' ther's generally somebody to sing a song and tell a joke, an' they commence goin' ther' more fur a pleasant time than for a drink, at fust. Ther's lots of likely boys goin' there that I wish to God 'd stay away, an' I've often felt like tellin' 'em so, but what's the use? Where are they to go to?"

"They ort to flee from even the appearance of evil," said Deacon Towser.

"But where be they to flee *to*, Deac'n?" persisted Joe Digg; "would you like 'em to come a visitin' to your house?"

"They can come to the church meetings," replied the Deacon; "there's two in the week, besides Sundays, an' some of 'em's precious seasons—*all* of 'em's an improvement on the wicked tavern."

"'Ligion don't taste no better'n whiskey, tell you get used to it," said the drunkard, horrifying all the orthodox people at Backley, "an' taint made half so invitin'. 'Taint long ago I heerd ye tellin' another deacon that the church-members ort to be 'shamed of 'emselves, 'cos sca'cely any of 'em come to the week-evenin' meetin's, so ye can't blame the boys at the tavern."

"Does the gentleman mean to convey the idea that all drunkards become so from justifying causes?" asked the lecturer.

"No, sir," replied Joe Digg, "but I do mean to say that after you leave out them that takes liquor to help 'em do a full day's work, an' them that commence drinkin' 'cos they're at the tavern, an' ain't got no where's else to go, you've made a mighty big hole in the crowd of drinkin'-men—bigger'n temperance meetins' ever begin to make yit."

"But how are they to be 'left out'?" asked the lecturer.

"By temp'rance folks doin' somethin' beside talkin'," replied the drunkard. "For twenty year I've been lectured and scolded, an' some good men's come to me with tears in their eyes, and put their arms 'roun' my neck, an' begged me to stop drinkin'. An' I've wanted to, an' tried to, but when all the encouragement a man gits is in words, an' no matter how he commenced drinkin', now ev'ry bone an' muscle in him is a beggin' fur drink ez soon as he leaves off, an' his mind's dull, an' he ain't fit fur much, an' needs takin' care of as p'tic'ler ez a mighty sick man, talk's jist as good ez wasted. Ther's been times when ef I'd been ahead on flour an' meat an' sich, I could a' stopped drinkin', but when a man's hungry, an' ragged, an' weak, and half-crazy, knowin' how his family's fixed an he can't do nothin' fur 'em, an' then don't get nothin' but words to reform on, he'll go back to the tavern ev'ry time, an' he'll drink till he's comfortable an' till he forgits. I want the people here, one an' all, to understand that though I'm past helpin' now, ther's been fifty times in the last twenty year when I might hed been stopped short, ef any body'd been sensible enough and good-hearted enough to give me a lift."

Joe Digg sat down, and there was a long pause. The Chairman whispered to the leader of the Glee Club, and the club sang a song, but somehow it failed to awaken the usual enthusiasm. After the singing had ended, the Chairman himself took the floor and moved the appointment of a permanent committee to look after the intemperate, and to collect funds when the use of money seemed necessary, and the village doctor created a sensation by moving that Mr. Joe Digg should be a member of the committee. Deacon Towser, who was the richest man in the village, and who dreaded subscription papers, started an insidious opposition by eloquently vaunting the value of earnest prayer and of determined will, in such cases, but the new member of the committee (though manifestly out of order) outmanœuvred the Deacon by accepting both amendments, and re-marking that in a hard fight folks would take all the help they could get.

Somehow, as soon as the new committee—determining to open a place of entertainment in opposition to the tavern, and furnish it pleasantly, and make it an attractive gather-ing-place for young men—asked for contributions to enable them to do it, the temperance excitement at Backley abated marvelously. But Squire Breet, and the doctor, and several other enterprising men, took the entire burden on their own shoulders—or pockets—and Joe Digg was as useful as a reformed thief to a police department. For the doctor, whose professional education had left him a large portion of his natural common-sense in working order, took a prac-tical interest in the old drunkard's case, and others of the committee looked to the necessities of his family, and it came to pass that Joe was one of the earliest of the reform-ers. Men still go to the tavern at Backley, but as, even when the twelve spake with inspired tongues, some people remained impenitent, the temperance men at Backley feel that they have great cause for encouragement, and that they have, at least, accomplished more within a few months than did all the temperance meetings ever held in their village.

JUDE.

GOPHER HILL had determined that it could not endure Jude any longer.

The inhabitants of Gopher Hill possessed an unusual amount of kindness and long-suffering, as was proved by the fact that Chinamen were allowed to work all abandoned claims at the Hill. Had further proof been necessary, it would have been afforded by the existence of a church directly beside the saloon, although the frequenters of the sacred edifice had often, during week-evening meetings, annoyed convivial souls in the saloon by requesting them to be less noisy.

But Jude was too much for Gopher Hill. No one molested him when he first appeared, but each citizen entered a mental protest within his own individual consciousness; for Jude had a bad reputation in most of the settlements along Spanish Creek.

It was not that he had killed his man, and stolen several horses and mules, and got himself into a state of most disorderly inebriation, for, in the opinion of many Gopher Hillites, these actions *might* have been the visible results of certain virtuous conditions of mind.

But Jude had, after killing a man, spent the victim's money; he had stolen from men who had befriended him; he had jumped claims; he had denied his score at the storekeeper's; he had lied on all possible occasions; and had gambled away money which had been confided to him in trust.

One mining camp after another had become too hot for
him ; but he never adopted a new set of principles when he
staked a new claim, so his stay in new localities was never
of sufficient length to establish the fact of legal residence.
His name seemed to be a respectable cognomen of Scriptural extraction, but it was really a contraction of a name
which, while equally Scriptural and far more famous, was
decidedly unpopular—the name of Judas Iscariot.

The whole name had been originally bestowed upon
Jude, in recognition of his success in swindling a mining
partner; but, with an acuteness of perception worthy of em-
ulation, the miners determined that the length of the
appellation detracted from its force, so they shortened
it to Jude.

As a few of the more enterprising citizens of Gopher
Hill were one morning discussing the desirableness of getting rid of Jude, and wondering how best to effect such a
result, they received important foreign aid.

A man rode up to the saloon, dismounted, and tacked on
the wall a poster offering one thousand dollars reward for
the apprehension of a certain person who had committed
an atrocious murder a month before at Duck Run.

The names and *aliases* of the guilty person were unfamiliar to those who gathered about the poster, but the description of the murderer's appearance was so suggestive,
that Squire Bogern, one of the bystanders, found Jude, and
requested him to read the poster.

" Well, 'twasn't *me* done it," sulkily growled the name-
sake of the apostolic treasurer.

" Ther' hain't nobody in Gopher that 'ud take a feller up
fur a reward," replied the squire, studiously oblivious of
Jude's denial; " but it's a nice mornin' fur a walk. Ye can't
miss the trail an' git lost, ye know. An', seein' yer hevn't
staked any claim, an' so hain't got any to dispose of, mebbe
yer could git, inside of five minutes."

Jude was accustomed to " notices to quit," and was able
to extract their import from any verbiage whatever, so he

drank by and to himself, and immediately sauntered out of town, with an air of bravado in his carriage, and a very lonesome look in his face.

Down the trail he tramped, past claims whose occupants knew him well enough, but who, just as he passed, found some excuse for looking the other way.

He passed through one camp after another, and discovered (for he stopped at each saloon) that the man on horseback had preceded him, and that there seemed a wonderful unanimity of opinion as to the identity of the man who was wanted.

Finally, after passing through several of the small camps, which were dotted along the trail, a mile or two apart, Jude flung himself on the ground under a clump of azaleas, with the air of a man whose temper had been somewhat ruffled.

"I wonder," he remarked, after a discursive, fitful, but very spicy preface of ten minutes' duration, "why they couldn't find somethin' I *hed* done, instead of tuckin' some other feller's job on me? I *hev* had difficulties, but this here one's just one more than *I* knows on. Like 'nuff some galoot'll be mean 'nuff to try to git that thousand. I'd try it myself, ef I wuz only somebody else. Wonder why I can't be decent, like other fellers. 'Twon't pay to waste time thinkin' 'bout that, though, fur I'll hev to make a livin' somehow."

Jude indulged in a long sigh, perhaps a penitential one, and drew from his pocket a well-filled flask, which he had purchased at the last saloon he had passed.

As he extracted it, there came also from his pocket a copy of the poster, which he had abstracted from a tree *en route*.

"Thar 'tis again!" he exclaimed, angrily. "Can't be satisfied showin' itself ev'rywhar, but must come out of my pocket without bein' axed. Let's see, p'r'aps it don't mean me, after all—'One eye gone, broken nose, scar on right cheek, powder-marks on left, stumpy beard, sallow

complexion, hangdog look.' *I'd* give a thousand ef I had
it to git the feller that writ that; an' yit it means me, an'
no dodgin'. Lord, Lord! what 'ud the old woman say ef
she wuz to see me nowadays?"

He looked intently at the flask for a moment or two, as
if expecting an answer therefrom, then he extracted the
cork, and took a generous drink. But even the liquor failed to help him to a more cheerful view of the situation, for
he continued:

"Nobody knows me — nobody sez, 'Hello!'—nobody
axes me to name my bitters—nobody even cusses me.
They let me stake a claim, but nobody offers to lend me a
pick or a shovel, an' nobody ever comes to the shanty to
spend the evenin', 'less it's a greenhorn. Curse 'em all!
I'll make some of 'em bleed fur it. I'll git their dust, an'
go back East; ther's plenty of folks *thar* that'll be glad to
see me, ef I've got the dust. An' mebbe 'twould comfort
the old woman some, after all the trouble I've made her.
Offer rewards fur me, do they? I'll give 'em some reason to
do it. I haint afeard of the hull State of Californy, an'——
Good Lord! what's that?"

The gentleman who was not afraid of the whole State of
California sprang hastily to his feet, turned very pale, and
felt for his revolver, for he heard rapid footsteps approaching by a little path in the bushes.

But though the footsteps seemed to come nearer, and
very rapidly, he slowly took his hand from his pistol, and
changed his scared look for a puzzled one.

"Cryin'! Reckon I ain't in danger from anybody that's
bellerin'; but it's the fust time I've heerd that kind of a
noise in *these* parts. Must be a woman. Sounds like what
I used to hear to home when I got on a tear; *'tis* a
woman!"

As he concluded, there emerged from the path a woman,
who was neither very young nor very pretty, but her face
was full of pain, and her eyes full of tears, which signs of
sorrow were augmented by a considerable scare, as she

"GET HIM—GET JOHNNY!" CRIED THE WOMAN, FALLING ON HER KNEES, AND
SEIZING JUDE'S HAND.

suddenly found herself face to face with the unhandsome Jude.

"Don't be afeard of me, marm," said Jude, as the woman retreated a step or two. "I'm durned sorry for yer, whatever's the matter. I've got a wife to home, an' it makes me so sorry to hear her cry, that I get blind drunk ez quick ez I ken."

This tender statement seemed to reassure the woman, for she looked inquiringly at Jude, and asked:

"Have ye seen a man and woman go 'long with a young one?

"Nary," replied Jude. "Young one lost?".

"Yes!" exclaimed the woman, commencing to cry again; "an' a husban', too. I don't care much for *him*, for he's a brute, but Johnny—blessed little Johnny—oh, oh!"

And the poor woman sobbed pitifully.

Jude looked uneasy, and remembering his antidote for domestic tears, extracted the bottle again. He slowly put it back untasted, however, and exclaimed:

"What does he look like, marm?—the husband I mean. I never wanted an excuse to put a hole through a feller ez bad ez I do this mornin'!"

"Don't—don't hurt-him, for God's sake!" cried the woman. "He ain't a good husband—he's run off with another woman, but—but he's Johnny's father. Yet, if you could get Johnny back—he's the only comfort I ever had in the world, the dear little fellow—oh, dear me!"

And again she sobbed as if her heart was broken.

"Tell us 'bout 'em. Whar hev they gone to? what do they luk like? Mebbe I ken git him fur yer," said Jude, looking as if inclined to beat a retreat, or do anything to get away from the sound of the woman's crying.

"Get him—get Johnny?" cried the woman, falling on her knees, and seizing Jude's hand. "I can't give you anything for doin' it, but I'll pray for you, as long as I've got breath, that God may reward you!"

"I reckon," said Jude, as he awkwardly disengaged his

hand, "that prayin' is what'll do me more good than anythin' else jest now. Big feller is yer husband? An' got any idee whar he is?"

"He *is* a big man," replied the woman, "and he goes by the name of Marksey in these parts; and you'll find him at the Widow Beckel's, across the creek. Kill *her* if you like —I hope *somebody* will. But Johnny—Johnny has got the loveliest brown eyes, and the sweetest mouth that was ever made, and——"

"Reckon I'll judge fur myself," interrupted Jude, starting off toward the creek, and followed by the woman. "I know whar ·Wider Beckel's is, an'—an' I've done enough stealin', I guess, to be able to grab a little boy without gittin' ketched. Spanish Crick's purty deep along here, an' the current runs heavy, but——"

The remainder of Jude's sentence was left unspoken, for just then he stepped into the creek, and the chill of the snow-fed stream caused him to hold his breath.

"Remember you aint to hurt *him!*" screamed the woman; "nor her, neither—God forgive me. But bring Johnny— bring Johnny, and God be with you."

The woman stood with clasped hands watching Jude until he reached the opposite bank, shook himself, and disappeared, and then she leaned against a tree and trembled and cried until she was startled by hearing some one say:

"Beg pardon, madame, but have you seen any one pass?"

The woman raised her head, and saw a respectable, severe looking man, in clothing rather neater than was common along Spanish Creek.

"Only one," she replied, "and he's the best man livin'. He's gone to get Johnny—he won't be gone long."

"Your husband, ma'am?"

"Oh, no, sir; I never saw him before."

"One eye gone; broken nose; scar on right cheek; powder-marks on left——"

"Yes, sir, that's the man," said the wondering woman.

"Perhaps you may not have seen this?" said the man handing her one of the posters describing Jude.

Then he uttered a shrill whistle.

The woman read the paper through, and cried:

"It's somebody else—it *must* be—no murderer would be so kind to a poor, friendless woman. Oh, God, have I betrayed him? *Don't* take him, sir—it must be somebody else. I wish I had money—I would pay you more than the reward, just to go away and let him alone."

"Madame," replied the man, beckoning to two men who were approaching, "I could not accept it; nor will I accept the reward. It is the price of blood. But I am a minister of the gospel, ma'am, and in this godless generation it is my duty to see that the outraged dignity of the law is vindicated. My associates, I regret to say, are actuated by different motives."

"You just bet high on that!" exclaimed one of the two men who had approached, a low-browed, bestial ruffian. "Half a thousan' 's more'n I could pan out in a fortnight, no matter how good luck I had. Parson he is a fool, but *we* hain't no right to grumble 'bout it, seein' we git his share —hey, Parleyvoo?"

"You speak truly, Mike," replied his companion, a rather handsome looking Frenchman, of middle age. "And yet Jean Glorieaux likes not the labor. Were it not that he had lost his last ounce at monte, and had the fever for play still in his blood, not one sou would he earn in such ungentle a manner."

"God's worst curses on all of you!" cried the woman, with an energy which inspired her plain face and form with a terrible dignity and power, "if you lay a hand on a man who is the only friend a poor woman has ever found in the world!"

Glorieaux shuddered, and Mike receded a step or two; but the ex-minister maintained the most perfect composure, and exclaimed:

"Poor fools! It is written, 'The curse, causeless, shall

not fall.' And yet, madame, I assure you that I most
tenderly sympathize with you in your misfortunes, whatever they may be."

"Then let him alone!" cried the woman. "My only
child has been stolen away from me—dear little Johnny—
and the man offered to go get him. And you've made me
betray him. Oh, God curse you all!"

"Madame," replied the still imperturbable parson, "the
crime of blood-guiltiness cannot be imputed to you, for you
did not know what you were doing."

The woman leaned against a tree, and waited until
Glorieaux declared to the parson he would abandon the
chase.

"It is useless," said he, striking a dramatic attitude,
and pointing to the woman, "for her tears have quenched
the fiery fever in the blood of Glorieaux."

"Then I'll git the hull thousand," growled Mike, " an'
I'll need it, too, if I've got to stand this sort of thing much
longer."

A confused sound of voices on the other side of the
creek attracted the attention of the men, and caused the
woman to raise her head. A moment later Jude appeared,
with a child in his arms, and plunged into the water.

"Now we'll have him!" cried the parson; "and you,
madame, will have your child. Be ready to chase him, men,
if he attempts to run when he gets ashore."

"Go back! go back!" screamed the woman. "They are
after you, these men. Try to——"

The law-abiding parson placed his hand over the woman's
mouth, but found himself promptly flying backward through
space, while Mike roared :

"Touch a woman, will yer? No thousand dollars nor
any other money, 'll hire me to travel with such a scoundrel. Catch him yerself, if yer want ter."

"But if you do," said Glorieaux, politely, as he drew his
revolver, "it will be necesary for Glorieaux to slay the
Lord's anointed."

" Follered, by thunder !" said Mike.

It was true. During the few seconds which had been consumed in conversation, Jude got well into the creek. He had not seemed to hear the woman's warning; but now a greater danger threatened him, for on the opposite bank of the creek there appeared a man, who commenced firing at Jude's head and the small portion of his shoulders that was visible.

"The monster. Oh, the wretch !" screamed the woman. " He may hit Johnny, his only son ! Oh, God have mercy on me, and save my child !"

A shot immediately behind her followed the woman's prayer, and Glorieaux exclaimed, pointing to the opposite bank, where Marksey was staggering and falling :

" Glorieaux gathered from your words that a divorce would be acceptable, madame. Behold, you have it !"

"Pity nobody didn't think of it sooner," observed Mike, shading his eyes as he stared intently at Jude, " for there's a red streak in the water right behind him."

The woman was already standing at the water's edge, with hands clasped in an agony of terror and anxiety. The three men hastened to join her.

" Wish I could swim," said Mike, "for he's gettin' weak, an' needs help."

The parson sprang into the water, and, in spite of the chill and the swift current, he was soon by Jude's side.

"Take the young un," gasped Jude, " for I'm a goner."

" Put your hand on my shoulder," said the parson. " I can get you both ashore."

"'Tain't no use," said Jude, feebly ; " corpses don't count for much in Californy."

"But your immortal part," remonstrated the parson, trying to seize Jude by the hand which held little Johnny.

" God hev mercy on it !" whispered the dying man ; "it's the fust time He ever had an excuse to do it."

Strong man and expert swimmer as the ex-minister was, he was compelled to relinquish his hold of the wounded

26

man; and Jude, after one or two fitful struggles against his fate, drifted lifeless down the stream and into eternity, while the widowed mother regained her child. The man of God, the chivalrous Frenchman and the brutish Mike slowly returned to their camp; but no one who met them could imagine, from their looks, that they were either of them anything better than fugitives from justice.